THE ONE SAFE PLACE

THE ONE SAFE PLACE

Tania Unsworth

ALGONQUIN YOUNG READERS 2014

Published by
Algonquin Young Readers
an imprint of Algonquin Books of Chapel Hill
Post Office Box 2225
Chapel Hill, North Carolina 27515-2225

a division of
Workman Publishing
225 Varick Street
New York, New York 10014

LIBRARY OF CONGRESS
CATALOGING-IN-PUBLICATION DATA
Unsworth, Tania.
The one safe place : a novel / by Tania Unsworth.—First edition.
pages cm
Summary: In a near future world of heat, greed, and
hunger, Devin earns a coveted spot in a home for abandoned
children that promises unlimited food and toys and the hope of
finding a new family, but Devin discovers the home's horrific true
mission when he investigates its intimidating Administrator
and the zombie-like sickness that afflicts some children.
ISBN 978-1-61620-329-0
[1. Abandoned children—Fiction. 2. Orphans—Fiction.
3. Survival—Fiction. 4. Science fiction.] I. Title.
PZ7.U44178On 2014
[Fic]—dc23   2013043145

10 9 8 7 6 5 4 3 2 1
First Edition

For Oscar, whom I love the most,
and Joe Ridley, my favorite

THE ONE SAFE PLACE

One

It was three o'clock in the afternoon before Devin was done digging the grave. He had really finished it at two, but had carried on for an hour longer, partly to make sure it was good and deep and partly to delay what was coming next. He stood in the bottom of it, resting. The hole was higher than his waist; a rectangle with uneven sides. Devin would have liked to straighten it out. It was too broken up and prickly. But it was the best that he could do.

He threw the shovel over the side of the grave and hauled himself out. There was a slight breeze at the top of the hill, and he stood for a few moments looking out over the valley. In the land beyond, his grandfather had told him, there had once been corn. They used to farm it with machines as wide as houses and it poured like gold, rushing and endless, into vast granaries.

That was more than fifty years ago, before it got hot. It hardly ever rained now except for massive storms that darkened the skies for days. Huge areas of land had become useless, the dry soil swept away by the wind or by sudden, treacherous floods that ripped everything in their path. The change in the weather had started slow, but then it had come fast, faster than anyone expected. But it wasn't just the weather that had changed, his grandfather said. It was people too. People had scattered. They lost homes and livelihoods, and desperation had turned their hearts as hard as the parched earth itself.

It was different on their small farm. The land was still good, a pocket of richness.

"We're lucky, then," Devin had said.

"We're fortunate," his grandfather corrected him.

It was important, his grandfather said, to keep to the right meanings of words or else they would be lost; blown away like the soil that had once grown enough corn to feed a nation. Other things also needed to be kept. Manners at table, the shine on the old silver vase. Every day, his grandfather fetched one of their books so Devin could practice his reading. They had five books. One was about farming, how to grow things and raise animals, and one was full of stories with no pictures except the ones the words made in your head. Another one had nothing but pictures, images of people who were dead now and places that were far away, and animals so strange they made Devin laugh.

"No," his grandfather said when Devin stumbled over his reading. "That's an *a*, not an *e*."

"But they're so hard to tell apart," Devin complained. "Both so pale they fade into the page . . . and they won't stop chirping, Granddad."

"Chirping?"

"Like the swallows," Devin explained.

When his grandfather smiled, his lips barely moved, as if his smile was another thing to be kept, guarded from view like a treasure. Instead you saw it mostly in his eyes. He reached out and touched Devin's hand, and the taste on Devin's tongue was half earthy, half sweet, like roots that had grown to fullness beneath the dark ground.

"Try again, Dev. Try again, my lad."

Devin hadn't thought his grandfather was old. He'd thought he was strong, as strong as the barn and the hills. He could labor all day until his shirt was wet through, but he'd never take it off and work naked to the waist because that was yet another thing to be kept: your standards. You had to keep your standards, he said, in such a shifting world. Since he'd been a boy, there'd been a thousand new inventions. You could do almost everything now just with the push of a button. But nothing had solved the problem of the heat, or the greed and hunger that had followed.

"Why not?" Devin had once asked.

His grandfather had squinted up into the blazing sun and pursed his lips.

"Nobody thought about the future, I guess. Too busy with other things."

✦ ✦ ✦

Devin couldn't delay any longer. He picked up the shovel and turned back down the hill, toward the farmhouse. The basket of apples was still there where he'd dropped it, the fruit scattered all over the yard. His grandfather was still there too, lying on the porch with his eyes wide open and his long arms flung out. For half a second Devin thought he saw the fingers of one hand move and he scrambled up the stairs, falling to his knees as he grabbed for it.

But the hand was as cold as ice.

Tears of grief and panic rose in Devin's eyes. But he couldn't cry. There was nobody left to be strong except for him. He shoved his palms into his eyes, pressing back the tears.

"I dug it the best I could," he told his grandfather. "It's good and deep. The coyotes won't find you. You'll be safe."

Devin stayed by his grandfather's side for a long while. The shadows were growing long when he finally rose to his feet. He went into the bedroom and took the sheet off the bed and spread it wide and white on the porch. Then he half pushed, half rolled his grandfather onto it, his hands shaking and his breath coming fast. His horse, Glancer, named for her shy, sideways look, nickered softly from the orchard, and Devin hesitated. Then he covered his grandfather with the sheet and began to sew the sides together as quickly as he could.

When he was finished, he fetched Glancer, hitched her to the low wagon and brought her round to the front of the house. His grandfather's heels banged on the porch stairs as Devin dragged him down, and each thud was like a blow to his heart. It took a long time to get the body into the wagon, but at last it was done and Devin slowly led Glancer up the hill, taking the shovel with him.

✦ ✦ ✦

It was nearly dark and his grandfather was just a dim shape at the bottom of the grave, the sheet covering him as pale as the wing of a moth. After the struggle to move the body, Devin thought filling in the grave with earth would be easy. But it wasn't. It felt like the hardest thing he had ever had to do. He stood holding the first shovelful of dirt, unable to move.

Burying his grandfather felt so final. And when it was done, he would be quite alone.

Although it was late, it was still hot. Devin put down

the shovel and wiped the sweat from his face, catching the scent of rosemary on his fingers. It made a long, sighing sound, and a flash of blue, very bright and clean, shot for a second behind his eyes. The herb grew wild here on the top of the hill. Devin's grandfather had pointed out the wiry plants, explaining that rosemary was the toughest of herbs, able to survive almost anywhere.

"Smells good, doesn't it?" He'd held out a sprig for Devin to sniff. "A long time ago, people used to place it in graves for remembrance."

Devin turned away now, searching in the gloom for the familiar plant. He found a bush and tugged a small branch free. For a second or two, he held it to his face, breathing in the scent, and then he tossed it into the grave and began shoveling in dirt as quickly as he could. "I'm sorry," he told his grandfather. "I love you, I'm sorry." He was crying now, his tears mingling with the dusty clods.

"I won't forget you. I never will, no matter what."

When the grave was all filled in, Devin collected rocks and placed them in a circle on top. Circles rang clear and they were always gold.

"Like the corn," he told his grandfather. "Remember you told me you saw it? When you were a boy?"

It was a comfort knowing he could talk to his grandfather, even though he was dead. And if he closed his eyes, he could even imagine that his grandfather was talking right back to him.

But that night, alone in his bed, he couldn't imagine his grandfather saying anything at all.

Devin woke before dawn and rose to do his chores. The chickens had to be fed and the wood collected and the cow watered and led out into the little field. He went as fast as he could, the bucket of water from the spring banging painfully against his shins as he stumbled across the yard.

The hay needed to be cut. It normally took him and his grandfather a full day and a half. Devin fetched his scythe and stood still for a moment, staring at the meadow. It suddenly seemed enormous. But he bent his head and set to work, not knowing what else to do, his arms moving automatically. By midday his hands were blistered and his breath was ragged with panic.

The grass was barely a quarter cut.

Leave a job undone, his grandfather always said, and it will just get bigger.

But Glancer's stall needed to be cleaned out and the vegetable patch weeded, and the apples were still lying in the orchard . . . Devin worked all day and into the night, every hour a little further behind.

Midnight found him setting traps in the field for rabbits, his fingers trembling with fatigue. What if he actually caught one? What then? He had never killed a rabbit before. His grandfather always did it, his big hands quick and merciful. Devin had grown a lot in the last year, but there were still many things he couldn't do.

His grandfather had gone before he could teach Devin everything. Perhaps like everyone else, his grandfather hadn't thought enough about the future. He had been too busy with other things. Devin dropped his head and wept, too exhausted even to wipe his face.

The next day was worse than the one before, because his grandfather was right, jobs left undone just grew bigger and bigger. He ate the last of the cornbread and some raw carrots; there was nothing warm to eat because he hadn't had time to fill the stove and light it. Despair began to creep over him.

He lay on his bed that night with his boots still on and his hands and face unwashed. A great silence came. It swept through the orchard and over the fields and trickled along all the veins and tunnels in his body, right into his fingers. He looked up through the window at the stars, but even they made no noise.

In the morning Devin got up and gathered provisions: boiled eggs, vegetables, a knife, his grandmother's locket, and the small handful of coins from the pot in the kitchen. The city was far to the north. His grandfather used to live there years ago and had described it to him—the buildings, the huge numbers of people. Devin had trouble imagining crowds. He visualized himself and his grandfather and then added all the people from the picture book. It came to about fifty or sixty, which seemed like an impossibly large number.

"You'll go there someday too, Dev," his grandfather had told him "When you're ready to leave."

"When will I be ready to leave?"

"When you know for sure how to come back again."

Devin didn't think that time had come. He didn't feel ready at all. But in the city he would find help, someone to work on the farm, perhaps. He couldn't do it alone, and the longer he waited, the more impossible it would become.

He went to the spring and filled up the large leather water carrier. Then he opened the gate to the field so the cow could roam free. There was nothing he could do for the chickens, but they were hardy creatures and he thought most would survive until he got back. Finally Devin went to the barn and led Glancer out. He took off her halter and stood for a long moment with his forehead resting against her nose, feeling her breath, the shiver of her skin. She had been his horse since before he could remember, and the beating of her heart was as familiar as his own.

"Go," he whispered at last. "I can't take you. Go."

The horse stood in front of the barn, not moving as Devin walked away, but when he looked back a moment or two later, she had already wandered off a little way, head down, her brown rump shadowed by the trees. From behind the barn, the rooster crowed purple and then fell silent.

Devin turned toward the north and began to walk.

Two

THE CITY WASN'T ANYTHING like his grandfather had described. It was more like something out of a nightmare.

It had taken Devin a week of walking over hard and desperate country to reach it. His farm lay in a tiny valley watered by a secret spring that flowed into a stream. Millions of years ago, the earth itself had slipped and formed this hidden place, surrounded on all sides by slopes of rock. The only way in or out of the valley was a narrow path that twisted between immense boulders. If you didn't know the valley was there, you would miss it completely. Inside, sheltered from the worst of the sun, there were trees and fields and meadows.

Outside it was different.

Outside it was dry and flat and empty. The earth had a weightless feel, rising in small clouds of dust as Devin trudged along, the water carrier bouncing at his waist, his eyes pinched against the glare of the sun. He stumbled over slopes of loose white stones, his feet slipping, sending the stones skittering and bouncing. Ahead lay a huge expanse where little grew except low, brittle shrubs the same color as the earth. The sky seemed far higher than normal, as if someone had scraped away at the underside of it, leaving nothing but a thin, burning shell. Eventually Devin came to a channel in the ground and clambered down into it. It was an old, dried-up riverbed. He could see where water had once smoothed and hollowed out the rocks.

On the second day, Devin saw the biggest coyote he'd ever seen in his life. It trotted across his path, ignoring him, its muscles moving like liquid beneath its hide. During the afternoon of the third day he saw buildings.

At first he thought he must have arrived at the city, because there were so many buildings; he counted nearly a hundred. From a distance everything looked orderly, almost neat; but as he approached, he saw tilting roofs and weeds creeping out through cracks in the sidewalks. Devin walked down a broad street with homes on either side. Drifts of dust had gathered on the doorsteps like silent visitors, and children's toys lay scattered in the backyards. Ragged clothes hung from a broken washing line. A row of poplar trees had been planted on the edge of town but they were brown and dead.

There was nobody around. They must have left a long time ago, Devin thought. And they had gone without picking up the toys or taking in the laundry, as if they knew they weren't ever coming back.

There was a main street, with bigger buildings, some with large glass windows so you could look inside, but there was nothing to see except some bottles smothered with cobwebs, and rows of empty shelves. There was a car parked on the street, its lid open. Devin knew it was a car because he had seen pictures of them. They didn't have a car at the farm, nor any machines or artificial lighting or screens or buttons, nothing that his grandfather called technology. It was foolish to rely on such things, his grandfather had said, because if they went wrong, you were stuck. You were better off relying on yourself.

Devin peered under the lid of the car and saw a mass of wires and dirt. It was hard to imagine that this battered old thing had ever moved. He reached up and closed the lid, not sure why he was doing it, only that it felt a little terrible to leave it gaping open like that.

The next day he came to a road. It was the straightest and flattest thing he'd ever seen in his life. Vehicles were moving along it, although they looked different from the car in the abandoned town. These were low to the ground and made no more sound than a whisper as they passed by, shrinking to dots on the horizon. They must be some of the new inventions his grandfather had talked about, Devin thought. He tried to see who was driving them, but he could sense only dim shapes inside. For a second he thought of trying to stop one, but he was frightened by their strangeness and their speed. How did people breathe, traveling so fast? Just looking at them made him dizzy.

Soon after, he ran out of water. He found a spot where more shrubs grew and began to dig, as his grandfather had taught him. He dug with his hands and then with a sharp stick; the hole was deep before he finally saw a thin layer of liquid seeping up through the gravel. He took off his shirt and wet it and squeezed it carefully into his carrier. The water amounted to barely half a cup, and it tasted orange-brown and gritty.

On he went, a lonely speck against the sky. More roads appeared, forking in various directions. Then on the seventh day he came to hills, empty at first but becoming greener. Plants meant water, he thought. Perhaps he was on the outskirts of the city at last.

To begin with, it seemed like a pleasant place, although strange. There were a great many trees. They weren't the trees he was used to but tidy things, regularly separated, their trunks surrounded by tiny fences. Then a large green space opened up. At first Devin took it for cloth, but then he saw it was grass, although unlike any that he had ever seen before. It was cut perfectly evenly and very close to the ground, but what astonished him most was the color—a green of such tingling, glassy richness that he immediately sank to his knees to examine it further. The ground was moist, although no rain had fallen in many days. Devin thought perhaps it was watered by underground streams or pipes, although why anyone would go to that trouble for mere grass, clearly not intended for the grazing of livestock, he didn't know.

A little farther along, he came upon houses. They were huge, the size of three barns, and they were surrounded by more of the strange grass, and their roofs were covered with great shining panels of something that looked like glass, only darker. The houses were all completely spotless. Even the borders of the flower beds were razor sharp.

Every single house was set back and every single one was surrounded by steel fences.

As he stared, the windows in one house seemed to move, the horizontal shutters gliding closed like eyes blinking shut. But he didn't see any people at all. It was very quiet.

A few cars passed him. They were larger than those he'd seen on the highway and had windows that weren't clear glass, but darkened to a whistling brown so that he couldn't see inside at all.

The city looked to be almost empty, Devin thought. But then, coming around a corner to the top of the highest hill, Devin saw he was completely wrong about this. These houses, these gates and pathways and stretches of perfect grass, were only a corner of the city, a tiny section, sheltered by trees. The rest of it—the real city—lay below him.

It was a vast jumble of buildings, one on top of the other, dusty and crowded. Some of the buildings looked half in ruins; others had huge pictures flickering on them. Great flocks of birds wheeled and darted overhead. In the middle of the confusion lay the thick brown stripe of a river, the water flowing low and sluggish around the legs of three great bridges that rose with a tangled arrangement of pillars and cables. A yellow haze obscured the farther horizon, and Devin heard a distant roar, made up of a million voices.

For a second, his courage failed him and he thought of turning back. But he was very tired and there was nowhere else to go.

✦ ✦ ✦

Devin made his way through a labyrinth of streets and found an alley as the sky grew dark. He curled up in a pile of dirty paper, his hands clutched tight against his chest. At dawn three boys, older than he was and far stronger, attacked him, keeping him face down on the ground while they searched his clothes. In three minutes they had taken everything: his knife, jacket, coins, the last of his food, and even his boots. They didn't find his grandmother's locket, because Devin had hidden it in the hem of one of his pant legs. He lay on the ground after they'd gone, too terrified to move for several minutes. Then he got to his feet and limped to the entrance of the alley.

He was in a street so crammed with people that he almost bumped into a woman walking past, leading a small child by the hand.

"Please," Devin said, his voice jerky with shock. "Please, they took everything. Can you help me?"

The woman looked at him quickly and her mouth went tight and her eyes swung away. She shook her head with a small, angry gesture and hurried on, pulling her child with her. A boy riding a two-wheeled vehicle with a huge box on the back swerved suddenly out of the crowd toward him. Devin stumbled back and half fell. "Need help?" the boy shouted in a laughing voice. "Call the POLICE! Ha!" And then he was gone, as quickly as he came.

Nobody else seemed to have noticed. Everyone was moving, jostling, hurrying. Most of the buildings nearby were run down, and the ground was littered with trash and pieces of brick. Devin joined the stream of people, not knowing what else to do.

He began to walk fast and then broke into a trot. The wide street met another, and then a huge crossroads of four streets met in a knot of dust and traffic. There were more two-wheeled things, and small, old-looking cars, and men dragging light carts as they ran along. So many people, faces upon faces. Devin whirled and ducked, unable to take it all in; the clamor and color, the flapping clothes and spinning wheels, the market stalls, the doors and dark openings, the noise of a thousand things clanging and clattering.

He was running now, his bare feet hot against the broken sidewalk, his skin burning with a hundred sensations at once, his ears ringing painfully, his head pounding. At last he stopped and crawled under a sheet of corrugated iron that was leaning against a wall. He crouched there for a long time, watching feet pass in front of his shelter, his hands pressed tight to his ears, his mind grappling with the reality that faced him.

His idea to get help with the farm had seemed simple when he was back home. Now that he was in the city, it was a different matter. He couldn't just go up to someone and ask. He might have if there had been three—or five—or even ten people here. But there were so many. He had no idea where to begin or whom to approach. You had to know people, he thought. Or else they would look at you like the woman with the child had. Or not look at you at all.

Devin was very hungry. He crept out from his hiding place and began to search for food. He scavenged scraps from vegetable stalls and bins, trudging the streets as the hours passed. Water was scarce. There were long lines of people waiting for their turn at a single faucet, and it ran out before he got anywhere near the front. He didn't understand why there was so little water when he had seen such green grass in the other part of the city, the area with the big houses.

He noticed other things too. Like the huge, new cars that sometimes appeared amid the old, ramshackle vehicles. Or the man he saw get out of one such car with shoes that shone and glasses that were black and a strange device attached to the side of his head that he seemed to be talking into. Or the tall building, covered with glass so clean and bright that it looked as if it had descended from the sky to land among the tatty, broken-down buildings around it. These things didn't look as if they belonged. Or perhaps it was the rest of the city that didn't belong. It confused Devin, although nobody else around him seemed to notice. The man who got out of the car, for instance, hadn't appeared to see a ragged old lady with bare feet sitting only a little way away on the sidewalk.

The whole place seemed lopsided, Devin thought. Out of shape and out of balance.

A little later, Devin spotted a man lying in the street as if he were very ill, perhaps even dead. But everyone was simply passing by. One lady actually stepped over the man's body as if it were invisible.

In the afternoon he came to a large, grimy-looking building. There was a word written above the main entrance: POLICE.

That was the word the boy had shouted. Devin stopped. The letter E had slipped a bit and was tilted to the right so that it made the wrong sound, more of a stutter than a chirp. Devin hesitated. He didn't know what the word meant or whether the boy had been right about getting help there. As he watched, a man came out and stood in the doorway. He was large and sweaty and his face was heavy with boredom. He glanced up and saw Devin and his eyes were suddenly hard and threatening and Devin was afraid. He ducked away and hurried down the street, his heart pounding.

His plan to ask someone to come back and cut his hay and patch his barn and help him trap hares seemed stupid now.

When darkness fell, he found his way back to the corrugated-iron shelter and tried to sleep. Even though it was night, the city remained alive with noise, but Devin could still hear the silence. It had followed him all the way from the farm, and now it was here in the city. He could feel it in the pit of his belly and all the way up to his chest.

It was the silence of knowing he was utterly alone.

✦ ✦ ✦

After a day or two, Devin became less fearful and more used to the hubbub of the streets. It was easy to make a pattern of the place in his mind. The shapes of the buildings sang a song, just like the stones in the old wall that circled the farm had done, and the colors around him wove themselves into a fabric as clear as any map.

But the silence never left him.

Nor did his hunger.

He was hungry when he woke up in the morning and hungry when he went to sleep; and all the time in between, he spent looking for food. He ate anything he could find. Scraps of bread, rotten fruit, a handful of potato peelings flung into the street. He had to be quick because there were always other people as hungry as he was. Many of them were children.

The children were all ragged and thin, and they kept their eyes on the ground, hunting for shreds to eat. It didn't seem as though anybody was looking after them. Perhaps there were simply too many children, Devin thought, and in this strange, lopsided world, nobody cared about them very much. Not the way his grandfather had cared about him. The other kids didn't speak to Devin. They didn't even look at him. The silence inside Devin grew until his whole body seemed to ache.

On his third day a girl caught his eye. She was delicate, with dirty reddish hair and pale skin speckled like an egg. What made him notice her was that she was the only person he had seen since arriving in the city who was actually looking up. She walked along slowly, her gaze fixed on some point along the rooftops. Then she turned a corner and was gone.

A day later, he saw her again. She was crouching alone in the middle of a large area between buildings, in an expanse of broken concrete and stunted weeds. Devin walked closer. The girl looked as if she was hunting for something, her fingers digging through a small pile of rubble. She was so intent on her task that she didn't notice when Devin came right up in front of her.

"What are you doing?"

The girl startled and got to her feet instantly. Her eyes were small and brown and showed no expression. Something glittered in her hand.

"What have you found?"

She didn't reply. Instead she simply turned her back and began to walk away. Inside Devin, the silence surged and pushed until it felt as though it would break the banks of his skin and carry him far away.

"Please!" he cried out. "Please talk to me! Somebody has to talk to me!"

Three

THE GIRL TURNED AROUND. She looked a little younger than Devin, about ten or eleven, although it was hard to tell because she was so slight. Up close, her face was even more covered with freckles than he'd first thought, and her hair was very long and matted. It was tied back with a piece of ribbon that was so chewy pink and crackling that it made him want to smile. She was too wild and odd-looking ever to be called pretty, he thought. But somehow, she was beautiful. She was the most beautiful person he had ever seen in his life.

She opened her hand and showed him what she was holding. It was a sharp piece of something that glimmered with iridescence. She tilted it one way and then another, and where it caught the light it made a line of rainbow so sharp it almost hurt the eye.

"I collect them," she said. "They're just bits. I've never found a whole one. Once I found half. They're mostly buried. You have to look."

"What are they?"

"Discs," she told him. "People used to use them to store information."

Devin had no idea what she was talking about.

"There's pieces of them lying around all over the place," she said.

Devin reached out and took the fragment. The rainbow shimmered with icy prickles that ran down the back of his neck. "It's strange . . . ," he said slowly. "I never felt anything like that before."

The girl nodded. "Well," she said. "Okay. So I answered your question."

She turned and began to walk away. Devin watched her as she went. "Hey!" he called. "You forgot your piece of disc! Hey!" She didn't turn. Without thinking of anything except that he couldn't let her out of his sight, Devin took off running after her.

The girl didn't slow down. When Devin reached her she gave him a quick look and then picked up her pace. She ran lightly, almost effortlessly, her knot of red hair bouncing against the nape of her neck. Soon she was running so fast that she was almost flying, dodging pedestrians, swerving this way and that to avoid obstacles, with Devin keeping pace beside her. They ran through crowded streets, down a long alley, and across an area of wasteland strewn with concrete blocks. At last she stopped.

They were standing in the shadow of a tall building perhaps eight or nine stories high. It looked as if it had been in a fire—one wall was entirely blackened—and the whole thing still smelled of soot. At one point, someone must have tried to repair the place, because there was scaffolding all the way up to the top. But the effort had clearly been abandoned. Through a broken window, Devin caught a glimpse of a dark and hollow interior.

"Can you climb?" the girl asked.

Devin bent at the waist, panting. "Sure," he said, thinking of the apple trees in the orchard.

But the girl hadn't waited for his answer. She had already swung herself up to the first rung of the scaffolding and was reaching for the second. Soon she was twenty feet above him. Devin followed. The scaffolding creaked and shifted under his weight, and he had to half jump to reach each handhold, his heart pounding. Halfway up he made the mistake of looking down and saw the earth tilt and shimmer in the heat. He stopped, terrified, the stink of the burned building filling his nostrils, his hands slippery and shaking. He looked up. The girl was already at the top. He saw her head appear over the edge.

"The last part is easier," she said. "Go to the left . . . grab that pole . . . that's it."

Devin took a deep breath and hauled himself up the last stretch. At the top he lay for a second or two without lifting his head, trying to get his breath back. Slowly he got to his feet. They were on the roof. A faint breeze lifted his hair and cooled his face. Below him and stretching all the way to the horizon was the city, shrouded in a golden veil of haze and dust. In the far distance, he could see the hills and woods he had traveled through all those days before, and nearer, the brown stripe of the river and the bridges, tiny from this distance, like things made out of matchsticks. But it wasn't this that made him draw in his breath and stare. It was the roof itself.

The girl had arranged boxes to sit on and an old mattress, covered with a faded sheet. Above it was a canopy, propped up on sticks, a shimmery piece of pale green fabric that fluttered slightly in the wind. All around lay boxes and containers filled to the brim with colored scraps that glittered when they caught the sun. To one side, there was a kind of washing line, a string stretched between two corners of the roof. From the line hung many more of the disc pieces. They glimmered and twisted, flavoring the breeze with the sound of far-off bells.

Devin turned and looked at the girl. She was standing with her arms folded, staring at him.

"If you tell anyone about this place, I'll kill you."

He nodded. "My name's Dev," he said. "It's short for Devin."

"Kit," the girl said.

"What's that short for?"

"Nothing. It beats being called 'kid.' That's all."

Devin frowned. A great tiredness came over him. He went to the mattress and sat down on it. It was quiet up here, but it was a different kind of silence from the one that had followed him from the farm. Above his head, the canopy fluttered gently. He lay back and stared at the sky through the gauzy green fabric.

"It's like the grass," he murmured. "But thinner . . . slippery . . ."

He closed his eyes, and in three seconds he was fast asleep.

He woke up a long time later. Kit was sitting across from him. He didn't know how long she had been there, watching him sleep. In her hand there was a miracle, a large orange that glowed with thunder. She tossed it up and caught it, then threw it to him.

Devin stared at it with disbelief. "Where did you get this?"

"Stole it. You've been asleep for hours."

Devin peeled the orange and divided it in half.

"Don't bother," Kit said. "I've had one already." She got to her feet and started emptying her pockets, bringing out handfuls of things, fragments of glass, screws, an assortment of bottle tops. While Devin ate, she sorted the items, examining each in turn, making little piles. When she was done, she put each pile into a different container.

"You've got a lot of stuff," Devin said.

Kit stared hard at him and shrugged.

"I collect." She reached into another pocket and pulled out a last item. "This one's a true rary," she said. "Never seen one of these before." In her palm was a tiny shell, delicately whorled. "You ever seen the ocean?"

He shook his head. "I had a book with a picture of it. It looks big."

"All that water . . . ," Kit said.

"My granddad told me you can't drink it, though. It's too salty."

"I wouldn't care about some stupid salt," she said. "I'd stick my head in and I wouldn't stop drinking until I died."

Devin got up and went to the edge of the roof to take in the view again. "Those trees," he said. "Over by the hills. I came through those when I first got here."

"You mean The Meadows?"

"Is that what they're called? The grass there, it's very green. I think they water it."

Kit stared at him, her eyes narrowed with suspicion. "Do you really not know anything or are you just pretending?"

Devin didn't know what to say

"The Meadows is where the rich live," Kit explained.

"Where do they get the water?"

"They own the water, idiot! How do you think they got rich in the first place?"

Devin thought of the sky dark with rain and the way the stream at the farm ran too fast to hold. "You can't own water," he protested.

Kit rolled her eyes. "Well, they do. They own it. They own control of it. Along with just about everything else."

"But how? How did they get everything?"

She shrugged. "I don't know. I guess they just grabbed it. And everyone else needs what the rich have, so they just go on getting richer. It's the way it is. The rich have a lot, most other people have a little, and then there's us. We don't have anything at all.

"Lots of kids in our group," she added.

"But don't they have homes?"

"Used to. Some of them had good homes before their parents died or weren't able to feed them anymore. Lots are runaways."

"What about you?" Devin asked. "Are you a runaway?"

Kit shrugged again. "My parents ran away from *me*. I came back one day and they'd left. Best day of my life."

"My granddad used to live here when he was young," Devin began. "He said it was different then. It changed when it started to get hot. People stopped looking out for each other and lots of things that used to be organized just turned into a big mess."

"Yeah?" Kit said without much interest. "Well, it's like this now. And it's not going to change. Some of the kids talk about getting out, how they heard about a kid who got adopted by rich people and went to live in luxury forever. Or that there's a home somewhere where they feed you and you can play all day and have everything you want. But it's just fairy tales." Kit's mouth set in a fierce line.

"Fact is," she said, "we're on our own."

✦ ✦ ✦

They spent the rest of the day on the roof. Along with the oranges, Kit had found a loaf of bread—completely stale, but whole. She fetched water from an old bathtub on the roof. It had been collected during the last rainstorm, and there was very little left. "You have to boil it," she told Devin. She showed him how to soak the stale bread in the water until it grew soft and could be eaten with a spoon. When the meal was finished, they sat under the canopy and talked. Kit wanted to know about the farm.

"My granddad used to say there was nowhere else like it. He said it was a place where all you had to worry about were ordinary things. Like whether the chickens were laying or how to mend a fence," Devin said. "I didn't know what he meant."

He paused. "Then I left and came here."

Kit made a face. "And now you know exactly what he meant . . ."

"I thought I'd get help with it," Devin said. "But there doesn't seem to be anybody to ask. I don't know who to go to."

"You're right," Kit said. "You can't trust anybody in this place."

"It will be getting so overgrown, and I don't know how the animals are doing. "

Kit looked away. "Don't think about it, Devin."

"I nearly went into that place that says Police," he said. "I thought—"

"You don't want to go there! They're not good people. They're criminals, some of them. They're supposed to keep law and order, but they only do things if you pay them. Like I said, we're on our own."

"I . . . guess so . . ."

To cheer Devin up, Kit started telling him about the time she'd been inside one of the houses of the rich. Her father had landed a temporary job doing the gardening there. While he was busy, she'd wandered inside. The first thing she noticed was how cool it was. There was a pad on the wall where you placed your hand and the temperature in the room immediately adjusted to your exact comfort. Everything adjusted, she said. The lights, the pillows on the chairs; even the windows automatically shuttered when the sun came in at a certain angle. The rich never had to lift a finger. In the bedroom, the closets were full of clothes arranged by color, all perfectly pressed, and there was a box with sliding drawers full of jewelry. Kit's eyes grew wide with longing at the memory. She'd pushed her hand right into the box and run her fingers through the treasures. In the kitchen, all you had to do was reach for the fridge—not even touch it—and the door swung open, and inside, it was the size of a small room, full of food that didn't even look real because there wasn't a mark or blemish on anything.

There wasn't a single thing inside or outside that house that was ugly or untidy.

"The rich don't like looking at anything messy," Kit explained. "It's like their cars. Ever notice how the windows are always dark? My dad said they're programmed to darken automatically so the people inside don't have to see anything that might upset them."

She paused. "I could have stayed in that house forever. But I had to leave. When I came out, my dad was waiting for me with a stick."

"He beat you just for going in there?" Devin was incredulous.

"Oh, no. He would have beaten me anyway. He beat me just for being alive."

✦ ✦ ✦

The next morning, Kit said she needed to go and get more food. Devin wanted to go with her, but Kit said he would only slow her down.

"You don't know anything," she said. "And you don't even have shoes. Anyone looking at you would think you're crazy." Kit shook her head. "No, there's an art to stealing. There's rules to it. Like stealing big and stealing small. Whenever I take something I always take something else that's much less valuable. That way, if I'm caught, I can hand back the small thing and they'll think it's all I took . . . You're not ready for any of that. I bet you can't even pick a lock, can you?"

He shook his head.

Kit led him to a box containing dozens of padlocks of different sizes and showed him how to insert a wire and fiddle with it until the lock came free.

"Practice on these while I'm gone," she told him. "I'll bring back something good."

But when she came back, three hours later, her hands were empty and her face was white. There was a large red welt on her forehead and the flesh around one eye was bruised.

"What happened?" Devin cried. Kit said nothing. She walked furiously across the roof, her fists clenched and her head down.

"Are you all right?" He reached out and, before she could stop him, gently touched the bruise on her face.

"Oh," he said, in distress. "Why does it taste like honey? It shouldn't taste of something nice."

She flung away from him in sudden fury. "Are you trying to be funny? Talking crazy like that! You did it before. I thought you were just tired. Are you nuts or something?"

Devin didn't know what she meant. She was just upset, he thought. It would be best if he didn't argue.

Kit went to the mattress and sat down with her knees pulled up to her chin, the shards of disc overhead casting patterns on her face. She sat there for a long time, staring at her boxes of treasures. Devin waited until he saw her shoulders relax before speaking again.

"I'm going with you next time," he said. "I don't want you to be hit again."

She lifted her head. "It's okay."

"No, it isn't."

"We'll both have to leave for a while anyway," Kit said, getting to her feet. "Look at the sky."

In the far distance Devin saw storm clouds, watery brown with blackened edges, like something singed. The breeze had completely gone and the city was held in a breathless, dusty hush.

"I think we've got till the evening," Kit said.

"No, the rain will be here sooner than that." Devin studied the sky with a farmer's eye. "Two hours, maybe less."

Kit was already busy, folding up the canopy and stowing it away. He helped her place lids on her boxes and stack the plates and camp stove. Together they dragged the mattress to one side of the roof and covered it with an old tarp, then arranged the bathtub and other containers in a long row to catch the rain.

"There's a place I go, where lots of the kids go, when it storms." She pointed across the city. "Over there. I think it was a school once. You'll have to follow me and be sure not to get lost because you'll never find it by yourself."

"'Course I will," Devin said. "Look at the streets in front of it. They almost join up in an X shape only not exactly, so the humming crackles a little around the edges. Plus the building itself is way more red than anything else for miles around."

This time Kit came right up to him, her eyes serious, almost frightened.

"What are you talking about? It's concrete and brick like all the other buildings. Dirty gray concrete."

"But it's different from the other buildings. They're all different. That's how you remember them, right? Once you've seen something, you can always remember where it is."

She searched his face. "You're not kidding, are you?" she said slowly. "I don't think you're crazy. Maybe you're just a fool."

But they were running out of time to talk about it. The sky had darkened to a dull yellow and the storm clouds were almost overhead. As they stood there, the first drops fell, huge and warm and very wet. For a moment or two they did nothing but enjoy the feeling of wetness on their skin, their faces raised to the sky, their arms stretched out. Then, as the rain fell harder, they ran to the edge of the roof and began climbing down the scaffolding as quickly as they could.

Four

BY THE TIME THEY got to the bottom of the scaffolding, the rain was falling in earnest. The streets were dark and full of frantic movement. Children, some half naked, whooped and danced in the spray, their skinny limbs gleaming wet, their mouths gaping. Shopkeepers were hurrying to lock up and bar their shabby storefronts, and tubs and troughs and barrels were being dragged out to catch water. It hadn't rained in a long time, and there was no knowing when it would rain again.

Within minutes the downpour had become a single, massive sheet of water pounding the ground so hard that the earth blurred and the streets turned into streams thick with dust and debris. People gasped and fled, struggling to breathe in the deluge. Even the mangy dogs had taken cover, scrambling for higher ground as best they could.

Kit and Devin ran, slipping and sliding, half blinded, calling out to each other although nothing could be heard above the massive roar of the falling water.

The abandoned school was already full of kids when they arrived. Everyone was crowded into the old gym, sitting on the floor alone or in groups. Two older boys were bouncing a ball and running up to dunk it through an empty hoop that hung crooked on the farther wall. Kit made her way through the crowd without talking to anyone and sat down in an empty corner, her bag clutched tight to her chest and her eyes wary. Devin sat down beside her, wringing out the sleeves of his shirt and trying to catch his breath. He looked around.

He recognized a few of the kids from his wanderings through the city. One boy in particular was familiar. He was taller than the others, maybe fourteen or fifteen years old, with dark, curly hair cut very short and a long, straight nose that gave him a haughty appearance. He was leaning casually against the wall, one hand in his pocket, the other playing with a plastic object that made a scraping noise and then produced a flame. Each time Devin heard the scrape, a tiny lavender star shimmered into his view.

Devin looked away, toward a group of three or four girls who were sitting together with their heads very close and their arms around each other. Farther away two boys scuffled. Right in front of him five more boys formed a circle, squatting with their pale, bony knees toward the center, playing some game with pebbles. One by one they shook their pebbles and threw them down. They didn't look at each other or even talk. When they had thrown their pebbles they picked them up and waited until it was their turn again. In the center of the circle there was a small pile of food. A slice of bread or two, a wedge of cheese, and a small, greasy patty that looked like it had been carried in somebody's pocket for a while.

Devin nudged Kit.

"What are they doing?"

She shrugged, not interested. "It's a game. They put food in the middle and whoever wins gets all the food."

"Have you ever played?"

She shook her head. Her whole body seemed tense.

"I don't play," she muttered. "I don't play with anyone. I'm better off alone."

The rain beat against the walls of the gym and darkened the interior. In the dim light, the children's faces gleamed pale. A smell of boredom and unwashed bodies hung heavy in the air.

"I hate it here," Kit whispered. "I can't breathe. I wish the rain would stop."

Devin looked up suddenly. The tall boy, the one who kept making the flame, was staring straight at him.

For a second their eyes met and then the boy looked away.

"Who's that?"

"I don't know," Kit said. "He's here sometimes. Gets enough to eat, by the look of him."

There was a sudden commotion among the group playing for food. A boy with sunken eyes and a ragged coat was trying to join the game. He had an apple in his hand and was pushing it forward. The apple was tiny and wrinkled, barely enough for a single bite.

"Butt out, Pesk," one of the gamers said. "I've seen nuts bigger than that."

"Unless they're your nuts," somebody else said and there was a burst of laughter.

The boy's eyes were fixed on the pile of food in the center. "I can play," he said. "I got something for the middle. That means I can play."

"Ah, let him," somebody cried.

Pesk squatted down and joined the circle. His knees were the boniest of the whole group, and Devin couldn't help noticing how hollow his chest was. When the pebbles came to him, he shook them for a long time.

"Come on, Pesk!"

The pebbles fell.

"Too bad, Pesk! You lose!"

Devin looked away, not wanting to see any more.

✦ ✦ ✦

The long afternoon passed. A few more children arrived. Some played quietly or talked or broke into petty fights, but mostly they just sat while the rain beat endlessly and the dim light grew even dimmer. At last it was completely dark.

When she was sure she couldn't be seen any longer, Kit rummaged in her bag and pulled out a roll. She divided it and pressed one half into Devin's hand.

"It has raisins!" she whispered in his ear.

Someone in the middle of the gym lit an oil lantern. By its flickering light, Devin could see the shapes of kids settling down for the night, arranging themselves under thin blankets, their bodies curled up on the floor. He ate quickly and lay down himself, his cheek resting on his hand, his eyes wide.

There was a boy lying next to him, his eyes glittering with unshed tears. It was Pesk.

Devin didn't say anything. The shadows made Pesk's eyes look even more sunken, like the dark holes in a skull. They stared at each other silently.

"D'you think it's true, what they say?" Pesk whispered at last.

"About what?"

"That there's a Home where they take you in? And alls you got to do is find it?"

"I don't know," Devin said.

"I think it's true. I heard they feed you alls the time

and you never . . . you never . . ." His voice trailed off. "They got new clothes there too. And so many toys you can play for just about forever."

"Shut up, Pesk!" somebody called out. "We're trying to sleep, here."

Pesk's mouth closed instantly, but his huge eyes never left Devin's face.

"Alls you got to do is find it," he whispered very quietly, as if talking to himself. He turned over, wrapped his arms around himself, and said no more.

Devin lay awake for a long time, listening to the rain. His hand crept to the hem of his pants where his grandmother's locket lay hidden. Inside were pictures of his grandparents when they were very young, taken not long after they'd first met. His grandmother had round cheeks and a smile that seemed to light up everything.

"She wasn't the prettiest girl I ever saw," his grandfather had told Devin, "but she was the loveliest."

Devin fingered the locket in the dark. It was solid gold and heavy, an oval shape, as clean and kind as an egg. He dozed briefly and woke before dawn, and while it was still dark he slipped the locket into one of the pockets of Pesk's ragged coat.

✦ ✦ ✦

The morning brought an end to the rain. Through the grimy windows of the gym, the sky was hard and blue again. In a little while, the heat would dry the earth, turning it to dust once more. Now that the rain had stopped, the gym was loud with the chatter of children waking up and getting ready to leave. Kit was already itching to get away.

"We got lucky," she said. "We could have been here for days . . ."

Out on the street, the sudden glare made them blink and squint.

"We should look for food," Devin said.

"I want to get back to the roof," Kit said. "I want to set up my stuff."

"I'll go for food. It's my turn."

She hesitated. But she was anxious to get back to her roof, to set up her home again and arrange her treasures. "Okay," she said finally, "But be careful."

"I'll be fine."

He trotted off, a map of the city clear in his head. Before, when he had roamed the city alone, the sights and sounds around him had overwhelmed him with their multitude. But he was ready for them now. As he ran along, making for a particular street with many market stalls, he found himself starting to take pleasure in the rattling, chattering kaleidoscope around him.

At the market he paused, savoring the sensations. On one side, a pyramid of lemons made a rough trilling sound, and on another, he heard the thunder of oranges and carrots arranged in piles below a dusty canopy. A man sweeping the ground with a broom sent a flock of crows wheeling through his mind. Things clicked and sang and flittered over his tongue: the buttons on a coat, an upturned basket, the faces of passersby, the feel of the sidewalk against the soles of his feet.

Devin almost forgot he was supposed to be looking for food. He walked through the market in a kind of daze. By a stall selling pieces of fabric he stopped, his eyes dazzled by all the tangled, tickling colors of the rainbow. He turned around and found himself in front of a long table heaped with loaves of bread. They had been baked not long before, and the smell was heavenly. How golden they were! Devin reached out and touched one, curling his hand against its rounded shape, feeling the thin crust and the warmth of the dough beneath.

A large hand gripped his shoulder so hard that he yelped.

"I've got you now, you little thief!" Devin was yanked backward, his cheek pressed against a greasy apron, and then shaken so hard that he almost bit his tongue.

"Right. Under. My. Nose," the baker grunted, shaking him some more. "You think I'm stupid, do you?"

"I wasn't stealing it," Devin cried when he could catch his breath. "I wasn't stealing!"

The baker's face flushed scarlet with rage. "Just admiring it, were you? Just fondling it with your grubby little hands?"

Devin was silent.

"I'm sick of you thieving brats," the man went on. "Every day it's the same. I have to have eyes in the back of my head. Tried reporting it, but what's the point? Nothing happens. The police used to do something . . ." He paused and his eyes narrowed. "Now we take matters into our own hands."

The grip on Devin's shoulder tightened. "I'm going to take you around to the back," the baker said, "and give you such a beating you'll never look at a loaf of bread again."

Five

"I wasn't stealing it. I've never stolen anything!" Devin cried in desperation.

The baker swung him around violently. "I'm going to teach you. I'm going to teach you a lesson you'll never forget."

"Let him go," somebody said.

The baker whirled around, still clutching Devin.

"What was that?"

"I'll pay for the bread."

It was the boy from the night before, the tall one with the flame who had stared at Devin. He held out his hand and showed two silver coins.

"He's my friend. Let him go."

For a second the baker hesitated, and then he shoved Devin away.

"You got lucky," the baker told him as he took the money. "Try it again and I'll have the skin off your back."

The boy took the loaf of bread and walked away. Devin hurried after him.

"Thanks," he said. "I wasn't stealing it, but he didn't believe me."

The boy said nothing. His eyes were very pale, a faded blue that looked as if it had been washed a thousand times.

"What's your name?"

"Roman."

"Mine's Devin."

The boy spun away suddenly and made his way through the crowds. He stopped in the doorway of a deserted storefront.

"Where are you staying?" he asked Devin.

Devin hesitated. Kit had told him not to tell anyone about the roof. "Nowhere, really," he said.

"That's what I thought," Roman said. He paused for a long time, staring into Devin's face.

"I'd like to pay you back for the bread," Devin said. "Only my money was stolen . . ."

"Never mind about that," Roman said. "I want to talk to you."

"Why?"

"I saw you in the gym last night. I watched you. You put something into that kid's pocket. Something valuable. Something you've been holding on to for a while. Why?"

Devin felt his face redden. "I don't know . . . I felt bad for him. I figured he could buy food with it."

Roman nodded. "That's what I thought. There was nothing in it for you. It was just kindness."

His words were warm, but there was something automatic in the way he spoke them that puzzled Devin.

"Some kids are born kind, but it's rare," Roman continued. "Most have to learn it. How do they learn it? By being treated with kindness themselves. I thought the moment I saw you that you must have come from a good home. Did you?"

Devin nodded. "There was me and Granddad, and when I was very little, there was Grandma too." He thought of his horse. "And animals. A horse and a cow and chickens and we were going to get a sheep . . ."

Roman nodded. "I knew it." He hesitated, staring at Devin for what seemed like a long time.

"Listen," he said quickly, as though coming to a decision. "You ever hear rumors about a children's home, a place where they feed you and keep you safe?"

"The boy—Pesk—was talking about it. But Kit says it's just a fairy story."

Roman put a hand on Devin's shoulder and leaned in close. "What I'm about to say is not a fairy story. It's the truth. Only you can't tell anyone about it. There is a home for children and it's great. They have everything. Playgrounds and a swimming pool and beds with clean white sheets and meals whenever you want and a ton of other stuff I don't have time to tell you about right now. They take in kids who have no home of their own. I know because I live there myself."

"Why are you telling me?" Devin asked.

"They can't take every kid," Roman explained. "They have to choose. And they only choose special kids." His hand tightened on Devin's shoulder. "I can take you there. Tonight. Think about it, Devin. Tonight you could be sleeping in a bed, with a full stomach, far from this filthy city, far from danger."

"I don't know," Devin said.

Roman straightened up and took his hand away. "Well, it's up to you," he said. "But don't think about it too long. I'm leaving tonight."

"Can Kit come too?"

"That girl you were with last night?" Roman frowned. "I don't think so. No. She's not . . . she's not right for the Home at all."

"Then I can't go," Devin said simply. "I'm very sorry. Thanks for asking me, though. And thanks for saving me from the baker."

"You won't change your mind?"

Devin shook his head. "Not if Kit can't come. There's no way I'm leaving her behind."

✦ ✦ ✦

Devin clambered up to join Kit on the roof. All her stuff had been put back in place.

"You were gone for ages," she said. "Get anything?"

Devin handed her the loaf of bread.

"A whole one! And it's fresh!" her eyes narrowed. "Did you steal it, Devin? I didn't think you'd be able."

"I didn't steal it." Devin sat down on the mattress. "It's a long story. I met a boy. He was at the gym last night. His name's Roman, and he bought it. I was going to be beaten by the baker and he saved me."

"You're not making sense," Kit said, tearing a chunk of bread from the loaf and stuffing it hungrily into her mouth. "Start from the beginning."

She listened in silence until he came to the part where Roman had told him about the home.

"That's nonsense!" she burst out. "It doesn't exist."

"But he said it did. He said he lives there."

Kit screwed up her face until her freckles almost merged into one. "Devin!" she cried. "He was messing with you. Only you would have believed him. You'd believe anything."

"I said I wouldn't go," Devin told her. "He said you couldn't come, so I said no thanks. I just walked away."

"You believed him about the home but you still walked away?"

He nodded.

"Because I couldn't come?" Her face looked as shocked as if he'd just slapped her.

"Yeah. And then he came running after me and said okay, you could come too, but nobody else. And he gave me the bread. And he said we have to meet him tonight."

"This doesn't make any sense. I don't know what this boy Roman is up to, but I don't like it. We'll just eat the bread and forget about it."

"Why?"

"Devin," Kit said softly. "You lived on a farm all your life, but even you have to know that people don't buy you bread for nothing. And people don't drive you off to homes where you can live happy ever after. Not in the real world."

Devin looked at her. She was wearing a different shirt, a ragged yellow tank that showed the top of her arms. Now he could see that there were marks all over her shoulders, a dense crisscross of scars and ugly lines of raised skin where she had been beaten. The marks were faded purple, and into Devin's ears came the sound of the farm rooster crowing, faint and far away like something in a dream. Kit saw him looking and raised her chin defiantly.

"Trust me," she said. "Good things don't happen in the real world."

"They must sometimes," Devin pointed out. "Maybe just one time in a hundred or a thousand. And if there's even just a tiny chance, don't you think we should take it?"

✦ ✦ ✦

They talked about it for the rest of the day without being able to decide what to do. In the end, they came to a compromise. They would go to the meeting place and Kit would make up her mind after talking to Roman and hearing more about the home. Kit was certain it would be nothing but a trick and they would return to the roof for the night. Still, when it came time to leave, she hesitated.

"If we do go, if it's real, I don't know what I should take with me."

"They probably have everything we need right there," Devin reminded her.

"But my raries . . ." She hovered over the small shelf where she kept her most prized finds. The shell was there along with an assortment of tiny porcelain dolls' heads, three old keys, and the golden nib of an ancient pen. Kit scooped them up and put them in the bottom of her bag.

"Okay, I'm ready."

It was dusk by the time they climbed down from the roof. They hurried through the streets, making for the place where Devin had last seen Roman. He was standing just where Devin had left him, leaning against the wall, half in the shadows.

"Come on," Roman said immediately. "We have to leave right this minute."

"We're not going with you until I find out more," Kit said. "I'm not leaving without some proof that it's not just a trick."

"There's no time," Roman said. "I'll explain everything later. You have to come now."

He turned and disappeared down a side street that was illuminated only by a few dim lights from neighboring buildings and the half-spent moon above the rooftops. The shadows fell long and dark over the sidewalk. At the far end of the street there was a car. It was large and gleaming and lit from the interior. A man was sitting in the driver's seat, his body nothing but a dark silhouette.

The passenger door was wide open, waiting.

Kit gripped Devin's arm.

"This isn't right," she said, shaking her head. "I don't like it."

Devin could feel her alarm, the beginning of panic.

"Look," he said, "You're right. We don't know anything about this. But I think we have to go. We can't stay in the city. Always hungry, having to steal, getting into fights and getting hurt. How long can we survive like that?"

"Okay, listen, this is a bad idea," Kit said, talking very fast, "I should just turn around and walk away from this. But here's the thing. You told that boy you wouldn't go without me and nobody's ever done something like that for me before. Not once. Not ever. This is a bad idea, but I can tell you've set your mind on it and someone's got to watch your back. You wouldn't go without me, and now I'm not going to let you go alone."

Kit marched forward and got into the backseat of the waiting car.

Six

DEVIN HAD NEVER SEEN anything like the inside of the car. The minute he got in, he was in a different world. Everything gleamed and the air was fresh and cool. As he sat down on the tan-colored leather seats, they made a tiny sighing sound as they shifted to fit his body. The windows—completely darkened—gave no view outside.

Roman had gotten into the front seat, next to the driver. There was a glass panel between the front and back seats. The car moved off swiftly and utterly silently.

Kit sat half curled up, her eyes wide and watchful. "I'm not going to close my eyes for a second," she whispered to Devin. "If anything happens, I want to be ready."

He nodded. "Me too."

But the cool air, the comfort of the seats, and the soft

vibration of the car as it sped onward soon lulled Devin into a doze and then into a deep sleep. He dreamed of his grandfather at the kitchen table at night with the light from the lantern making a circle of gold. His grandfather had the book open and was teaching him to read. "No, that's not it," he said to Devin in his quiet, patient voice, "you're getting all muddled up aren't you?"

"I am," Devin said. "I'm really muddled up, Granddad."

Devin looked down and the whole farm was suddenly there below him as if he were flying. And it was set inside another, bigger circle of gold that glowed bright at the edges and kept the dark away.

"You have to try again, Dev," his grandfather said, turning the page. "Go back, try again, go back."

"I can't, I don't know how! I don't know!"

Someone was shaking him, calling his name. It was Kit. His eyes shot open. It was early morning; they had been driving all night. The car windows had lightened to clear glass and he could see they were far from the city, traveling on an empty road. Beside the road he saw thin lines of crops. They were soybeans, one of the few plants that could be cultivated on such dry soil, although even these were stunted and half withered.

"You slept for hours . . ."

Devin wasn't listening. He was too busy staring outside, where a row of hills made a pattern against the sky, interrupting the steady clicking of the horizon with a series of soft thuds. He looked up and noticed by the sun that they were traveling west. The road forked and they turned away, moving southwest now, past great heaps of tumbled rocks.

A tray slid out from the panel in front of them and there were two glasses of a shimmering pale yellow liquid. Kit eyed the drink. "Better leave that alone. It's all bubbly. We don't know what it is."

"But I'm so thirsty, Kit."

"Okay. But I'll try it first."

She took a wary sip and her face shivered with astonishment. "I never had a bubbly drink before."

The car turned off the main highway and began to wind along through trees and hedgerows. The road narrowed until it became a single lane. Finally it petered out completely. In front of them was a stone arch with words carved across the top:

Gabriel H. Penn Home for Childhood

In a second, the car had passed beneath the arch and entered a long and shady driveway.

Kit cast a look at Roman sitting in the front seat. "He was telling the truth," she whispered. "There really is a home. It really exists."

❖ ❖ ❖

The driveway wound around in a wide curve. To their left were bushes and tall trees; on their right, a huge meadow, surrounded by a low fence, where three or four horses were grazing. As the car came around the top of the curve, Devin and Kit saw a group of buildings built around a courtyard, with a tower at the center. Above the tower, the sky was full of dark flecks; a vast flock of birds, which darted this way and that in sudden groups and clusters.

The car pulled up alongside the buildings and entered the courtyard with the tower. The walls around them were golden stone, faded with age and covered with patches of creeping ivy. The courtyard itself was paved around the edges, and there were beds of flowers on both sides, bright, heavy, rich-looking blooms that Devin had never seen before. They must need a lot of water, he thought. He had never heard of anyone wasting water on flowers. The extravagance of it astonished him.

The car stopped and the children got out.

Instantly the air was full of the sound of the birds twittering in their hundreds. A small girl who must have been waiting in the shadows ran forward and attached herself to Roman's side. She was six or seven, round-faced and blond, with a large yellow bow pinned to the side of her head. She peeped around Roman at the newcomers.

"Have you got a match?" she asked Devin in a sweet, clear voice.

He shook his head.

"Not even one?" the girl begged, "not even a teeny tiny baby one?"

"That's enough, Megs," Roman said, patting her on the head. "Leave them alone. Go on now." She darted off obediently, her yellow bow bouncing against her curls. Roman turned back to Kit and Devin.

"I have to go. Mrs. Babbage will be along to show you to your rooms."

"I can't believe we're here," Kit said. "You were telling the truth. Who runs this place? How long do we get to stay? How many kids are here?"

But Roman didn't seem in the mood to talk. He looked down at the ground, not meeting their eyes.

"I have to go," he repeated. "Mrs. Babbage will look after you."

As if on cue, a woman came out from one of the buildings facing the courtyard and pattered over to them. She wore a cardigan that drooped almost to her knees, and her thin hair was pinned back in a bun no bigger than a walnut. Her face wore an expression of kindness.

"Right on time!" she cried, as if the children had planned their own arrival. "You poor, dear things, you must be ever so tired."

"Not really," Kit said. "What is this place? Do you run it? Can we look around?"

"There's plenty of time for all that, plenty of time. You must rest. Your rooms are ever so nice." And she led them away, across the courtyard, into another building, and up a winding stone staircase.

They found themselves in a small bedroom with whitewashed walls and a patchwork quilt on the bed.

"This will be your room," Mrs. Babbage said, turning to Devin. "There's a bathroom over there, and your pajamas are laid out. Clean clothes in the closet. You jump into bed and have a little sleep and when you wake up you'll feel ever so refreshed."

Devin and Kit could only stare, dumbfounded.

"You're next door," Mrs. Babbage continued, turning to Kit.

"You mean I get a room too?"

Mrs. Babbage made a high-pitched tapping sound at the back of her throat which Devin thought was probably a laugh.

"Of course! All our children have their own rooms."

She darted into the hall, followed by a bewildered-looking Kit. Devin was left alone.

It was very quiet. The walls were stone, and no sound from the outside, not even the twittering birds, could penetrate them. Devin stared at the quilt on the bed. The scraps of fabric formed a complicated pattern that instantly imprinted on his mind. Large, interlocking stars were connected to each other by smaller ones, the whole piece worked in a hundred different shades of red and blue. But it was the shapes in between the stars that Devin looked at. They leapt out at him, a jagged arrangement of triangles that looked just like stairs rising and falling, turning back on themselves, leading nowhere, deceiving the eye . . .

✦ ✦ ✦

It was close to noon when Devin woke up.

His clothes had vanished from the chair where he'd left them. He went to the closet and found a pair of brand new jeans and a navy shirt. Then he went to find Kit.

For a second or two he didn't recognize the girl sitting on the bed next door, staring out of the window. Her hair was clean and hung in gleaming, blood-red waves almost to her waist. Her ragged clothes were gone, and she wore a green dress with a scarlet sash that matched her hair. When she saw Devin, she ducked her head, embarrassed.

"You look . . . so different," Devin said.

"There was nothing to wear," she muttered, "except this dress."

"I slept," Devin said. "I didn't think I would."

"Me too. Then I got up and had a shower. A shower, Devin! The water just kept on coming out. And it was warm!" She paused. "What is this place? It's not like anything I've ever seen before. There's nothing like this in the city, not even The Meadows."

"We had books at the farm," Devin said. "There was one with a picture inside that looked kind of like this place. It was a school, from a long time ago."

Kit stroked the quilt on her bed. "It's so lovely . . ."

Through the window, Devin could see hills in the distance, and nearer, surrounded by trees, he glimpsed water, too blue to be an ordinary pond.

"I think it's the swimming pool!" Kit cried, following his gaze. "Can you imagine?"

Devin couldn't. The swimming pool took his breath away. He wondered how many gallons of water the pool held. And all of it—every single valuable drop—was there just to give pleasure.

"I keep thinking there has to be a catch, but whatever it is, I don't care," Kit said.

"What do we do now?"

"We're supposed to go the dining room for lunch," Kit said. "That Babbage woman told me. After that someone is supposed to show us around the place."

✦ ✦ ✦

A separate building, off the courtyard and half-covered in ivy, housed the dining room. From its open windows came the noise of chattering, the clatter of knives and forks, and the smell of cooked food. Kit and Devin entered and found themselves among twenty-five or thirty children seated at long tables. At one end of the room, a table was covered with piles of plates and steaming dishes. They saw meat and pies and mashed potatoes and sandwiches, fruit of all kinds, and a large cake with white frosting. In the middle of the food stood a castle made of jelly, red and wobbling slightly under its own weight.

A boy seated near the door caught sight of them and immediately got to his feet.

"New kids, right?" He was skinny, with long, dark hair that hid half his face. He spoke fast, as if his words were trying to catch up with his thoughts.

"I'm Luke. I'm going to show you around. After you've had your lunch. I wouldn't show you around before you've had your lunch. That wouldn't make any sense."

"Excuse me?" Kit said.

Luke made a visible effort to check himself. "Sorry," he said. "I get a bit hyper around this time of day. Must be all the sugar, although that's never been proved, the link between sugar and hyperactivity. But you can't count it out." He gave himself a little shake and rapidly opened his eyes and squeezed them shut several times.

Kit stared at him uncertainly.

"Am I doing it?"

"What?"

"The thing with my eyes."

"Uh-huh."

Luke nodded. "Can't always tell. Best to know."

After Kit and Devin had heaped their plates with food, they sat down at one of the tables next to Luke and another boy.

"This is Malloy," Luke told them. "He's a pain in the neck."

"Hi, new people!" Malloy said. "Guess how many boiled eggs I can get into my mouth at the same time?" His face was perfectly round except for his ears, which stuck out on either side like the handles on a jug. "Three!" he announced.

"Triggered my gag reflex," he added. "I barfed all over the floor."

"Malloy likes to share," Luke said.

But Kit and Devin were too busy eating to pay attention. For several minutes, all they could think about was the food disappearing into their mouths. Luke and Malloy watched them in fascination.

"You can always tell the new ones," Luke commented.

"Like you'd know anything about feeling hungry, rich kid."

"Ever noticed how 'Malloy' rhymes with 'annoy'?" Luke said, his eyes twitching.

"Ever noticed how 'Luke' rhymes with 'puke'?"

Devin ate furiously, not really listening to the other boys. It was only when his hunger was completely satisfied that he was able to lift his head and look around him.

The cafeteria was filled with kids of all different

skin, hair, and eye color, all different ages from little ones to teenagers. But they were alike in the way they were dressed, the boys in neat jeans, the girls in the same sort of party dresses that Kit was wearing. Devin was reminded again of the pictures in his book, the ones that showed kids from a long time ago.

Most of the children seemed quiet and orderly, but three or four were making no effort to behave themselves. They had taken over the huge jelly castle and were busy demolishing it, attacking it with spoons, cramming it into their mouths, flicking pieces at each other and laughing wildly. As he watched, one small girl stuck her entire hand into the wet, wobbly mass, shrieking with excitement.

Devin glanced around to see if anyone else had noticed. But nobody was even looking. He looked in the other direction and saw Roman sitting next to the little girl, Megs. Devin wanted to catch Roman's attention, but the older boy's head was down. He was staring at his plate as if he didn't want—or didn't expect—anyone to speak to him. As Devin watched, Megs tugged at his arm, her face tilted toward him, smiling. Roman patted her gently, pushed his plate away, and stood up.

"Hey, Roman!" Devin said as he passed by.

Roman carried on as if he hadn't heard.

"What's up with him?" Kit asked Luke through a mouthful of spaghetti.

Luke shrugged. "Knows you don't like him."

"Why wouldn't we like him?" Devin asked, astonished.

"He's not exactly popular around here," Luke said, making a face. "Let's just leave it at that."

✦ ✦ ✦

Lunch was almost over and most of the children had left.

"I've got to show you around now," Luke told Kit and Devin. "You coming, Malloy?"

Malloy shook his head. His cheerful expression had vanished. "I just got the message from Karen."

Luke's face fell. "That's too bad . . . I'm sorry, Malloy. But maybe it's not for that. Maybe it's for something else."

"Unlikely," Malloy said, staring down at his hands.

Luke nodded. "Yeah. But you'll be all right. You haven't done it too many times."

"Will you keep an eye on Fulsome for me, Luke?"

"'Course I will . . ."

"I thought he was looking kind of pale this morning, not his usual self . . ."

Luke drew a deep breath. "Okay," he said, turning quickly to Kit and Devin. "I guess it's just us on the magical mystery tour."

"What was all that about?" Devin whispered to Kit as Luke led them out.

She shrugged, not interested. "Who knows?"

Devin stared back at Malloy. He was still sitting at the table, his shoulders hunched.

But Kit was hurrying Devin along. "Come on! I can't wait to see around this place!"

They stepped into the courtyard and suddenly he could hear the noise of the birds again. The sound was a collection of sharp threads, gray in the center but lightening to a dull violet at the edges, a mass of clotted knots that spread across the sky like . . .

"Hey, you okay?" Luke asked as Devin stared upward, dizzy and transfixed.

. . . like a net. A huge net, he thought. And they were all trapped underneath it.

Seven

THE COURTYARD AND THE tower were in the center of the Home. Around them, pathways led in all directions toward a variety of attractions. Kit and Devin followed Luke around the back of the dining room and saw a playground with swings and a slide. A little way off, a fountain in the shape of an elephant blew bubbles out of its trunk. The bubbles drifted away toward a circular track with wooden cars arranged in a row.

"Go-carts," Luke said.

Around the corner, Devin saw a huge, brightly colored shape, soft around the edges and curiously pudgy, with fat, leaning towers and a large inner area, the size of twenty beds.

"Bouncy castle," Luke said, as if reading from a list. "There's also tennis and basketball courts farther

down, next to the large meadow. On the other side of
the meadow there's a climbing wall and tree houses with
zip lines."

"What are zip lines?" Devin wanted to know.

"Devin doesn't know what any of this stuff is," Kit
said. "I know about it. I mean, I've heard about it, but
he just knows stuff about farms." Her eyes were shining.

She was right, Devin thought. He had never owned
toys. The farm had been his playground. The barn had
been his castle, Glancer had been his steed, and a piece
of whittled wood had been his sword.

They continued to walk. Although it was hot, there
was shade under the trees, and a gentle breeze followed
them as if, like all the other things in the Home, it had
been expressly provided for their comfort and ease.

"Here's something you can relate to, Devin," Luke
said.

They had stopped by a small farmyard. Devin could
tell at once that it was just for show, not a working farm,
but he couldn't help admiring the large pigsty and the
pair of goats in the enclosure beyond. He sniffed deeply,
inhaling the familiar scent of hay and manure. The
breeze ruffled the grasses in the meadow, and he smiled
to himself, wondering how such a soft, whispery noise
could be colored so very red . . .

"Look at that!" Kit cried. Devin turned and saw
horses. Not living ones, but brightly painted wooden

creatures that rose and fell, galloping fixed and stately around a glittering platform roofed with gold.

"I want a ride on that!" Kit declared.

"If you want a ride, you can ride a car too," Luke said. "They're copies of old ones—real low-tech classics, except they're sized for kids. There's about ten of them in the garage.

"They can get up to twenty-five miles per hour, sometimes thirty," he added without excitement.

A little later, he led them past a group of kennels. Kit stopped, transfixed.

"Are those . . . puppies?" she asked. "Can we play with them?" She ran over to their enclosure and fell to her knees, her hands groping among the tumbling creatures.

"You can probably have one if you want," Luke said, uninterested.

Devin was puzzled. He knew that Luke had been at the Home for a while, but surely not long enough to get bored with everything in the place. Kit picked up one of the puppies, a mottled scrap of brown and white patches, all tongue and wagging tail. She pressed her face against it.

"I'm going to call him Frisker!"

"Whatever," Luke said.

✦ ✦ ✦

As they walked, Devin observed several adults, dressed in dark green. Some were tending to the flower beds; others passed by pushing carts or carrying supplies of one sort or another. They were staff members, he thought. He remembered the way his clothes had been silently removed and the huge amount of food that had appeared in the dining room. There must be dozens and dozens of staff at the Home, working behind the scenes, keeping everything orderly. He smiled hesitantly at a man walking down the path toward him with a pile of towels. But the man didn't smile back.

Devin also saw plenty of children; some seemed odd to him. One boy was walking along clutching a teddy bear to his chest although he was at least fourteen years old. A girl was crouched beside a bush, completely still, her arms wrapped around herself. That was the other odd thing about the kids. Apart from one or two, the majority of them were just sitting or standing around.

Despite all the marvels surrounding them, very few children were actually playing.

A great stillness hung over the place. From somewhere far away came the sound of music, tinkling and repetitive, the notes pink and apple green, as pale as fingerprints on a window.

Da dumdee dumdee, dum dum dum . . .

"And now . . . big drum roll, please . . . the swimming area!" Luke announced.

The swimming pool was a complicated arrangement consisting of one main pool and several smaller ones leading into it. Waterfalls cascaded down piles of rocks, and there were water toys everywhere. But only one boy was enjoying the place. He was about twelve or thirteen, broad shouldered, with a square, strong-looking face. He stood waist deep, holding a red plastic pistol in one hand. As Devin watched, he suddenly squirted himself in the face, laughed loudly, and then, seeming not to notice that he had an audience, did exactly the same thing over again.

"Who's that?" Devin asked.

"That's Ansel," Luke said, without looking.

"Why's he doing that?"

"I don't know. Don't look."

"Why not?"

Luke turned away abruptly. "Just don't, okay?"

Ansel squirted himself in the face for a third time. "Come on," Luke said roughly and hurried them away.

✦ ✦ ✦

A girl sat under the shade of a large cedar tree. She was sucking the tips of her long hair and staring blankly at the ground.

"Hi, Missie," Luke said.

Missie frowned. "Hi, yourself, rich kid. How come you get to show the new kids around? It's not fair."

Luke's eyes twitched rapidly. "You want to do it?"

"No. I'm just saying, Genius."

"Don't pay any attention to her," Luke told the others. "Missie's always crabby."

"I'm not crabby," Missie argued, tossing her saliva-wet hair. "It's everyone else that's so stupid and cheerful."

Luke rolled his eyes. "Missie's the sort of person who could be driving a car down a one-way street and if she saw twenty other cars all going the opposite way, she'd think they were the ones going in the wrong direction."

"Of course I would," Missie retorted. "If they were."

"Why'd she call you 'rich kid'?" Kit asked, after they had walked on a little way. "Malloy called you that too."

Luke stopped abruptly. "Okay," he said. "Let's get it over with. I come from The Meadows. My parents were billionaires."

Kit's eyes widened. "What happened?"

"The money wasn't theirs. They stole it. The plan was sheer genius. They got millions and millions from rich people who were hoping to get even richer. Greed makes idiots out of people, that's what my dad always said."

He looked down at the ground, scuffling the dirt with his shoe. "The trouble is, they got caught. The judge gave them ten sentences of fifty years each. That's a total of five hundred years in jail for each of them."

"But won't they be . . . dead before that's done?" Devin asked, bewildered.

Luke rolled his eyes. "'Course they will. The judge was making an example of them. If you steal money from the rich, nothing can save you. Don't you know anything?"

Kit shook her head. "He doesn't. It's not his fault."

"So what happened to you?" Devin asked Luke.

"I ran away, spent some time on the street. I was trying to figure out a way to bust Mom and Pop out of jail. Might have done it too, only I met Roman."

"You met him like we did?"

"Oh yes," Luke's voice went low. "We all met Roman."

There was a confused silence. Devin reached out instinctively and touched Luke's arm. It was tense, tight as a stretched rope. Devin tasted burned rubber and peppermint—a fleeting sensation, half bitter, half sharply sweet.

"What about the genius bit?" he said. "Why did Missie call you that?"

Luke made a laughing sound. "My IQ is off the charts. Apparently. Truth is, I just figured out a way to ace the test. It's all a matter of probability, and once you've factored in the psychology of the questions it's totally predictable and you can calculate to within a percentage point what the correct answer is. Doesn't make me a genius."

Kit stared at him. "You found a way to cheat the IQ test?"

"Not cheat. Decode. Slight difference, although it amounts to the same thing."

✦ ✦ ✦

It was late afternoon. Shadows striped the green lawns and collected in pools under the trees.

Kit stopped at a narrow path that wound between low trees. Their trunks were curled and knotted like clumps of writhing snakes. "Where does this go to?"

Luke hesitated. His twitching face was suddenly quite still. "We don't need to go down there," he said quickly. "I have to take you to the Recreation Hall." And he nudged them away, down another path.

They entered a gym with a high roof. A bunch of ropes with harnesses attached hung from the ceiling. They were there so kids could swoop from one end of the gym to the other, although none of the five or six kids in the gym was doing that. They simply stood around aimlessly. Luke hurried Kit and Devin on to farther rooms, all stuffed with toys. There were dress-up chests bursting with costumes, a small mountain of musical instruments, thousands of tiny plastic blocks in all colors of the rainbow spilling out of tubs, and stuffed animals that looked like mice dressed in clothes. One room contained three trampolines; another had something Luke called paintball and a gigantic doll house, five stories high, fully furnished down to the last tiny detail.

"Oh!" Kit cried, running forward. "It has everything."

"We don't have time to stop," Luke said. "It's getting late."

As they turned to leave, Devin halted suddenly. He had the strangest sensation of being watched. He looked around—the room was empty. There was a window set high in the far wall. It didn't face the outside and he could see nothing through it, but he had the briefest impression of a shadow behind the glass. The shadow moved and was gone.

Devin hurried after the others, who were now back in the gym. He noticed that there was a walkway around the upper portion of the gym, level with the tops of the ropes. The feeling of being watched grew to a certainty. There were people up there. Not children but adults, five or six of them, keeping so still you might not know they were there unless you were looking.

"Who are they?" he asked Luke. "What are they doing?"

The reason they were all so still, he now realized, was because they were all extremely old, older than he imagined it was possible to be. They looked like scraps held together by cobwebs and spit. Only their eyes, glittering slightly, showed that there was life inside their brittle husks. One or two stood leaning on sticks. The rest were sitting in wheeled chairs, their shrunken faces surrounded by pillows. On each face was a look of utter concentration.

Devin suddenly noticed another thing. Just a few moments ago, when they'd passed through the gym, none of the children there were moving very much. But now they appeared in a fever of animation. They were running to climb up the ropes; a few had already managed to get into the harnesses and they were swooping to and fro, screaming and whooping. The eyes of the old people passed slowly, very slowly, from one child to another.

"Who are they?" Devin repeated.

"They're the Visitors," Luke said.

Frisker wriggled wildly, jumped out of Kit's arms and scampered through the doorway. Kit immediately ran after him.

"Visitors?" Devin repeated.

Just then, Malloy came into the gym. He was holding a huge ice-cream cone in each hand. As he trotted along, he gave a slobbering lick first to one cone and then the other, his head turning rapidly from side to side. His tongue hung out, and there was ice cream all over his chin and down his shirt. His eyes were bright, almost feverish.

"Hi, Malloy," Devin said uncertainly. Luke immediately shoved him in the ribs.

"Don't look at him!"

"Why not?"

Luke gave him another shove, even harder than before.

"Because we don't. We don't look. It's the Rule."

"I don't understand," Devin said helplessly. "What's going on?"

Luke's whole face convulsed in a massive twitch. "Look, Devin, I haven't been straight with you. There's stuff I haven't told you. But I've stopped trying to explain things to new kids because they just don't believe me. They usually have to find out for themselves. You'll know more when you go to see her."

"Mrs. Babbage? Does she run the Home?"

"Not Mrs. Babbage. The Administrator. She lives in the tower. Remember the sign when you came in? The Gabriel H. Penn Home for Childhood? Well, she's Penn's daughter, and she never lets you forget it." He drew a deep breath. "Listen, Devin. This isn't a good place. They do stuff to kids here . . . bad stuff. I hate to have to tell you that. I don't even like to talk about it."

"So why don't you just leave?"

"That's the thing," Luke said heavily. "We can't."

Eight

DEVIN FOUND KIT IN her room after supper.

"I don't like it here," he said. "Luke told me nobody can leave, but I think we should try."

Kit was arranging her bed for the night, folding down the quilt carefully and plumping the pillows. She didn't look at him.

"You were the one who wanted to come. You said we should give it a chance."

Devin told her about Malloy and the ice cream and what Luke had said to him while she had been chasing Frisker.

"You know what I think?" Kit said, sounding angry. "I think Luke is crazy. I mean, just look at him, the way he twitches all the time. Why should we believe what he says? I didn't think this place existed, Devin, but it does. And it's amazing."

She fell to her knees and pulled a box from under the bed.

"I wasn't going to show you this, but look." She took a tiny golden jug from the box. "I took it from the dollhouse," she said. "Isn't it the rarest of all raries?" She rummaged further in the box.

"Remember my rule? Steal small and steal big?" Inside the box lay the rest of the dollhouse dinner service, a glittering trove of plates and crystal glasses, each no bigger than a fingernail.

"Have you ever seen anything so beautiful?"

The note of longing in her voice was the same as when she had told him about the house in The Meadows.

"Kit, I just know there's something going on here," Devin said helplessly. "Something bad for us."

She looked at him steadily, her eyes fierce amid the starry speckles of her face.

"Okay," she said. "Let's say you're right and there's something bad here. My question is, how bad could it be? Because I can take bad, Devin. I've taken it all my life. I'm kind of an expert at it. But today I got fed and I got this dollhouse stuff and best of all, I got Frisker. So what I'm thinking is, if this place really is bad like Luke says and I gotta start taking it again, better here than in the city or anywhere else."

She looked sad for a moment and very lost. Then she brightened.

"Let's talk about Frisker," she said. "I'm going to start teaching him tricks tomorrow. Like sitting and fetching. You lived on a farm, Devin. How do you get dogs to do stuff like that?"

"I never had a dog," he said. "But I have a horse. I've had her forever. She's so smart and good. I taught her loads of things. I even taught her how to dance! Some evenings, after chores, Granddad would play his guitar and I'd put on shows for him."

"What did he play?"

"Mostly green stuff," Devin said, "sometimes blue . . ."

Kit made a face. "You're crazy," she said. "You know that, don't you?"

✦ ✦ ✦

It was very late, and the only sounds were the sighing of the moon and the scratch of ivy against the window of Devin's bedroom. He lay wide-eyed, watching the shadows on the ceiling.

After a while, he got out of bed and went to open the window.

He stood for a long time, inhaling the night air. The grounds of the Home were spread beneath him, the trees pooled in darkness, moonlight glittering on the roof of the carousel. He was too far away to see the wooden horses themselves and wondered if they were still turning around and around with nothing but shadows to ride them. Over to his left loomed the Administrator's tower, paler than the other buildings, almost luminous in the moonlight.

Devin's thoughts kept returning to Malloy. How strange he had looked, greedily devouring the ice cream. Luke had told him not to look, but Devin knew Luke had seen Malloy too and had shuddered.

And yet Malloy had been fine at lunchtime. Devin had liked him then, even hoped they'd be friends.

Devin returned to bed with an uneasy mind, and it was a long time before he fell asleep.

✦ ✦ ✦

It was almost noon when he woke up. Someone was knocking at his door.

A girl appeared.

"I'm the messenger," she said. She paused, waiting for him to do or say something. She had long brown hair in a center part and fingernails bitten down so far there was hardly any nail left at all. "Oh, yeah, sorry," she said. "I forgot you're new. Sorry. I'm Karen. I'm the one they always ask to give the message."

"Who always asks?"

"Mrs. Babbage or the Administrator. I don't know why they ask me. I don't want to do it."

"What's the message?"

"Oh sorry, forgot to explain that too. The message is

always the same. You have to go see the Administrator. Normally I just turn up and say 'I'm the messenger' and everyone knows what I mean."

"So I have to go to the tower?"

She nodded. "Sorry . . ."

Devin pulled on his jeans and went outside. The birds were still there, swooping to and fro around the tower. He paused at the door, not knowing whether to knock or not. He pushed it gently and it opened.

He'd been expecting to find himself in a large area, with a staircase, perhaps. Instead he was standing in a narrow corridor, more like the hallway of an ordinary house. On one side was a coat rack, on another an umbrella stand and a place for boots. The walls were painted a dull plum color, and a faded rug in the same shade ran all the way from the entrance to a wooden door at the far end of the hall.

Devin went down the corridor and through the wooden door into an even smaller room, barely bigger than a closet. It was perfectly square, without windows or furniture or decoration of any kind.

The door closed behind him.

Next second, the floor shifted beneath his feet and the whole room seemed to tremble. Devin cried out in alarm and reached to steady himself. A band of light appeared. It ran all the way around the room and as he stared, it moved down toward the floor and disappeared. There was a long, low hissing sound, and then the wooden door opened again.

Devin was shocked to see that he was now at the very top of the tower, standing in an enormous circular room. Comfortable armchairs surrounded a fireplace. Pictures hung on the curved walls: scenes of mountains and cows, and a lady in a bonnet sitting in a field. There were little tables crowded with knickknacks, and a beautiful old rug covered the floor. Half the wall on the farther side of the room was devoted to books, all bound in the same dark leather and all exactly the same size. At one side of the room was a gleaming wooden desk, empty except for a big bowl of blue marbles.

A woman sat perched on the front of the desk, staring intently at a piece of paper.

She was dressed in an immaculate white shirt and navy skirt without a single crease or sign of wear. A small key on a silver chain hung around her neck. Her dark hair was all one shape without a strand out of place, and it was very shiny. Her skin was shiny too, pale and polished and perfectly smooth. She looked, Devin thought, as if she were waterproof, as if nothing—not sweat or dirt or tears—could stick to her even for a second.

She raised her head at last and looked at Devin. There was no expression at all on her face.

"Well," she said. "So Roman has redeemed himself."

Devin didn't know what to say. She spoke extremely

clearly, her *s*'s particularly sharp, sizzling in the air above her head.

"Sit down."

He looked around and chose a high-backed chair next to a metal stand with a blanket draped over the top of it.

"You look fairly healthy," she commented. "Some of Roman's finds arrive in very poor shape indeed. But you're too thin. You're not eating enough."

"I am . . . it's just that I didn't have much before, when I was walking and then when I was in the—"

"Yes," she said, cutting him off. "You must eat more. Our food is excellent. Nothing synthetic or processed. We did a lot of research before we got it just right."

"Please . . ." Devin faltered. He looked down. He was squeezing his hands together so tightly it almost hurt. "Please can you explain what I . . . this place . . . ?" His voice trailed off.

"Remarkable," the Administrator said, ignoring his words. She was studying the piece of paper again. Devin suddenly heard a noise; a scraping, shuffling sound coming from somewhere very close by. He half turned.

"Bye-bye," someone said in a low, dusty, unhappy voice.

Devin looked around the room, startled. He could see no one apart from the Administrator.

"Bye-bye," the voice said again, even more wretchedly than before.

The Administrator strode forward and whisked the blanket off the metal stand next to Devin's chair.

"Be quiet, Darwin!"

A bird huddled on the floor of a cage. It was pale gray all over except for its tail, which was red, and a flash of white around its eye. But its feathers were dull, and there were large bare patches, as if the bird had been pulling them out. It shuffled toward Devin and gave him a sorrowful look.

"This is an African grey parrot," the Administrator stated. "It is the most intelligent of all the parrots and capable of learning hundreds of words and mimicking almost any sound. It can be taught to count and even to hold simple conversations." She gave Darwin a long, blank stare. "Unfortunately," she said, "Darwin fulfills none of these expectations. He refuses to learn anything. He has mastered merely one word."

The parrot ducked his head as though ashamed. "Bye-bye, bye-bye."

The Administrator replaced the blanket over the cage. "He deserves to be kept in the dark," she said. "Perhaps it will encourage him to try a little harder."

"But why don't you just let him go?" Devin asked, in distress. "If he's such a disappointment . . ."

"Because he is a failure," the Administrator said very sharply. "And I don't like failure, Devin. He serves as an example of the consequences of disappointing me."

She turned back abruptly to the paper she'd been studying. "You were brought up on a farm."

He nodded. It seemed the Administrator didn't ask questions. She just made statements. Perhaps this was because she already knew the answers, Devin thought. Or perhaps she was simply not very interested.

"Remarkable," she repeated. "It appears you have extremely unusual sense perception. Blending of just two senses is rare, but in your case all five appear to overlap to some degree. This level of synesthesia occurs in only one out of ten million individuals."

Devin hadn't eaten breakfast and he was starting to feel faint.

"What's syn . . . synesthesia?"

The Administrator dipped her fingers into the bowl of marbles on the desk and stirred them with a noise like teeth chattering on a cold night.

"The way I look, for example," she said. "It causes you to hear a sound."

"Tight and high," Devin said automatically. "Like something thin stretched out. But how do you know all this about me?"

She stared at him for a second. Her eyes were the only thing about her face that didn't shine. They were flat black, and they reflected nothing.

"Your brain was scanned," she said casually. "In the elevator coming up here."

"I saw a light. But I didn't know what it was."

"Of course not. The Home is designed to look old-fashioned. The furniture, the decor. The same goes for the entertainment. The pony rides, the carousel, the tree houses, the food. No detail has been overlooked for our clients. It's exactly what they remember." She lifted her chin proudly. "My father planned it that way."

"Is your father here?"

She glanced away. "No. My father is a genius," she announced. "He lives alone and rarely ventures out. His time cannot be wasted on ordinary things. Idle chit-chat, the keeping of dates, the dull demands of friends and family—one cannot expect them of a genius. He is above such things, and rightly so."

Devin was feeling fainter than ever. The curved wall of the room seemed to ripple slightly.

"You said . . . clients," he said. "Who are they?"

She frowned very slightly. "Visitors" she said. "I meant the Visitors."

"The old people? I saw some yesterday in the gym."

The Administrator smiled to herself.

The air prickled and shimmered before Devin's eyes. He leaned forward, his head down, his breath coming quick and shallow. "Could I just have a glass of water?" he whispered.

She waved her arm. "Yes, all right, go. Get what you need. But remember that you have to eat more. I need you to be healthy, Devin. You're the most unusual child I have ever come across. I'm saving you for something special."

✦ ✦ ✦

The elevator whisked Devin down with a long hiss like the sound of breath being expelled. In the hallway below, he half ran toward the front door, desperate for air. It was early afternoon and very hot. He stood still for a moment or two, leaning against the wall of the tower, trying to catch his breath.

He didn't know what she'd meant by those last words. Or by anything else she'd said. None of it made sense.

As he stood there, he noticed something by his foot, a tiny scrap, gray and curled. He peered closer and saw it was the body of a baby bird. There was another one not far away and then a third, lying close to the wall, in the shadow of the stone. He looked up. The birds must be nesting in the cracks and crevices of the tower. But there was not enough space there for all the hatchlings. They must jostle and shove in a frantic fight for life, he thought.

The birds were not singing at all. They were shrieking.

Devin turned blindly and ran.

Nine

DEVIN RAN ACROSS THE courtyard, through an archway, and down a path. He ran fast, thinking only of finding Kit, his breath fighting his throat. A boy was kicking a ball around on the grass, passing it skillfully from foot to foot, flicking it up to bounce against his knee and then his head. Devin recognized him from the day before; Ansel, the boy in the pool with the red water gun.

When he saw Devin coming, he caught the ball neatly and jogged over to the edge of the field. He stopped and gave a friendly smile.

"I'm Ansel," he said, tucking the ball under his arm. "You're new, right?"

Devin nodded, still panting.

"You like soccer?"

"I never played before."

Ansel looked amazed. "For real? I was hoping for some shooting practice."

"You're really good," Devin told him.

Ansel's face lit up with shy pride. "Thanks," he said. "It's the only thing I am good at. I was useless at school. But my dad taught me how to play. In the evenings, you know? Just him and me . . ." He smiled, a little sadly. "If you think I'm good, you should have seen my dad. He could've played in front of the world."

"In front of the world?"

Ansel nodded. "They used to, you know. Can you imagine?"

"Where's your dad now?"

"He got sick," Ansel said. "He didn't have enough money for the medicine . . ." His voice fell away.

"I'm sorry," Devin said. "Really sorry."

"Thanks."

They stood in silence.

"Have you seen Kit?" Devin finally asked. "She's new too."

"I don't know. What does she look like?"

"You saw her yesterday," Devin said. "At the pool . . ."

A spasm crossed Ansel's face. He shook his head.

"But you did!" Devin insisted. "You looked right at us. You were standing in the water and you were—"

"I don't remember!" Ansel burst out. He had flushed

a deep red and his hands were clenched into fists. He suddenly looked almost overwhelmed with rage.

"You're not supposed to look!" he shouted. "You're not supposed to tell!"

"I'm—I'm sorry," Devin stammered. "I didn't mean—"

"I just want some shooting practice, that's all!" Ansel continued furiously. "I just want to play soccer!" He gave the ball a kick so powerful that it flew into the air and smacked against the goalpost with a noise like a gunshot.

"I'm sorry," Devin repeated. He turned and ran back to the courtyard.

Kit wasn't in her room. He stood for a second or two, sick with disappointment. Her bed had been slept in but not made up. Half a dozen dresses lay strewn over it. Devin knelt and looked underneath the bed. The box containing her collection of dollhouse raries was still there. That meant she was here too—somewhere. He got to his feet and went to the window. Lunch must be over by now, but maybe she was still in the dining room.

✦ ✦ ✦

Kit wasn't in the dining hall or the pool or the gym. Devin hurried along, searching everywhere, his body drenched with sweat. Under the shade of a tree he spotted a small, familiar shape and rushed forward.

"Frisker!"

The puppy raised his head eagerly, already knowing

his name. His tiny stump of a tail wagged enthusiastically. Devin scooped him up in his arms.

"Where's Kit?" he whispered, pressing his face against the puppy's warm side. "Why did she leave you here?"

He walked on, Frisker trotting by his side. The sun dipped toward late afternoon. At last he found her in a little meadow, sitting by herself in the long grass. She was half-turned away from him, her long red hair falling in a gleaming sheet over the side of her face.

"Kit!"

Frisker whimpered, hesitating. Devin ran forward. "I've been looking for you everywhere!"

She held a small mirror in one hand and was staring at herself, lost in concentration.

"Kit?"

She looked up at last, smiling, seeming bewildered. It was her; he knew every freckle on her face. But her eyes were wrong. It wasn't the color or the shape. He couldn't find words for what it was, yet somehow it changed the look of her more than any bruise or burn. He took a horrified step backwards.

"Is that your doggy?" she asked, in a soft, dazed voice.

She bent her head without waiting for an answer. Her eyes returned to the mirror and she began running her fingers over her face, slowly, very slowly, as if uncertain of its shape.

✦ ✦ ✦

Devin had been sitting hunched up by the gates to the large meadow for a long time when Luke found him.

"Hey, buddy, you all right?"

Devin didn't answer. Luke squatted beside him and shook his head. "Stupid question. Stupid. Saw Kit, didn't you? That's why we don't look . . ."

Devin lifted his head. "What's going on here, Luke? What's happening?" His voice rose with panic. "You have to tell me!"

"All I know is they do weird things to kids." Luke said. "I don't know why they're doing it and I've been driving myself crazy trying to figure it out."

"Who's doing it?"

"Who do you think?"

Devin remembered the sound of the Administrator's fingers as they stirred the bowl of marbles.

Your brain was scanned in the elevator coming up here.

"Roman's part of it too," Luke said. "He goes into the city to find new kids and brings them back here. I hate him almost more than I hate the Administrator."

He rose to his feet. "Come on," he said. "I'll show you something."

Luke led Devin back past the soccer field, taking the path that ran by the side of the swimming area. The pool was empty of people, the water sparkling in the setting sun. It was quiet. Luke stopped. They were at the path

Devin had seen the day before, the one that ran between the low, knotted trees.

"We never go down here," Luke said, "unless we have to."

It was darker there, the way shadowed by the trees. Devin had never seen anything like them before; their branches were so interlocked that it was impossible to tell where one tree ended and another began. He followed Luke uncertainly. The path continued for a hundred yards and then opened out onto another courtyard. It was much smaller than the main one and contained a single building.

Luke stopped twenty feet away and stood looking up at it.

"This is where it happens," he said. "We call it the Place."

At first glance, the building looked like all the others at the Home. It was made of the same yellow-colored stone, and the same ivy crept over its weathered surface. But there was one difference. Only the third story had windows. Below was simply empty wall, apart from the narrow entrance. It made the place look odd, unfinished, like a face left blank where the nose and cheeks should be.

"What happens here?" Devin asked.

"It's hard to explain," Luke said. "Karen came to see you this morning, right?"

Devin nodded.

"You had to see the Administrator. That's because you're new. Normally when you get the message, you have to come here. Inside it's all modern, and it's set up like some sort of lab. There's a big chair and you have to sit in it and they give you an injection. I don't know what it is, but it's terrible. It hurts, Devin. Your whole body hurts. You're in pain and you dream and all your dreams are bad ones. Really bad ones."

Luke's whole body had become completely still, tensed up as if caught in a single massive twitch.

"Horrible dreams that you can't really describe or explain why they were so bad, even though you—" he broke off abruptly.

"I shouldn't think about them, I shouldn't think about them. But my mind gets into a loop, you know? Everything gets scrambled."

"Can't you wake yourself up?" Devin said.

"No, it feels like you can't. Everyone else can see that you're acting strangely, but you don't know what you're doing. While it lasts, there is no 'you.' You can't remember who you are." He broke off again, shaking his head in frustration.

"I can't describe it, there's no use trying."

"Is that what was happening to Malloy yesterday?"

Luke nodded. "Yeah. He was in the Dream. You saw how weird he was. Ansel was the same way when we saw him in the pool. That's why we don't look. Kids who are in the Dream act strange, and you don't want to see them; it reminds you of being that way yourself. And nobody wants to know what crazy stuff they did, so nobody tells."

"Kit?" Devin whispered.

Luke nodded. "They got her fast. I was surprised."

"How long will she . . . How long does it last?"

"Two days," Luke said. "It's never longer than two days. She'll be back to normal then."

"But why? What's it for?"

"Like I said, I don't know. I think it's some kind of experiment they're doing on us. Something to do with the cognitive sciences, certainly behavioral in some way, although I've never heard of any method that—"

Devin wasn't listening to Luke anymore. He was staring up at one of the windows at the top of the Place. The sun had dipped below the level of the roof, and with the glare gone, he could make out the details of brick and glass more clearly. He grabbed Luke's wiry arm.

"Did you see that?" he asked.

"Where?"

"I saw something, in the window. Up there, the one in the middle . . ."

Luke shaded his eyes and peered. "I don't see anything. What was it?"

"Something moved," Devin said. "I saw it for a second."

"What?"

Devin didn't answer. The truth was, he wasn't sure exactly what he'd seen. It had been small and thin, not pressed completely flat against the glass but slightly bent. Had it been a claw?

He pushed the thought away.

"Probably just a trick of the light or something." he said.

❖ ❖ ❖

It was growing dark as they made their way back to the courtyard and their rooms. Devin had many more questions, but he could see that talking about the Place and what went on there had upset Luke. His nerves seemed frayed to snapping.

A pale moon showed itself above the treetops. It shone on the horses quietly grazing, the neat pathways, and the ivy-covered walls with a peaceful, steady light. From the dining hall came the faint clatter of dishes, ordinary and comforting.

"It all looks so . . . normal," Devin said.

"Yeah," Luke agreed. "You'd never guess it was anything but a paradise. But every inch is wired, Devin. They've got sensors, devices everywhere, keeping track of us. The whole place is fake, like that wall of books in the Administrator's office. I was there once and I saw part of it slide back. There's a control panel behind it. Some alarm had gone off—it wasn't anything but a glitch, I guess. She told me to leave, but just before the elevator door closed I saw her switch the alarm off from that panel.

"The books are fake?" Devin was surprised. "All one thousand and ninety three?"

Luke looked startled. "You counted them? You must have been there a long time."

Devin shook his head. "They were right in front of me."

✦ ✦ ✦

Luke went back to his room and Devin went to eat supper. As he ate, a great weariness came over him. He longed for sleep, his mind almost overwhelmed with the events of the day. He had left the dining room and was just about to enter his dorm when he saw Roman coming across the courtyard. Megs was trotting behind him like a ghost, her dress and hair turned to gray in the moonlight.

Devin stopped, and Megs immediately ran to him. "Did you find me a match? Roman's got a lighter, but he won't let me hold it. He keeps it in his pocket."

Devin stared at Roman in silence.

"I trusted you," he said at last.

Roman's eyes were as pale as river pebbles washed by endless flow. He held Devin's gaze.

"Yeah," he said softly. "Yeah, I'm good at that."

Ten

DEVIN CAUGHT SIGHT OF Malloy next morning in the dining room. Malloy was cramming his mouth with scrambled egg, little flecks of it spraying in all directions. His eyes were closed as if he was in a kind of rapture. There was a mountain of egg on his plate, smothered with lashings of maple syrup and dollops of chocolate sauce.

He was still in the Dream, as Luke had called it. Devin looked away, feeling slightly sick.

After breakfast he wandered the grounds of the Home. The toys and entertainment no longer filled him with wonder or even enthusiasm, and he understood why there were so few children actually playing. Knowing you were part of some painful experiment made it hard to enjoy anything much. For all its novelty, a stifling air of sameness hung over the Gabriel H. Penn Home for Childhood. The same heaps of food in the dining room, the same sort of clothes worn by everyone, the same tinkling notes carried on the breeze.

Dumdee, dumdee, dum dum dum . . .

He saw Mrs. Babbage, hurrying along with a pile of bed linens in her arms. She stopped when she saw him.

"You're ever so pale, Devin dear," she said. "You need a treat! Go get yourself something from the ice-cream truck. You can hear it now."

"Is that what that music is?"

Mrs. Babbage's lips tightened into a smile.

"Yankee Doodle! It's such a popular tune, they play it over and over."

"Mrs. Babbage?" Devin said, finding hope in her friendly tone.

"What is it, dear?"

"This place . . . ," he began, his words tumbling out in distress. "The Administrator . . ."

"You'll have been to see her by now," Mrs. Babbage said. "Doesn't she do a wonderful job? She keeps it all ever so perfect, doesn't she? Oh yes, everything has to be just right.

"You'd think Mr. Penn would have come to admire it," she continued. "He built the Home, you know. The whole thing was all his idea. But he's not been back, not even once. I find that very strange, I must say."

"I'm worried," Devin said. "I'm worried about Kit."

Mrs. Babbage tilted her head to one side. "Oh, you mustn't worry. Kit is perfectly fine! I'm sure of it. She's such a pretty little thing. I'm sure she'll get adopted very, very soon."

"Adopted?"

Mrs. Babbage seemed surprised by his question. "Didn't anyone tell you?" she asked. "From time to time the children here get adopted. By lovely people, Devin. People who adore children. Wealthy people."

"Who are they?"

"Why, the Visitors of course! That's what they're here for!"

Devin remembered how the eyes of the old people had traveled from one child to another in the gym, and how the kids had suddenly perked up and started playing when the Visitors were there.

"Run along to the common room—it's next door to the dining room—and you'll see pictures of all the kids who've been adopted. Why, I don't think it will be long before you'll be joining them. And Kit too. Perhaps together! Wouldn't that be something?"

Devin nodded, a little bewildered by this news.

"Run along now and take a look," Mrs. Babbage urged him.

The common room was a large, comfortable space, full of deep sofas and shelves loaded with books and jigsaw puzzles. A girl was sitting reading in one corner, her legs carefully crossed at the ankles. A fly buzzed drowsily against the window. On one wall there was a large corkboard, almost entirely covered by photographs.

The photos were all of children and old people together. The old people didn't look particularly frail. They were the sort of elderly types whose faces still looked pretty much the same as when they were young, only more wrinkled. His grandfather had been like that, Devin thought, and tears rose in his eyes. He took a deep breath, blinked them away, and turned back to the corkboard. The children in the photos were all smiling. Some were hugging their adopted parents, while others played with kittens or held wonderful-looking toys, such as miniature cars and big, round, brightly colored hoops. One was standing on a stretch of sand in the sunshine, holding a large shell toward the camera while an older couple clapped and beamed.

Devin looked from one picture to another. After what Luke had told him the day before, he'd wondered why the children in the Home didn't rebel. Now he knew. They were hoping to be adopted, to find a family and a home.

His thoughts were interrupted by the girl sitting reading.

"You don't look special," she said abruptly, giving him a scornful glance.

"What do you mean?"

She licked her finger very delicately and turned the page of her book. "She thinks you are for some reason."

"Who? The Administrator?"

"Roman's back on her good side for finding you. That's what I heard."

Devin stared at her. She was about thirteen, with long, dark hair that hung in odd-shaped curls around her face and lay completely flat everywhere else. Her nails were red. Devin could see the scribbly lines of the marker pen she had used to paint them.

"I'm Devin," he said.

"Yes, I know," she said, rolling her eyes. "And you've made friends with Luke, haven't you? I'd be careful about that. He's nearly Spoiled, you know."

"You mean because he used to be rich?"

She rolled her eyes again. "No. Spoiled. Don't you know anything?"

He shook his head.

"It's not good to be Spoiled," the girl said with a smug look.

"I don't know what you're talking about," Devin said. "I have to go. I have to be somewhere . . ."

Back outside, Ansel was on the soccer field again, kicking his ball around, despite the heat. There was something almost robotic in the way he charged to and fro, but he came panting up to Devin the minute he caught sight of him.

"Hey, friend," he said in his straightforward way. "No hard feelings about yesterday?"

He wiped his hand on his jeans and held it out. Devin took it and they shook solemnly.

"No hard feelings," Devin agreed. "I'm sorry I upset you. I didn't understand about . . ."

"It's okay. I find it helps to exercise after I've been in the Dream. You know, run around a bit. It used to be I could take the edge off after an hour or two, but recently . . ." He broke off, his face creased with worry. "Recently it's been harder. I've been forgetting things. Not just during, but after, when I'm back to normal. An hour can go by and I don't know what happened. I just don't know. Does that ever happen to you?"

Devin shook his head.

Ansel bounced the soccer ball a couple of times, his head low.

"Did they really play in front of the whole world?" Devin asked, trying to cheer him up.

"You bet!" Ansel said, immediately brightening. "My dad said the crowd roared so loud you could hear it from twenty miles away. Imagine that. Everyone together, feeling the same thing."

"You'll have to teach me to play sometime," Devin said.

Ansel grinned. "Never played soccer!" he said. "How've you lived?"

Devin watched him jog away, moving the ball along with small, lightning movements of his feet.

✦ ✦ ✦

Devin decided to visit the small farmyard. It made him feel homesick, but it was a good sort of homesickness— if such a thing was possible. It reminded him of happiness and of belonging. He walked along, keeping his head down. The day before, he'd been frantic to find Kit, but now he didn't want to see her, wherever she was. He thought of the rapt way she had stared at herself and how in that moment she'd seemed not beautiful at all, but consumed by a kind of greed that was almost ugly.

The farmyard was all the way on the other side of the Home. Devin took the route that led behind the dormitories. He passed the ice-cream truck and the recreation hall and then paused by the entrance to the corn maze. He could hear voices, thin and inquiring. A group of Visitors was approaching, two or three men and a woman in a motorized chair that made a whining, wheezing sound as it rolled along. Devin remembered how the old people had stared at the kids in the gym, the concentration on their faces. Without hesitating, thinking only of avoiding them, he plunged into the maze.

The maze was made of corn, the stalks rising to a

height two or three feet above his head. It wasn't ripe yet—the ears were still tightly wrapped—but the leaves were tired and dry-looking, and they made a shifting, rustling sound that seemed to come from every direction, despite the stillness of the air. Devin trotted rapidly down the first dusty path, and, within seconds, the entrance was lost to view.

Inside the maze, the rustling was much louder. Grass made a red sound when the breeze passed over it, but the sound of the corn was a dull, speckled mustard that was not nearly as nice. He turned left at a fork, heading for the center, which was marked by a flag, visible above the tops of the plants. He was just about to slow down when he heard the Visitors again, the old lady's voice high-pitched, excited.

"Are we having an adventure? Oh dear, oh dear."

They must have come into the maze behind him. Perhaps it was part of the tour. Devin set off running again. The path twisted and then forked once more, seemed to double back on itself, and then continued in the wrong direction. Ordinarily he would have had no trouble at all finding his way through, but panic had seized him.

"Oh dear, oh dear, dear, dear . . ."

The voices were behind and then in front, cutting him off. He thought it must be his hearing. Old people couldn't move that fast. Devin was sure they hadn't seen him entering the maze. But still, he wanted to get away from them.

He turned around frantically and retraced his steps. The second fork again—had he turned left or right? Every turn looked exactly the same. He plunged left and then left again, feeling sure that he was on the right track until he came around a narrow corner and saw he had arrived at a dead end.

He stood very still, listening. There was no sound but the rustling of the corn. Then he heard it, the faint, ugly whine of the motorized chair. It was growing louder by the second.

Devin turned blindly and pushed his way into the hedge of corn, stepping deep into the tight, dark forest, moving as quietly as he could. He thought he could hear voices, but they were distant and soon vanished. His heart was beating hard. He put his hand on his chest to steady himself. They had gone, he thought. He was safe. They hadn't found him.

But so what if they had found him? Now that he was calmer, Devin began to feel a little silly, cowering in the dark. He couldn't imagine how he could have thought he was lost. The maze was simple; the exit was only a few turns up ahead. He was just about to push his way out of the corn and forget about the whole thing when he stopped short.

Someone was walking on the other side of the hedge.

He saw shoes. The corn stalks were too thick to see more than a vague shape of a figure. But the shoes he saw. They were men's shoes, shiny and elegant, the toes slightly tapered, the laces tied in a perfect bow. They were moving extremely slowly, coming toward him. There was a cane too. Devin saw the tip of it, a dull gold color, as it was placed by the side of the shoes.

He froze instinctively, his breath catching in his throat.

The shoes were very close now. Devin was near enough to see the tiny puff of dust as the cane came down with each slow step.

The shoes came level with his hiding place, and then they stopped. Devin slowly raised his eyes. Then the corn was moving in front of him, being parted. He saw the cane first and then the man holding it, using it to push the plants aside.

The man's face was all bones, as if the juice had been sucked clean out of it. He wore a dark suit that hung from his shoulders the way clothes hang on a scarecrow that is made of nothing but stick and straw.

"I see you," the Visitor said in a soft, playful, sing-song voice.

For a moment, Devin was too terrified to speak.

"Playing hidey-and-seek, are you?"

"I was just . . . I was just . . . ," Devin stammered.

The old man lowered his cane.

"Just having fun?" He chuckled lightly, the sound crackling in his throat. "Just playing, were you?"

Devin stared at him.

"I got left behind," the Visitor explained. "Old legs not what they used to be." His throat crackled again. "Not like yours, eh?"

Devin crept out of the corn.

The Visitor waved his cane. "Well, run along, then, don't worry about me."

Devin tried to smile, but he couldn't. The man was staring at him with a fascination that was almost disturbing. Devin turned and hurried away, not looking back even once. But he could feel the man's gaze on him watching, watching until he disappeared from view.

Eleven

Malloy and Luke were at the farmyard when he arrived, still shaken from his experience in the maze. He could tell at once, by the easy way Malloy held himself, that he had recovered from his visit to the Place and returned to normal. But what he was doing still seemed a little crazy. He was down on his hands and knees with his face pressed up to the fence of the pigsty. Through the cracks in the fence, Devin glimpsed the snout of a piglet. Malloy, he realized, was trying to kiss it.

"Malloy! I'm Devin, remember?"

Malloy turned his head and grinned. "Meet Fulsome," he said, getting to his feet.

The piglet was only half grown but extremely fat. Its eyes were squeezed to pinpricks, and its tight pink belly almost scraped the ground. At the mention of its name it lifted its head and began to turn around and around on the spot, grunting in excitement.

"Poor impulse control," Luke commented. "Just like Malloy."

"Why's he so fat?" Devin wanted to know.

"He's not fat!" Malloy protested. "He's pleasantly chubby."

"No, he's fat," said Luke. "He's a lump of lard. Malloy feeds him scraps all the time."

"Here, Fulsome!" Malloy called. At once the pig came waddling over. "How many fingers am I holding up?" Fulsome grunted three times. "Good pig! And now?" The pig gave a single snort.

"Yes! What about now?" Malloy asked, putting both hands on top of his head. Immediately the pig, fat as he was, raised himself on two legs and began strutting around in the mud.

"Incredible!" Devin laughed.

"Malloy and that pig are soul mates," Luke said.

"I've got a thing for animals," Malloy boasted, pulling a large piece of toast from his pocket. "Watch this!" He positioned the toast in his mouth, bent down and allowed Fulsome to attach his jaw around the other end. For a few seconds, boy and pig were face-to-face, both steadily munching until Fulsome tossed his head impatiently and snatched the remaining bread away.

"Gross, right?" Malloy said.

"Sick," agreed Luke. "Get him to do something else."

"Throw that stick," said Malloy.

Luke picked it up and tossed it to the far side of Fulsome's pen. "Fetch it, Fulsome! Fetch it!"

The pig stared hard at Luke. Then he trotted over, took the stick in his mouth and returned it with a shake of his tail to Luke's feet. Luke tossed him a scrap and Fulsome gobbled it greedily.

"He's amazing," Malloy said lovingly. "Cheers me up."

"Everything cheers you up," Luke pointed out. "He's always happy," he added, speaking to Devin. "That's because unlike everyone else around here, he thinks his parents are going to come and get him."

"That's right, Professor Twitch," Malloy said. "They'll find me, all right. And if I could just get out of here, they'd find me a whole lot faster."

❖ ❖ ❖

Malloy's parents, Devin learned, were Nomads. He had no idea what this meant until Luke explained that Nomads were people who had given up on the city and on struggling to make a living and instead lived in the middle of nowhere in tepees made out of sticks. They wanted to live close to nature because they thought the only way the planet could be saved was if they wandered around admiring rocks and trying to communicate with Mother Earth. Luke sounded rather scornful when he said this. Devin glanced at Malloy, but Malloy simply nodded.

"Yup, that's pretty much it," he agreed. "It's kind of cool. Not much to eat, though . . ."

The other thing Nomads did was take long treks into the wilderness. Most of the time, they stayed in their camps, but every so often, they went off by themselves to a far-off canyon or the top of a mountain.

"It's to gain wisdom," Malloy explained solemnly. "It's really important to us."

Only adults went on the treks, so Malloy's parents had left him with the rest of the camp when the time came for them to set off. They were gone for a long time. The treks were hazardous, with dangers of all kinds, including hunger and thirst and the perils of unfamiliar terrain. When Malloy's parents still hadn't come back after two months, other people in the camp started shaking their heads, first in worry and then in sorrow. A month after that, the whole group had to break camp and move on to find food. Malloy went with them, but he slipped away the first night and returned to the ruins of the old camp. He waited alone for his parents to come back.

"I knew they just got lost," he explained. "My dad has a terrible sense of direction and my mom does everything he says cuz she thinks he's great. I figured they were out there, walking in circles, making each other laugh like they always did . . ."

Behind Malloy's back, Luke glanced at Devin and shook his head.

Malloy had waited in the camp for seven or eight days, living on tiny scraps of leftover food and searching for plants that were safe to eat. At last, hunger drove him to move on. One day he walked three miles to the south, finding nothing but dust and rocks and coyote tracks. He came down a bank of loose stones and found himself by the side of an empty road, stretching far into the distance. A single car, the sunlight glinting on its polished sides, was coming toward him. When it reached him, it stopped and the window glided down silently.

"Need a ride?" somebody said.

It was Roman.

"He was on his way back from the city," Malloy explained. "Only I didn't know that then. He asked me where I came from and who my parents were. Then he said he would take me somewhere they could keep me safe while they looked for Mom and Dad. Instead, he brought me here."

He paused. "I know they're still out there. I know it."

Luke squeezed his shoulder quickly. "Of course they are! And they'll find you, any day now. Right, Devin?"

Devin nodded.

"You'll be back in your teepee, eating gophers and getting wisdom and all that Nomad crap," Luke said. "You'll see."

"Gophers are really good," Malloy said, immediately cheering up. "Especially when they're all crispy . . . little bit of sage . . . you should try 'em." He looked from Luke to Devin. "When Mom and Dad do get here, I bet they take you away too. I won't leave without you guys."

"Good to know, my man," Luke said, a touch sadly. "Good to know."

✦ ✦ ✦

"You don't think Malloy's parents are really going to come get him, do you?" Devin asked Luke.

"If I was going to quantify the level of certainty, I'd estimate the probability would be infinitesimally low."

Devin just stared at him.

"No," Luke said. "No, I don't think they're going to come get him. I doubt they're even still alive."

They were talking in Luke's room. It was so untidy that it was a while before Devin could even locate the bed underneath all the clothes and snack wrappers. Pieces of paper lay scattered everywhere. Even the desk was a mess, with one entire edge splintered and ragged. The minute Luke sat down at it, he began automatically plucking at the wood, his fingers nervous and busy.

Devin noticed a smallish, framed photograph among the scraps of paper on the desk. It showed a smiling man in a sailor's cap and a woman with sleek blond hair by his side.

"Is that your mom and dad?"

Luke nodded. "On our yacht," he said with a curl of his lip. "The good ship *Swindler*."

"You've seen the ocean?"

"Sure," Luke said, his fingers tugging frenetically at the edge of the desk.

"Listen, don't tell Malloy what I said about his parents," he said abruptly.

Devin shook his head. "No, 'course not."

"Believing they'll come back keeps him happy, and Malloy, well, he cheers everyone up."

"I won't say anything," Devin assured him.

"The trouble is," Luke continued, "he won't stop nagging me to help him escape. He doesn't want to be adopted. He doesn't think he needs it."

"I was wondering about that," Devin said. "I don't see any fences in this place. So what's stopping us from leaving?"

Luke gave him a horrified look. "I didn't tell you?" He rubbed his forehead, very agitated. "I'm losing it, I swear. My mind's so scrambled . . . Look, whatever you do, don't try to leave."

The reason there were no fences, Luke explained, was that the Home was surrounded by twelve posts. Anyone trying to pass them would activate a laser. It wasn't strong enough to kill; it would simply disable with extreme pain. A week after Luke arrived at the Home, another new kid tried to cross. The pain was so bad she couldn't even scream; she just lay there on the ground until the staff came to pick her up.

"Malloy wants me to figure out a way to get around the posts. I've been trying, but so far, no luck."

Devin bent and picked up one of the many pieces of paper scattered on the floor. It was covered with mathematical equations, all of them tiny and set close together. They filled up the whole page, even the margins, and Devin could see that they'd been written by someone pressing down so hard on the paper that it was half curled up from the pressure.

"Does this have to do with figuring out the posts?"

Luke glanced over uneasily. "No, that's nothing. I just play with numbers, that's all. When I get stressed, you know?"

Devin's eyes swept over the room. There were hundreds of similar pages.

"It's hard to turn off," Luke said. "Sometimes I'm up all night doing it. But it's just math, you know? It's not like I'm going crazy or anything."

✦ ✦ ✦

It was particularly hot that evening—a dry, stifling heat that seemed only to intensify as darkness fell. A few children were in the pool. They stood up to their chests, not moving, trying to stay cool. Devin joined them. He had never been in such deep water. The stream at the farm had only come just above his knees, and it had felt different against his skin.

"The water's pure," his grandfather had told him. "It comes straight from the heart of the earth. You can drink it all your life and never get sick."

Devin thought of the colored pebbles at the bottom of the stream and how he had fished for them and then arranged them in lines so they would make songs, the notes trickling golden like the stream itself.

Luke and Malloy were in the pool too, as well as Missie and Karen, who seemed to be friends. The scornful girl from the common room was with them, her hair pinned up carefully on top of her head. Devin had found out from Luke that she was named Vanessa. A chunky, sandy-haired boy with a blank expression stood a little way apart, swirling the water slowly with one hand.

The only light came from two or three low torches planted nearby. The water was as dark as oil, and odd, flickering shadows traveled across the surface. The children stood in inky circles that slowly spread out to join one another and rang softly with a strange reluctance. Devin thought they sounded almost sticky.

"I'm so hot," Missie complained. "Even the water's hot. Why can't they make the water cool?" She flung her arms out, splashing.

"It's better if you keep still," Karen said.

"I know that, Smarty Pants," Missie said.

"Yeah, sorry." Karen whispered. "Sorry."

Missie splashed again.

"Stop doing that!" Vanessa cried.

"Why? You scared your hair will get wet?"

"You are so immature," Vanessa said, in a superior tone of voice.

"You okay, Malloy?" Luke asked. Malloy's mouth was turned down. Little beads of water clustered in his hair and shimmered slightly in the dim light.

"Just thinking about being in the Dream," Malloy said. "I always dream about eating. My whole body is begging to stop but my mouth won't let me. It makes me feel . . . ashamed. And what I'm eating makes it worse. It's all weird, disgusting stuff. Liver and seaweed dumplings and deep fried giblets and swan tongue sandwiches with the crusts cut off . . ."

"Coming from someone who likes to eat gophers, that's a bit much," Luke muttered.

"What's it really like, being in the Dream?" Devin asked, although a big part of him didn't want to know. The kids looked at each other and nobody answered.

"It hurts," Missie said, finally. "Sometimes more, sometimes less. Afterward I want to punch things and kick people and stamp on ants."

"Poor ants," Karen murmured, "They haven't done anything."

"They run around, don't they? They exist."

"That doesn't make any sense," Karen said feebly.

Malloy interrupted them. "Being in the Dream is weird. It's confusing, mainly. You dream that you're in a room, only you don't know where. Except, of course, you're not really there at all. Instead you're running around the Home acting weird." He paused. "That's just the start of it, though, cuz while you're dreaming that you're there in that room, you dream you fall asleep and then the really bad dreams come. The really nutso ones. They're like . . . dreams within the Dream. And they're terrible."

"I had this one dream," Luke said. "It was about animals. Or parts of animals. Their heads. I'd killed them, and cut their heads off and stuck them all over the wall. They were stuck there, but in the dream, I was stuck too. I was sitting in a chair and I couldn't move any part of my body at all. All the animals were looking down at me. Some looked like they were screaming, others just looked . . . sad. Like they knew I'd murdered them."

"My dream doesn't sound that creepy, but it was," Karen said timidly. "I dreamed I was knitting a scarf."

Missie rolled her eyes. "I wish I dreamed I was knitting."

"But it was horrible," Karen protested. "I couldn't stop. I'd been knitting the scarf for ages and ages, fifty years or a hundred, maybe. I'd started making it for a little boy but the little boy died. I don't know how I knew that, but you just know things in dreams, don't you? He'd died, but I kept on knitting the scarf for him. It was very long. I looked down and it stretched all the way to the door and I could see it curling around down the corridor. And . . . and it was wet." Karen's voice dropped very low, almost to a whisper. "It was all wet with crying."

"When I say it out loud," she continued, "it doesn't seem like much, but it's the feelings, you know? All the dreams have such terrible feelings . . ."

A deep silence fell over the children.

"That's nothing!" Malloy burst out. "I'll tell you what's really creepy."

The others all looked at him apprehensively. Devin wasn't sure he wanted to hear about another bad dream.

"People who can fart the alphabet!" Malloy spluttered. "I mean, that's just wrong."

There was a stunned silence and then a wild splashing as Missie and Karen shrieked with laughter and Luke dived on Malloy, trying to dunk his head under water. Even Vanessa smiled, although she pretended not to. Only the sandy-haired boy seemed unaffected. He stayed quite still, his face expressionless.

When the hubbub had died down, Devin asked the others about the silent boy. His name was Pavel, and he'd stopped speaking about a week earlier.

"He's really close to being Spoiled," whispered Missie.

"I heard that word before," Devin said. "What's being Spoiled?"

"Shhhh. Not so loud."

Vanessa waded across the pool and climbed out. Devin watched her pale body disappearing into the dark.

"She used that word too. 'Spoiled.'"

"Don't pay any attention to her," Luke advised. "She thinks she knows everything. She thinks she's so grown up, but she's not."

"She curls her hair," Karen informed him. "Only she forgets to do the back of it."

"But what is being Spoiled?" Devin persisted. "What's it actually mean?"

No one replied.

"Being in the Dream . . . ," Malloy began unwillingly. "It does something to you. It messes you up. After a certain number of visits, you go . . . strange."

"When kids first arrive here," Luke said, "they're normal. But little by little they start to change." He glanced around. "It's true of all of us, whether we want to admit it or not. After a while you go completely weird. Like Pavel. And Jared, the boy with the teddy bear. And Megs." He paused. "Ansel too. He's different, not in control . . ."

"What happens to you after you're Spoiled?" Devin asked.

"Everyone gets adopted," Karen said, "sooner or later. Only I hope with me it'll be sooner. I've been here for three months. Jared's been here ten months. Megs has been here for ages."

"How many visits does it take to get Spoiled?" Devin asked.

Luke's arms were wrapped around himself so tight it looked as if he might crack his chest.

"Depends on the kid. Twenty seems about . . . average."

Devin stared at him, thinking about what Vanessa had said. He wondered how many visits to the Place Luke had made. But the urge to ask questions had suddenly left him.

Twelve

THE NEXT MORNING WAS so exactly like the one before that Devin felt he had been at the Home for years rather than just three days. On his farm there had been constant activity, seasons of growth and labor, colors that sang with different voices as the months turned. And the city was full of movement too; to stay still there was to die. But here time seemed to pause. Time and the children too, all of them in limbo, waiting.

The only new activity was in the small meadow where staff members were setting up tents. Mrs. Babbage was overseeing the job.

"We're having a campout!" she told him. "We'll sing songs and roast marshmallows over the fire and sleep under the stars. It's ever so much fun. I'm sure you'll love it, Devin. The Administrator wants everyone to be involved."

"So everyone has to do it?"

"Everyone wants to," she corrected. "It's a group activity. We have group activities of all sorts. Last week we had sports day. There were all sorts of races, and the winner got a medal and so did everyone else."

"Why would you get a medal if you don't win?"

"We're all winners here, Devin."

Devin looked at her carefully. She was so kind, so warm and chirpy, despite her timid manner and droopy clothes. Devin couldn't believe she had any idea how bad it was for the kids in the Place. He thought maybe she was just dim.

He smiled politely and walked on.

✦ ✦ ✦

Devin was passing by Kit's room and saw that the door was ajar. Kit was sitting on the floor with her arms wrapped around her knees, her head down. Frisker was curled up against her ankles. Devin knew at once that she was back to normal.

"Hey, you okay?"

She looked up at him with a tear-stained face and then buried her head again.

He went over and sat down beside her, not saying anything. He could see the top of her shoulders as she leaned forward, the old scars and welts clearly visible above the neckline of her pale green dress. They sat together in silence for a while.

"Can you talk about it?" Devin said at last.

Kit sniffed and wiped her nose.

"She wanted to see me early," she said. "I had to go to the tower. You weren't up yet. When I got there, she looked angry."

"The Administrator?"

Kit nodded. "She said Roman shouldn't have brought me because . . . because I wasn't right for the Home. She knew I'd been badly treated. She said I was damaged."

Devin clenched his fists.

"I thought she was going to send me away and I'd lose Frisker and . . . and everything. But then she started talking about a shortage of something and how it couldn't be helped. I didn't understand. Not that it mattered much. I don't think she's the sort of person who cares if you understand or not."

Devin nodded.

"She said it helped that I was 'unusually attractive,' which I thought was really stupid, but I didn't argue because I wanted to stay so badly. She told me to go to this special building and I had to go right away."

"I've seen it," Devin said.

"They gave me a shot," Kit said. "Then I had this horrible feeling . . . You know how sometimes when you're just going to sleep and you think you're falling and you kind of jerk awake?"

He nodded again.

"It was like that, only it lasted for ages, that feeling of falling, and I didn't wake up. I dreamed a lot. Bad dreams mainly, really bad ones."

Kit said the dreams were strange because in the past, sometimes she had nightmares where everybody was looking at her. But in the Place, it was just the opposite; she dreamed that nobody was looking at her. It was as if she was invisible, but instead of feeling glad about this, she felt terrible, lonely and ignored and full of sadness. In the dream she came to a hall of mirrors, but even she couldn't look at herself. She crouched and covered her head, overcome by panic and shame. She kept having this same dream, over and over until she thought she might go crazy.

"I hope I never have to do it again," she said. "Because I don't know if I can take it."

"You probably will have to do it again," Devin told her. "All the kids here have done it lots of times."

Kit looked at him with anguish on her face. "But why, Devin? What's it for?"

Devin wondered what he should tell her. Everyone he'd asked had a different theory. There was Luke's idea that the whole thing was a scientific experiment. He said some of the other kids agreed with this, although a few of the younger children were convinced that magic was involved, that it was some sort of spell or enchantment and the Administrator was a witch in disguise. Karen had just shrugged her shoulders. She didn't know and she didn't like thinking about it. Thinking about it made it worse, she said. Vanessa—source of all gossip and rumor—claimed she'd heard that it was all a test.

"A test?" Kit asked when he explained this to her.

"To see if we're . . . ready for adoption," Devin said. "But I don't think that can be right. I mean, who would do that just to—"

"That's it!" Kit interrupted. "That's got to be it." She scrambled to her feet, her face suddenly eager. "It's a test to see who's ready for adoption. Or to get us ready for adoption." She picked up Frisker and buried her face in his fur. "That's it, isn't it, Frisk? And when I do get adopted, I'm taking you too."

"I don't know," Devin said. "It just doesn't sound right. I think Luke's idea makes more sense."

"I can take it if it's a test," Kit went on, ignoring him. "I can take a hundred visits to that place if it'll make me ready for adoption."

"But it's bad," Devin protested. "It makes people strange. The other kids call it being Spoiled . . ."

But Kit wasn't listening to him. She wasn't even looking at him. She was playing with Frisker as if he hadn't spoken at all. For the first time since they'd become friends on the city rooftop, Devin felt distance between them.

"There's a campout tonight," he remarked awkwardly, trying to change the subject. "We have to go. It's a group activity."

"A campout!" Kit exclaimed brightly, her voice a little too loud. "Wonderful! Great!"

✦ ✦ ✦

The campout was neither wonderful nor particularly great, despite the fact that Mrs. Babbage kept hovering around, clapping her hands and telling everyone that it was all "ever so much fun!" There was a fire and there were marshmallows on sticks and small lanterns inside every tent. But none of the children looked like they were enjoying themselves.

Devin was sitting next to Pavel, who had been sent to the Place that morning and was now in the Dream once again. He had caught a couple of moths fluttering over the dusky grass and was slowly pulling them apart, flicking the scraps of wings into the fire with a contented, almost peaceful expression on his face. Devin looked away, repulsed. Everyone else had also averted their eyes, although Devin sensed that there was something more to it than simply not liking to look at poor Pavel. He saw how the children shrank away, their bodies still, almost frozen. Devin was reminded of a rabbit he had once seen, caught in the open, under the shadow of a gliding owl. The animal hadn't tried to run or hide. It had simply stayed there, rooted to the spot with fear.

The children were like that. They didn't just dislike seeing someone in the Dream. It seemed to terrify them.

On the other side of Devin, Luke poked angrily at

the fire with a stick, the light making his eyes look dark and sunken. Kit sat in silence, her face expressionless. Only Malloy seemed to be making the most of the group activity. Having grown up as a Nomad, he was an expert at cooking over an open fire, and he was busy wrapping small packages in leaves and placing them carefully among the coals. He left them there to cook for a few minutes, then fished them out again.

He wriggled his way in between Devin and Luke and offered them each a package. They were very hot, and the boys had to pick the leaves off carefully before eating them.

"That's kind of good," Luke said, chewing. "What is it?"

"Grubs, mostly," Malloy said. "And some mashed potato to hold it together."

Luke made a terrible face and spat.

"Lots of nutrition in bugs," Malloy informed him. "Mom makes a great beetle-chip cookie. Not what you're used to, though, is it, rich kid?"

"Not exactly."

Kit had been quiet all evening, but now she seemed to come to life. "What's it like living in The Meadows?" she asked eagerly. "I bet it's lovely. Everything you want."

"I guess so," Luke said, frowning. "But when you're used to something it just feels ordinary. I spent a lot of time at school. I qualified for Hi-Speed Learning. Not many kids qualify because the program can mess with your head. But once they hook you up you can cover a whole grade in a month."

Pavel had finished with the moths and had started picking at a large scab on his knee, levering a fingernail underneath it with deep concentration.

"Hurts so good," he remarked in a small, sticky voice to nobody in particular.

He can talk when he's in the Dream, Devin thought. The realization disturbed him almost as much as what Pavel was doing, although he didn't quite know why.

Mrs. Babbage jumped to her feet and waved her arms. "Time for songs!" she announced.

"Oh, no." Luke groaned.

Devin didn't know any songs, and he wondered how Mrs. Babbage was going to persuade the kids to start singing. She didn't even try. Instead, music began to play from speakers hidden somewhere nearby and he heard a recording of children's voices.

The recording went on and on. The song was all about walking in the woods with backpacks on, and there were many verses. After it was over, another song began, and then a third. The children sat stiff with boredom. There was a movement beyond the fire, and out of the corner of his eye, Devin saw three or four Visitors, standing and nodding to the music. One was extremely fat and unable to nod because he didn't appear to have a neck. His head merely bobbed to and fro on the flabby layering of his many chins. The moment the other children caught sight of the Visitors, most of them began singing as heartily as they could.

"Hiking! Hiking! Hiking all the day!

"We have stout boots and we know the way!

"The world is full of great de-light . . ."

"Until you get a big bug bite!" Malloy sang in Devin's ear. He rolled his eyes and grinned.

The Visitors wandered away and the children stopped singing. Mrs. Babbage turned the music off abruptly.

"Tents, everyone!" she called.

Devin was sharing a tent with Malloy, Luke, and Ansel. Kit was in the tent next door with a couple of other girls. After they had all crawled inside, Malloy made an announcement. "Nobody go to sleep," he said. "I want to go look at the posts again."

Luke groaned slightly. "We've tried this before, Malloy. I can't figure out what sets off the lasers, let alone how to keep it from happening."

"We haven't tried using fire."

Luke looked thoughtful. "True."

They waited in silence, listening to the voices and rustling of children in the other tents, the footsteps of adults passing to and fro. At last all was quiet. Malloy stuck his head out of the tent cautiously. "Eagle One to Eagle Two," he said. "We have clearance."

"No one out there at all?"

"That's a negative, Eagle Two."

"Stop talking like that," Luke hissed in irritation.

"Order acknowledged. Over and out."

They emerged and made their way quietly through the camp. Kit stuck her head out of her tent and then hurried to join them. As he passed the fire, Luke picked up a stick. It was still burning slowly, the tip white with heat. They left the camp and passed by the farmyard, Devin stumbling along on the uneven ground. Where the path ended, they pushed through bushes, Malloy leading the way. He stopped about ten feet from the first post, and they stared up at it. It was made of slender steel, and a red light flickered on the very top, casting a weird, unearthly glow.

"That shows it's active," Malloy told him.

Together, Luke and Malloy had tried throwing different things past the posts, trying to see what set the lasers off. They'd thrown plates and toys, handfuls of earth, rocks and sticks. Malloy had once even flung his underpants. But nothing worked. In the end, Luke had concluded that the posts were only triggered by living things. This meant they were probably heat sensitive, and if so, it might be possible to cross them by somehow masking the natural warmth of their bodies.

"Only safe way to tell if they're heat sensitive is with this stick," he said.

"Go on, then," Malloy urged, "Throw it over!"

Luke swung his arm far back and hurled the glowing stick. For half a second they watched it, bright against the dark sky. It flew past the post and landed in a dusty patch on the far side. They waited, holding their breath.

"Nothing!" Luke said in disgust. He sat down heavily on the ground and began chewing his lip.

Malloy was still peering after the burning stick. "It's gone to join all the other stuff," he remarked. "Wonder if it'll set my underpants on fire . . ."

"I don't get it," Luke said. "If it's not triggered by heat . . . perhaps it's set off by a heartbeat."

The others sat down, disappointed. Devin leaned against the trunk of a tree and looked up. The sky was clear and the stars looked very close, as if they were hanging like decorations from the branches. He gazed at them, marking their familiar places. Kit crept up and joined him.

"What do they look like to you?" she asked him.

"Why'd you say that? They're stars."

"Tell me."

"Well, okay," Devin said uncertainly. "It's the sound first, isn't it?"

It was a keen, sharp sound like a knife running over stone, although it didn't feel as if it would cut him. It was more like a long, tingling shiver in his fingers, and then immediately afterward came the echo, and the echo sent out circles, like ripples on the surface of a still pond when a stone is thrown. The circles were gold, but only faintly, so that he felt them more in the back of his eyes and on the tip of his fingers, like something slippery that he couldn't get ahold of for more than a second.

"That's why you keep looking at stars, isn't it?" Devin said. "Because you feel you can almost hold them." He stopped, a little out of breath, feeling foolish for describing something so very obvious. Kit was staring at him with a peculiar expression on her face. Luke and Malloy stared at him too.

"What?" Devin said.

"Do you hear sounds and feel stuff when you look at everything?" Kit said at last.

"Not everything. Lots of things are sort of flat and don't make any noise at all."

"It's, like, your imagination, right?" Luke suggested. "You see and hear things in your mind. That's what it is."

"No, of course not!" Devin protested. "It's just what's there, it's not made up." He looked from one to the other. "Don't you see it too?"

"You don't understand, do you?" Kit said. Frisker shifted in her arms and she gripped him tighter. "We don't hear or feel anything when we look at the stars."

"Color is just color!" Malloy burst out. "Sound is just sound, taste is just taste; shapes don't have feelings, and feelings don't have shapes! But it's like you've got them all twisted and tangled.

"It sounds kind of cool, though," he added kindly.

"There! You said it sounded cool," Devin argued, "So you do feel sounds . . ."

Malloy shook his head. "Just a figure of speech, Strange Boy."

"I thought everyone saw things the same way," Devin said in a low voice. "I didn't know I was different."

"It's like a secret power!" Kit said, very excited. "Only, secret powers have to be useful, like X-ray vision or invisibility. What's the use of hearing colors and feeling noises if—"

She was interrupted by the sound of rustling. It was coming from a bush on the other side of the post. The children froze. In the sudden silence, the rustling came again. A cautious nose and pair of long ears appeared between the leaves and then, after a second or two, a small hare hopped into view, looked around, lifted a long back leg, and gave itself a good scratch.

Frisker leaped out of Kit's arms.

"Frisker, no!"

The puppy bounded forward, past the post, barking at the top of its tiny lungs. The hare vanished. Kit ran forward a few steps. She was almost at the post now.

"He went through!"

"Doesn't mean you can too," Luke said in a sharp voice. "Don't go a single step closer."

"Please, Frisker," Kit begged. She dropped to her knees. The dog looked at her, barked again, and raced back. "Good boy!" Kit cried, but Frisker swerved and tore past her, hurtling through the undergrowth in high excitement.

"What if he goes back past the posts again? I'll lose him," Kit wailed.

Ansel was standing by himself a few feet away. He had followed the others when they left the camp but had taken no part in the conversation, seeming uninterested in the posts or Devin's talk of stars. There was a dull look on his face, and he moved sluggishly, as if he was half asleep. Even the drama with Frisker had failed to rouse him, but now he lifted his head. The dog had appeared again, tearing down the path. He was four feet away when Ansel suddenly moved with instinctive, lightning speed. He leaped forward and dived head first toward the dog, catching him in his arms, his face smashing hard into the ground.

He scrambled to his feet, grinning. For a moment, he looked like his old self.

"You got him!" Kit cried, rushing forward. "That was amazing."

"Knew all that goalie practice would come in useful one day!" Ansel said.

"You're completely obsessed with soccer, you know that?" Luke said.

Ansel handed Frisker back to Kit. "You're hurt!" she cried. There was a large graze on Ansel's cheek. It was already oozing blood, and Kit rummaged for a hand-kerchief and wiped it gently. "It's nothing," Ansel said, although he held still while she looked after him, his eyes fixed on her face.

"You know what this means, don't you?" Luke said. "Frisker crossed the post without setting off the laser. That proves that it's not triggered by heat or a heartbeat. It must be wired to respond only to humans. Otherwise it'd be going off all the time when animals cross. I was thinking we could somehow fool it, but I don't see how we can stop being human."

Malloy stared at the ground and rubbed his head.

"It's a shame Frisker isn't trained in search and res-cue," he said, glancing at the puppy. "He could search for someone to rescue us."

Malloy's face grew thoughtful. "Do you think any animal could get past the posts?" he asked Luke.

"Seems that way," Luke said. "Come on. We've got to get back. We don't want them to catch us wandering around."

They turned to leave.

"Hey!" Luke called. "Where are you going, Malloy? The camp's in the other direction."

"I just have to visit with Fulsome," Malloy said. He trotted off and disappeared down the path toward the farmyard.

The others walked back quickly, worried that they had been missed. But the camp was quiet. Two or three of the tents had lights on inside; the rest were dark. Devin was a little behind the others. Passing between two tents, one in darkness, the other lit from within, he heard low voices.

"She rode all day on her horse; it carried her far away to a castle by the sea . . ."

It was Roman's voice. Devin paused and heard Megs whisper, "What happened to the Princess of Fire then?"

"The Red Witch's armies were all around the castle and there was nothing to eat," Roman replied. "The Princess of Fire got very hungry. In the end she only had one sandwich left."

"That's real bad."

"Yes, it was. She decided to eat one half of the sandwich the first day and then one half of that the next. At last she was down to a single crumb that couldn't be cut in half no matter how small the knife she used."

"And then she was rescued?"

"Yes. The Black King came and fought all the armies. Nobody could stop him. He saved her."

"You're good at stories, Roman. Really good."

"I used to tell them to my little sister."

"She was lost . . ."

"Yes." Roman's voice was suddenly fierce. "But you won't be. I won't let it happen to you."

Devin suddenly felt uncomfortable about eavesdropping and continued on to his own tent. He crawled inside and found Ansel already asleep. Luke lay wide-eyed, his hands clenched into fists on his sleeping bag.

"Did you see Malloy?" he whispered.

"No."

"I wish he'd come back," Luke muttered. "He was upset about the posts. Not many people can tell when Malloy's upset. But I can. I know him. If I could just figure out how those posts operate . . ." His voice trailed off.

Devin closed his eyes and thought of Roman and Megs and the armies of the Red Witch and the broad back of his grandfather, knee deep in the meadow, cutting hay for Glancer. Then he slept, deeply and without dreams, only stirring slightly when Malloy entered the tent sometime later.

"That pig's a genius, I tell you," Malloy told him. "Fulsome will get us out."

But Devin had fallen back asleep again.

Thirteen

DEVIN WOKE EARLY. There was a thin film of dew on the outside of the tent. He stared at it carefully. It made the tent fabric glitter a bit, he thought, but perhaps he was the only one who saw it that way. It also made a ticking sound, which he felt on the back of his hands, but again, he didn't know if that was normal or not. Since the conversation about the stars, everything he saw and heard was suddenly up for question. How strangely everyone had looked at him! But he knew they were telling the truth. Hadn't the Administrator told him he was unusual? He'd been feeling too sick at the time to pay real attention. But she'd said he was one in ten million and she'd used a word for it, something scientific. Devin didn't remember what it was. Luke would probably know, but Devin didn't want to ask him. He didn't want to be one in ten million.

It made him feel lonely.

His thoughts were interrupted by the sound of Mrs. Babbage clapping her hands.

"Time to wake up! Rise and shine, everyone!"

"What the heck?" Malloy grunted in outrage, burrowing deeper into his sleeping bag.

"Everyone up! I have a special announcement." There was a flustered edge to Mrs. Babbage's voice, and Devin crawled over to the tent flap and stuck out his head. Around him, other bewildered children were starting to emerge, their hair tangled from sleep. Mrs. Babbage stood by the remains of the campfire, waving her arms in anxiety.

"Everyone up!"

In a little while, they were all standing around her, blinking and rubbing their eyes.

"I have a special announcement," Mrs. Babbage repeated. "The special announcement is that the Administrator has a special announcement. She wants to see all of you at once. You have half an hour to clean yourselves up. I want teeth brushed and clothes clean! She won't be pleased if you look untidy. Hurry now! Hurry!"

✦ ✦ ✦

By eight o'clock, they'd gathered in the courtyard, buzzing with chatter and questions. The staff members had assembled as well. Devin had been right, there were many more of them working at the Home than it seemed. The Administrator's announcement must be really momentous, he thought, to make them stop work like that.

All eyes were fixed on the tower. Mrs. Babbage was hovering by the door, frantically smoothing her hair and adjusting her cardigan.

The door opened and everyone fell silent.

The Administrator was wearing a suit so sharp and white that the light seemed to bounce clean off her. The suit had no visible buttons or pockets, and the lapels were broad, spreading like wings against her chest. She held herself stiff, as if gripped by great excitement.

"Late last night I had news of the utmost importance. We are about to receive a visit." Her hands were pressed together almost as if she was praying. "In the history of the Home, it has never happened before. It is an honor of the highest kind."

"What's she talking about?" Kit whispered in Devin's ear.

"An honor!" the Administrator repeated. Her voice rose. "We are about to receive a visit from none other than Gabriel H. Penn himself. Inventor, founder, and president of this home!"

Mrs. Babbage's hand shot up and covered her mouth. Murmurs filled the courtyard.

The Administrator waited for her news to sink in, then held her hands up for silence.

"My father must have the best experience possible. His visit must be perfect in every single way." There was an edge to her voice that held everyone's attention. "The grounds will be groomed down to the last blade of grass," she continued, addressing the staff. "Surfaces will be wiped and repainted if necessary. All trash will be removed. Windows will be washed. Every floor will be swept and every piece of glass and cutlery polished. The Home must look like a paradise."

She paused. "There is no dirt in Paradise. There is no untidiness."

She turned her focus on the children.

It was so quiet in the courtyard now that not a single whisper or rustle could be heard. Even the flock of birds above the tower, disturbed, perhaps, by the unusual size of the crowd below, had fallen completely silent.

"You will be perfect in dress and perfect in manners. My father does not wish to see brawling children and he does not wish to see crying children. Above all, he does not wish to see dirty children. No scabs, sores, or runny noses. Clean, washed faces, and clean, washed hands and—"

She was interrupted by a soft sound coming from the far side of the courtyard. It began as a snuffling and grew to a series of throaty grunts. The Administrator paused abruptly and frowned. The grunting came louder and more eager, then rose to a crescendo of snorts and squeals.

A fat, foul-smelling, and familiar shape charged headlong into the courtyard.

Fulsome's skin, normally the color of well-chewed bubble gum, was half hidden beneath a rich coating of mud, manure, and old leaves. A thistle dangled from his left ear. His legs dripped an oily substance, and there was a large stick wedged firmly in his mouth.

When he reached the center of the courtyard, he stopped, grunted, and looked around inquiringly, then began to turn excited circles on the spot.

In the dreadful silence, two things were instantly obvious. The first was that Fulsome had been rolling in the rankest, filthiest substances he could find. The second was that this rolling had only partly wiped away the words written large in black marker pen on his side. And what remained was clear enough for everyone to see.

CA . L   OUT   ARMY   P . L ICE!

WE   . R . PRIS . N . RS   H . RE.

H . LP!!!!!!!

For half a second, the Administrator, Mrs. Babbage, and the entire crowd of staff and children appeared completely paralyzed. Malloy's eyes bulged with horror. Luke's face froze midtwitch. Then all the children (and some of the staff) broke into a huge shout of laughter that nothing, not the Administrator's terrible glare nor Mrs. Babbage's flapping arms, could prevent.

"Oh Fulsome, Fulsome!" Malloy shrieked, bent double with laughter.

He stopped laughing, however, when the pig, tiring of showing off, took a firmer grip on the stick between his teeth and advanced confidently into the crowd.

"Oh no," he said, "Oh no, oh no, he's coming straight at me. She'll know I'm the one to blame."

He darted behind Devin and stood cowering, tugging on Devin's shirt in an effort to hide himself. But Fulsome had other things on his mind. Not long before, he had received a tasty treat for depositing a stick of roughly this length and weight at Luke's feet. He trotted through the crowd, which parted eagerly to let him pass.

He reached Luke, but Luke ducked away at the last moment and the stick fell to the ground at Ansel's feet instead.

"Ansel Fairweather!" The Administrator's voice cut through the hubbub like a knife.

"You are to report to my office at once!"

✦ ✦ ✦

They were meant to be tidying their rooms in readiness for the great Mr. Penn's visit, but Devin, Kit, Luke, and Malloy were too busy wondering what had happened to Ansel to do much work. After issuing her order, the Administrator had turned on her heel and disappeared into the tower, and Ansel, with the eyes of the crowd fixed pityingly on him, had trailed in after her. The children dispersed, and a staff member, still grinning, led Fulsome away.

"Bet they hose him down," Malloy commented. "He hates to be washed. It isn't natural for a pig, you know."

"What were you thinking, pulling a stunt like that?" Kit asked.

"It was such a genius idea," Malloy said. "After you'd gone back to the tents last night I went to the pigsty and took Fulsome out and I wrote that rescue note on his body. Even though he's little, there's a lot of room on Fulsome's body. He's chubby, you know.

"Not fat," he added hastily, "just nicely chubby."

Kit rolled her eyes.

"I led him to where we'd been sitting, near the posts," Malloy continued. "I looked him straight in the eye and I told him to go fetch. But I meant fetch help, not an old stick. I should have been more specific, I guess. I mean, even Fulsome can't read minds.

"One little word," he mourned, "between triumph and disaster . . ."

"You really think that if you'd told him to fetch help, Fulsome would have come galloping back with a rescue team?" Kit asked.

"Something like that, yeah."

"You're a moron, you know that?"

Malloy slumped forward, his head in his hands. "I should go, shouldn't I? I should go and own up and say it was me. It's not right for Ansel to take the blame."

Devin didn't know how to answer. It was awful thinking of Ansel being punished for something Malloy had done, but he didn't want to say that.

"I'd go like a shot," Malloy said, "except I'm too much of a coward. I'm more chicken than chicken pot pie. I'm more chicken than fried chicken with a side of chicken. I'm more chicken—"

"Okay, okay," Kit said. "We get the point."

"I should go," Malloy repeated. "Do you think I should go? I really ought to go . . ."

✦ ✦ ✦

Whether Malloy would have owned up or not, it was already too late. Ansel had been sent to the Place. Perhaps it was a punishment, or perhaps it was simply his turn again. As usual, it was Vanessa who had all the information. She sat in the common room looking self-important. Devin noticed that she had undone the top two buttons of her shirt, perhaps in imitation of the Administrator. She fingered the neckline, showing off her marker-made red nails.

According to Vanessa, Ansel had been sent to the Place. But he hadn't gone willingly.

"You mean he put up a fight?" Luke asked.

Vanessa shook her head. It hadn't been like that. "It

was more like he went crazy," she said. "He yelled things nobody could understand and fell down and wouldn't get up. Two staff members had to pick him up and take him away."

Malloy hung his head and went very quiet. He trailed off to the farmyard in search of Fulsome, and nobody else felt in the mood for talking. Devin wandered by himself for a while. The Home had become a scene of frenetic activity in preparation for Gabriel Penn's visit. Staff members were everywhere. The lawn mowers were out in force, leaf-blowers blasted the pathways; buckets and mops filled the dining room; hedges were being trimmed, horses brushed, and gravel raked. The air was full of the smells of fresh paint, soapy water, and cut grass. But the children themselves were stiller than ever. They moved listlessly, fearful of messing up their clothes, bewildered by the turn of events.

A small girl was swinging alone in the playground. Devin could see at once that she was in the Dream. She plunged back and forth, rising so high that her seat jerked in the air and hung slack-chained for a second before hurtling back down again. One of her shoes had fallen off. Her hair flew back, and her eyes were closed as if the swing was carrying her to a different world, a place so full of joy that she would stay there forever if she could. Apart from the heavy, rhythmic creak of the swing, there was no sound.

Jared was sitting alone on one of the benches by the carousel. Devin stared at him curiously. Nobody seemed to know Jared very well. They always referred to him just as "the boy with the teddy bear," and sure enough, there it was, sitting beside him on the bench. Jared was a tall boy, but he had his knees up so his legs didn't touch the ground. As Devin passed by, Jared waved at him, then picked up the bear and made it wave too, waggling the bear's paw playfully. Spoiled, Devin thought with a stab of pity and fear. He waved quickly and hurried away.

It was early evening when he got back to the courtyard, and he stopped, astonished. The courtyard had always been an impressive area, but now it was transformed. An army of staff members must have been working on it all day. The driveway had been raked—Devin could still see the lines in the gravel—and the expanded flower beds were an explosion of color. Torches had been planted all around the open area, and moths flickered in their pools of light, and the curved walls of the tower were striped with twisted shadow. It looked beautiful, Devin thought. Almost magical.

As he stood there, a car pulled up. It was different from the car he'd arrived in, far larger, with a sleek silver ornament on the hood, in the shape of an eagle. In the same instant, almost as if she had been waiting behind the tower door, the Administrator appeared on the threshold.

She had changed her clothes. Instead of her usual severe skirt and shirt, she wore a dress, pale blue and floaty. The pretty, rather girlish barrette pinned in her hair made her whole face look softer. She stepped forward and then stood waiting, her arms by her side. The car stopped and the front door opened and a man got out.

Devin held his breath. Was this the famous Gabriel Penn?

He was wearing a navy jacket with gold buttons and had a cap on his head. Not Penn, Devin thought. Just his driver; Penn must be still in the car.

Devin was too far away to hear. He stepped a little closer, keeping to the shadows. The Administrator said something and the driver shook his head. "I've been instructed . . . ," Devin heard him say, and then, ". . . purely a business visit . . ."

The Administrator glanced at the darkened windows of the car: ". . . a meal," she said, "all prepared . . . I was expecting . . ."

The driver shook his head again and spread his hands. He turned and got back into the car and in a second it was moving away toward the adult accommodations on the other side of the courtyard.

For a second or two, the Administrator simply stood there, watching it leave. Then she turned and Devin got a glimpse of her face, lit by the torches. Was it pain and disappointment that he saw? Was it rage?

It was impossible to tell. Her face was as blank as a slammed door.

Devin knew she couldn't see him, but her gaze seemed to find him as he shrank back against the dark wall.

I need you to be healthy, Devin.

He hurried back to his room and lay down on his bed, hugging his pillow, his insides hollowed out by dread.

I'm saving you for something special.

Fourteen

DEVIN COULDN'T SLEEP, AND after a while, he stopped trying. He sat, fully dressed, on the edge of his bed, watching as dawn crept over the sky. There was a tiny knock on the door.

"I'm the messenger," Karen said.

Devin nodded.

Karen twisted her hands together. "I'm sorry," she said. "I'm so sorry."

"You don't have to apologize. It's not your fault."

"I know. It's just that I'm always the messenger. It makes me feel . . ."

"It's okay," Devin said. "I'll be fine. Look out for Kit for me, will you?"

He left the room and went downstairs. The courtyard was empty. There was still dew on the grass, the faintest trace of moisture. It would be gone soon, when the sun rose. Devin looked up into the clear blue sky, wondering suddenly what it had been like to live in a world where clouds were common, everyday things. Where all kinds of plants grew without any help and there was always hay for the horse and grain for the chickens. It hadn't been as easy as that on the farm—they'd had to work for everything—but it had been better there. A pocket of richness, his grandfather had called it. There were seasons on the farm; spring brought a scattering of flowers in the hedgerow, and autumn, color to the trees. And one January morning, when he was very small, his grandfather had woken him up to show him a miracle: a glittering sheet of ice, paper thin, on the top of a bucket of water by the back door.

The farm was different from the outside, hidden and protected. It was as if it had been forgotten by time itself and simply left to its own blessed devices. Perhaps there were other spots like it, but Devin did not know of them. And whatever happened at this place, however confused his mind and terrible the dreams, he would hold on to the memory of the farm. A pocket of richness, the one safe place in all the world.

Mrs. Babbage was at the door of the tower.

"You're to report to the East Building," she said.

She meant the Place, of course. He followed her down the path, around the field with the small hill, and up toward the recreation hall and the turning with the strange, twisted trees. She didn't say anything to him as they walked. He thought perhaps that dim as she was, she understood he was afraid and felt a little sorry for him.

The entrance to the Place was open, and they went inside.

It was just as Luke had described it. The walls were white and shining and there was a room with nothing but screens and monitors and glass panels and a staff member in a white coat who led him to a chair without saying anything. The Administrator was there. He saw her at the back of the room behind one of the glass panels, looking intently at something, her hand held up as if to say "wait." Then she murmured something into a black button in front of her mouth and her hand came down.

Devin didn't see the needle going into his arm. He barely even felt it.

✦ ✦ ✦

He was awake, he felt almost sure of it; but he didn't know where he was. The pieces wouldn't fall into place. There was a ceiling above and light coming in and the vague shapes of furniture around him, but none of it fit together.

He didn't know where he was, but he felt that he should know.

Even worse, he didn't know who he was—his name, his age, his past, or his future. These were basic things—the most basic things of all—but they simply wouldn't come to him. Yet they felt very close, like words stuck on the tip of his tongue or a familiar tune whose notes refused to play. He was someone; everyone was someone unless they were dead. Was he dead? Was this what death was like? Not knowing who or how or even what you were?

A crack had opened in the universe, and he was falling through empty space without a single memory to clutch onto.

I am someone! I am someone! Help me!

Panic engulfed him, and for several moments he lay paralyzed while his mind whirled, battered by fear and confusion like a bird beating its wings against the bars of a cage. In a little while he became aware of a sound, a low, rasping noise like air squeezed through ancient, leaking bellows.

It was his own breath.

It sounded that way because his body hurt so much. He was not dead, then, he thought. Surely the dead didn't feel such pain. He was lying in a bed under a single white sheet, but it felt as though there was an iron board pressing down over the whole length of him. His throat was dry, his muscles ached, and all the joints in his body felt locked, as if they'd been tightened by invisible screws.

He turned his head and saw that the room he was in was high up; he could see fields through the window and something that glittered as it turned, catching the sun. He could tell by the light that it was midmorning. On the other side of the room were two doors. One was half open, and he could just see the edge of a bathroom seat and the side of a small sink. Apart from a table by the bed and a single chair, very large and comfortable looking, the room was empty.

There was the sound of keys and the door to the room suddenly opened. A woman came in. He felt sure he knew her, but equally sure he had never seen her before in his life. She had a pinched-looking face and was carrying a tray with a glass of clear liquid. He managed to raise his head slightly. As he did so, the pillows rose up behind him with a small hissing sound so that in a few seconds he was half-propped up with his neck and shoulders supported.

"Where am I?" he said with difficulty. His voice sounded odd in his ears, although he didn't know why.

"Right where you're meant to be," the woman said irritably. She came over and put the glass of liquid on the bedside table and went out of the room again without looking at him.

He stared at the glass. He was very thirsty. He lifted his hand and reached for it. There appeared to be a large gold ring on his middle finger. He stared at it stupidly for a second or two, then grasped the glass and drank it down.

Almost immediately, most of his pain seemed to ebb away. He sighed, his breath rattling in his throat. His fear retreated too. It was still there, but only slightly, a shadow at the edge of things. His thoughts became muffled; the walls of the room lost their sharpness and grew vague and spongy. He dozed.

The light changed and changed again. He dreamed.

He dreamed he was on an empty plain. No trees grew there or plants of any kind. The sky was low and hard, curved like the inside of a tin mug turned upside down to catch a beetle. A boy was sitting on the ground a little way ahead with his back to him and the hood of his jacket up. He couldn't see the boy's face, but a terrible misery radiated from him, a stink of desperate sorrow and regret beyond all power to comfort. He didn't want to keep walking, but he couldn't help it. He was close to the boy now, close enough to hear him crying.

He left me, he left me . . .

There were tears running down his own cheeks; grief clutched his heart.

It's too late, too late, too late . . .

The boy's small shoulder in its blue jacket was just below him. He reached out his hand.

✦ ✦ ✦

159

He woke up and he was back again in the dream of the room with the single chair. Someone had come in and left a tray of food for him.

The food looked strange. A single fried egg lay on a white plate. A tiny tomato that had been scooped out to form a bowl lay to the right of the egg. To the left, three slices of mushroom had been placed in a fan arrangement, each slice overlapping its neighbor with perfect regularity. He stared at it dully. It didn't seem like a meal that had been cooked in the ordinary way, he thought. It was more like something that had been put together with tweezers by a person holding their breath.

He ate in a daze, without tasting.

The light changed. It grew dark outside.

He thought he was awake and standing by the window but he must have been asleep, because there was a man outside looking in at him and he knew that was impossible. The room was high up. The man would have to be fifty feet tall. He was an old man with cheekbones as sharp as knives, and he stared at him through the glass.

"I'm dreaming," he cried to himself in terror. "I'm dreaming!"

The lights went off and the man went away.

Time stood still and then suddenly passed. "Where am I?" he asked the woman with the pinched face. "Please . . . tell me my name."

"Wouldn't you like to know?" she said, handing him

another glass of liquid. "Drink it up now like a good boy . . ." She was smiling, her whole face lit up with satisfaction.

"That's it," she said. "Drink it all up and have a nice little sleep."

He didn't want to sleep. The boy would be there, waiting for him. He didn't want to see the boy or touch him. But wanting had nothing to do with it. He slept and dreamed of the empty plain again. There was a trail of small footprints in the dust. They ran across the ground with skips and hops and he followed their path, his own feet dragging, his heart flooded with anguish.

The footprints ended and the boy was there. His head was down, hidden by the hood of his jacket, and his shoulders twitched as he sobbed.

He left me. He hasn't come back.

"Who left you?" he said, and touched the boy's shoulder.

The boy turned his head and looked at him and he staggered back in horror.

He had the wrong face. Not the innocent face of a child, but that of an old man, the old man who had been looking in through the window. The same sagging, pitted skin, the same pale, watery eyes. And he was staring at him with a look as cold and distant as the stars.

He tried to scream, but for a long moment, no sound came. Then, like bats bursting from a cave, his shrieks came thick and fast and seemed to have no end.

Fifteen

DEVIN WOKE IN HIS bed at the Home, under the quilt of patchwork stars. For a second or two he could barely believe it, and then he was overcome by relief. He pulled his knees up to his chest and hugged himself as hard as he could. He was back, he was safe. He was himself again.

But the feeling of the dream wouldn't quite go away, and after the relief passed, a strange unease came over him. He felt mysteriously changed. It was as if someone had crept into his home while he was away and used everything and moved everything around and then, just before he got back, returned them to almost the right places. Almost, but not quite. Devin couldn't identify what it was, but he knew something was different.

Tears rose in his eyes and ran down his face. They

tasted of dark-blue dust. Did everyone taste tears that way? It didn't seem to matter anymore. Nothing he felt or did seemed to matter. Before going to the Place, he'd told himself he would hold on to the memory of his farm, whatever happened. But he hadn't been able to. A great feeling of helplessness washed over him, and for a little while he lay in his bed without moving, simply crying.

He heard a scuffling at the door and wiped his eyes quickly. Luke was outside, with Malloy and Kit.

"Welcome back," Luke said. "We missed you."

"Fulsome was all sad!"

"Frisker too," Kit said gently, and held out the puppy for him to pet.

Devin looked from one to the other, so glad to see them he thought he might cry again.

"Thanks," he said. "Thanks. I missed you too."

✦ ✦ ✦

They sat down and told him what had been happening while he'd been in the Dream. There wasn't much to report except that Megs had succeeded in setting fire to her doll's hair, using one of the courtyard torches, and after that, all the torches had been removed. The main news was that since her father's visit, the Administrator had introduced a number of annoying new rules. For a start, there was now a dress code.

"We have to wear socks," complained Kit. "And if you have long hair you have to keep it tied back."

"And you have to keep your room tidy," Malloy chimed in. "They come around and check."

They'd also heard from Vanessa that the Administrator wasn't happy with the group activities. Vanessa claimed to have heard the Administrator lecturing Mrs. Babbage about arranging a better one, a scavenger hunt with objects for the kids to find all over the Home. Since then, Mrs. Babbage had been scurrying around frantically, trying to set it up.

"Complete waste of time," Luke commented. "It'll be pathetic . . ."

At lunch Devin was glad to find he was hungry. He heaped his plate with macaroni and cheese and sat down with the others. He didn't want to talk much. It was enough just to sit there and listen to the chatter.

"Mac 'n' cheese is such a useless food," Missie announced.

"You don't have to eat it," Kit informed her.

"That's not the point. The point is . . . Karen, why are you sitting so close? I can't move my elbow . . ."

"Sorry about that, sorry." Karen hunched her shoulders and shifted away.

"The point is that it's boring. Mac 'n' cheese is boring. It's a boring, boring food." Finding no agreement, Missie glanced at Pavel sitting silently at the other end of the table.

"It's boring, right, Pavel?"

Pavel, of course, said nothing.

"Can't you say anything at all?"

Malloy flicked a drip of cheese at Missie. "Sure he can," he said. "He's just waiting until there's something worth saying."

Missie pushed some food into her mouth with an angry gesture. "All I'm saying is that it's dull." She chewed and swallowed. "It's the food equivalent of watching paint dry. No, it's worse than that. It's the food equivalent of a jigsaw puzzle, one of those huge ones with nothing but sky." Her voice quivered with indignation. "Or nothing but sky and windmills."

Devin wondered why nobody told her to be quiet. He could tell she was annoying everyone. But perhaps Missie's endless grouching was simply her way of getting through the day, her way of surviving. And perhaps the others knew this, whether they realized it or not. He gazed at the faces around the table.

Look at the way Malloy stuck up for Pavel just a minute ago, he thought. Everyone's got a weakness, but we cover for each other and we make allowances, for Pavel, for Missie, for poor Jared who wants to stay a little boy forever . . .

He suddenly saw that they were a team. And that he would never feel lonely again, because he was one of them now.

Mrs. Babbage made her pattering way to the food table.

"If I could have everyone's attention," she bleated. "Attention . . . everyone . . . ?"

It was a while before the chattering died down, but finally there was quiet in the room. Mrs. Babbage looked around and gave a big smile. "I have wonderful news to share with you," she said. "Ansel Fairweather has been adopted!"

There was a second of silence and then a sigh rippled around the room, half of pleasure, half of envy.

"In a little while," Mrs. Babbage continued, "you will be able to see the photograph of Ansel with his new parents in the common room. I'm just on my way now to pin it up."

Someone started clapping, and in a second all the children had joined in. Devin glanced at Kit. She was clapping harder than anyone else, her lips bunched up and her eyes shining.

✦ ✦ ✦

The others had finished lunch. Only Devin and Luke were left at the table. Without being asked, Vanessa came over and sat down with them.

"You were weird," she announced, staring at Devin.

"What do you mean?"

"In the Dream. You were so immature."

Devin felt his hands begin to tremble.

"Hey!" Luke interrupted. "You're not supposed to talk about it. It's the rule."

"It's not my rule," Vanessa retorted. "I've got my own rules."

"What . . . what did I do?" Devin faltered.

Luke gave him a nudge in the ribs. "Don't ask!"

Vanessa smiled a small, superior smile. "You touched everything and you smiled and your breath went all gaspy and you stared at the sky like you'd never seen it before."

"I did?"

"You licked the grass. You ate some dirt. I saw you!"

Luke stood up suddenly and shoved his dinner tray at her. "Shut up! Shut your mouth!" he yelled.

The tray slid across the table and hit Vanessa in the chest. She stood up at once, brushing herself off in an exaggerated way.

"You are so pathetic," she said.

"I don't know what's wrong with her," Luke said as she marched away. "I don't know why she's so mean. It's like she thinks she's better than any of the kids here and doesn't want anything to do with any of us.

"Don't pay any attention to her," he added. "Don't listen to a word she says."

Devin nodded, but it was hard not to feel disturbed. His uneasiness of the morning had returned, seasoned with a new feeling of shame. It wasn't his fault that he'd acted "weird," as Vanessa had put it, but he couldn't help wishing he'd been able to have more control over himself.

It was evening. Devin and Malloy were at the gates of the large meadow, watching the horses and talking. Malloy was wondering whether it would be possible to get past the laser posts on horseback if the rider lay very low. That way, the posts might fail to detect the presence of a human. Devin thought it sounded far too risky, although he had his eye on the largest of the horses, a piebald mare that looked strong and eager. She reminded him a little of Glancer.

"I've gotta get out of here, I've just gotta," Malloy said. "My mom and dad, they're not very . . . Well, to be honest, I don't think they'll find me without some help. Luke's sure they will and I always agree with him, but I kind of only do that because I can tell it cheers him up. The truth is, my mom and dad couldn't find their way out of a paper bag."

Devin didn't say anything. He watched the sun dip behind the trees and the golden rumps of the horses and the long, whistling grass.

"Luke says there's a control box in the Administrator's office," Malloy went on.

"He told me about that," Devin said.

"She wears the key for it around her neck. I bet it controls the laser posts." Malloy paused. "We'd have to get that key, but how? And even if we did, Luke says for sure there's a code we'd need to know before we could disarm the posts . . ." His voice trailed off.

Devin had never seen him so serious. He'd thought Malloy couldn't be serious to save his life.

"Guess I'm just gonna have to fly out of here," Malloy said, grinning suddenly. "Have to lose some weight, though." He patted his stomach. "Never going to get liftoff with this belly.

"I tell you what," he went on. "When I do get out of here, I'm taking that bird with me."

"Bird?"

"That parrot of hers." Malloy clenched his fists. "Poor thing. Poor tatty old thing. Why does she have to treat it like that?"

"She hates failure," Devin said. "She told me that when I saw her on my second day here. I think she keeps the bird to scare us. To show us that she's never going to stop punishing anything or anyone who disappoints her."

"Nah," Malloy said. "I think she just likes hurting things. When I get out of here, I'm taking that bird and I'm going to the jungle where it came from and I'm letting it go free. Won't that be great?"

Devin nodded, smiling.

"I can just see it now," Malloy said. "Me and that bird in the jungle . . . all the animals everywhere . . . kind of like heaven."

"But where is the jungle?" Devin asked.

Malloy paused in his reverie. "Not sure," he admitted. "But wherever it is, I'm gonna find it."

✦ ✦ ✦

Malloy had left, and Devin stood alone by the gate, watching the sunset. He was so still, the piebald mare grew curious and wandered over, pushing her head toward him. Devin stepped onto the first rung of the gate and leaned over to pet her nose. She was wearing her bridle, and without thinking, moving automatically, he took it in one hand, climbed to the top of the gate, and slipped quickly and easily onto her back. She startled slightly and half wheeled, and he leaned forward to pat her neck, whispering to her. He nudged his heels against her sides and she took off at once, with a long stride that in seconds had become a gallop.

They raced around the large meadow, the wind whipping Devin's hair. Faster and faster they went. He thought if he went fast enough he could outrun the memory of his bad dreams and that terrible word *spoiled* and all that it meant. And for a while, with the blurred trees roaring as they flashed past and the sky ringing golden and his heart thundering to the beat of the mare's hooves on the dry earth, for a little while it really felt as though he might.

Sixteen

THERE WAS A NEW sense of tension in the Home. Perhaps it was all the recent rules or perhaps it was the sight of the Administrator herself. Before, she had mostly kept to herself in the tower, but now she seemed to be everywhere, checking the work of the gardeners, inspecting the kitchen, circling the courtyard with a narrowed eye as if judging the angle of the buildings themselves. She had also started carrying Darwin around on her shoulder. Darwin looked worse than ever, more like a clot pulled out of a filthy drain than a bird. Perhaps, since her father's visit to the Home, it was even more important to remind everyone what would happen if they failed her. Or perhaps Malloy was right and she simply enjoyed tormenting the creature.

Mrs. Babbage tagged along behind. She kept nodding,

her hands fluttering with anxiety as the Administrator issued orders.

"This is not up to standard, Babbage!" the Administrator said, her words carrying the length of the dining hall. "I simply won't have it. Sort it out!"

Kit had also changed since Devin had been in the Dream. She was quieter, her fierceness turned inward, and Devin noticed that she no longer asked as many questions as before. He found her in her room the next day before breakfast. She was lying on her stomach on the floor. Arranged around her were items from the dollhouse. There were a lot of them; Devin had no idea that she'd stolen such a vast hoard.

In addition to the tea service, her collection now included three lamps; a table; a vase of flowers; a harp which, though tiny, still had all its strings; a perfectly formed, real crystal chandelier; two oil paintings no larger than a fingernail; a desk; a trunk with a minuscule lock; a four-poster bed; a violin with a bow the size of a needle; and eight chairs with velvet seats and curly wooden backs.

Kit was staring raptly at something in the palm of her hand when Devin came in. She held it out for him to see. It was a tiny box with a glass lid, containing several rows of real shells, none larger than the head of a pin.

"Can you believe it?" she said. "It's a collection inside a collection . . ."

Devin wondered why she'd taken so many things. After all, she could have played with them in the dollhouse whenever she wanted. He sat down on the bed, rubbing his head. He hadn't slept much the night before.

"Kit," he said. "When you . . . came back . . . did you worry you'd have the same dreams? That they'd follow you even though you were back to normal?"

Kit shrugged slightly. She lowered her head so her chin was resting on the floor and her eyes were level with the dollhouse furniture.

"My granddad said if you want to dream of something good, you just think about it really hard before you fall asleep. I've been trying to do that, but I'm worried it won't work and instead I'll dream about—"

Kit interrupted him. "You know what's amazing? If you get down low like this and kind of squint your eyes, you can almost imagine all this stuff is life size. You can see how it would be if it was real, if you lived in a house with it all around you. And nobody would punish you if it got lost or broken because there was so much of it."

"I guess so," Devin said uncertainly. He looked down at his hands. "It's just that if I can't stop thinking about the bad dreams, then I'll dream them again, won't I? Even if I'm trying to think about good stuff like the farm and Granddad . . ."

Kit jerked to her knees abruptly. "Stop talking about

it, then!" Her face was pinched with anger. "The trouble with you is that you need to grow up!"

Devin stared at her. Kit got to her feet and smoothed her dress down, her hands agitated. "Sorry for telling the truth," she said furiously, catching sight of his wounded expression. "But it's not about sitting around feeling sorry for yourself. It's about doing what it takes."

"What it takes?"

"To get adopted."

"To maybe get adopted," Devin said.

"Why maybe? It happened to Ansel. You saw his photo, didn't you?"

Devin nodded. They had all been to the Common Room to look at the photo of Ansel. In the picture he was sitting at a table with two women who, although old, were still beautiful. One had silvery hair that fell to her shoulders in luxurious waves. The other was wearing a white skirt and held a tennis racquet. Behind them, slightly out of focus, there was a shelf with what looked like several trophies, large and golden.

Lucky Ansel, Devin had thought. He's gone to a sporting family.

But as Devin had looked from Ansel's face to the faces of the women and back again, something tugged at the back of his mind, a vague sense of oddness. He frowned—he couldn't decide what it was. Perhaps it was simply that the last time Devin had seen Ansel, he'd seemed so dazed and shattered. But in the picture there was no sign of it. He looked strong and happy again.

"It happened to Ansel," Kit repeated. "And it will happen to us too. But you've got to get tough, Devin. You've got to do what it takes."

✦ ✦ ✦

Mrs. Babbage was in the dining room at breakfast with pencils and paper and a bunch of cloth bags slung over her arm. She stood by the door with a frazzled look on her face.

"I've worked very hard on this . . . it's all set up . . . ," she muttered as she distributed the bags and papers.

Malloy was busy demolishing a plateful of French toast as Mrs. Babbage passed by and handed him a bag.

"Thanks, Mrs. Cabbage!"

She stopped uncertainly. "I don't think I heard that," she said.

Malloy chewed and swallowed. He grinned. "I just wanted to say thanks, but my mouth was full. Sorry to be rude, Mrs. Cabbage."

Mrs. Babbage looked even more uncertain. She glanced around. Luke, Devin, and Kit were staring at her with completely straight faces.

"My hearing must be going. Never mind," she said, and went on her way. Devin couldn't help grinning, although he thought it was perhaps a little cruel to mock Mrs. Babbage. She couldn't help it if she wasn't very clever.

Luke was looking at the paper Mrs. Babbage had handed him. It was a list of all the things they were supposed to go find on the scavenger hunt.

"Three stars, a four-leaf clover," he read. "Five things with eyes (humans not included!), six blue objects that are also circular, something beginning with the letter Q, something that rattles, three yellow things that are rectangular or square . . ." He groaned. "This is going to take hours."

He was interrupted by the clap of Mrs. Babbage's hands as she called for order.

"You will do the scavenger hunt in pairs," she announced. "Partners have been assigned. I have the list here."

Devin's heart sank. He knew it was too much to expect he would be paired with one of his friends, and sure enough, he wasn't.

"Luke and Karen," Mrs. Babbage announced, going down the list. "Malloy and Megs, Missie and Pavel, Kit and Jared . . ."

He was going to get a kid in the Dream, he knew it. A whole day spent trying not to look at or hear or even notice some kid acting strange. Now that he'd been in the Dream himself, now that he'd gone through the whole awful thing, he could barely glance at someone else going through it without feeling sick. Please, anyone but a kid in the Dream, he thought. Anyone . . .

It wasn't a kid in the Dream. It was worse.

"Devin and Roman," Mrs. Babbage said.

✦ ✦ ✦

Everyone trailed out of the dining room except for Roman and Devin.

"You going to carry the bag or should I?" Roman said.

"You carry your own bag," Devin said.

Roman pushed back his chair and stood up. He looked at his watch.

"Better get started. It's going to take a while."

"Not really. It's obvious where everything is."

Curiosity flickered in Roman's pale eyes.

"Are you going to be like this all day?" he asked.

"Like what?"

"Like you'd rather die than talk to me." He paused. "I know what the other kids call me. They call me Traitor. Is that what you call me too?"

Devin had heard Roman called that and worse. The kids at the Home shared a passion in their dislike of him. Vanessa never failed to stare at him as he passed, her eyes narrowing malevolently. Devin had seen one boy actually spit at him. Even Malloy joked about feeding him to Fulsome, though as Luke pointed out, Fulsome would probably turn up his snout in disgust. Nobody could forget that it was Roman who had lured them there with his talk of good food and endless play. The worst of it was that Roman himself knew what it was like to be in the Dream. He'd been there himself. Vanessa had told Devin all about it.

"Roman's been five times. That's what I heard," she had said. "I keep count."

"Of everyone?"

She nodded. "Yes. Five times for Roman. Megs is fourteen times. That's because she looks so babyish."

"Really?"

"Oh, yes, didn't you know? The younger you look, the more times you have to go."

She paused, brushing her curled hair away from her face with a careful, ladylike gesture. "I seem older than I am," she told him. "Don't you think so?"

Luke had wondered why Vanessa always acted so mean. Now Devin thought he knew.

"Yes," he said kindly. "Yes, a little."

"A lot," she corrected. "In fact, I don't look like a kid at all. I don't act like one, either."

Roman had been in the Dream five times. So he knew how bad it was. But he kept bringing kids back from the city. Maybe he'd made a deal with the Administrator, Devin thought. Maybe if he brought enough new kids in, he wouldn't have to go to the Place anymore himself.

In that case, he really was a traitor. Not that Devin would ever say it out loud.

He looked away. "I don't call you anything at all," he said truthfully.

Roman's mouth twisted. "No," he said. "No, you wouldn't. You're too good for that."

Devin wondered whether he was making fun of him, but Roman wasn't smiling.

"Come on," Devin said, a little roughly. "Let's get this over with." He looked at the list Mrs. Babbage had given him and then closed his eyes. It was easier to see the map in his head when his eyes were closed. He waited and sure enough, the colors and shapes swam into view, growing clearer as his mental gaze ranged over the intricate pattern of the Home. At last they were all in focus.

"There's a soccer ball with stars on it in the shed . . . ," he told Roman, "blue plates in the dining room . . . plus a blue Frisbee also in the shed, a pack of yellow playing cards in the common room on the shelf under the books . . . Needles have eyes, don't they? There are some in the drawer also in the common room."

Roman let his breath out in a soft whistle of surprise but said nothing.

After half an hour, although all the other kids were still searching, Devin and Roman had found almost everything on the list. The only thing left was the four-leaf clover. Roman said there was a big clump of them on the hill in the small meadow.

"I know because she told me once."

Devin knew without having to ask, who "she" was. No doubt "she" and Roman had many little cozy chats, he thought. He walked faster, longing to be done with the hunt and Roman's company.

There must have been thousands and thousands of four-leaf clovers growing in the clump on the top of the hill. In fact, there was nothing but four-leaf clovers there. Devin bent down and picked one and thrust it into his bag. Done. He turned to leave.

"She wanted them so she had them planted," Roman said in a low voice. He plucked a handful, closing his fist tight around the green sprigs. "Kind of misses the whole point of finding one, doesn't it?" He glanced at Devin. "Four-leaf clovers are only lucky because they're rare. Plant a whole clump and they're just weeds." His fist opened and the clovers fell.

"I'm going back," Devin said. "We've found everything."

"I was a bit like you once," Roman said abruptly. "People thought well of me. I used to go to school. It wasn't a great school but it had a baseball team."

Devin didn't know why Roman was telling him this or why he should stay to listen. But there was a strange look on Roman's face. At first Devin thought he was angry.

"I played catcher," Roman said in a tight, hard voice. "You know what a catcher is?"

Devin shook his head.

"The catcher has to have a lightning arm and an even faster mind," Roman said. "He has to know the whole game inside and out, and he can never relax because he's involved in every single play. The pitcher might get more attention, but it's the catcher who's the true leader. He's got everyone's back, and from where he stands, he can see the whole field."

He paused. "I was the best catcher that school had ever had."

He spoke so seriously and so sadly that Devin almost felt sorry for him.

"Why did you do it, then?" he said sharply. "Why did you become a traitor?"

Roman's face lost all expression. His pale eyes gazed blankly down the little slope.

"I guess everyone has their price," he said.

Seventeen

DEVIN AND KIT HAD been at the Home for nearly two weeks now, although it seemed much longer. The days blurred into each other and it was hard to keep track of the time. Some of the kids knew how long they had been there, others appeared to have lost all sense of the weeks and months. Luke didn't seem to think that anyone had been there much longer than a year, apart from Roman and Megs. Nobody knew when they'd arrived.

Nothing disturbed the monotony of the days except for the occasional group activity and visits to the Place, which Devin learned happened about once every two weeks or so. He wasn't expecting to have to go again for a while, so it came as a shock when he got the message barely four days after his last visit.

"Too soon," Luke said, looking worried. "Kids never have to go again that soon."

All the way to the Place, Devin kept the images of field and farmhouse tight in his mind. And as he allowed himself to be led to the chair to wait for his shot, he imagined himself in his favorite place of all, the barn. It was dark and sweet in there, the refuge of mice and small creatures. Up in the beams over the door, swallows made their nests. The walls were old, and sunlight sent a hundred golden threads through the chinks and cracks in the wood . . .

Devin closed his eyes as the needle went in.

I remember the barn. I am there, I am there.

But then he woke and his memories were gone. In their place was nothing but pain and confusion. He lay very still, crying silently, the tears dripping down the side of his face onto the pillow.

This time he didn't turn his head or speak when the woman came in with the drink that took away pain. She put it down on the bedside table.

"Down in the dumps are you?" she said. "Dear, oh dear."

He waited until she had left before reaching gratefully for the drink. His hands trembled. He twisted, trying to get a better grip on the glass, but his fingers were wet with tears and the glass slipped and fell, tumbling onto the floor, the liquid drenching the sheet and carpet.

He heard himself groan—a long, low, terrible sound.

He needed the drink. He couldn't endure another moment without it. He lifted his head from the pillow and called out to the woman, his voice reedy with panic.

"Help! Come back! I spilled it."

But nobody came.

After a long struggle, he managed to shift his legs over to the side of the bed. Slowly he sat up. A bolt of pain shot through him from the base of his spine, then ebbed as he gasped and panted. He rested his feet cautiously on the floor and swayed upright. He could see out the window. There were fields and buildings and a great number of birds wheeling in the sky. He rubbed his eyes. His fingers were sticky from the liquid that he'd spilled. He turned toward the door that led to the small bathroom.

It was hard to walk. He had to go carefully. His whole body felt as though it might break at the slightest misstep. Without the numbing effects of the painkiller, the pain was severe, but his mind also felt sharper. He found himself able to think and even form vague opinions. There was something wrong, for example, very wrong, with the way his feet moved. His head was too heavy; his arms seemed to dangle far below him. But he was too busy to pay these things more than passing attention.

He shuffled by slow degrees toward the bathroom

and stopped when he reached it, leaning against the door, out of breath with effort.

At the sink he reached out and turned on the tap. He lifted his head and stared at the wall above the sink. It was blank. Shouldn't there be something there? There was a bar of soap in a small dish by the side of the sink. He reached for it automatically. It smelled of something. He brought it up to his face, breathing in the scent.

A long sighing sound, a flash of blue—very bright and clean.

Smells good, doesn't it?

He reached for the name and like a miracle, he found it. Rosemary.

It helps improve your memory. A long time ago people used to place it in graves for remembrance.

The soap smelled of rosemary. And in an instant, like a door unlocked and suddenly thrown open, everything came back to him. It was just as if his grandfather had returned from the dead and was standing at his shoulder, his collar straight and his eyes calm. *You are Devin,* his grandfather said. *Wake up! Remember!*

In the same moment, he knew what was missing from the space above the sink.

It was a mirror.

Devin dropped the soap in shock. He lifted his hands and looked at them.

They were not his hands.

But he could feel the hands! He could feel the smear of soap on the tips of the fingers, a slight itch in the right palm, the way the ring—shaped like an eagle—chafed against the skin.

But they were not his hands. And these legs—long and bony; these dangling arms; this heart pattering weakly in his chest; this breath itself, coming in short, fearful gasps . . . None of it belonged to him. He brought his fingers up to his face and groped his cheeks frantically. All of it was unfamiliar, the features of somebody else, somebody old and weak.

He was dreaming, Devin told himself desperately. It was just another dream. But he knew it wasn't. It was too real and detailed to be a dream, and his body hurt too much. He staggered against the sink.

He didn't know how long he stood there, sick to his stomach, his senses reeling in confusion. What should he trust, his mind or this withered body? Where did he really exist?

You exist where I am, his grandfather answered. *In your memory, in your love. Remember when you were small and used to hold my hand to walk?*

Devin nodded. "Yes, I remember."

Hold it again. Hold on as long as you need to, Dev. I won't let you fall.

Devin closed his eyes and took a long, deep breath.

He was Devin. He used to live on a farm, and now he

lived at the Home for Childhood, where terrible things were done to kids . . . and where something terrible had just been done to him. There was an explanation and he would find it.

The tap was still running. He thrust his hands under the stream and splashed his face, shuddering at the feel of his slack and pitted skin. He wanted to wriggle away, out of this body, as ugly as a cuckoo in another bird's nest. But he forced himself to stay calm. He dried his face on a hand towel and tottered back into the main room.

He looked out the window and at once recognized the view. It was the Home, of course. There was the tower, the wheeling birds, and there was the carousel, still turning. He was in a room at the top of the Place. He'd never left it.

But that wasn't possible. Of course he'd left it! That's what happened at the Place: You went in and then you came out and for two days you were in the Dream. You didn't remember it, but everyone else could see you perfectly clearly . . .

Yet he was here. At least his mind was here, all his thoughts and memories and feelings.

Then who was the boy—the Devin—that was running around down there?

He breathed deeply, keeping the panic at bay, trying to think.

They've swapped us, he thought. Me and some old man. I have his body and he has mine.

It was the only explanation that made sense. No wonder they kept it a secret. The thought alone was enough to drive anyone half crazy. Devin reached his bed and saw the glass still lying on the floor where it had fallen. He bent painfully and picked it up and put it on the table. There was a large wet stain on the carpet where the drug had spilled. He tugged at the sheet on the bed, pulling down a corner to cover the stain, and then made his way to the large chair on the other side of the room. He sat down.

There was a rattle at the door and he closed his eyes, lolling his head as if lost in sleep. He had to act like he was in a daze, he thought. He had to look as if nothing unusual had happened.

He smelled food. It was the woman with a tray holding his lunch. He heard her place it heavily on the table.

"I dunno why they bother giving you this fancy stuff," she grumbled. "But the clients can't miss their creature comforts, even if they're not here to enjoy them."

He knew that voice! He half opened his eyes for a second. How could he not have recognized Mrs. Babbage before? But this was not the Mrs. Babbage he knew. Gone were the smiles and placating gestures. This Mrs. Babbage was hard and complaining.

"Wants everything perfect, she does," she muttered. "Worse than before, ever since *he* came . . ."

She leaned toward him, and he felt her breath against his cheek.

"Bon app-e-teet!" she said, drawing the word out with relish.

She's not stupid at all, Devin thought. Not even slightly dim. She was actually enjoying his suffering. It was the only fun she got in life.

He heard her footsteps going away and then the rattle of the door being locked. He glanced at his meal, an elaborate arrangement of baby carrots and delicately sliced meat. It smelled good, but Devin had no appetite. The thought of eating, of thrusting food down his throat into someone else's body, suddenly seemed almost disgusting.

He had to get out of the room. Kit had taught him to pick locks back in the city, using a piece of bent wire. Could he do it here? The thought made his heart pound weakly and he pressed his knotted hand against his chest, trying to still himself. There wasn't any wire in the room, nothing he could use. There was only the bed and the chair and the small table. The lights were even set into the ceiling.

Devin didn't know how long he sat there, sunk in dismay, his gaze fixed dully on the gray carpet. After a while a tiny object came into focus, something that lay half on the carpet and half off. He hadn't seen it before, but it was late afternoon now and the light had changed. The beams of sunlight coming in through the window were lower, and one of them had found the object where it lay in the shadows and made it glitter.

Devin leaned forward for a better look. He lifted himself out of the chair and with a great effort got to his knees and crawled over to the object.

It was a hairpin.

Mrs. Babbage, Devin thought as his hand closed eagerly over it. It must have fallen out of her bun on one of her trips to and fro.

It was harder than he thought to pick the lock. This wasn't because it was particularly difficult, but because his old hands shook so much. It was a while before he could steady them enough even to insert the pin into the lock, and then it took a good ten minutes of fiddling before he heard the click of the door coming free. He hauled himself to his feet, opened the door, and looked out cautiously.

He saw nothing but an empty corridor with white walls. A thin strip of gray wool carpet ran down the center, and there were three doors—all closed—on the same side as his room. At the end of the corridor was another door, larger and without a doorknob. Devin took a deep breath and stepped out into the hall.

His feet were bare. They were horrible to look at, huge blue-veined things with gnarled yellow toenails. But he was glad because having bare feet meant he could walk quietly. He crept along, keeping to the wall. When he got to the first door, he paused. He could hear something. He leaned his ear closer to the wood, listening. Someone inside was wailing very softly, with a sound as formless as the wind.

They have another kid in there, Devin thought. Someone else who's been swapped. He remembered his first sight of the place, how he'd seen something moving at the window. He'd thought it was a claw, but now he knew it wasn't. It was the hand of someone very old, pressed up against the glass . . .

He walked on past the other doors. When he got to the one without a doorknob at the end of the corridor, he paused and listened. But he couldn't hear anything. He pushed the door and it swung open. He was standing at the top of a flight of stairs. There were no windows. Instead, the staircase was bright with a cold, harsh light that cast no shadow. There was nowhere to hide if anyone came up the stairs toward him.

Devin took a firm grip on the stair rail and began slowly easing his way down.

✦ ✦ ✦

The stairs led to the ground floor. The corridors were wider down here, although equally white and clean looking. There were a great many doors leading into rooms that looked like offices. Devin shuffled along, not sure what he was looking for and desperately afraid he would be caught. He saw a door made of metal that was polished as bright as a mirror, and a wide lobby with chairs. Everything was lit with the same artificial light.

He passed a hallway that he recognized—it led to the room where he'd sat for his shot—and turned away hastily. Then, just ahead, he heard the sound of footsteps. Someone was coming around the corner, walking briskly. Without thinking, Devin pushed open a door to his left and ducked inside. He held his breath until he heard the footsteps pass by, and then glanced around to see where he was.

He was in a pleasant-looking room with a big vase of yellow roses on a low table and a lot of soft chairs. A large portrait of a man in a gray suit hung on the far wall, and a table in one corner held a variety of drinks and crystal glasses. A neat pile of magazines lay on the table, and Devin walked over to take a look.

Up close, he realized they were brochures, not magazines. He picked one up. There was a photograph on the cover. It was a picture of the Home, the large meadow with the courtyard and tower in the background, and a soft, sunny haze on the grass. In large letters above the photo, he read the words *An Introduction*.

Devin opened the brochure. Inside were more photos

of the Home: children playing on the go-carts and the climbing wall and a big close-up of one of the horses on the carousel, its wooden mane tossed back, its teeth bared.

Are you low? Are you bored? Devin read. *Have you lost heart?*

Has the passing of time sapped your strength and dulled your spirit?

We offer the solution!

Simply press RE-PLAY!

Devin turned the page.

WHAT IS RE-PLAY?

The Re-Play Treatment is a unique remedy for the depression of old age. As the years pass we forget how to play. But play is essential! It energizes us, increases optimism, eases burdens and provides joy. Now, thanks to the pioneering genius of our founder, Gabriel H. Penn, you can experience that joy again.

Actually experience it.

Just as you remember.

Devin stopped reading. He thought back to his meeting with the Administrator and the way she'd smiled when he mentioned the Visitors.

They weren't visiting the Home looking for kids to adopt, he thought, with a shock of understanding. They came to become kids again. Literally. To run and jump and throw and catch. To eat marshmallows around a campfire and swim in the pool and put a jigsaw puzzle together.

They came to play. And the kids were their toys.

Numbly he replaced the brochure on the pile, his eyes traveling across the room to the portrait on the far wall. He'd seen that face before. He'd seen it in his nightmare of the little boy. And he'd seen it in the window of his room. He'd thought a giant was peering in at him, but it was worse than that. It was his own reflection.

Devin stared down at the ring on his hand. An eagle, just like the one on the hood of the large sleek car . . .

I'm saving you for something special.

What could be more "special," Devin thought, than to swap bodies with the great Mr. Gabriel Penn himself?

But why me? Devin thought. Why swap with me?

Because he was different, he saw the world in a way that others didn't: richer, far more colorful, alive with sound and sensation. But there was more to it than that. It was also because of the farm. He'd been sheltered there, kept from knowledge of the outside world and all its fears. That made him different too. The Administrator had called him the most unusual child she had ever come across. Unusual enough to persuade her father to visit the Home at last and try out his own invention for himself.

She had used him as bait, he thought. A worm held dangling to catch a rare fish.

Devin didn't know how he made it back to his room without being discovered, because he made no effort to be careful. He shuffled along toward the stairs as fast as he could, his heart bursting with effort, shooting pains running up his back at each lurch of his hips. He knew he looked grotesque, Gabriel Penn with bare feet trying to run down a corridor and managing only a wheezing, panicky trot. But he was past caring what he looked like. He just wanted to get back to his room, curl up in the bed, and wait out the long hours until he was free again.

He reached his room at last. The minute he was inside he reached up and placed the hairpin on the tiny ledge of the doorframe. Then he sank down, exhausted.

Luke would figure it out, he thought. Luke and the others would know what to do.

Eighteen

THE TROUBLE WAS, LUKE didn't believe him. Malloy and Kit were no better.

"Sounds like just another dream," Malloy said. "A really bad one. Sometimes they do seem totally real . . ."

Kit nodded. "You just have to suck it up, Devin. I told you before."

"But it wasn't a dream," Devin cried. And he started explaining it all over again.

They were sitting in the small meadow. Devin had gathered them there because it was out of the way and he knew they wouldn't be overheard. He had spent the rest of his stay at the Place lying on his bed, pretending to sleep when Mrs. Babbage came in and out but fighting real sleep with all his might. He didn't want any more nightmares. He'd kept his gaze away from the window and his reflection, counting the minutes, his mind struggling with the knowledge that as he lay there helpless, Gabriel Penn had taken over his body and was using his mouth to talk, his legs to run. There was a stranger in his skin and the thought of it left Devin weak with outrage and horror.

Finally, at the end of the second day in the Place, a deep sleep came over him, too strong to fight. The shot they'd given him was wearing off, and it was the sleep of return. The minute he'd woken in his own bed, he had run to find the others. But now they wouldn't listen.

"I saw the brochure!" he insisted. "They're selling this place as a kind of treatment for old people . . . They're selling us."

Luke frowned and rubbed his forehead. "It can't be right, Devin. A couple of visits ago, they forgot to bring me the drink. Doing without it for a whole morning didn't make me remember anything. It just hurt like hell."

"Maybe it's not just the drink," Devin argued. "Maybe there's something in the shot that makes you lose memory, and the drink just helps it along."

"Then why would it happen to me and not to you?"

Devin was tempted to say that his grandfather had come back from the dead to help him, but he didn't think it would be very convincing.

"I don't know, it just did."

"It happened when you smelled the soap," Kit said. She turned to the others. "His senses are different, remember? Everything is stronger for him. Maybe the smell was strong enough to break through." She turned to Devin. "Is rosemary special for you in any way?"

He thought of the grave at the top of the hill.

"Yes," he said. "Yes, it is."

"So they're swapping us with old people?" Malloy cried out incredulously.

Luke was silent. "I suppose it's possible," he said at last.

"No it's not!" Malloy burst out. "It's impossible times ten."

"Okay," Luke said, talking very fast. "I once did this Hi-Speed course on the biology of the brain. And in theory, it is possible—"

"You're telling me that people can go around swapping their bodies?"

"Not swapping bodies!" Luke snapped. "It's not that. It's swapping minds. I know that sounds like the same thing, but it's not. It's completely different."

"I don't get it," Malloy argued. "Why is swapping brains any different?"

Luke jumped up in agitation. "No! Not brains!" he cried. "I said minds!"

"But how do they do it?" Devin said. "How do they swap our minds?"

Luke sat down, but he kept on talking just as fast as before. Devin tried his best to follow, but it was hard. Luke seemed to be saying that Gabriel Penn—or a team of scientists working for him—could, in theory, have found a way to see all the connections that made up a person's mind and they could have developed a method—using a combination of biology, chemistry, and technology—to transfer one person's mind patterns into another person's brain, at least for a while.

"So you're saying it is possible," Malloy said slowly.

Luke nodded to himself, caught up in thought. "Amazing, really, completely amazing . . . and very cool."

"It's not cool!" Malloy half shouted. "It's terrible! It's . . . it's like stealing your soul."

"Yeah, that too," Luke said.

Devin glanced at Kit, but she had her head down and was tugging at the grass, pulling out clumps and flicking them away.

Things were starting to be clearer to Devin now.

The reason the Home was so old-fashioned wasn't just because the Visitors liked to remember the past, it was so they could actually experience the past. The group activities weren't for the children; they were only organized to provide extra play for the Visitors. Even the name of the Home itself now made sense. It wasn't a home for children but for childhood: the Visitors' childhoods.

It was obvious now why the kids became "spoiled."

Over time, it must be devastating to a child's mind to be treated like that. No wonder Pavel had been struck dumb and Jared had started behaving as if he were five years old.

"We act crazy when we're in the Dream," he said. "But it's not us, is it? It's the Visitors who are acting crazy."

"Yeah," Malloy agreed, looking as if he might be sick. "They probably can't believe how good it feels to be a kid again."

"But why do we have the dreams?" Devin asked. "Why do we have such bad dreams?"

"My guess is that they're leftovers," Luke said. "Really negative emotions can actually change the makeup of the brain itself. We're using their brains, remember? So the Visitors must leave bits of themselves behind—the bad bits."

Devin thought of the little boy in the dream with his terrible old man's face who had sobbed as if his heart would break. Who was he? And what had he done to become a leftover in Penn's brain?

"Now do you agree that we've got to escape?" Malloy cried. "We can't go to the Place again, not knowing this."

Luke nodded. "Bad as it was before, this makes it ten times worse."

Devin glanced again at Kit. She had gone pale but she was still plucking at the grass, taking no part in the discussion.

"Kit? What do you say?"

She gave him an odd, defiant look. "I don't know," she said, "I don't know. I have to think about it, okay?"

"What's to think about?" Malloy demanded. But Kit just shook her head and refused to answer.

✦ ✦ ✦

Devin found her later that day, down by the kennels. She had taken Frisker to visit the other puppies, and all four dogs were tumbling wildly, frantic with joy. Devin couldn't help smiling at the sight. Kit was smiling too, and it gave him hope that she'd come out of whatever strange mood she'd been in.

"You okay?"

She looked at him and then looked away.

"Sure," she said tightly. "Why wouldn't I be?"

"We'll get out of here," he said. "Don't worry. We'll figure out a way. Luke's smart, and so is Malloy in his own way. And you're tougher than anyone."

"What if I don't want to get out?"

Devin stared at her.

"I'm not going anywhere," she said.

"But they're using us! Kit, weren't you listening?"

"I can take it. Like you say, I'm tough. I'm staying until I get adopted."

"By . . . a Visitor?"

She shrugged.

"Why would you want to be adopted by the same

people who've been doing this terrible stuff?" Devin protested. "People who've used you like that could never really love you."

Kit jumped to her feet, her fists clenched. "Love! Who said anything about that? I've never been loved and I've gotten along just fine."

Devin wanted to tell her she was wrong about never being loved, but he couldn't find the words.

"Love!" she repeated in a scornful voice. "Listen, the people who'll adopt me will be old, very old. That means they'll die soon; and when parents die, their children inherit all their stuff."

"So it's about that," Devin said quietly, thinking of her dollhouse furniture and the way her face had looked as she imagined it being real and all hers. "It's just about having stuff."

"You don't understand!" she cried. "Of course it's about having stuff! Rich people don't get hurt, Devin. They don't get beaten. For the first time in my life I'll be safe."

She scooped Frisker into her arms, and before Devin could say anything, she hurried away, her shoulders hunched, her face buried in the puppy's soft fur.

Nineteen

THE RULE AMONG THE children was that nobody should look at anyone in the Dream. But over the next couple of days Devin made a point of watching them carefully. There were currently three: a boy named Corey, a tall girl with long, blond hair, whose name he didn't know, and Missie.

Now that he knew that there were Visitors' minds inside their bodies, their behavior, which had seemed so odd before, made perfect sense. He remembered his aching limbs back in the Place and tried to imagine what it would feel like to be old one minute and very young the next. It must be thrilling, he thought. It must be the best feeling in the world.

In the beginning, the children in the Dream could barely keep still. Missie turned cartwheels on the lawn, her skirt around her ears, her shoes tossed off. Corey ran from one attraction to the other, jumping on the trampoline and randomly kicking at things as if to test out the strength of his legs. The blond girl simply hopped from one foot to the other, apparently astonished at her own balance. They were like new lambs, he thought, or colts: giddy with energy, amazed at the working of their own arms and legs.

After this first stage of euphoria, they seemed to settle down a fraction. But they still moved in a state of wonder, as if their bodies were suits of fabulous clothes to be touched and admired.

All of them, without exception, spent a lot of time simply gazing around. But they didn't look at things the way that Devin had noticed children—real children— looked. Real children observed the world in an open, matter-of-fact sort of way. But the Visitors peered and stared, marveling like tourists in some new and incredible land.

They didn't play like real children, either. They were not intent and businesslike with their toys. Instead they seemed incredulous, examining each item as if they could barely believe their eyes. It was understandable, Devin thought. It had been decades, after all, since they had last held a building block or watched a model train chugging around a track or dressed a doll. He had never seen such toys himself before arriving at the Home, but he realized how familiar they must seem to the Visitors, as familiar as the nests in the barn and Glancer were to him.

In the dining room, they always heaped their plates up high. It puzzled Devin slightly, until he remembered the tiny, careful meals he'd been given during his visits to the Place when he'd been in the body of Gabriel Penn. After half a lifetime of eating balanced, healthy food, the Visitors couldn't get enough roast beef and bread and butter and chocolate cake. They ate for the joy of it without fear of weight gain, crumbling teeth, or getting enough vitamins.

Devin could understand it, but even so, their selfishness sickened him.

He glanced at Corey. The Visitor that had taken over his body had a sharp knife and was carelessly carving his initials into the wood of the dining room table. That knife could slip and cut the small hands that held it. But what did the Visitor care about that? There would be a moment of pain, but someone else would bear the scar forever.

Devin turned his head away, unable to watch any longer.

He thought of what Vanessa had said about how he had behaved when he was in the Dream. How he'd licked the grass and touched everything. It was Gabriel Penn who had done those things, carried away by the novelty of Devin's mixed-up senses. It made Devin feel small and almost worthless, as if he didn't really belong to himself any longer.

You have to keep your standards in a world where everything is slipping and sliding.

His grandfather was right. He was Devin. He belonged only to himself. And he would fight to keep it that way.

Devin pushed back his chair and went out into the courtyard.

The sunlight was almost blinding. According to Luke, it hadn't rained here for weeks and weeks. The longer the time between rainfalls, the fiercer the storm would be when it came. But there was no sign of it now. That wispy cloud he had seen days ago had disappeared.

A car pulled up in the driveway on the other side of the courtyard. Devin shaded his eyes, watching it. Then Roman appeared from one of the buildings with Megs trailing behind him. The door of the car opened and Roman got in. It reversed, turned, and started back down the driveway toward the main gates. For a little while Megs gave chase, her yellow bow bobbing wildly. Then she stood still, a forlorn little figure staring and waving as the car disappeared from view.

Roman must be off to the city to get more victims, Devin thought. He'd wondered whether the boy had turned traitor to avoid going to the Place, but now it occurred to him that there was nothing stopping Roman from simply staying in the city and never coming back.

Unless he was being paid.

He was doing it for the money, just like the Administrator. While the kids suffered, they were both happily raking in the cash.

✦ ✦ ✦

Devin needed to take his mind off things, if only for a short time. He went to the farmyard and stood watching the animals. Fulsome nosed his way over to him and nudged his leg. Devin rummaged in his pocket and found a piece of leftover cheese that he had saved for him.

"How many fingers am I holding up?" he asked the pig. But Fulsome just stood there, waiting patiently for his treat. Only Malloy could get him to do tricks. The boy had an understanding of animals that seemed almost magical. It was probably his Nomad upbringing, Devin thought. He liked the sound of Nomads. The way they lived didn't seem so different from his grandfather's ideas. Perhaps one day Malloy would take him to visit one of their camps.

Perhaps.

Devin tossed Fulsome the cheese and turned away. He wandered off toward the courtyard. Passing by the kennels, he heard voices. The Administrator and Mrs. Babbage. They were coming down the path in the opposite direction. Devin didn't think he could bear to see them. He ducked behind the kennel wall.

"He was told to come back tomorrow." That was the Administrator talking. Devin could only just make out the words.

Mrs. Babbage mumbled something in reply.

"He was told to find at least two," he heard the Administrator say. "Although I have serious doubts—"

They had stopped on the path. Devin shrank back against the wall, praying that they wouldn't look in his direction.

"I'm well aware of that, Babbage!" the Administrator snapped. Her voice lowered. Devin could hear only a phrase or two. She seemed to be talking about Visitors—new Visitors—and then there was a mention of "things being not up to standard." He kept as still as he could, listening.

"I won't have this sloppiness . . . certain individuals . . . no longer . . . I want it put right, a clean sweep . . ."

Mrs. Babbage murmured a question.

"Do try and keep up!" the Administrator snapped. "It's perfectly obvious! It's only because we've had such a shortage that I've tolerated it." Her voice lowered again. ". . . the teddy bear for one . . . wretched little fire . . . long overdue . . ."

"I thought you said she was not . . ." Mrs. Babbage's voice was plaintive.

"I don't care what I said!" the Administrator said, suddenly loud. "He makes no effort! He has not kept his side of the bargain, so I feel no obligation to keep mine."

Devin heard her heels clacking against the path as she strode away and then the softer, more rapid patter of Mrs. Babbage's shoes as she hurried to catch up.

He had the feeling that whatever it was they'd been talking about was important. He just wished he could have heard more. He might have if he'd had the courage to creep nearer. But he'd been too frightened of being discovered.

Kit would have made sure she heard the whole thing, he thought. At least the old Kit would have. The old Kit wasn't afraid of anything. But as he hurried back toward his room, he wondered whether this was true.

He was starting to think that he didn't know her as well as he'd thought he did.

Twenty

DEVIN WASN'T THE ONLY one who was wondering about Kit. He soon found out that Luke and Malloy had been watching her too. The two boys had told Devin to meet them in the small meadow. They wanted to talk about escape.

Devin waded through the long grass, threaded with wild flowers. The others were already there, Luke with a sheaf of papers in his hand, Malloy lying on his back and staring at the sky with a piece of grass in his mouth.

"Where's Kit?" Devin asked as he approached. Malloy sat up and glanced at Luke.

"We didn't ask her to come," Luke said, without looking up from his notes.

"Why not?"

Malloy grimaced. "One of Luke's theories. And I have to admit he's got a point."

"What?" Devin demanded.

"Sit down," Luke said. "Okay, this is kind of hard to talk about . . ."

"Awkward!" Malloy chimed in.

Luke gave him a look and Malloy fell silent.

"It's to do with that stuff we were talking about before," Luke explained. "You know, the bad dreams and how we thought they were leftovers from the Visitors. Bad stuff that had happened to them which had become part of their brain?"

Devin nodded. "I remember."

"It got me thinking," Luke continued. "When Roman first told you about the Home, back in the city, did he ask you about where you'd come from and if your home had been happy?"

Devin nodded again.

"He asked me too," Luke said. "Have you noticed how every kid in this place has come from a good home? Bad things might have happened to us, but we've all . . . we've all been loved. You, me, Malloy, Ansel and his dad. Karen had an aunt who looked after her, Missie was in a great family until her parents were killed in a car crash on the highway . . . My point is that we were all selected for that reason."

"But why?"

"So the Visitors won't be uncomfortable when they swap with us. Because we have no bad leftovers. Don't you get it? Being treated badly when you're a kid must do something to your brain, warp it in some way. Kit is the only one here who doesn't fit the pattern. Roman made a mistake with her; she wasn't meant to come along, was she?"

"I said I wouldn't come if she didn't." Devin felt his face grow hot. "But I don't know what you're saying. Are you saying Kit's brain is warped? Because if you are, you're wrong."

"I'm not saying that," Luke muttered, looking away. "It's just that we don't know her like you do. And Malloy and me have been thinking . . . wondering . . . if we can trust her."

"This is wrong!" Devin burst out. "It's wrong and . . . and unfair. Kit would never do anything to hurt us!"

"Are you sure? Really sure?"

Devin paused. He thought of Kit's desperation to be adopted, how she said she would do whatever it took. Did this include gaining favor with the Administrator by betraying her friends? He shook his head.

"I'm sure," he said. "I know her. I'm sure."

"Well, we're not," Luke said. "And we can't take the chance."

"I'm sorry, Strange Boy," Malloy said, looking unhappy. "Really sorry . . ."

A tense silence fell. "So are you in or are you out?" Luke said abruptly.

For a second, Devin considered walking away. But there was time to convince them that Kit could be trusted. He sat down stiffly, apart from the others.

"I'm in," he said. "What's the plan?"

+ + +

The first thing to decide was whether to tell the others in the Home about what was really going on in the Place. Devin and Malloy felt that it was only fair that they should know, but Luke pointed out that it might lead to unrest, which would put the Administrator and the staff on high alert. He thought their chances of escape would be better if they kept it to themselves for now. After a moment of thought, Devin agreed to this on the condition that when they did get out, they would take all the others too.

"We can't leave anyone here," he insisted. "Not even one."

"I see your point," Luke agreed, "but it's going to make it harder."

The talk turned to the laser posts, the control box, and the key.

In order to get a large number of children out of the Home, they would have to disarm the posts. To do this they would need three things: access to the control box, the key to unlock it, and whatever code was almost certainly needed to turn the posts off. There was a fourth requirement: enough time after the posts were disarmed to effect a mass escape. But since this would depend largely on luck, they decided to focus on the first three.

Only the first seemed doable. To gain access to the control box, they would have to get the Administrator to leave her office and stay out for as long as it took. They thought it might be possible with some sort of diversion, although it would have to be a major one.

The key was a different matter. It hung around the Administrator's neck, and she had never been seen without it.

"Could we simply attack her?" Malloy wondered. "Knock her out or something?"

"I suppose so," Luke said, "although it would be risky. She's probably got alarm buttons all over the office, and if we took one step toward her, she'd set them off. Besides . . ." He looked around at the others. "No offense, but none of us is exactly that strong."

Malloy punched him in the shoulder.

"Ow!"

"Strong enough for you?"

But even Malloy had to concede that they had a better chance of escape if they could get the key without having to attempt force.

That left the code. Luke was hoping that it was a long, complicated one because that meant that it was probably written down somewhere. But where? And how would they get the time to look? How many people knew it? The Administrator of course, and perhaps Mrs. Babbage . . .

Gabriel Penn must know it too, or know where it's kept, Devin thought. He invented this whole place, after all.

Penn had returned within a few days of his first visit, and there seemed no reason to think he wouldn't come back again very soon. Was there any way to find the code then? He kept the question to himself, partly because it seemed like a very slim possibility, but mostly because the thought of having to return to the Place terrified him.

I'm not strong enough, he thought; not brave enough either.

After a few more moments of talk, the boys got up and walked back to the courtyard. Apart from the diversion idea, it didn't seem as though they'd accomplished much, and the knowledge seemed to hang heavily on all of them. Luke was particularly depressed. He walked along, his mouth moving soundlessly as if in deep and frustrating conversation with himself.

Just before they got back, he stopped and turned to the others.

"Not a word to anyone, right?" He looked hard at Devin. "You promise?"

Devin paused, and then nodded.

In the common room, Vanessa was holding court on the sofa. She had news.

"Roman's back with a new kid. That's what I heard."

"Boy or girl?" someone asked.

"Boy," Vanessa said. "But very short," she added disdainfully. "He looks way younger than he is."

"Where is he now?"

Vanessa smiled knowingly. "Where do you think?"

The new boy was in the dining room, eating as if his life depended on it. Which in fact it probably did, Devin thought, staring at the wispy figure hunched over a plate of steak. He was tiny, with a delicate manner and very pale skin. He wasn't wearing the usual neat jeans and shirt that all the boys in the Home wore, but had apparently kept on the clothes that he came in: a suit, shirt, and large red bow tie.

The suit was slightly threadbare and a little too small—the boy's wrists showed at the ends of the sleeves. But the shirt collar was straight and the bow tie very bright, a singing shade like the wind in the grass. If you saw him from a distance or didn't pay too much attention, you might imagine that he wasn't a homeless street urchin at all, but a boy from a good home—perhaps even from The Meadows itself.

"Hi," Devin said, sitting down next to him. "I'm Devin, what's your name?"

The boy wiped his mouth carefully on his napkin. "Caspar John Friedrich Farrilly. Are seconds permitted here?"

"You can eat as much as you want. Did you come from the city?"

Caspar nodded. He looked down and brushed the front of his jacket.

"Don't you like the clothes they gave you?" Devin said.

"Oh, I'm not taking off my suit," Caspar said quickly. "I might not be able to get it back."

"Okay," Devin said a bit uncertainly.

"This suit is absolutely vital," Caspar continued in the same grown-up tone. "It's my Edge. Is that pie? We're allowed dessert, right?"

Devin nodded and Caspar made a beeline for the food table. His suit really was getting small for him, Devin thought. In addition to the too short sleeves, the seams were stretched at his shoulders.

Malloy had wandered up, and now, as Caspar returned with a heaped plate, he gave him his customary grin. "Eat much more and you're gonna be busting out of those pants. You might want to think about putting some elastic in the waist there."

"Oh, I have," Caspar said very seriously. "Believe me, I have. But it turns out elastic is hard to find in the city."

Malloy looked at Devin and raised his eyebrows.

"This suit's my Edge," Caspar explained. "You have to have an Edge, don't you? Some people are fast or strong or good at thieving or big enough to push other people out of the way. I don't have any of that. I just have this suit."

"I don't get it," Malloy said.

Caspar put down his fork. "What do I look like to you?" he asked.

"Kind of stuck up, if you must know," Malloy said.

"Malloy!" Devin said. "No, Caspar, you don't . . ." But Malloy's comment seemed to give Caspar satisfaction.

"Stuck up! Exactly. Here's how it works. I stand on the corner looking lost and a bit scared and I tell people that my chauffeur failed to pick me up and I need to get back to my home in The Meadows only my cash was stolen by some ruffian kid. And it works. Not always, but just enough. They pat me on the head, look worried, and give me money. Of course, you can't do it in the same place too many days in a row. You have to move around. But even when that doesn't work, the suit can usually help me get what food I need. People don't suspect a kid dressed like me could be hungry enough to steal."

"That's genius," Malloy said.

"Thank you," Caspar John Friedrich Farrilly said with great dignity. He tugged at his cuffs. "All the same, I'm glad to be here. You may have noticed that I am slightly on the short side, although my mom used to tell me it didn't matter. 'You're big inside,' she'd say. 'A big spirit is better than great height.' She never explained to me why I couldn't have spirit *and* height, and every single night, I prayed to grow. But lately I've been doing the opposite. I've been praying to stay small enough for this suit. Every night, I hang up the jacket so it won't crease, and hope I can still fit into it tomorrow." He looked down at the half-demolished pie on his plate as if seeing it for the first time. "I guess I won't need to do that anymore," he said slowly. "Now that I'm here, I guess I'm safe."

Devin and Malloy exchanged glances.

He'd find out soon enough what lay in store for him at the Home. Perhaps Devin could break it gently to him as he showed him around.

"You want a tour?" he asked.

"Definitely!" Caspar exclaimed. "This place looks incredible!"

✦ ✦ ✦

As it turned out, the tour ended much sooner than Devin anticipated—in the common room, after barely fifteen minutes.

"We sort of hang out in here," Devin said, waving his arm over the place. Caspar went over to look at the books. He pulled one halfway out and then looked up at the wall.

"What are all those pictures?" he said.

Devin hesitated. He understood now why Luke had been so reluctant to tell him about the Home when Devin first arrived. It felt almost cruel to destroy Caspar's happiness at being there.

The boy had replaced the book and was now peering at the photographs.

"Who are those people? And the kids—are they kids from here?"

Devin nodded unwillingly.

"I know him," Caspar said, pointing to one of the photos. His whole face had changed.

"Saw him just two days ago . . ." Caspar's voice was very low.

Devin looked at the picture. "You know Ansel?"

Caspar nodded.

"You saw him in the city? That must have been a while ago. Before he got here."

"No, I told you," Caspar muttered. "I saw him two days ago."

"You can't have," Devin said. "Ansel was adopted from here over a week ago. He went to live with the ladies in the picture. He went to be their son. You must have met someone who looked like him, that's all."

Caspar shook his head. "No. It was him. I'll never forget that face. Not as long as I live."

Devin looked around to make sure they weren't being overheard. A couple of the younger children had entered the common room and were starting a jigsaw puzzle. "Let's go to my room," he said. "You can tell me about it there."

According to Caspar, he had seen Ansel, or a boy who looked very much like him, in the old school gym in the city where the children went when it rained. Although it hadn't rained in weeks near the Home, Caspar had been pleased about this big storm in the City, because it had given him a chance to wash his shirt.

"I have a secret place where I hang it up," he explained. "You have to keep your shirt white, or your suit doesn't look as good. I get the shirt wet in the rain and then it dries again and it's clean."

But Caspar didn't like being in the school gym, partly because he was frightened of some of the other, larger boys and partly because his suit jacket scratched against his bare skin and he was worried—as always—that while he was away, someone would find his shirt and take it. He sat in the darkest corner, with his knees pulled in to his chest, watching and waiting for the rain to be over.

He knew most of the other kids by sight, particularly a gang of four older boys who were occupying a space right in the middle of the gym, staring threateningly at the other kids and shoving those who got near. But one boy in the gym was new to Caspar, and he watched him carefully. The boy was big and good-looking, but he seemed dazed. He sat with a blank look on his face, hugging a backpack to his chest as though it contained something very valuable. He didn't seem to know that in the city if you had something valuable, you kept it hidden. Nor did he seem to know that he had attracted the attention of the gang. He just sat there in a dream.

"He didn't have an Edge," Caspar said. "No Edge at all."

Caspar had felt bad for the boy, but by the morning, he'd forgotten him. The sun was out again and he needed to see if his shirt was still where he'd left it. He was planning to start telling his story about the chauffeur and the stolen cash in a different part of the city. It was time he found a new place. People were beginning to look at him very suspiciously, and just the day before, he'd been chased down the street by a man who'd given him money in the past and realized he'd been tricked.

The shirt was where he had left it and it was already dry. Caspar breathed a sigh of relief, put it on carefully, and set out.

He was crossing a small parking lot surrounded by abandoned buildings when he saw the boy again. The gang was surrounding him, trying to get his bag. Caspar immediately ducked into the shadow of a wall. One of the gang shoved the boy hard in the shoulder, almost knocking him down, another swung a fist into his face, a third snatched at the bag, yanking on the straps. Caspar wondered why the boy didn't just give it up. But he wouldn't. He clutched the bag against his chest as if it was more than merely valuable, as if it was part of his body itself.

Caspar heard a yell of triumph. They had the boy on the ground now and had tugged the bag free. The biggest gang member opened it and looked inside. Then he flung it down again with a howl. Whatever he'd been expecting, food or money, clearly wasn't there.

It seemed to drive the gang into a fury. Caspar shrank back against the wall, his heart pounding and his hands sweaty. They were laying into the boy now, powered by disappointment and rage. The boy was still on the ground, his hands over his head, his body curled up.

"What did you do?" Devin asked. Caspar hung his head.

"Nothing," he whispered.

He'd squeezed his eyes shut and put his hands over his ears, trembling in the shadow of the wall. After a long time, he looked again. The gang was gone. The boy lay on the ground without moving, his backpack by his side. Caspar crept toward him. There was blood on the boy's head, and his eyes were closed. Caspar put his hands under the boy's shoulders and dragged him inch by inch into one of the nearby buildings. It was cooler in there, the light filtered through windows thick with dust.

He hesitated, then took off his jacket, bunched it into a pillow and slid it under the boy's head.

"He bled on it. But luckily only on the inside." He opened his jacket and Devin saw the huge stain, dark against the gray silk lining.

Caspar gave the boy water, although he didn't drink much. Then he carefully washed the boy's face and sat down beside him. He sat with him all afternoon. In the early evening, just as the light was starting to soften, the boy died.

"I don't think he was in pain," Caspar said. "He didn't look like he was in pain. I went out and got his backpack. You'll never guess what was inside."

Devin was silent.

"A soccer ball," Caspar said. "All that for just a plain old soccer ball."

Twenty-One

"I'm not listening to you!" Kit half-shouted. She shoved her hands over her ears. "Go away, I'm not listening!"

"You have to listen," Devin said. They were in Kit's room. He had gone to find her as soon as he could. Frisker was curled up in a ball on the bed. When Kit started shouting, he leaped up and began to bark, his yelps tiny and squeaking.

"You have to listen," Devin said again. "Ansel is dead. He never was adopted. There is no adoption. We stay here until we're all useless, Spoiled, whatever you want to call it, and then they dump us back into the city and they don't care whether we live or die."

"It's a lie. That new kid is just causing trouble. Or maybe he did see someone who looked like Ansel.

Or maybe Ansel has a brother. The real Ansel's been adopted." She stared at Devin almost pleadingly. "You saw his photo. That's the proof."

Devin didn't reply. He reached into his pocket and took out the picture, smoothing the creases. "I took it from the wall," he said quietly. "Something always bugged me about this picture and now I know what it is. Do you remember the campout? How Ansel caught Frisker? He fell on his face and had a big scrape on his cheek. You wiped it yourself."

Devin held the picture out for her to see. "Look at his face. There's not a mark on him. They faked the photo. They faked all the photos on that wall. They did it to keep us quiet and well behaved."

Kit's face went as red as if Devin had slapped her. Then all the blood drained from her cheeks and the whole upper part of her body seemed to cave in on itself. She sank to the floor.

"I knew it," she wailed. "I knew, I knew. All along, right from the start. The minute I got here I thought, this place stinks worse than the leather of my dad's old belt."

She was crying now, her face blurred and twisted.

"I didn't know what was wrong," she sobbed, "but I could feel it. I just didn't want to think about it. I wanted Frisker and good food and nice clothes and . . . and I wanted to be adopted. The more you tried to talk to me, the angrier I got because you were spoiling it, Devin. But I knew you were right. Deep down I knew it."

"It's okay," Devin said helplessly. She had stopped crying, but there was still despair on her face. He sat down on the floor beside her. "It's okay," he repeated.

"No," she said, "no it's not. I lied to myself. I thought I was tough, but that's only on the outside. Inside, I'm nothing. The Administrator was right, Devin. There's something wrong with me. I'm damaged."

Devin thought about her, the whole of her. Her fierce, freckled face, the way she ran and climbed and looked toward the sky, her skilled thievery and love of beauty, her sparkling rooftop and the scars upon her back. All her daring and her passion and her weakness and her sorrow.

"You're not damaged," he said. "You're perfect."

Kit buried her head in her hands and burst into tears again.

"Don't cry," Devin begged. "It's going to be okay." He knew he had promised to stay silent, but he couldn't help himself. "We're planning to get out, to get everyone out. It's not just talk anymore. We haven't gotten very far with the plan yet, but we will." And he told her all about the diversion, and their idea of possibly attacking the Administrator to get the key, and the difficulty with the code.

"I've got an idea about how to do it. It might work . . ."

Kit's head was still buried in her hands, but she had stopped crying. And Devin could tell she was listening, because she had gone completely still.

✦ ✦ ✦

Of the three boys, Luke seemed the most devastated by Devin's news. Malloy cried when he heard about Ansel and crept off silently to mourn on his own. But he had never wanted to be adopted and wasn't too surprised to find out it had all been a hoax. Luke, on the other hand, seemed to turn in on himself; his face grew tighter and his twitching worsened. He became morose and then downright mean.

They were still talking about Caspar's story next day in the dining room, although they were careful to avoid being overheard.

"You haven't told anyone else, have you?" Devin asked. "I don't know what would happen if everyone knew."

Malloy shook his head.

"No one. Although I think Roman might have a clue. Luke and I were crossing the courtyard yesterday and talking about it and I turned around and there he was. He might have overheard.

"Rotten sneak," he added.

"He doesn't matter," Luke muttered. "Nobody talks to him except for Megs, and she probably wouldn't pay any attention. Too busy trying to set fires."

"Sooner or later, someone's gonna hear, though. Like

Vanessa," Malloy said. "Once she knows, there's no stopping it. The good news is that I've got a great idea for a diversion."

Malloy's idea unsurprisingly involved his friend Fulsome. According to Malloy, the pig was virtually psychic and the two of them could communicate without words. Besides, he said, the diversion would be a chance for Fulsome to redeem himself after the fiasco in the courtyard.

Luke listened to him chatter on without saying anything.

"He nearly saved us last time," Malloy said, "only I didn't give him complete instructions."

Luke suddenly banged his fist hard on the table. "Are you a moron? Are you a complete idiot?"

Malloy looked astonished. Luke had always been sarcastic with him, but never unkind.

"I can't believe you're even thinking of using that stupid pig again," Luke cried. "This isn't a game, Malloy. This isn't another one of your jokes. Ansel died. Don't you get it? He died."

Luke pushed away from the table and strode out of the room, his whole body jerking as he went. Malloy's mouth was open.

"It will work," he said sadly, "I mean it will probably . . . I thought he trusted me . . ."

"I'll go and talk to him," Devin said.

Luke didn't answer when he knocked on the door of his room. When Devin pushed it open, papers swirled and rustled around his feet. The floor was covered with Luke's notes and calculations. He had obviously shoved them all off his desk, along with the photograph of his parents. Devin spotted it lying half under the bed. There was a crack in the glass over the picture.

Luke was sitting at the empty desk, his head sunken into his shoulders.

"What do you want?" he muttered without looking up.

"Are you okay?"

"Oh, great. Never been better."

"Why'd you throw everything onto the floor?"

"Because it's trash."

"It's all your work," Devin protested. He knelt and started to gather up the papers.

Luke was biting his bottom lip so hard that Devin thought he might draw blood.

"It's trash," he repeated. "Like our escape plan. Malloy says himself that he's a chicken. That's who's going to get us out of here? A chicken and a pig? I'm never getting out."

"You have to," Devin said. He picked up the photograph with the cracked glass and placed it carefully on the desk. "You have to so you can bust your parents out of jail, remember?"

Luke made a sound that was meant to be a laugh but sounded more like a rattle.

"My dad! I've been thinking a lot about him. He stole more money than he could possibly spend in ten fabulous lifetimes. But he wouldn't stop. He just kept going and going. He told me that greed makes idiots out of people. Well, that makes him the biggest idiot in the world, doesn't it? Except that he's not. I'm the biggest idiot in the world."

"Why would you say that? How can you think that?"

"I should have seen it!" Luke cried. "I should have figured out what was going on here. If I had, I might have saved Ansel. He was a good kid. He didn't deserve what happened to him . . . But they tricked me, they made an idiot out of me, and I'm supposed to be some kind of genius?"

"You are a genius," Devin said simply. "You're the smartest person I've ever met."

"Yeah? And how many people have you met, Farm Boy? It must be all of ninety-three."

Luke slumped, his head and shoulders on the desk, his long hair covering his face.

"We'll work it out," Devin said, his words tumbling out with anxiety. "You really are a genius, and Malloy's a kind of genius too with animals, and now that Kit understands we have to get out, she'll help. She's amazing, you know, she's—"

"You told Kit?" Luke had raised his head and was staring at him. "You told Kit about the escape?"

Devin fell silent.

"That's great. Just great. You promised not to tell her, but you did."

"I know," Devin said. "I broke my promise. I'm sorry."

"A lot of good that does. The damage is done. Where is Kit, by the way? I haven't seen her all day."

Now that Devin thought about it, neither had he. The last time he'd seen her was the night before, in the dining room. She had sat by herself in a corner, picking at her food. Since then there had been no sign of her at breakfast or at lunch.

"I haven't seen her either," he admitted.

"So let me get this straight," Luke said. "You run off and tell Kit all about how we're going to create a diversion, possibly attack the Administrator, try to disarm the posts, and get everyone out, and then Kit mysteriously disappears for hours and hours. I'm not liking the sound of this, Devin. I'm not liking it at all."

But Devin had stopped listening. He was looking out the window to the courtyard below. The door to the tower had opened and Kit had come out. She was walking right toward their rooms and there were two security guards, one on either side, walking along with her.

"Oh, no," whispered Luke. "They're coming this way."

Twenty-Two

THEY HEARD THE ENTRANCE door below bang open and then heavy steps on the stairs. Luke grabbed Devin's arm. "Don't say anything, not a word. I'll tell them it was all my doing, that I influenced you, forced you into it . . ."

The steps came down the corridor toward Luke's room and passed by. Devin ran to the door and listened. "They're going down to the end of the hall. They're going to Kit's room."

There was a rattle of keys, the sound of the footsteps coming back and down the stairs again. Devin flung open the door and ran to Kit's room.

"Let me in!"

"They've locked the door," came her voice. "Hang on a sec."

He heard a scratching at the keyhole and the door opened.

"That lock is pathetic," Kit said. "A cross-eyed sloth could pick it.

"With one arm tied behind its back," she added. She looked at Devin and Luke.

"What are you staring at? Are you going to come in or not?"

"Where've you been?" Devin asked. She closed the door behind him and dragged a chair over, wedging the top of it under the door handle. "Just to be on the safe side," she said.

"Where did you go?" Devin asked again.

"For a long time, nowhere. I was too nervous to eat breakfast and I sat here for a couple of hours kind of psyching myself up."

"For what?" Luke demanded.

"I'll tell you if you let me just talk, okay?"

She had sat on her bed for a long time, Kit told them. She was thinking through everything she had to do. At last she was ready. She got what she needed from the drawer in her dresser and slipped on a dress with deep pockets. Then she took a deep breath and went out look-ing for Mrs. Babbage.

After a long search, Kit found her in the laundry room, counting towels.

"I need to see the Administrator," Kit said. "It's very important."

A look of annoyance flickered over Mrs. Babbage's face, quickly replaced by a smile.

"What's it about, Kit, dear?"

"I can't tell you."

"The Administrator is ever so busy," Mrs. Babbage said. "She can't be disturbed. You don't want to get into trouble do you?"

"You're the one who'll get in trouble if you don't let me see her," Kit said. "Believe me."

Mrs. Babbage hesitated, her eyes narrowing.

"All right," she said at last. "I'll let her know you're coming. But I do hope, Kit, dear, that it is important. I'd hate to see you punished, you know."

Kit didn't bother replying. She went at once to the tower.

The Administrator was sitting behind her desk, her hair shining as if it had been polished strand by strand. Kit made a note of what she was wearing: an icy pink shirt with the top three buttons undone. She stepped forward.

"You said it was important," the Administrator stated.

"Yes." Kit glanced over to the small birdcage. The cover was off, and she could see Darwin on his perch.

He was wiping his beak against the bars of the cage, over and over, making a rasping, clacking noise. The Administrator didn't seem to notice the sound. Perhaps it had been going on for so long that she had simply gotten used to it. Kit felt a stab of pity for the bird, and then shook it off. Pity made you weak, she thought. She had to be strong.

"I'm waiting," the Administrator said. Kit walked forward until she was almost at the desk.

"It is important. Important to me," she said in a rush. "It's about getting adopted." She put her hands on the desk and leaned forward. "I really want to get adopted, I mean I really want to and . . . and I want to tell you that I'll do whatever it takes to get to the top of the list."

The Administrator stared at her. Kit leaned even further forward. Her hands moved fast, but not as fast as they could, she made sure of that.

"This is not what I would call—" the Administrator began. Then her eyes widened. "Open your hand!" she snapped. "I saw you. Open it now!"

Kit appeared to tremble slightly. She took a step back and hung her head. Slowly she uncurled her fist. In her palm were four blue marbles from the bowl on the Administrator's desk. The Administrator pushed back her chair and strode around to the front of the desk.

"You dared to come in here and disturb me so you could steal from me?" she said in a low voice.

Kit made a wailing noise and pitched forward. "I'm sorry!" she cried, clutching at the Administrator, "I'm sorry! They're so pretty and I . . . I can't help myself . . ."

The Administrator stiffened in disgust as Kit's arms went around her in a hug. The Administrator's arms shot up, jerky as a robot, and Kit heard her gasp. For a split second they stayed like that and then Kit let go and fell back. "I'm sorry," she said again and began to cry.

The Administrator brushed herself off with both hands. "You will go to your room," she said. "You will not come out. You will not eat. You will stay there until further notice."

"Yes, yes, I deserve that," Kit mumbled, wiping her eyes.

The Administrator was still frantically brushing at herself as if she could wipe away even the memory of having been touched.

"Oh," Kit cried. "You dropped something, your necklace. Under the desk there. I'll get it!" And without waiting for a reply she dropped to her hands and knees and groped under the desk. "Here it is," she said, handing it back. The Administrator took it without a word, her eyes fixed furiously on Kit's face. Two security guards had appeared.

"Take her to her room," the Administrator ordered the guards. "And make sure you lock the door."

✦ ✦ ✦

Devin and Luke stared at Kit. Her eyes were shining with triumph. She rummaged in the pocket of her dress and pulled something out. It was a little silver key.

"Remember my rule, Devin? Steal small and steal big? The Administrator was so busy thinking about me taking the stupid marbles that she didn't notice that I got this!"

"But what about when she sees it's gone?" Devin exclaimed. "She's bound to . . ."

Kit smiled. "I noticed that key and that chain around her neck the first time I met her. I saw that the chain was thin but the clasp was quite big. I notice things like that. I also noticed that the key looks a lot like one of the keys I brought with me from the city—from my special collection. When I grabbed her I undid the chain and threw it under the desk. Then I pretended to find it, and while I was under the desk, I swapped her key with mine. She won't notice the difference. People don't really look at their keys, do they? Not till they have to use them."

There was a stunned silence and then Luke stepped forward.

"I doubted you," he said simply. "I shouldn't have and I'm sorry."

"'S okay," Kit said, sounding very embarrassed but also very pleased.

Luke took the key and examined it carefully.

"You're right that people don't look at keys, but she

might. So we don't have much time. If we're going to do this, we have to do it soon."

"What do you mean, 'if'?" Kit demanded. "We've got everything we need except the code." She looked at Devin. "You had an idea about that, didn't you?"

"Kind of," Devin said hesitantly. "You see, they don't know that I've figured out what they're doing and they don't know I can move around the place. Maybe the code is somewhere in there and maybe I can find it."

"It's a big maybe," Luke said skeptically, "but I guess it's the best plan we've got."

"Only problem is," Kit said, "Devin's got to go to the Place again before we get out."

They were all silent. "It's okay," Devin said at last. "Don't worry. I'll be okay."

✦ ✦ ✦

Devin spent most of the next day wandering around aimlessly. He'd spoken bravely the day before, but he didn't feel brave. There was an ache in his throat, and his hands were sweaty, no matter how many times he wiped them on the front of his shirt.

The sky was just as blue as always, but the color had hardened as though covered by a thin film of burning ice. When Devin stared up, it seemed to glitter slightly, sending out a thin whine, as faint and insistent as a mosquito. He had heard this sound before. It was the noise of the sky being stretched tighter and tighter, like skin over clenched knuckles. They should have had a storm days ago, he thought. Instead it had just grown hotter.

Devin felt stretched too, pulled tight between desperate hope and terrible fear. He wanted more than anything to be sent to the Place again, but he also dreaded it with all his heart. He walked slowly up to the top of the hill where he had found the four-leaf clovers with Roman. The tower was on his right, just below him. To his left lay the maze and carousel. As usual, there was nobody riding the golden horses. Their manes flew back, and their eyes were wild, but they were trapped, speared through the heart by rigid poles, forced to turn in the same tight circle forever.

The mirrors at the top of the carousel flashed as they caught the sun and made the same noise as the sky, only louder. On the farthest edge of the horizon, where it met the line of trees at the perimeter of the Home, there was a blurring in the air as if someone had smudged it with the tip of a finger. Devin felt the muffled drumbeat of a headache against his skull.

Above the tower, the birds wheeled and scattered. There was something different about their flight and a new urgency to their shrieking. Birds had knowledge, he thought. They could feel the disturbance in the atmosphere. The strange heat, the tight, unbreakable sky.

Devin sat down in the long grass, watching them. He could sense disturbance in the weather too, just like the birds. He'd always assumed everyone had this ability, but he'd also thought everyone could see colors and sounds in the same way that he did. Kit had told him otherwise. A "power" she'd called it. A secret power.

Was it possible to have a power without realizing it?

Devin turned and lay on his stomach and rested his throbbing head in his hands. For most of his life there had been only his grandfather to explain things to him. What other powers might he have that he didn't even know about?

A breeze ruffled the grasses in the meadow. It was a feeble thing, almost spent already. From the other side of the grounds, the notes of the ice-cream truck tinkled faintly, half lost in the heat.

In a little while they would be laying out supper in the dining room. And then it would be night and another day gone. Devin didn't know how much more waiting he could take. What if Gabriel Penn never switched with him again? Maybe he was tired of it. Maybe he was dead. Old people did die suddenly sometimes. Devin rested his cheek against the ground and thought of his grandfather lying on the porch of the farmhouse, his big empty hands, his open eyes . . .

He felt a vibration in the earth, distant at first but growing stronger. Devin raised his head. Someone was toiling slowly up the hill toward him, head down.

It was Karen.

He waited until she was right in front of him, panting in the heat.

"It's okay," he said. "You don't have to say it." He got to his feet and brushed himself off.

Karen hung her head. "I'm sorry," she whispered, "I'm sorry, so sorry . . ."

"Don't be," Devin said. And he meant it. The hammering in his head was stronger than ever. He took a deep breath and set off walking toward the Place.

Twenty-Three

HE WAS IN THE room at the top of the Place again. He opened his eyes and knew it instantly. He didn't need the rosemary soap this time to identify his location or remember who he was. The memory of the scent had wedged itself too tightly in his mind to be easily dislodged. All the same, he knew he couldn't afford to take the drugs that Mrs. Babbage would bring.

When she entered with the glass of liquid, he waited until she had gone and then got up and poured it down the sink. He had to do this as fast as he could because the temptation to drink it was very strong. Being inside somebody else's body felt worse than ever. Before, he'd been numbed a little by shock, but now the full horror of the situation washed over him. He longed to grab at his own flesh and tear it away as if it were some repulsive animal that had latched on to him and wouldn't let go. Yet, at the same time, he couldn't bear to touch himself. He stood shaking, nausea rising in his throat, his breath ragged with panic.

The code, he thought. The code.

In a little while he felt calmer. He went to the door and reached up for the hairpin on the ledge, his fingers groping through a thin layer of dust. For a second he thought it was gone, but then his fingers brushed against it and he heard himself wheeze with relief.

Devin didn't know where he should start looking for the code. He lurched slowly down the stairs, clinging to the rail with both hands. He'd seen offices on his last visit to the Place; perhaps he should begin there. At the bottom of the stairs, he turned left and shuffled into the first empty room he came to.

On the desk was a large screen. The moment he saw it, Devin felt a fresh clutch of panic. If the code was anywhere, it was surely in here, but he had no idea how the things worked. Why hadn't he thought of this before? He didn't even know how to turn it on. He stared at it. The screen was as thin as a piece of paper, and there were no buttons anywhere. He brushed his hand across the glass, and then tapped it a couple of times.

Nothing.

He walked around the desk to look at the back of the thing, feeling stupid and helpless. It was completely blank.

Perhaps he should go to the room with the brochures and the portrait of Gabriel Penn. Perhaps there was something there that might help. He crept down the corridor, not sure exactly where the room was. He'd ducked into it so quickly before . . . He looked into one room and then another, eventually finding it more from luck than anything else. It was the same as before except that the roses were red this time instead of yellow. Devin looked around, not knowing what to do next.

There was a low dresser with a number of drawers, and he was just about to go and have a look at it when he heard the sound of footsteps and then the Administrator's voice, loud in the corridor outside.

"If you'd like to follow me, please!"

The footsteps grew louder.

"This is our meeting room . . ."

Devin stood paralyzed. He had to hide. But where? If he'd been himself, if he'd been a boy, he would have simply dropped to his knees and crawled behind one of the huge chairs. But Gabriel Penn's old body simply couldn't bend fast enough. He'd be caught before he got halfway to the floor. He looked around wildly, saw a tall screen with a pattern of dragons and flowers on it, and staggered behind it, ducking his head only a second before the door to the meeting room opened.

"Please make yourselves comfortable," he heard the Administrator say. How different her voice sounded! It was almost soft. There was a sound of murmuring and shuffling and sighing and the plumping of cushions and gasps of relief as several people settled themselves into the chairs. The screen had three separate panels, joined together with hinges. Devin put his eye to the gap between two panels and peered through. The room was filled with six or seven Visitors, all seated. He could see the Administrator. She had a bundle of brochures and was handing them out, one by one. A staff member was busy serving drinks.

"I'll have water," he heard one woman say in a thin, querulous voice. "With bubbles. But it has to be the right kind of bubbles. Small bubbles. I must insist on the kind with the small bubbles."

"Scotch and soda for me," a man croaked. "Only hold the soda—heh-heh-heh."

"Perhaps we should begin," the Administrator said.

Through the gap in the screen, Devin watched her flat, black eyes as they ranged over the room.

"You have seen our facilities, the operations room, and the accommodation. And I've run through the process of what we offer here. If you have further questions, now is your opportunity to ask them."

"I want to know how much the whole damn thing costs!" It was the man who'd ordered the scotch and soda. "It can't be cheap."

"It isn't," the Administrator said without hesitation.

Then she named a sum so high that Devin wondered if he'd heard correctly.

The man gave a long whistle.

"Please consider what's involved," the Administrator continued smoothly. "And consider that this is a unique opportunity. We are the only place in the world to offer this service. The technology exists nowhere else but in this building. And after experiencing our Re-Play Treatment, one hundred percent of our clients agree that it was worth every penny of the cost. Their lives are, quite simply, transformed."

"But isn't it . . . I mean . . . isn't it . . . against the law?" Devin couldn't see who had spoken. The voice was low and rather timid. But he saw the Administrator smile.

"Technically, yes, it is," she agreed. "But the money you pay includes a fee that frees you from any legal responsibility whatsoever. Besides, I'm sure you'll agree that such trivial laws hardly apply to people such as yourself."

The Visitors exchanged glances and small, knowing smiles.

"Let me also take this opportunity," the Administrator continued, "to reassure you that the children at our Home are all in the best of health and couldn't be happier to be part of the program. They've told me on many occasions that they actually look forward to being of help to you. They consider it a great privilege."

Behind the screen, Devin clenched his fists tight. The room was filled with happy chatter.

The Administrator let them talk for a while and then clapped her hands. "If nobody has any more questions, I'd like to direct you to my office for further refreshments and the signing of contracts . . ."

With a seemingly endless amount of shuffling and sighing and heaving of limbs out of chairs, the whole group rose to their feet and exited the room. For a moment after they'd gone, Devin could hardly move from sheer rage. How easily the Visitors had accepted the Administrator's lies!

It's because they don't care, he thought. They just don't care about us.

But Devin couldn't afford to waste time with anger. It was late in the day and he was no nearer to finding the code than he had been before. And with the Place milling with Visitors, the chances of being caught were higher than ever. With a sinking heart, he decided to return to his room.

✦ ✦ ✦

Devin sat on the edge of his bed, too tired and anxious to shudder any longer at the sight of his bony knees and shriveled legs.

He hadn't been able to find the code. He'd failed.

He sat without moving for a long while. It grew dark outside. There was a quiet click as the lights in the room came on automatically. Devin raised his head. He was directly opposite the window, and in the glass he saw his reflection again. The face of a stranger. The face of Gabriel Penn.

He stood up and slowly stepped forward, forcing himself to look and not turn away. Gabriel Penn had once been handsome, and there was still a shadow of something fine and strong in the sharp lines of his cheekbones and the set of his broad forehead. But time had all but destroyed whatever attractiveness he might have had—time and a thousand heartless choices that had put money before kindness and ambition before love. It was a hard, shut-off face without a trace of kindness or feeling. Devin remembered Penn's first arrival at the Home, how he'd left the Administrator standing there without even bothering to get out of the car to greet her. Even his own daughter meant nothing to him.

But as Devin watched, something seemed to tremble behind Penn's cold eyes. Was it just a trick of the reflected light? Devin walked forward until he was close enough to the glass to put two hands up against it. He stared, searching.

There it was again, behind the eyes: the faintest flicker of heartache, a yearning for something—or someone—that was long gone and never to return. It was as feeble as a flickering candle, but it brought a gleam of humanity to Penn's face, like a light at the end of a long, dark tunnel.

Or maybe, Devin thought, he had it the wrong way around. Maybe it was a light at the start of the tunnel. All the way back to where Gabriel Penn had begun. And suddenly he knew who the boy was in the dream.

He had to find him again. He had to sleep.

He turned away and drew back the white sheets of the bed and lay down. He was frightened, but strangely calm. He closed his eyes.

There was no empty plain this time. Instead he dreamed of the farm, and it was more beautiful than it had ever been. It was morning and spring, the fields new green and the stream running fast and the air full of dandelion spores drifting on the breeze. Devin clattered down the steps of the porch and ran across the yard, looking for the little boy. He wasn't in the barn or the orchard. Devin ran around the side of the farmhouse.

He found him sitting on the stone wall, his small legs dangling. No old man's face this time, but the soft skin and wide blue eyes of a five-year-old child. He had a dandelion in his hand and was blowing on it, his little cheeks puffed out.

"You're him," Devin said. "When he was little. You're Gabriel."

The boy stared at him and then smiled. "It's not Gabriel, it's Gabe."

"You're in his head . . ."

"I'm part of him," the boy said.

"So you know . . . you know things about him." Devin said. "I need your help, Gabe."

"Are you lonely like me?"

Devin shook his head. A wind was picking up. The trees on the top of the hill swayed, and the long grass bent and sighed. "Do you know where the code is?" he asked. "Do you know how I can find it?"

"Is this a game?"

"Yes," Devin said. "A game . . ."

"Only I never get to play anymore. Not even ever. He grew up and left me behind."

"Please tell me. It's important."

The boy laughed, his face lit up with merriment. "But it's so easy! An easy game! It's not a mirror, silly!"

"I don't understand."

"You just stand and wave!" the boy cried. "And then you use the ball!"

The wind was even stronger now. It whistled through the stones in the wall and whipped the hair around Devin's face.

"What do you mean?"

But the boy bowed his head and twisted his hands in his lap.

"I miss him," he whispered. "I miss him bad."

"He misses you too, Gabe."

And with the strange insight that sometimes comes in dreams, Devin knew he spoke the truth. Gabriel Penn had lost all touch with the child he used to be. But he longed for him. Perhaps his childhood was the only time in his life that he'd ever been happy. He'd invented a way to swap minds so that people could feel like kids again, but it hadn't been enough for him. He must have known that it wouldn't get him any closer to the boy he once was because he'd never tried it for himself until now. Perhaps old age had made him desperate.

"But no matter how many times he swaps with me, it's not going to work," Devin said. "He'll never find you. He's done too many . . . terrible things."

"Then I'm lost," the boy said. "Where can I go? Can I stay here?"

"This is my farm." Devin said. "You don't belong here. You're a part of him."

"But now I'm a part of you too, aren't I?"

The idea should have been disturbing, but it wasn't.

He's innocent, Devin thought. Just an innocent little boy.

The wind had dropped and the meadow was starry with wildflowers. Blossoms drifted in the shady orchard. Down at the stream, the water ran clean and tawny, turning paddling feet to gold. There would come a day when a basket of apples would be dropped in the yard, and a grave dug amid the rosemary. But that was not today and today would last forever.

"Okay Gabe," Devin said, very gently. "You can stay here."

✦ ✦ ✦

It was morning when Devin woke. He lay very still for a moment or two, thinking. Most dreams, he thought, were perfectly clear when he was dreaming them. It was only when he woke up that they got muddled and confused. But this one was different. This one had made no sense while he was asleep. But now it did. Realization rushed over him. He heaved himself up.

It was hard to wait until he could get out of the room again. It seemed to him that Mrs. Babbage was being particularly slow when she came with his drink and breakfast. She took a long time arranging everything on the table, then came over to the chair where he was pretending to sleep and peered at him, her face very close.

"Nothing to say for yourself? Going to sleep all day are you?"

But at last she was gone and the corridor outside was quiet. Devin made for the stairs, his bones creaking and groaning. He didn't waste any time going into offices, but headed straight for the metal door he'd seen on his previous visit to the Place.

It's not a mirror, silly!

Devin stood in front of it. The metal was smooth and looked massively thick. There was no handle on the door and no buttons on the wall beside it.

You just stand and wave!

Devin raised his right hand, palm out and rested it against the frame of the door. He felt a soft vibration as invisible sensors briefly scanned his skin. A green light flickered above the door, then the metal slid back. Devin stepped inside.

It was a large room, completely empty apart from a huge table in the center with a top made of black glass. He shuffled forward uncertainly, and as he did, colors appeared on the surface of the table. Devin gaped in astonishment. A model of the Home had risen before his eyes, although it wasn't made of anything but light. Devin could see right through it. There were the court-yard and the tower, the outlying meadows, the farmyard, maze, and recreation building, all perfectly propor-tioned, floating in the air.

And there were the twelve laser posts arranged like the numbers on a clock.

Devin hobbled nearer, his heart pattering, missing a beat or two and then fumbling on again.

Stay alive, Gabriel Penn! Devin thought. Stay alive just long enough!

The model of light seemed to get clearer as he got nearer to it, the edges losing their shimmer. Details emerged. Devin could see the carousel now, and the tree houses and even the wretched ice-cream truck in its spot behind the long hedge. Penn left nothing to chance, he thought. Everything about the Home was planned, down to the last blade of grass.

He reached out and then stopped. What was it the boy had said? Something about a ball. He must need it to activate the model. He bent, grunting from the effort and peered underneath the table. Perhaps there was a drawer down there, hidden below.

Not a drawer but a small shelf. Resting on it was a white globe no larger than an egg. Devin reached for it, squeezing it slightly in the palm of his hand. At once numbers shimmered into view above the model, dozens and dozens of them, arranged in rows and columns. Devin's eyes locked onto them.

Then they vanished. The code was gone.

"Someone's been a very naughty boy," a voice said.

Devin whirled around. Mrs. Babbage was standing in the doorway.

Twenty-Four

"WE CAN'T ALLOW YOU to look at that, now can we?" she said. "That wouldn't do at all."

There was another white ball in her hand. She tossed it into the air and caught it playfully.

"I knew you were faking," she said. "I saw you peeking, Devin dear."

Devin couldn't say anything. His voice was stuck in his throat.

Mrs. Babbage looked at him, her head tilted to one side as if she were about to tell him off for having his elbows on the table during lunch.

"I don't like to think what's going to happen to you now," she said. "But we can't have anyone knowing what really goes on here, can we?"

Devin didn't try to deny anything. He knew it was no use.

"I won't tell anyone," he said. "I mean it. I just want to get out."

Mrs. Babbage walked forward, her sandals making a slapping sound on the floorboards. The light from the model cast green shadows on her thin cheeks.

"No kid has ever woken up in here," she said. "I wonder what makes you so different."

She was only four feet away. Devin was a grown man, but he was old. He knew he could no more tackle her successfully than if he were a toddler.

"The Administrator doesn't have to find out," he said, although he could tell it was useless to plead with her.

"Her?" Mrs. Babbage's lips pursed up so tight her mouth disappeared.

It sounded, Devin thought, as if all the hatred in the world had been crammed into that single word.

"She does nothing," Mrs. Babbage continued, "except order people around. And since that father of hers showed up, she's been even worse. Nothing's good enough for her, and I've had enough of it."

She paused. An expression of cunning dawned over her features.

"Actually, it would serve her right if I didn't tell . . ."

She smiled, showing her small gray teeth. "Why should I? She's done nothing for me."

"That's right, you don't have to tell," Devin said.

Mrs. Babbage shot him a gleeful look. "I wouldn't get your hopes up, Devin, dear. I'll tell her all right, but only when I'm ready. Perhaps in front of that wonderful father of hers. She wants him to think she runs this place perfectly . . . Well, my news would show her up, wouldn't it? Pay her back for how she's treated me."

She took his arm. "You must be very tired," she murmured in his ear. "I think it's time you went back to your room for a nice little rest."

Devin let himself be led away.

✦ ✦ ✦

Someone was calling his name. A girl, her voice high and sharp.

"Devin!"

The word floated above him, rippling and distorted. He swam up toward it, his limbs heavy, his hands beating the darkness.

"Devin!"

He opened his eyes with a start. Kit was tugging on his arm as if she could physically drag him out of sleep. He was on his bed in his room at the Home; he was back from the Place. He turned his head and saw Malloy and Luke standing nearby.

"He's awake!" Malloy cried.

"You've been asleep for hours," Kit said. "What happened? Did you get the code?"

Devin sat up, bewildered. He shivered slightly.

"Did you get it?" Luke insisted.

"Give him a minute," Malloy chimed in. "He's still foggy."

Devin shook his head. "I'm okay . . . I looked for the code everywhere. I nearly got caught. It was hard . . . I couldn't hide, couldn't get down on my knees . . ."

"Okay," Luke said. "Take your time. Start from the beginning."

Devin drew a deep breath and told them what had happened. How he'd searched the offices and overheard the Administrator's meeting with the Visitors and found Gabriel Penn in a dream when he was still a small and trusting boy.

By the time he got to the part about the model of light and the little white ball, the others were on the edges of their seats with tension, and when he told them about the code appearing and then disappearing, they exploded.

"What?" Luke shouted.

Malloy covered his face with his hands.

"I can't believe it!" Luke cried. "If only you'd had more time!"

Devin stared at them in confusion.

"At least you tried, Devin," Kit said softly. "You tried your best."

"But . . . I saw it!" Devin said. "Didn't you hear me?" He drew in his breath sharply as understanding dawned.

They don't know what I can do. Until this moment, even I didn't know.

Kit had told him the way he saw things was like a secret power, and now he understood what she meant. It wasn't a power like X-ray vision or invisibility; it wasn't nearly as interesting or as incredible as that. But it had been exactly the power he'd needed when he came across the security codes for the Home.

"I can memorize things, complicated things," he said, his words tumbling out in a rush. "I can do it really, really fast. I didn't think it was anything special. But it is, isn't it? Remember how surprised you were, Luke, when I told you how many books there were in the Administrator's office? And the scavenger hunt—I knew where everything was without having to hunt like everyone else. And before that, in the city, I would never get lost, Kit, because I'd seen all the buildings from your rooftop. I had memorized them all. I only got a glimpse of the code for a few seconds, but it was enough."

Devin had to stop for breath. "The numbers were in the shape of a square," he continued more calmly. "Twelve columns of twelve numbers, 144 in total. The first column read 01, 33, 19, 02, . . ."

Luke scrambled for a piece of paper. "Hang on. Let me get a pen."

He wrote steadily while Devin dictated. At last he put down his pen.

"How did you remember all that?"

Devin felt embarrassed. "I don't know," he mumbled. "I can just do it. Numbers and letters, they make different sounds for me, and they're different colors too, so they stick in my mind. They kind of make a pattern . . . like a map. And then there are all the shapes in between the numbers—they make another pattern. And some of them I feel on my skin too . . ." His voice trailed off. "Don't you understand?"

Malloy was shaking his head. "No," he said. "We really, really don't, Strange Boy."

"It's like a page of words," Devin said, trying again. "If they were just random words, you'd never remember them, would you? But if the words made a story, it would stick in your head. I think that's how I remember things—because everything makes a kind of story for me."

There was a short silence. They still didn't understand, Devin thought. He couldn't explain it. But perhaps it didn't really matter.

"I thought you were a fool," Kit said. "I was so wrong."

Luke was staring at the piece of paper, gnawing on his lip. "Never mind about all that," he said. "I've got to think. You realize there are too many numbers here? You can't possibly have to enter each one of them to shut down the laser posts . . . unless it's a code."

"A code for a code?" Malloy piped up.

"Shut up! Let me think!" Luke tapped his pen against his knees, his eyes narrowing to slits. "Twelve columns . . . twelve numbers in each . . . twelve laser posts . . .

"Got it!" he said, sounding almost disappointed. "It's actually kind of lame. See if you can guess. What else has twelve?"

"Twelve eggs in a carton?" Malloy suggested.

"Oh, just tell us!" Kit snapped. "This isn't a math quiz, Luke."

"Twelve months in a year," Luke announced. "Look, the first number of the top row is 01. That's January. Next 02, that's obviously February. So the code changes every month. You don't have to enter all the numbers, just the ones in the column for that particular month. There's twelve numbers in every column, one for each of the twelve laser posts. Very simple."

"For a genius . . . ," Malloy said.

They all looked at each other. "So that's it. We've got everything." Kit said. "You figured out a diversion, Malloy?"

"I guess so."

"So when are we going to do it?"

"How about tomorrow? That gives us a little more time to plan," Luke said, his eyes starting to twitch.

"We can't wait," Devin said. "Mrs. Babbage said she wouldn't tell right away, but she's only waiting until she can humiliate the Administrator as much as possible. She might have told already. We have to go as soon as possible."

Kit looked at her watch. "It's now or never," she said. "I say we go during lunch."

✦ ✦ ✦

Kit told Devin to grab a backpack and fill it with things they might need later, once they were out. Warm clothes, a flashlight and penknife, any camping equipment he could find. Devin stood in his room after the others had left and tried to concentrate on the task.

In the two days he'd been away in the Dream, it had grown even hotter. Despite lavish watering, there was a brittle, dried-out quality to the plants in the courtyard. The leaves on the trees made a rasping, insect sound when the breeze stirred them, and the sun was small and pale, as though it had shriveled in its own heat.

Sweat prickled on his face despite the coolness of the room.

He grabbed his bag and started stuffing it as fast as he could.

The light had turned a pale, sickly yellow. It made the faces of the children in the dining room look drained of all blood. Kit, Luke, and Devin sat in front of their food, hardly speaking.

Caspar sat at the next table. He was working his way through a huge sandwich and looked a little healthier, although he was still wearing his suit.

I hope he can run in it, Devin thought.

"Get your stuff under the table!" Kit said, pushing her backpack out of sight. "Mrs. Babbage is coming!"

They did as they were told. Each had a bag except for Malloy. Luke was keeping Malloy's for him because he was busy. When Mrs. Babbage entered, Malloy was walking around the dining room, pausing by each table to whisper something to the kids sitting there. The instant he caught sight of Mrs. Babbage, he straightened up and put on his most innocent expression. But she wasn't looking at him. She made her way to the front of the room and clapped her hands for silence. She was staring straight at Devin, and when she caught his eye she gave him a tiny wink.

"Did you see that?" Kit whispered. "Has she told already? Is it too late?"

"I have an announcement," Mrs. Babbage said. "A lovely announcement!"

The room stilled.

"I have just heard from the Administrator that Megs, Jared, and Pavel have been adopted! They will be leaving for their new homes tomorrow. So all of you have plenty of time to say good-bye and wish them good luck with their new lives."

There was a scraping of chairs as the kids in the dining room rose to clap. Devin, Kit, and Luke rose with them. Out of the corner of his eye, Devin noticed Roman pushing his way toward the door; he looked quickly back at Mrs. Babbage. She was staring at Devin with a strange little smile on her face. He felt certain she was about to say something to him, but she walked right past and out of the dining room without another word.

As soon as she was gone, Malloy hurried over to their table. "I told everyone to hang around. Said there was going to be a show." He looked very nervous.

"Oh, God," Luke said. "You'd better have something good planned, Malloy. This has to work, it has to . . ."

"Stop it!" Kit said fiercely. "This is going to work and we're going to get out of here. But we've got to keep our heads and not panic. I know we can do it."

"What if you're chicken? What if you're more chicken than chicken soup?" Malloy said.

Kit gave him a long, hard look. "Then you pretend you're not. You pretend so hard it comes true."

Dessert had been laid out on the buffet table and kids were already helping themselves to it. "Okay, Malloy," Kit said. "You've got fifteen minutes, max. Can you be ready in fifteen minutes?"

Malloy paused, his eyes wide. Then he nodded.

"Remember where we're going to meet?"

"Hill outside, behind the maze and bushes."

"All right, then. Go!"

Malloy turned without another word and left the dining room.

Twenty-Five

THE MINUTES TICKED BY, five and then ten. Devin, Kit, and Luke sat in silence, not looking at each other.

"He's not going to be able to do it, is he?" Luke whispered in agitation.

Kit looked at her watch for the tenth time.

"It's been fifteen minutes already . . ."

"Shut up Luke! You're losing it."

The kids around them were finishing their dessert and starting to get up from their seats.

"He'll do it," Devin said. "I know he will."

Kit nodded, her lips tight.

There was a commotion at the window. Someone called out and kids were suddenly raising their heads to look. Devin heard a few gasps and then a muffled squeal of laughter.

"This is it!" Kit said, grabbing her bag. The dining room was abuzz with talk.

"I don't believe it!"

"You've gotta see this!"

"Is that animal driving a car?"

The doorway was jammed with kids all trying to get out at once. They spilled into the courtyard, pushing and shoving to get a better look. Kit, Luke, and Devin followed behind, keeping close to the building. For a few seconds they couldn't see anything, and then the crowd parted and they saw a red miniature car.

Malloy was in the passenger seat. He had raided the dress-up box and found himself a tuxedo and a shiny black top hat. He was grinning with terror. Fulsome was sitting next to him, hooves planted on the steering wheel of the car as if he were driving. Malloy had dressed him in a tiny white shirt with the top two buttons undone, and on his head, slightly askew, sat a dark, glossy wig.

The resemblance was unmistakable.

"It's her!" Karen whispered.

"Oh my goodness!" Caspar exclaimed.

The children stared in disbelief. Around and around the courtyard went the car, Malloy steering it with his left hand. From the corner of his eye, Devin saw staff members running toward the commotion.

"This will get her out," Kit said. "It has to."

But there was no sign of the Administrator. Kit, Luke,

and Devin eased their way behind the crowd, making for the door to the tower. Behind them, the car stopped in the center of the courtyard and Malloy got out. He stood uncertainly as if half paralyzed, then scuttled around to the other side of the car and opened the door.

"We have arrived, My Lady," he told Fulsome in a voice that was meant to be grand but came out in a frightened squeak. A ripple of laughter ran around the courtyard.

Fulsome descended. He ambled forward and then stopped to have a look around him. His wig had slipped even further, exposing a large pink ear, and his shirt was now missing several buttons. His stomach strained against the fabric and his thick front legs almost burst the seams of the arms.

But the pig had dignity, there was no denying it. If Fulsome was humiliated by his appearance, he gave no sign of it. He walked with his snout up, his tail perky, and his eyes alive for good things to eat. He was so gloriously proud that he made it look as if he wasn't dressed as the Administrator at all.

He made it look as if *she* were dressed like *him*.

"Good old Malloy," Luke muttered. "I'm sorry I doubted him."

"Seems to be a pattern with you . . . ," Kit said. But Devin could tell she only partly meant it. The three of them were close to the tower by now, keeping to the wall and moving slowly to avoid notice.

"Would you care for a stroll, My Lady?" Devin heard Malloy say. Mrs. Babbage had now joined the throng along with several more staff members. "Get that disgusting animal out of here!" her voice shrilled. There was a scuffle around the pig, and suddenly Fulsome had broken through and was charging around in the flower beds.

"You go, Pig!" somebody yelled. In a minute, twenty kids had taken up the cry.

"Go, Pig! Go, Pig! Go, Pig!"

Fulsome, excited by the attention, got up on his hind legs and turned on the spot. Vanessa forgot to be grown up and gave a hysterical cheer. Somebody grabbed Jared's teddy bear and flung it high into the air. The cries of the crowd became a roar.

GO-PIG! GO-PIG! GO-PIG! GO-PIG!

"Stop it at once," Mrs. Babbage said, apparently addressing Fulsome himself.

PIG! PIG! PIG!

Malloy stood in the middle of it all, waving his hands vaguely as if horrified by the ruckus he'd created. Mrs. Babbage turned to a pair of burly staff members. "Do something! Catch it or something!"

Kit, Luke, and Devin had reached the tower. They stayed around the side of it, keeping to the shadows.

"Why isn't she coming out?" Luke said. "This whole thing is pointless if she doesn't come out."

The two staff members had decided to use trickery to

catch Fulsome. Someone had fetched a large bread roll and was now waving it in the pig's direction. Fulsome stared at it thoughtfully. He took a couple of steps forward and sniffed.

"Don't do it!" a kid cried.

But Fulsome was not one to ignore any kind of food. He took another two steps. He was now almost within grabbing range of the man holding the bread.

"No-o-o-o," wailed the crowd.

The door of the tower banged open and suddenly the Administrator was there. Peering around the curved wall, Devin caught only a glimpse of her, her body rigid, her hands clenched into fists. For a second she stood there, perfectly still, and then, with terrifying speed, she moved.

When Fulsome had run loose before, the Administrator had thought Ansel was responsible. But she was not fooled now. Four or five swift strides brought her to her target. Her arm shot out and seized Malloy around the neck so tightly that his top hat fell off and his eyes bugged out.

A dreadful silence fell. The only sound was the gasping bark of Malloy trying to breathe.

Slowly, very deliberately, the Administrator bent her shining head as if to whisper something in Malloy's ear. But before she could say a word, she was interrupted by Mrs. Babbage, sounding full of panic.

"Visitors!"

She waved her arms frantically, pointing.

Devin looked out past the courtyard to the large meadow and the gates beyond. Five large cars had appeared in a line, moving up the driveway.

It was another group, eager for a tour of the Home. Business was certainly booming.

The cars were still distant, and they were moving very slowly in order not to jar the fragile, ancient bodies of their passengers. But in a very few minutes they would be pulling in to the courtyard. And then the Visitors would step out, not into the orderly paradise they were expecting, but into a scene of total chaos.

Exactly the same thought must have occurred to the Administrator. Her head shot up and, for a second, her whole body froze.

Then several things happened almost at once.

Malloy wriggled wildly and freed himself from the Administrator's grip. He leaped toward the miniature car, yelling for Fulsome. The pig halted in his tracks and then plunged after him, knocking a staff member to the ground. Mrs. Babbage screamed. Fulsome's wig flew off and several children made a dive for it.

Malloy jumped into the car and took off recklessly down the path toward the corn maze with Fulsome crammed in beside him. All the children immediately stampeded after them, followed by the members of staff.

In sixty seconds, the only people left in the courtyard were Mrs. Babbage and the Administrator. Kit, Luke, and Devin shrank against the wall of the tower. If the Administrator had turned, she would have seen them, but her attention was fixed on the convoy of cars, which was advancing steadily.

"What's she going to do?" Devin whispered.

"I bet she'll try to head them off," Kit said. "There's another place for cars to park behind the dining room. She'll try to redirect them there, then get them into the building quickly before they have a chance to see anything."

As they watched, the Administrator gathered herself. She straightened, flicked an invisible mark off the front of her shirt, and nodded to Mrs. Babbage, who scuttled off without another word. Then the Administrator began to walk—very fast but with no apparent haste—across the courtyard and down the driveway toward the approaching cars.

Kit grabbed her bag. "Now's our chance. Come on."

The three of them made a dash for the tower door.

✦ ✦ ✦

"Can we lock it?" Kit panted, slamming it closed.

Luke fumbled with the handle. "Not sure . . ."

"Never mind, then, leave it. Get in the elevator."

Luke punched the button for the top floor. They crowded together, perfectly still, their bodies tight with tension, their faces looking desperately white in the elevator light's glow. In the few seconds of silence as the elevator rose, they heard a soft, whimpering, scratching sound, very close. Luke's whole body jerked.

"It's just Frisker," Kit said, patting her backpack. "You don't think I'd leave this place without Frisker, do you?"

The elevator hissed and the door slid open and the Administrator's office was laid out before them.

Kit put her bag down carefully on the floor and rummaged in her pocket for the key to the control box. She pulled it out and tossed it to Luke.

"It's up to you now," she said.

Luke was at the Administrator's desk. "There's a button here somewhere that opens the panel hiding the control box . . . I saw her press it . . . ah, here it is."

A small rectangle slid open on the wall of fake books.

Luke had unlocked the control box and was hunched over a sheet of glass. Small lights were blinking on the surface in an apparently random pattern, but Luke didn't seem disturbed by this. In fact he looked calmer than he had in days. He rubbed his hands together.

"Pretty basic stuff," he murmured. "It uses touch recognition but there's an easy way around that . . ."

Kit and Devin clustered around him, watching. His fingers flew over the glass, swiping and tapping. The small lights began to form a line. "I thought so," Luke muttered. "It's completely predictable. You'd think they would have installed something a bit more advanced."

"Just get on with it," Kit said. "You need the code yet?"

"In a minute. Okay . . . I'm in. Give me the numbers."

Kit pulled out the piece of paper with the code and began dictating to Luke. His fingers hesitated. His eyes scanned the screen anxiously.

"What's the matter?"

"Slight glitch. I can enter the numbers but I don't know which laser posts they correspond to. I could find out but it's going to take me a couple more minutes."

"Does it matter? Just put them all in. Then all the posts will go down."

"Okay, keep going."

Kit continued to read the numbers aloud, and this time Luke's fingers flew across the glass panel. "That's one out . . . that's two . . . that's three . . ."

Frisker whimpered again in Kit's bag and made a scrabbling noise as he tried to get out. Kit hesitated, the paper shaking slightly in her hand.

"That's four out," Luke said. "Eight to go. We'll be out of here in—"

He was interrupted by a piercing noise, half whistle, half roar. Devin's hands shot up to cover his ears.

"Security alarm!" Luke shouted.

"What did you do?" Kit was yelling herself.

"Nothing! Someone else must have set it off." He

banged at the glass panel with his fist. "I can't go on. It's overriding everything."

"You have to!" Kit screamed. "Try!" The alarm had risen to an earsplitting shriek.

"It's no good!"

Devin ran to the window that overlooked the courtyard. The alarm suddenly stopped. In the silence he heard Luke's voice, babbling in panic.

"We've got four down, but which four? Which ones? There's no way to tell."

"I don't think it matters anymore," Devin said quietly. "Take a look at this."

Far below they saw a crowd of people: the children and all the staff members and Mrs. Babbage, her thin hair out of its bun and hanging in disheveled strands. The Visitors who had arrived in the convoy of cars were standing to one side in a huddle, looking completely bewildered. In front of them all, the Administrator stood, her hands on her hips. Even from this distance she looked terrifying.

Everyone's head was turned in exactly the same direction.

They were all looking up at the top of the tower.

Twenty-Six

KIT, LUKE, AND DEVIN shrank down, away from the window.

"What did we do to set off the alarm?" Kit whispered, her back to the wall.

Luke shook his head. "No, I told you, I don't think it was us. I was careful. I know how these systems work. Something else must have happened."

Devin raised himself and peered out the window again. "They're still there, just looking."

"How can they see us?" Kit said again.

"I'm not sure it's us they're looking at," Devin said, staring down. It seemed to him that the gaze of the crowd wasn't fixed on their window, but at a point somewhere above them. "I think they're looking at something else."

"It doesn't matter," Kit said. "We're still trapped

aren't we? The minute we walk out of here, they'll see us. Even if they didn't, we don't know which posts are down and which are still active. We don't know what direction to run in." Her fists clenched. "She's not going to get me again. I'll trash this place before I let her get me again."

Devin had risen to his feet and was levering the window upward. The casing was a little stiff, and he had to shove hard. Luke made a grab for him. "What are you doing? They'll see you!"

But Devin had the window open and was leaning out. Immediately, the eyes of the crowd below turned in his direction. Then they turned back to a spot just above him. Devin leaned out farther, craning his neck, trying to see what they were looking at. The top of the tower was about twenty feet above him, invisible from this angle. Before the others could stop him, he scrambled out through the window onto the broad ledge, turning and inching sideways.

He knew better than to look down. He shuffled along the window ledge until he came to the end of it. The wall of the tower was irregular here, with several large chunks of masonry missing. If he judged it just right, he could find enough footholds to climb to the top of the window, which jutted out far enough to provide a perch for him. He put out a foot, found a crack in the wall, and hauled himself up, his hands scrabbling to hold on.

Below him, he heard Kit calling to him, but he couldn't make out the words.

The wind was stronger up here than he thought it would be, a harsh white roar in his throat, tugging at his insides and battering his body. His jacket blew up and whipped at his shoulders with a sound that was half a shout and half a scream. He sucked in his breath, found another foothold, and swung upward again. Three more feet and he would be at the relative safety of the perch. His hand was slippery; he tried to wipe it against his shirt, found himself off balance, and for one terrible moment felt himself about to fall. Somehow, he clung on, face crammed against the sandy stone, heart hammering, too frightened to continue but equally certain he could never make it back.

His grandfather's voice was a whisper in his ear.

Try again, Dev, try again, my lad.

Devin's foot found the next step. His arm reached out and grasped the perch, and he heaved himself up and lay there panting. Then he stood up carefully. The roof of the tower was still a good ten feet above him, and he could see that he had no chance of climbing any farther; from that point on, the wall was perfectly smooth, without a single foot- or handhold. But now that he was higher, he saw what everyone below was staring at so intently.

It was Roman. Devin remembered how he'd slipped from the dining room after Mrs. Babbage had made her announcement. He must have been climbing the tower while Malloy was still running around the courtyard with Fulsome.

Roman was standing on the edge of the roof. Heat haze blurred his outline, making his body shimmer and appear to sway. But his face was as fixed as stone.

Devin looked back down at the courtyard. Nobody had moved. They were all still staring up. From this distance, their faces were nothing but pale smudges.

He shuffled to the edge of his perch. "Roman!"

The boy glanced down at him without expression, as though he had reached a place beyond recognition or even surprise. He looked away.

"Roman! What are you doing?"

The wind blew Roman's shirt tight against his body. He took another step forward. He was almost at the very edge of the roof now.

"Don't!" Devin cried, reaching one arm hopelessly toward him. "Don't!"

Below him on the ground, many of the children covered their faces with their hands. Someone had left and come back with a megaphone and was shouting something into it. But the words were lost on the wind. Devin looked back at Roman.

"*Why?*" Devin asked.

But even before the word was out of his mouth, he knew.

"It's because of Megs isn't it?" he said. "It's all because of Megs. You didn't do any of this to protect yourself, or for money. You did it for Megs."

Roman lowered his head and looked down at Devin, as if for the first time. His eyes had a bruised appearance, like he'd been grinding his fists against them. "We arrived here together, over a year ago," he said in a dull voice. "She reminded me of . . ." He paused, unable to speak for a second or two.

"I had a little sister once, but I lost her. In a flash flood behind our house after a storm. I was holding on to her but she . . . she slipped through my fingers. I saw her face before she went under. She was crying out for me." He lifted his right hand and stared at it. "I had hold of her . . ."

Devin remembered the conversation he'd overheard the night of the campout. "You couldn't save her but you thought you could save Megs."

"Megs was normal when I met her. Just a sweet, normal little girl. But they changed her. I saw her getting disturbed . . . all the fire stuff . . . I couldn't stand to see it. I promised myself I wouldn't lose her like I lost my sister."

"The Administrator told you Megs wouldn't have to go to the Place anymore if you went out and found more children."

A terrible resignation spread over Roman's face.

"Yeah. But I didn't find enough kids. She said I wasn't useful to her anymore. I should have known she'd break her promise.

"They'll dump her back on the streets," Roman said, as if talking to himself. "And she'll die. All by herself in a corner somewhere."

"No," Devin said, "she won't if—"

But Roman wasn't listening to him any longer. His right foot had crept over the edge of the roof. "I'm a traitor," he muttered. "But I wasn't like that before, I wasn't that person . . ."

"You're still not," Devin said. "It's not too late."

Roman shook his head.

"We need you," Devin pleaded. A sudden gust of wind caught him and pinned him to the side of the tower. He waited for it to pass, his cheek pressed tight against the stone, his mind groping for the right thing to say.

"You were on a baseball team," he said. "You were the catcher," he said.

He didn't wait for Roman to reply but carried on, his words tumbling out. "Luke's in the office, he's disabled four of the laser posts but we don't know which ones. If we run the wrong way we'll be caught. You said that from where the catcher stands he can see the whole field. Do you remember that, Roman?"

The boy swayed slightly on the lip of the roof.

"We need you, Roman," Devin said softly. "We need you to be the catcher again."

Roman's lips tightened.

"Where are they? Can you see?"

Roman seemed to shudder and his shoulders dropped. He stepped back.

"Yes," he said. "I can see them all. Most of them still have their lights flashing. But the ones behind the farmyard and the meadow—those are out."

"You sure?"

He nodded. "You should head over there."

"Thanks, Roman, thank you . . ."

"Wait. You'll never get past that crowd in the courtyard." There were several loose bricks scattered over the roof of the tower and Roman bent and picked one up. "I told you the catcher's got a lightning arm," he said grimly. "Watch this."

He leaned back slightly, his shoulder curving into a long, smooth swing, and flung the brick into the courtyard. Devin heard cries of alarm, saw children scattering. Roman bent and got another brick. "I'll get her with this one," he said. He aimed and sent it hurtling down. Devin watched it fly straight at the Administrator, standing motionless below.

"It hit the ground right next to her!" Devin cried.

The Administrator was stumbling backward. Another brick was already in Roman's hand. His body was steady, his face full of concentration. The brick sailed toward Mrs. Babbage, who gave a thin scream and bolted for the shelter of the dining room. Staff members jumped to hustle the old folks away.

"You'd better hurry," Roman shouted. "I can't hold them off forever. Once I'm out of bricks, they'll be back."

"What about you?"

"I'll manage. Get out of here!"

Another brick went whistling through the air. Devin ducked his head and scrambled down the footholds to the window ledge below. He slid through the window feet first.

"It's clear behind the farmyard," he panted. "Roman's on the roof, he could see. He's keeping the crowd away, but we don't have much time."

They grabbed their bags and bolted toward the elevator. Outside, the courtyard was completely empty. The Administrator couldn't have been far away, Devin thought, but nobody dared to brave the open with Roman still on the roof hurling his missiles. As if to prove his point, a brick slammed down and hit the ground twenty feet from where they stood.

"Come on!" They took off running toward the farmyard.

"Get the others!" Devin cried. "Tell everyone you see . . ."

Kit was ahead, her braid bouncing against her back as she raced.

The rest of the children were in a bewildered group behind the buildings on the far side of the courtyard. The minute they caught sight of Kit and the others, they rushed forward.

"What happened to Roman?"

"Is the Administrator dead?"

"Where are you going?"

"Come with us! Just run!" Kit yelled. "We'll explain later . . . Everyone's gotta get out of here!"

They moved off in a herd, running as fast as they could, Jared still clutching his teddy bear, Karen whimpering as she tried to keep up, Caspar trotting along stiffly, Pavel silent, as always.

Devin peeled off to the side. "Devin!" Kit shouted. "Where are you going?"

"The mare," Devin said, "I want to get the mare."

"It's the wrong direction!"

But Devin had already turned and was racing toward the large field. Kit hesitated and then handed her backpack with Frisker inside to Missie and ran after Devin. It was a good quarter of a mile down the long driveway to the horse's gate, but they didn't see anyone as they flew along, side by side. Then, from the corner of his eye, Devin saw the cars of the Visitors turning down the smaller driveway on the other side of the Home. They were heading for the exit, he thought, leaving in a hurry. For a second he imagined the Administrator's utter fury and he stumbled slightly. Kit caught his arm.

"You're crazy, you know that?" she panted. "We could be out of here by now."

They reached the gate and Devin flung it open. From the other side of the field, the mare lifted her head. "Here," Devin called to her. "Here, to me . . ."

She came at a trot, her face eager. Devin reached for her neck as she turned, prancing a little with excitement. She was missing her bridle, but it didn't matter. He grabbed her mane and swung himself up onto her back, leaning down for Kit.

"I can't," Kit said, her face twisting in fear, "I don't know how."

"It's okay," Devin said. "It's easy, I've got you." He grabbed her under her arm and pulled her up, her legs scrambling and slipping against the side of the horse.

"Hold on," he said.

"Wait! Devin stop! Devin! "

The mare broke into a canter. Devin heard the lovely chestnut sound of her shoes striking the gravel of the driveway. "Hold on!" he cried again. Kit jolted wildly behind him, but then she steadied and found her balance.

"Go around," she said in his ear. "There'll be people in the courtyard, go around by the pool."

They had to slow down among the trees but instantly picked up speed again once they reached the path by the swimming pool. At a small fork, Devin came to a stop. He caught a glimpse of four or five staff members coming at a run on their right, and Devin automatically turned the horse left.

They were at the head of the path leading to the Place. Devin hesitated and then urged the mare on at a walk. From his high vantage point, the twisted trees looked smaller and the way less dark, but there was still a memory of terror in those knotted depths. Neither Devin nor Kit spoke, and even the hooves of the mare fell silent on the shadowed path.

They reached the clearing at last and stopped.

The Administrator was standing in the doorway of the Place, twenty feet away. Roman was there too. She had his left arm pinned against his back. His right arm dangled, horribly bent and crooked. The bone was shattered; Devin had seen enough animals with broken limbs to recognize that immediately. But perhaps more terrible than this was the sight of the Administrator's hand closed in a tight grip around the injured arm. Roman was strong and almost as tall as she was, but he wasn't struggling. Even the smallest movement must cause him agony.

The Administrator's head whipped around.

"Stop right there," she told Devin.

"What have you done to him?" Kit cried.

"Nothing," she said. "I found him like this.

"He'll never throw again," she added with satisfaction.

Devin suddenly noticed Darwin. The bird was clinging by one claw to the Administrator's back. He must have been dislodged from her shoulder in the struggle with Roman.

"Get down off the horse," the Administrator ordered. "All I have to do is give the signal and twenty staff members will be here. You'll be sorry if they have to take you by force."

"You can't stop us," Kit cried in a high voice. "We'll run you over!"

The Administrator's expression changed. It became conspiratorial, almost friendly.

"Kit," she said smoothly, "I believe I underestimated you."

"Yeah," Kit said. "A lot of people make that mistake."

"I knew you were different from the others when you arrived," the Administrator said, her voice calm, her eyes never leaving Kit's face. "But I must confess I didn't understand you."

"You said I was damaged!" Kit burst out.

"Don't talk to her," Devin said. "Don't listen . . ."

"Then, when you stole my key—I didn't notice until far too late, by the way—I realized what sort of person you are. Someone who does what it takes to get what they want and who succeeds at it." She paused. "We're alike that way, you and I."

"That's not true!" Devin burst out. "She's nothing like you!"

"All your friends may have escaped," the Administrator continued, ignoring him. "But it hardly matters. Most of them had become useless anyway. I shall simply find new children. You could help me run this place, Kit. Together we could make it even better than before."

"What about Mrs. Babbage?" Kit said.

"Mrs. Babbage is packing her bags. She was a servant, a nothing, a sniveler who ran away at the first sign of trouble. With you it would be different. You could find the children. Roman was very unsatisfactory in the job. His heart was never in it. But I know they'd trust you. You'd be a great success. Then later, when you're older, you can have a full partnership in the business. Think about it."

Kit said nothing. In the silence, Devin heard Darwin give a muffled croak. He had regained his perch on the Administrator's shoulder and was settled in hunched obedience, his eyes closed to slits.

"I know what you dream of, Kit," the Administrator said. "This place makes more money than you can ever imagine. You'd have everything you've ever wanted."

Behind him on the horse, Devin felt Kit grow very still.

"You're right," Kit said.

Devin twisted, trying to face her, struggling to understand. "Kit!" he whispered. "Kit!"

"We are alike," Kit said. "We both have disgusting, rotten fathers."

The Administrator jerked as if she'd been shot.

"How dare you?" she said in a voice so thick with loathing that Devin could taste it like vomit in the back of his throat. "How dare you?"

"The difference is," Kit continued, "I got away from mine. Which makes me the opposite of you. So thanks for the offer, but I'd rather die."

"How dare you?" The Administrator repeated, as though unable to form any other words. "Get down from the horse and get inside now!"

"Or what?" Kit said.

The Administrator squeezed Roman's arm so tightly he cried out and his legs buckled.

"Or I'll break his other arm."

Looking at her face, Devin was certain she meant it.

"I want this place back up and running. Fresh kids, tighter rules, a new standard of excellence . . ." On her shoulder Darwin shifted uncomfortably, interrupting her flow of talk.

"Disgusting creature!" she cried in a shrill voice, batting at him with a furious sweep of her hand. Devin couldn't account for what happened next. Perhaps Darwin was spooked by the Administrator's rage. Perhaps he saw something in the twisted trees that frightened him. Or perhaps (as Malloy would later claim), being the most intelligent of all parrots, he understood human language better than anyone had thought.

Whatever the reason, he lunged at the Administrator's face in a furious clump of wings and feathers and stabbing beak. She cried out and threw up her hands, but the bird continued to attack as though making up for the long years behind bars, for all the darkness and the scorn and the neglect.

Roman, freed from the Administrator's grasp, fell forward onto his knees, then staggered to his feet, his broken arm pressed to his side.

"Can you run?" Devin shouted to him. "Get to the farmyard—we'll meet you on the other side!"

The parrot was circling above the Administrator's head now, beating the air with awkward, heavy wings. For a moment it flapped and struggled, fighting to keep airborne. Then it righted itself and, with a flick of its tail, soared above their heads.

"Bye-bye!" Darwin screamed.

"Go!" Kit yelled in Devin's ear. Devin looked for Roman and saw he'd gone. The Administrator was still cowering, her hands covering her face. Devin dug in his heels and they took off down the narrow path on the far side of the clearing, the mare's hooves raising great clouds of dust. They reached the entrance to the corn maze and plunged inside. Devin led the mare through it unhesitatingly, Kit clinging to him, gasping as the stalks whipped at her legs.

They reached the farmyard at last, and the bushes beyond it, and saw the outline of the nearest laser post.

Between the distant trees Devin saw a flash of bright red and heard the tooting of a horn.

"It's Malloy in the car!" Kit shouted. "They're through! It's safe!"

✦ ✦ ✦

The whole group had gathered together on top of the hill just beyond the perimeter. Almost all the kids were there. After a few minutes, they saw Roman coming toward them. He was stumbling and pale, but his head was held high.

Like a catcher, Devin thought, after a game hard won.

"You okay?" Devin asked him.

Roman slumped to the ground, panting. "I will be," he said, grimacing with pain.

"We've got to get a splint on that arm . . . It looks bad."

"In a minute, okay? Just need to catch my breath."

Devin sat down beside him. He gazed down at the buildings of the Home.

"Back on the tower," Devin said, "you could have hit her with that brick. You could have killed her if you'd wanted to."

"Probably."

"Why didn't you?"

"She made me into someone I wasn't once already," Roman said. "I wasn't going to let her do it twice."

"She'll just start again with new kids. She said she would. Nothing's stopping her is it?"

"Maybe, maybe not."

Devin stared at the buildings. Something was different. "The birds are gone," he said.

Then as he watched, he saw a flicker at the window of one of the buildings. It came again, a yellow streak that darted out, retreated, then appeared once more. A second streak appeared, as red as breath, and into Devin's mind came a trembling, sighing sound that ran like fingers down the back of his neck. A thin plume of smoke rose in a wavering column. He heard the small sound of glass breaking at a distance, and suddenly the window of the building was alive with flame.

"Megs," Roman said. "Before I went up onto the tower I gave her my lighter. I never saw her look so happy."

The other children had caught sight of the fire and stood open mouthed, watching as flames swirled furiously above the roofs and licked the walls of the Home. Then up the hill came a small figure. Her bow was gone and her cheeks were covered in soot. Roman held out his good hand.

"Give it back now, Megs."

She hesitated and then placed the lighter in his palm.

"You did good, but never again, you understand? It's done, it's over."

She nodded, very solemn. "Will everything be gone, Roman? Will all of it burn clean away?"

"Look how fast it's taking hold," Kit said. "It's been so dry, no rain for ages. I don't think there'll be as much as a pile of sticks left by morning." She was standing next to the mare as she spoke, stroking the animal's neck, her fear gone now. She turned to Devin.

"I still can't believe you stole her. I thought I was the best thief in the world, but she's better than anything I ever took."

"What do we do now?" somebody said.

"I'm hungry," Missie whined. "I didn't have any lunch. Did it occur to anyone to bring food?"

She looked at the motley group of kids: Malloy with an arm around Fulsome's neck, Jared and Vanessa and Karen disheveled and silent, Caspar with his mouth agape, Luke pacing and gnawing on his lip.

"I didn't think so," she said.

"We should get away from here," Luke said. "I don't want to get blamed for burning that place down."

Kit hoisted her pack onto her back. "Nor me. Come on, Frisker."

"Where are you going?" Malloy said.

Kit shrugged. "Back to the city, of course. You coming?

"I can't go to the city," Malloy wailed. "Fulsome will get eaten."

Luke stopped pacing. "Let's be honest, we don't have much of a choice."

"There's nowhere else to go," Karen whispered.

"The city again." Caspar's shoulders sagged. "I'm going to need a new suit, aren't I? Where am I going to find a new suit?"

Roman shook his head in weary disgust. One of the younger children started to snuffle and then cry.

"We could go to the farm," Devin said. His hand tightened on the mare's mane.

"All of us could. And the mare and Fulsome. I left because it was too much for one person, but together we could get it running again."

Nobody said anything.

"Maybe we'd find the cow, and the chickens that are left can't be far away," Devin continued, his words quickening with excitement. "And Glancer might still be there . . . There's a stream and a barn and a place to grow vegetables and you can catch rabbits. But best of all, it's not as hot there. The hills protect it . . ." His voice trailed off. The others were staring at him doubtfully.

"Sounds made-up," Missie announced.

"Yeah, kind of hard to believe, Strange Boy," Malloy added.

Devin shook his head. "No. What happened to us here is what's hard to believe. Life in the city is what's hard to believe. My granddad was right. At the farm all you have to worry about are ordinary things."

He glanced at Kit. "There isn't anywhere else like it. It's . . . it's a true rary."

She hesitated, her face full of doubt and hope.

"You won't have to gather stuff anymore because everything you need is right there," Devin told her, his voice soft. "It's the one safe place, Kit."

She looked at him with troubled eyes, and for a second he thought she would walk away. Then her shoulders relaxed.

"Sounds like something I should try, then." She turned to the others. "Who's in?"

"Me!" Malloy said, "Fulsome likes the whole idea."

Luke nodded, considering. "It's a plan . . ."

Everyone was suddenly talking at once.

"Will we plant seeds?" Caspar inquired. "Will we chop wood? I suspect I'll be excellent at chopping wood."

"I hope we find the chickens," Karen murmured. "I think I'd like chickens."

Devin listened to them talk, his mind ranging ahead. It would be a very long walk, and they'd have to keep out of sight, avoiding roads. We came from the west, he thought, then we turned southwest . . . Through the window of the car he'd seen hills that thudded yellow-soft, one after the other in a long line. Devin lifted his hand and tapped out their rhythm against the mare's warm neck until he was sure of the tune. That was the way they should go.

ACKNOWLEDGMENTS

With special thanks too my friends Bonnie Tenneriello and Andrew Sofer for their incredibly clever advice, my niece Isobel Jones and her support and enthusiasm, and my husband, David, for his unfaltering love. Thanks also to Elise Howard, whose editing made all the difference, and Rebecca Carter, the best agent in the world.

S. J. LAIDLAW

FIFTEEN LANES

TUNDRA BOOKS

Library and Archives Canada Cataloguing in Publication

Laidlaw, S. J., author
    Fifteen lanes / S.J. Laidlaw.

Issued in print and electronic formats.
ISBN 978-1-101-91780-0 (bound).–ISBN 978-1-101-91782-4 (epub)

    I. Title.

PS8623.A394F54 2016   jC813'.6   C2015-901054-3
                                       C2015-901055-1

Published simultaneously in the United States of America by Tundra Books
of Northern New York, a division of Random House of Canada Limited,
a Penguin Random House Company

Library of Congress Control Number: 2015931503

Edited by Sue Tate
Designed by Rachel Cooper
The text was set in Bell MT

Printed and bound in the United States of America

Tundra Books,
a division of Random House of Canada Limited,
a Penguin Random House Company

www.penguinrandomhouse.ca

1 2 3 4 5   20 19 18 17 16

Penguin
Random
House

TUNDRA BOOKS

*How can I dedicate a book to girls who may never
have the freedom, education or leisure to read it?
How can I not?*

noor

What I remember . . .

I was asleep on the floor under Ma's bed when I was awakened by the creaking of rusty springs straining under the weight of a heaving mattress. I feared it would break and crush me so I slithered out. This was not allowed. I was never to come out from under the bed until Ma said. I didn't know why I had to stay quiet, or why I couldn't sleep in the bed with her at night, like I sometimes did on hot afternoons. My heart pounded as I emerged.

The terror of being caught in the darkened room eclipsed my earlier fear. Too late, I realized the rashness of my disobedience. Without looking, I knew Ma was not alone. The deep grunting of her visitor punctuated her own soft mewling. I scuttled on all fours toward the curtain that separated our small section of the room from the other three occupants. I was not accustomed to seeing it closed, though it didn't surprise me. Its soft rustle always accompanied the heavy footsteps of her guests. I moved quickly, brushing against clothes that hung from a low peg on the wall next to the bed. They hadn't been there when I fell asleep. I recognized Ma's crimson skirt with the gold-sequined border. I resisted the urge to touch it, though the diaphanous fabric held endless fascination. I had no desire to touch the man's clothes. Their smell of sweat and earth was trapped in the fetid air around the bed.

Only when I reached the curtain did it occur to me to worry about who might be with Deepa-Auntie on the other side. I went cold when I heard an unfamiliar male voice. If it had only been Deepa-Auntie I wouldn't have hesitated. She was kind, not like the other two aunties who shared our room. Deepa-Auntie gave me sweets and never scolded me. She called me her beautiful baby, though my too-dark skin proved her a liar. Deepa-Auntie couldn't have babies. That part of her was broken. I liked to pretend she was my real mother. I even called her Ma, but only when my own was not around.

I reached for the edge of the curtain, listening hard to the voices. Deepa-Auntie was using her sex-me voice. That's what Ma called it when Deepa-Auntie shouted to the men who passed by under our window. I don't know why Deepa-Auntie's shouting made Ma angry. She got angrier still when the men came inside and went behind Deepa-Auntie's curtain. Ma stood in the street, where Deepa-Auntie was not allowed to go, and cajoled the men to come inside. They often did, but when they saw Deepa-Auntie it was her they wanted.

The man with Deepa-Auntie sounded angry. He called her bad names and said he would bring police to arrest her if she didn't let him do what he wanted. Her voice quavered. No one at Binti-Ma'am's house talked to the cops. Not ever. Police were wicked, even more wicked than Binti-Ma'am. They arrested mummies and put little girls in cages. Real cages, not like the barred window boxes the aunties sat in at Binti-Ma'am's, which overlooked the street but were open to the bedroom. Police cages had bars on all sides.

Deepa-Auntie said she'd never let anyone put me in a cage. I asked if she meant a police cage or Binti-Ma'am's cage. Ma said it made no difference because Deepa-Auntie couldn't even keep herself out of a cage. Besides, she said, Deepa-Auntie, with her pale-pale skin and slanted eyes, was not "our kind." I wasn't sure what our kind was, but when Deepa-Auntie got a beating I was the only one who could make her smile again. Nothing I did made Ma smile, so I thought Deepa-Auntie may not have been Ma's kind but maybe she was mine.

I held my breath and slid silently under the curtain. I did it so carefully I imagined the curtain barely stirred, but when I glanced up, Deepa-Auntie was looking right at me. Her eyes went wide and her lips pressed together. I think she wanted to say something but only her eyes told me to go back.

Deepa-Auntie wasn't wearing any clothes; neither was the man who loomed over her. I felt embarrassed. I'd seen Deepa-Auntie without her clothes many times but not like this, never like this.

The man clutched a fistful of her hair and tried to kiss her. Deepa-Auntie's face twisted away. The man yanked her hair so hard it stretched her neck back and I thought it might snap. Deepa-Auntie's eyes rolled back in her head. She let out a sound like the whoosh of a sugarcane press. I wanted to shout at the man to let her go. Kissing wasn't even allowed. Everyone knew that. But I kept silent. I would be in far bigger trouble than him if I was caught roaming at night.

I crawled toward Deepa-Auntie's bed. To get past them and reach the door, I had to slip under the bed and out the other side. I pretended I was invisible, a cockroach, just part of the landscape. If the man raised his head he would see me. I worried he could hear my thudding heart.

As I got closer I saw Deepa-Auntie's cheeks were wet. I wasn't sure if it was sweat or tears. I couldn't think of anything I could do to make her smile. I mouthed the word *chootia*—stupid—it was the worst word I knew. I added a few threats. If words could pierce flesh, that man would have run from the room screaming.

I reached her bed and dropped flat on my stomach. The cold cement chilled my body through the thin fabric of my dress but its worn smoothness made it easy to slide. I was almost completely under when the mattress juddered and there was a loud exclamation of surprise. A huge hand wrapped round my ankle. Without thinking, I shrieked.

I was jerked backwards and my head cracked on the metal bed frame. The man let go of my ankle only to grab my arm and swing me up to his eye level. I dangled helplessly in his clutch and whimpered in fear as much as in pain. (The next day, when Ma took me to the hospital, we were told that I should have had stitches right away for the gash on my head. By then it was too late. To this day I have a bald patch under my hair.)

Ma appeared on Deepa-Auntie's side of the curtain and slapped me hard across the face. This shocked me into silence. I still wanted to cry so I bit down on my lip to hold it in. A man stepped out behind Ma and shouted at her. He towered over her with his fist raised. His arm was as sinewy as a buzzard's neck. Ma would have got the better of him if he'd tried to hit her. He wanted her to give him his money back, which showed how little he knew. Only Binti-Ma'am had money. Ma couldn't give him what she didn't have. He shoved Ma back toward her bed. She got tangled in the curtain that was still half closed.

Ma looked angry rather than frightened as she scrabbled behind her to push the curtain aside. I didn't want her to leave me but I knew enough not to call her back. Deepa-Auntie was sobbing now, much louder than I was before. I wanted her to stop because this would only make things worse.

Suddenly the lights came on. Seconds later, Binti-Ma'am and her son Pran pushed through the curtain nearest the door. The man holding me let go and I dropped to the floor. I tried to scoot back under the bed but I was grabbed again, this time by Pran. He smacked me, once on each cheek, even though I was no longer making noise and my head was already bleeding profusely. The last thing I saw, as he dragged me out the door, was Binti-Ma'am pummeling Deepa-Auntie with a mop handle. Ma was nowhere in sight.

Pran carried me down the hall. I realized immediately where he was taking me. I struggled and pleaded hysterically. As he threw open the door to the kitchen cupboard, I heard the rats scuttling behind the wall. They'd wait for him to lock me in before they crawled through the holes to attack me. I begged for mercy one last time. He laughed.

It was years of this before I finally understood it was what he wanted. He fed on fear like a mosquito feasts on blood. The more I fought, the more he enjoyed it. Eventually, I learned to submit quickly, but on that night, when I was five years old, I still had hope.

2

Grace

I feel I ought to give this day a dramatic name, like in a murder mystery. I could call it *Before the Apocalypse* or *The Beginning*. More than anything I'd like to give it a soundtrack. The shark's music from *Jaws* would capture it nicely, except that would imply that I had a sense of foreboding, and honestly I hadn't a clue.

I knew I wasn't in for a great school year. We'd been back in class only three weeks but that had been long enough to get a pretty good idea of what I was in for. I'd been trying desperately to ingratiate myself with a group of girls who'd made it very clear I wasn't welcome. Madison, the queen bee, questioned my motives. According to her, I was a snob who, in the three years we'd all been together at Mumbai International School, had never shown the slightest interest in being friends until I had no other options. She wasn't completely wrong.

I was never under the illusion that I was too good for

Madison, or anyone else for that matter, but it was true that for the first time in my fifteen years I was out of options. The summer break had seen not only the departure of my über-popular brother Kyle to university but the move of my best and only friend, Tina, back to her home in Singapore.

Tina and I had been inseparable since our very first day of school, when we'd met at orientation three years earlier. Ours was by far the longest friendship I'd ever had. To be perfectly honest, it was the only friendship I'd ever had. Losing Tina had been a painful and unexpected blow. I'd had time to get used to the idea that Kyle would be leaving, but Tina and I had always talked of graduating together. In fact, we'd made a lot more plans than that. This year, for example, we were going to start dating. I wasn't entirely sure how we were going to find boys to date, since none had ever shown the slightest interest, but that didn't faze Tina. She said the only thing we had to worry about was finding boys who got along well with each other since we weren't going to sacrifice our own time together just because we had boyfriends. We also had to find boys who were serious about school. Both of us were in the International Baccalaureate program, which was mega-challenging, and Tina said we only wanted boys who would not hinder our studies. She was mainly talking about me when she said that because Tina could pull straight As standing on her head. Tina was determined I was going to get good enough grades that I could apply to the same universities as her. We were going to apply only to the top schools. Like I said, we made a lot of plans.

The one thing we never planned on was the possibility of her moving away. It never occurred to us, though I don't know why. Before Mumbai, my family had moved every couple of years. I'd gone to four different schools on three continents by the time I was twelve. I was so used to the idea that relationships, like schools and homes, were at best temporary that when we first arrived in Mumbai and Dad announced we wouldn't move again until I graduated I thought he was joking. And I was not amused.

To my mind, spending five years in one place was unbelievably risky. What if I didn't like the school? What if no one liked me? The latter was a distinct possibility. At my previous schools I'd always hung on the fringes of groups, never really fitting in. No one ever picked on me; it was more like I was invisible, which at the time I thought was almost as bad as being bullied. I knew it was my own fault I had no friends, especially since Kyle slid into every new school like he'd been there his whole life, proving it could be done. I was just too shy.

The one thing that kept me from giving up completely was the chance that things would be better at the next school, that I'd hit the right combination of kids, or I'd figure out the secret to fitting in. Moving gave me hope. Dad's decision to stay in Mumbai meant the end of hope. Perhaps that's what gave me the unprecedented courage to make the first move with Tina.

I liked the look of her immediately long black hair tied in a messy knot on top of her head and cherry-red, horn-rimmed glasses. She looked dorky and bold at the same time. I didn't approach her immediately, though. I waited through the tour of the ground floor (gym, pool and playing field), the second floor (offices, cafeteria and library), the third floor (humanities classrooms), the fourth floor (foreign languages and arts classrooms) and the fifth floor (science labs). Only when we got to the top floor, Fine Arts and Theatre, did I finally work up the nerve.

By this time I'd had more than ninety minutes to prepare my opening line. I was convinced it was the perfect combination of witty, yet sincere. I sidled over to her and waited until I caught her eye.

"Rockin' goggles."

That's what I said. You can see why I wasn't more popular, right?

She burst out laughing.

I couldn't believe it. It was like a solar eclipse or a meteor shower. Not only had she understood my humor but she'd laughed out loud. No one had ever done that before, unless you counted my parents' dutiful fake laughs or my brother's bemused groans. But this was different. Tina laughed for real.

So Madison was right when she said I wasn't interested in being her friend until I had no other options. There was even a grain of truth to her accusation that I thought I was superior. I did feel elevated. But I never thought I was better, just luckier. I didn't care that Tina and I weren't part of any particular group, or that some kids probably considered us losers. I never even thought about it. I had a friend, a best friend. I never wanted another.

Uppermost in my mind, as I dragged myself to the cafeteria on a Friday, the day after saying good-bye to my brother at the airport, was how much I wished Dad would get transferred again. I wanted to leave this school, these girls and this country. I wanted another do-over. I could see Madison and her posse at the usual table. There wasn't a chair for me, though there was room for one. This wasn't the first time this had happened. I suspected they got rid of empty chairs before my arrival, to discourage me. It worked. I was discouraged. I almost walked right past them to the library, but then I remembered Kyle.

My brother loves to give advice. It's partly an inherited trait, being my mom's favorite pastime as well, and partly his conviction that, with guidance, I, too, could become popular. It's irritating and flattering at the same time. The night before, as we drove to the airport, he'd given me a final pep talk. Though I was mired in my own misery, one thing he said stuck.

"You don't try hard enough, Gracie. You assume people aren't going to like you. You've got to take more risks, put yourself out there."

I didn't state the obvious—that it's a lot easier to put yourself out there when you're smart, good-looking and athletic, like Kyle—because I knew he was partly right. My heart pounded with anxiety even when I was called upon in class to answer a question I knew the answer to. I hated being the center of attention, at any time, for any reason. Even at home I was happy to let Kyle monopolize our parents. He cast a long shadow, and I was content to hide in it.

With Kyle in mind, I dragged a chair from a neighboring table, dropped my schoolbag on the floor next to it and sat down. For the past week, Todd Baker, a boy in the year ahead of us, had been the subject of lunchtime conversation. Today was no exception. I did my best to look interested.

"He pretty much asked me out," said Madison. "I'm just not sure I want to go."

"What did he say—exactly?" asked Kelsey. You could tell she was trying not to sound skeptical. While Madison was undeniably the queen of our little group, her popularity quotient

When Deepa-Auntie corrected Ma about the lice, Ma's face turned purple. I worried she might shave off my hair again just to teach Deepa-Auntie a lesson. Instead she told Deepa-Auntie to mind her own business. I went to school, braids and all.

Ma walked with me but stopped when we were still half a block away.

"You can go on from here," she said.

I looked down the road. Tears pricked the backs of my eyes. I stared straight ahead and made my eyes wide so the air dried my tears before they could jump out. I knew I should be grateful that Ma was sending me to a fee-paying school and not a government school like all the other children in my neighborhood. "Why would I send her to a school where the teachers never show up and there aren't even any toilets?" Ma responded to the many who questioned why she was wasting money on a girl-child.

Ma wanted the best for me, even if it meant I was going to a school where I wouldn't know anyone. Maybe if I thanked her she would walk with me the whole way and not make me go alone.

I started to speak but Ma had already turned away. I didn't even have time to ask her if she would fetch me at the end of the day. I wasn't sure I knew the way home. Ma walked quickly. In seconds she'd created a distance between us that seemed too wide to carry my small voice, though perhaps it was the set of her shoulders that silenced me.

I trudged the final few steps. When I reached the schoolyard, it was already crowded with children and their parents. Some children had not just one parent with them but two.

Papas and mamas held their children's hands and talked to them in soft voices. They didn't shout, even when it was time to go into the classroom and some children cried. I looked at my shiny shoes. They didn't make me feel like laughing anymore. I knew if Ma had been there she would have told me to stand up straight and pay attention, so that's what I did.

Teacher told the parents they needed to leave, so the children could "get settled." This made the crying children cry louder, and some who hadn't been crying joined in. Things got very noisy, and I thought Teacher had made a bad decision sending the parents away because there was no one to hit the children to quiet them. Still, I was relieved to see the parents go. I was the only child without a parent, and several of them had been eyeing me strangely.

Teacher stood at the front of the classroom and held up her hand, just like a traffic cop, so I understood this meant stop what you're doing. It took a bit of time for the crybabies to control themselves. Finally, they took notice as well. Teacher said we'd made a good start to the year. I wondered what a bad start looked like.

Then she said we were going to take our seats according to *the alphabet.* I was frightened because I didn't know what *alphabet* was, so how could I know where to sit? There were so many desks, in perfect straight rows, side by side, from one end of the classroom to the other. Their shiny wood surfaces beckoned, and I imagined if I sat at one I would already be smarter. I was certain the children who came from mama-papa homes would know *alphabet*, and my ignorance would be discovered. Teacher would send me home and tell me not to return.

All the children clustered at the back and I hid behind them.

Teacher called out the name of the first child and pointed to a seat at the front, right next to the window. I was glad I didn't get that seat because the window was very large and looked out on a cement playground with three leafy mango trees on one side. If I sat there I would be tempted to look out the window all day long. We had only two small windows at Binti-Ma'am's and both were enclosed with bars. If you looked out those windows, men in the street shouted rude things. Our street was always crowded, especially at night when the bootleg bars opened, and there was not a single tree in sight. It was never enticing to look out our windows.

An empty playground with three mango trees sparked the imagination. I could picture myself sitting on a wide branch, though I'd never climbed a tree in my life. I'd shimmy along to the plump mangoes and pluck all I could eat. At home I plucked only spoiled mangoes from the trash that had been discarded by the fruit-wallah when they were too rotten to sell. Perhaps I would even see a parrot or a monkey perched in the branches above me. Ma said parrots were common in Mumbai, just not in our neighborhood. Monkeys and even leopards could be found on the outskirts of the city. Ma said I was lucky not to have to worry about leopards but I thought it might be nice to see a leopard. They couldn't be any more frightening than Pran.

Teacher called out the second name and that child took the seat immediately behind the first. By the time she came to Noor Benkatti, I knew exactly where to sit. Before I took my seat I counted rows and desks so I wouldn't forget where it was the next day. I already knew how to count from running errands for the aunties. I was second row from the window, third seat from the front. I felt very proud and grown-up as I walked straight to the desk behind Gajra Bawanvadi. I smiled at her just before I sat down and she smiled back. I still didn't know *alphabet* but I'd learned something even more important. School was not so different from home. I just had to keep quiet, watch carefully and do what everyone else did.

The rest of the morning passed swiftly. I didn't understand much of what Teacher said but Gajra sat with me at lunch and gave me a samosa because her mother had packed not only dahl and a thick, flaky paratha but two samosas as well. I told her I forgot my lunch. I wish I'd told her I always ate so much at breakfast that I never had room for lunch. That would have saved me from having to think up a new lie the next day and the day after that.

But I really wanted that samosa. It had meat in it. I never got meat at home. That morning, like every other, I'd had only a handful of rice for breakfast. My stomach, usually resigned to the meager scraps it received, roiled when confronted with dahl, a paratha and meat samosas as well. If I hadn't filled it with Gajra's samosa I'm quite certain it would have made itself heard in the afternoon lesson.

After the first few days, Gajra didn't bother to ask if I wanted to share her lunch, she just divided it in half as if we were sisters. She even started bringing an extra paratha so I could share her dahl. It was the most wonderful food I'd ever tasted, but my stomach wasn't used to such vast quantities. For almost two weeks I had constant diarrhea. One day Ma followed me into the latrine and watched as I squatted over the hole and did my business.

"What's that?" she demanded, pointing at the foul-smelling pile I'd just expelled.

"It's my shit, Ma," I said. Sweat beaded my forehead. I hoped she wouldn't notice in the tiny, dimly lit confines.

"I know that, stupid girl. Don't try to trick me. What's that in your shit? Have you been stealing food?"

The smell of the room was making me dizzy. I scooped a cup of water out of the bucket and cleaned my bottom, then I scooped a second, planning to wash down the evidence. Ma seized the cup. She held it aloft, not even minding that she was wasting the water that splashed down, soaking the blouse of her sari. She smashed it three, four, five times on my back and shoulders. I bent over, shielding my head. As long as she didn't hit my face none of my new school friends would ever know.

Finally she grew tired. She had a new baby weighing heavily in her belly. She cradled it and panted. "If Pran finds out you've been stealing food you'll get far worse. Do you understand?"

I nodded, keeping my eyes down.

"Answer me, Noor. Do you understand?"

"I understand, Ma." I didn't look up, or let the tears fall, until I heard the door close behind her.

The next day she got up before I left for school. I'd rarely seen Ma awake before noon. She couldn't have had more than an hour of sleep since her last customer left. She handed me a small packet of biscuits as I went out the door.

"For your lunch," she said.

I ate them on the way to school and was already hungry again before the lunchtime bell, but I told Gajra the lie I should have told her in the first place. "I ate so much this morning, four dosas and dahl makhani and eggs. I almost fell asleep in our lesson I was so stuffed." I puffed out my flat stomach and rested my hand on it. "I couldn't eat another bite."

Grace

Dinner that night was an awkward affair. My parents were trying their best to engage me in conversation but fifteen years of being *the quiet one* was a habit that was hard to break. Don't get me wrong, I love my parents. They're great people. But we're as different as strawberries from a lima bean. They're smart, good-looking and athletic. Sound familiar? If I didn't have my dad's hazel eyes, I would have been sure I was adopted.

"How was school?" asked Mom.

"Fine."

"Did anything exciting happen?" asked Dad.

"No."

"What was the most interesting thing you learned?" he persisted.

That Madison hated me. "Nothing."

"So, who are you eating lunch with these days?" My dad's not a quitter.

"Just a bunch of girls."

"It must be hard without Tina," said Mom sympathetically. "Have you heard from her recently?"

This was a sore point. Tina had missed our last two scheduled Skype chats because she was hanging out with new friends. She had a boyfriend now too, which made me feel even more left behind. "A couple of weeks ago. We're both pretty busy."

There was a long silence. My parents exchanged glances. They were debating whether to challenge me. I'd been home directly from school every day since term started and I was home every weekend as well. I was the walking definition of *not* busy.

"I got a message from Kyle," said Mom. "Only that he arrived safely." She couldn't keep the wistfulness out of her voice though she was putting on a brave face. "I imagine there's a lot going on. He'll write more when he settles in."

"Absolutely," agreed Dad. "And he'll start football practice soon. He's going to have to work hard to keep up his grades."

"He'll be fine," said Mom. "He's always been good at managing his time."

"I bet he has a girlfriend before long," said Dad.

"It will be strange not to know his friends," said Mom.

"We can always meet them when we go home on vacation this summer."

"That's true, but I wish we'd taken him to school."

"We can Skype him this weekend."

They continued like this for the next fifteen minutes, talking about the kid who wasn't there, instead of to the one who was. I didn't blame them. Mom and Dad wanted nothing more than to talk to me. I was the one who pushed them away. I always felt bad about it afterwards but I couldn't stop myself. The way they hovered over me, always worried I'd have no friends, or do poorly in school, drove me crazy. I was the sole reason they'd decided to stop moving. It was my academics and social isolation they were concerned about. Even when I had Tina, they went over the top trying to make her feel welcome, like they didn't trust me to hang on to her friendship by myself. Of course, it turned out they were right.

I sat for a few more minutes listening to them talk about Kyle. Finally, using the homework excuse, I retreated to my room. Bosco, the family Bichon, was already asleep on my bed. Someone must have put him there. Bosco was way too lazy to jump up on furniture by himself. I didn't care how he got there; I appreciated it. Kyle was Bosco's favorite, but with Kyle gone I was happy to take his place.

"Shove over, Bosco," I said, flopping down beside him and reaching for the TV remote. Friday used to be my favorite night of the week. Tina and I had a well-established routine. We'd sleep over at my house or hers and watch old Bollywood movies long into the night, then all day Saturday we'd hang out at the club. One of the weird advantages of Mumbai being such an overcrowded city, with few public facilities, was that everyone who could afford it joined expensive health clubs, with everything from swimming pools to tennis courts. Our families were no exception.

My room felt unfamiliar without Tina in it, as if all the furniture had been slightly rearranged to hide a major theft. Even my bed felt wrong. I switched on the TV, a present from my parents two Christmases earlier. It was bigger than the one in the family room. They, too, had loved my Friday night routine—it was more proof that I had a friend and was happy. The TV was a bribe to make Tina enjoy spending time with me. It was one of many. For three straight years our fridge was stocked with fresh sushi, even though Tina was the only one who ate it. And she and I always got first dibs on rides. That used to bug Kyle. Even if he'd asked for the car first, if we decided at the last minute that we wanted to go somewhere, he had to cadge a ride with a friend.

For the next few hours, I watched TV while trying not to think about Madison. It was an epic fail. Our conversation replayed in my mind at least a hundred times. I imagined a million things I should have said to calm her down before she demanded I never sit with them again. Why did I have to go and mention Anoosha? Why didn't I immediately reassure her that she was every bit as hot as Anoosha? Who cared if it would have been a big, fat lie?

"The fact is, I'm not sure anything I said would have helped, Bosco." I know exactly how lame it is that I talked to my dog but it's not like I had anyone else. "I think she was looking for an excuse to get rid of me. She didn't like me." I hated the way my voice cracked when I admitted that out loud. "They never included me, not in conversations, not in weekend plans. It wasn't getting any better."

Bosco lifted his head and dropped it in my lap.

"I don't know what's wrong with me. Kyle says I have to be more outgoing but when I try to join in, it never works out." I buried my hand in his soft white fur and scratched his ear.

"Do you think I should apologize again? I could text her right now. But what if she didn't answer? I wouldn't know if she was ignoring me or just hadn't seen my text."

Bosco stood up and resettled himself on my lap.

"What do you think, Bosco? Time to start on my Asian History paper? I'm pretty sure the Mughal invasion of India isn't going to be any more confusing than Madison." I gently slipped out from under him and scooted to the edge of the bed to take my laptop off the bedside table.

I was doubtful that Mughals were going to distract me, so when my cellphone bleated from my schoolbag several hours later I was almost as shocked by the fact that is was nearly eleven o'clock as I was by receiving a text on a Friday night.

Bosco, who was pressed up against me, raised his head and growled.

"Who do you think it is? Tina's too busy with her new boyfriend to be texting me on the weekend. Do you think they broke up? I don't wish that on her, but we were *both* supposed to get boyfriends this year and I'm not even close."

Bosco gave me a thoughtful stare.

"I know. It's weird, right? Who could it possibly be?"

I had a flutter of anticipation as I slid off the bed and walked to my bag to dig out my phone. I carried it back, clicking through to the message at the same time. It was from an unknown caller. I opened it.

Hi. What u up 2?

Could it be someone I knew? That seemed unlikely. I could probably count on two hands the number of people who even had my number.

"What should I say?" I asked Bosco. "Should I ask who it is? It must be a wrong number. Should I admit I'm chatting with my dog and doing homework on a Friday night? I'm not sure which part of that would sound more pathetic."

Listening to music, I typed. What are you doing?

I waited.

Thinking about u.

I smiled. "That's so cheesy it's sweet. But he's definitely got the wrong girl, if it is a *he*."

Do u know who you're txting?

The girl I'm crushing on

"The wrong girl all right." I sighed and tried not to feel jealous of the girl who should have been getting these messages. Bosco put his head in my lap again and I stroked his head as I thought about whether to fess up. It was so nice to actually be communicating with another human being. It had been weeks since I'd done anything in the evening other than watch TV and do homework. But it was only going to get more embarrassing if I let it continue.

Its Grace, I texted finally.

McClaren, I added.

I waited again.

Gracie ive waited 2 yrs to tell you I like u. I no who u r!

I stared at the name, Gracie. Only my family called me that.

Who is this?

Don't u no? ☹

I stared at Bosco as if he might have a suggestion. "I have no idea who it is. Do you think I could have a secret admirer?" As unlikely as that was, I couldn't help but feel a warm glow of excitement. In my head I knew it had to be some weird mix-up, but what if it wasn't? What if someone actually did like me? Tina liked me. Could lightning strike twice?

Sorry I really don't know who u r.

Its todd

No freaking way, positively no freaking way! I didn't think there was more than one Todd at our school but it was just too coincidental. I had to be sure.

Todd who?

There was a long pause this time.

Gracie, ur killing me. I w8t 2 yrs till yr brothrs out of the way to finally get up the nerve to ask u out and u say todd who?

I gave this some thought. I'd always thought there was bad blood between Todd and my brother. Could this have been why? Did Todd want to ask me out and Kyle didn't want him to? But why? Kyle wanted me to have a social life. He was always bugging me to be more sociable. He'd even tried to drag me to a couple of his cool-kid parties. I'd chickened out, of course, but that wasn't his fault.

"What do you think, Bosco?" I gave him a questioning look, only to discover he'd dozed off. "Some help you are." I ruffled his ears. He opened an eye and closed it again.

None of it made sense, but what if it was true? Guys can be weird about other guys. Maybe Kyle thought Todd was too old for me. Todd was a jock, and from the little I knew he'd had a number of girlfriends. Maybe Kyle thought he was too experienced for me, or a bit of a player. I felt the tiniest flame of annoyance as I considered the possibility that Kyle was being overprotective. It wouldn't have surprised me. No one in my family trusted me to do anything on my own.

Why would Kyle stop u? I had to ask.

Dunno u hav 2 ask him. What music u listening 2?

Crap! The truth was, I listened to angry indie girl bands. I didn't want to tell him that. It's not that I was trying to impress him. I just didn't want to un-impress him so quickly.

What music do u like? I was pleased with myself that I'd managed to dodge his question without lying.

U listen to indie doncha?

Crap again! Another message came in before I could figure out how to respond.

U want to watch me play sometime? We hav r 1st match nxt Sunday.

I tried to remember what season we were in. Cricket, maybe?

Wat u playin? I decided to be honest. Perhaps he'd find it charming.

Ha! Wat u do for fun?

Read, swim, movies. I was honest again.

Want 2 see a movie sometime?

He couldn't begin to imagine how much I wanted that. Ever since Tina left, the only people I'd gone to movies with were my parents. Even Kyle never wanted to go with just me, and I refused to go with his gang of boisterous friends. I'd had some hope at first that Madison's group might invite me some weekend—they often talked about going to movies right in front of me—but the invitation never came. After today, it wasn't likely it ever would.

Was I doomed to spend the rest of my high school years with no one to hang out with but my parents? Was Todd offering me an alternative? If so, it couldn't have come at a better time. As bad as I'd felt when Tina left, today had been a new low. It was one thing to miss my best friend but quite another to feel like a social pariah.

I wasn't sure if I wanted to date Todd. The fact that Madison was under the impression they were starting something gave me serious qualms. I had no desire for revenge. Quite the contrary, I still clung to the faintest hope we could somehow make up. At the same time, she couldn't have been clearer that she had no interest in being friends. And Todd did. Maybe I didn't have to spend the year lonely and bored.

I needed to clear up a few things though.

R u goin out with anoosha?

No! Not since last year. Why, do u want to go out with me? ☺

R u asking?

I looked at the screen. I wasn't really going to send that, was I? Of course I only meant it as a joke. I added a happy face.

R u asking? ☺ I typed

It still looked like an invitation. From a desperate girl. Who had no friends. I deleted it.

Maybe to a movie sometime . . . I hit send.

U dont like me? ☹

Didnt u just ask Madison out?

Madison who??

Ha! After the grief she'd put me through, he didn't even know who she was! My phone tweeted again.

So u dont like me? ☹

Surely a guy like Todd wasn't really worried that an average-looking, morbidly shy girl wouldn't like him. He had to be fishing for compliments, not reassurance. Despite that, his question stirred something in me. What if he wasn't as confident as he pretended? I'd seen Kyle fake it enough times to know that some guys were good at hiding their insecurities.

It was a relief that Madison's relationship with him was all in her head. That didn't stop me from feeling guilty though. Obviously she had a crush on him. But I couldn't help feeling a glimmer of satisfaction that the very guy Kelsey said would never be interested in me was the guy who was. The symmetry of it was almost poetic. And wildly coincidental. Unfortunately, the wildly coincidental aspect didn't occur to me until later.

I do like u. I typed it and hit send before I could change my mind. I gave a little squeal at my own boldness. Bosco pricked an ear and woofed.

"I don't really know if I like him," I confided to Bosco, "but I think I could. He's really cute, and Kyle said I need to take more risks."

U don't really like me. u r just sayin that

I shot Bosco a guilty look. Bosco flipped onto his back for a belly rub. I laid the phone on the bed so I could text and rub at the same time.

Im not. I don't know u vry well but I want to get to no u. I lik what I do no of u

U don't

I DO!!!

How can I believ u when it took u so long to say it?

I'm shy

2 shy 2 kiss me?

Bosco pawed the hand that had frozen on his stomach. My own stomach was doing somersaults. I'd never kissed a boy in my life. Even the idea made my whole body feel tingly. It wasn't a pleasant sensation, but it wasn't entirely unpleasant either.

"I think this is it, Bosco. I think this is the opportunity Kyle was talking about. My life will never get better if I don't change. I need to take risks."

I could feel the sweat beading on my forehead and collecting under my arms. If Todd had seen me just then, kissing me would have been the last thing on his mind.

"What should I do, Bosco?" He'd rolled over again and was watching me intently. "I have to go for it, don't you agree? Maybe Madison will understand. If Todd likes me, it would never have worked out for her anyway. And it's not like she and I are best friends. I just want a life, Bosco. Imagine what Mom and Dad will say when I come home with a boyfriend. They'll have to stop worrying that I'm a social reject. Kyle might be angry at first, but when he sees how happy I am . . ."

I looked at the clock on my side table: a minute to twelve. I picked up the phone and cradled it in both hands, almost as if it were the boy himself. Just like Cinderella, on the stroke of midnight, my life was about to change.

If I'd only known how much . . .

noor

Ma is a devadasi . . .

Deepa-Auntie and I were in the washing room, doing dishes. It was my job. Even on school days, dirty dishes would be left there, awaiting my arrival. The single bucket of water, which had to last me two days, was also my responsibility. Along with the dirty dishes, I collected money from the aunties to pay for the water.

The space in the washing room was too small for us to crouch side by side so Deepa-Auntie couldn't really help me. That wasn't why she was there. It was a humid Sunday afternoon with not a breath of wind, so there were no customers. The aunties had arisen, as they always did, around one o'clock in the afternoon, to bathe and eat. Most had gone back to sleep. The men would come later that evening, when the temperature dropped, which meant more customers squeezed into fewer hours. Deepa-Auntie wanted to enjoy the temporary respite, so she had to hide where Pran wouldn't find her. He always considered a lull in customers his own chance to take a turn with her.

He could have had any of the aunties. Some would have appreciated the opportunity to win favor with Binti-Ma'am's son—even Ma would have agreed—but Pran's cold eyes always fell on Deepa-Auntie. Ma said Deepa-Auntie's golden skin was both her good fortune and her bad. I wasn't sure it was Deepa-Auntie's skin that held Pran's interest. He didn't have the restless hunger of the men who came at night. Usually he looked tired, even bored. Only if Deepa-Auntie cried and begged him to choose another did he light up, and Deepa-Auntie always cried.

"I grew up on a farm," said Deepa-Auntie. It was the beginning of a story I'd heard variations of many times. I never tired of hearing it, nor she of the telling.

"We were very poor but I didn't know it. When the rain came it was so heavy it dripped through our grass roof. Mama caught it in buckets and joked that it would save me a trip to the river, though in the rainy season I never had to go as far as the river to fetch water. It filled the cistern in our front yard and was so plentiful we'd throw full buckets over ourselves when we bathed.

"I never went to school. Only my younger brothers went. I didn't mind. I was happy to have them out of the house. They were always chasing the chickens and stealing eggs. They never took a turn milking the goat, or helping Daddy hitch the bulls to the plow. The house was peaceful without them. I enjoyed the time alone with Mama and my baby sister, Yangani. I carried Yangani everywhere on my back, even while doing chores. Daddy called me 'little mother,' and I dreamed about the day I would have my own babies. My blood had not yet come when the man took me and brought me here."

Deepa-Auntie always stopped her story at this point, though she arrived there in a slightly different way each time. She never told me what happened between the day a man came to her village with promises of domestic work and the day she ended up in our house. Many times I'd seen the scars on her body. I pretended not to notice. Though I was nine and in the 4th class at school, she thought I was too young to know the truth. We colluded in this, my feigned innocence and her delusion that anyone could remain uncorrupted in that house.

With the dishes done, I sat back on the floor, trying to stay clear of the drain so I didn't get my kameez wet. It would take hours to dry and I didn't own another. I wanted to go outside but I couldn't leave Deepa-Auntie.

"Tell me about Yangani," I said.

Deepa-Auntie smiled at the memory. "She was the most beautiful baby in the village. All the other girls were jealous of me and would beg to hold her. I'd let them, but Yangani would always cry until they gave her back. After I taught her to walk, she followed me everywhere."

We both jumped when the door suddenly opened. It was only Ma, with my sister, Aamaal, who was born three years earlier.

"What are you doing in here, Noor? If you're done with the washing up, you should do your homework."

I was already finished my homework, as Ma well knew. It was the first thing I did when I got home from school every day, such was my pleasure in studying. Ma also took pride in my schoolwork. Every year I won firsts in Math and English. She secreted each medal into the hem of her skirt as if they were made of real gold and not just gold-colored tin. Her real concern was not too little time spent on homework, it was too much with Deepa-Auntie.

"I'm telling her about my farm," said Deepa-Auntie. "Didn't you also grow up on a farm, Ashmita-Auntie?"

"No," said Ma. "I didn't. And if I had I wouldn't waste my time thinking about it since I'd be smart enough to know I would never live there again."

"How can you be sure, Ashmita-Auntie? The voyage of life is very long with many bends in the river. So many things can happen. Who knows what course it might take?"

"It's not so long for us," said Ma.

"Why do we never visit your home anymore, Ma?" My breath quickened to ask.

The last time we'd been to Ma's village was for the birth of Aamaal. Before that we'd gone once a year. On our final visit, Ma and Grandma had argued behind closed doors, and when we left, Grandma didn't walk us to the main road, where we waited in silence for a bus. Ma hadn't spoken of Grandma since. I never asked, but I missed those visits. For those few days, I could laugh as loudly as I wanted and run far and fast. No one shouted at me, or beat me. I risked a beating now, asking Ma about these visits, but she was far less likely to let her anger loose with Aamaal beside her. I didn't begrudge Aamaal her favored status. With her golden skin and thickly fringed eyes, anyone could see she was going to be a beauty. She was my mother's child in a way I could never be.

"You should not waste your time thinking about the past, Noor."

"Please, Ma."

She frowned.

"Please, Ma," Aamaal echoed. For once I was happy that she always copied me.

"They only wanted our money, Noor. In my village the elders pretended it was something else, a sacred duty. Maybe there was a time when that was true but it was many years ago. When my mother dedicated me to the temple, it was for money, not religion, not even tradition."

"I don't understand."

"Grandma felt it was time for you to learn your history, your calling. We didn't agree. She's a devadasi, as am I."

It was the first time I'd heard the word that dropped like a stone from my mother's lips. I understood it was significant. "Am I also a Devadasi?"

Ma laughed mirthlessly. "The foolish hen tells you life is a twisting river like the one in her mountain homeland. Do you see such a river flowing past our house? There is only the open sewer carrying foul waste discharged from bodies too numerous and worthless to count. Perhaps it goes underground when it passes the great mansions of South Bombay, or slinks, like a thief carrying treasures, when it courses through the sleek neighborhoods to our north. It makes no difference. When it empties into the sea it's still shit, and the destination was never in question. You were born into your fate, Noor. I may forestall it but you can't escape it. We can only hope your next incarnation will be more forgiving."

She stroked her belly where another child was already growing inside her, though the bump barely showed. "I'm going to lie down. Look after your sister." She pushed Aamaal through the doorway and closed it behind her.

"What's a Devadasi?" I asked Deepa-Auntie.

"I'm not sure, though I know several women here are also devadasis and they all speak Kannada, like your ma. I don't think we had Devadasis in Nepal."

"If Ma and Grandma were devadasis, am I also one?"

"You are whatever you choose to be, Noor-baby. Someday we'll leave this place. I'll pay off my debt to the fat one and her pig-faced son and we'll go back to my village. We'll climb the hills of my homeland, follow the egret's flight to my father's herd. We'll see him first as we crest the hill overlooking my home. He will be watching for me, as he's done every day since I left, and will run to greet us, shouting the news of my return. Even my worthless brothers will laugh with joy. We'll take them presents like they've never seen—a cooking pot made of the strongest iron for my mother, and bells for each of our goats, so my father will never have to search long for them when they stray. But the greatest gift will be for Yangani."

"What will that be?" I asked. I already knew the answer.

"It will be you, of course. A new sister for her to play with and love. She will follow you as she once followed me, or perhaps she will be grown and you will walk side by side, sharing secrets as sisters do."

I wanted to ask her how she could have such optimism. We knew not one woman who had escaped the trade. The few who had managed to buy their freedom continued to work alongside us. Rejected by their families, who were ashamed of what they'd become, regardless of the circumstances, they survived in the only profession they knew, among the only community that would accept them.

"Do you want me to check if Pran has gone out?" I asked.

"Perhaps we could sit out in the window box for a while. Men won't bother with us on such a hot day."

"Thank you, my love. I'd like that."

The window box was the only outdoor freedom Deepa-Auntie was allowed, and of course that had all the freedom of sitting in a shop window. Unlike the other aunties, not to mention myself, she couldn't come and go from the house as she pleased. She had to ask permission and be escorted by Pran or Binti-Ma'am. Her only outings were infrequent trips to the temple to pray, and she always returned home more disheartened than when she'd left. I often stayed in on the weekends, when I'd have preferred to play in the street, because it cheered her to have my company. I didn't realize until years later that Deepa-Auntie was not so many years older than me and my friends.

Taking Aamaal's hand, I left Deepa-Auntie and went into the hallway, pausing for a moment to listen to the voices of the house. I could hear murmurings from the second floor. One of the aunties barked with laughter, which was enough to confirm that Pran wasn't upstairs. I put my finger to my lips to silence Aamaal and led her down the short, narrow passage to his room. We had to pass Binti-Ma'am's room. There was no danger of awakening her. She slept deeply in the afternoons, knocked out by the heat and her own bootleg booze.

I leaned my ear against Pran's door. Aamaal's hand sweated in my own. How quickly she had learned to fear him. I shook my head to let her know he wasn't there, though I didn't speak, as it was possible he'd heard us come out of the washing room and was deliberately keeping silent, waiting to pounce. Aamaal tugged at my hand and I let her lead me back down the hall to the washing room. I stuck my head in and gestured to Deepa-Auntie to come out. I still didn't dare speak.

The three of us crept as silently as we could to the ladder leading to the second floor. Deepa-Auntie had one foot up when the door to Pran's room flew open and he raced out.

"Where do you think you're going?" he demanded.

Deepa-Auntie started to cry.

Grace

I was nervous going to school on Monday but it was happy nerves. I realized it was possible that things wouldn't work out with Todd, but just the fact that he liked me made me feel like a brand-new person, prettier, more confident. As I entered the building, I smiled at kids and said hi to the receptionist, like it was completely normal for me to speak to an adult even when I was not compelled to.

Todd and I had texted all weekend. It turned out we liked a lot of the same music and we shared a passion for Bollywood films. Like me, he was studying Hindi so he could watch them without subtitles. We agreed to a Bollywood movie marathon that coming Friday night, just like I used to have with Tina. It was all I could do not to share my excitement with my parents but I wanted to see their look of amazement when I brought him home. He wasn't only good-looking, he was smart and funny and surprisingly wise, in a teenage boy way. I told him a bit about what happened with Madison, not his part in it of course, but just that I'd said something thoughtless that upset her and she didn't want to be my friend anymore. It felt so good to tell someone. I told him how Madison's group made me wonder if I was even capable of making friends. He said that was ridiculous and I couldn't let other people get inside my head like that. Nothing he said was a revelation, but just hearing it from someone else made me feel stronger.

By Sunday evening the conversation had taken a romantic turn, though perhaps *romantic* isn't quite the right word. At some point we got more playful, flirted, talked about sex and crossed a line. Just thinking about it made my stomach churn. I never would have thought I'd do something like that. I deleted all of his texts immediately and made him promise to do the same. I was horrified that anyone might read them—or worse, see them. I don't even remember what I wrote. It was like I was channeling someone else, someone sexy and fearless.

We'd agreed to meet for lunch and show the whole world we'd become a couple. I'd got up early and dressed carefully. I'd left my hair down, instead of scraping it back into a ponytail the way I usually did. I'd brushed it until it fell in one shiny waterfall almost to my waist. I'd put on makeup, which I almost never did, and wore the dress Tina and I had picked out before she left. She'd insisted on buying it as a going-away present. She'd said to save it for my sixteenth birthday but I knew she'd understand why this occasion was more important. It clung to my body, accentuating what little I had in the way of curves. When I looked at myself in the mirror I felt different, more sharply defined, as if my whole persona had gone from black-and-white to color.

The only thing weighing me down now was Madison. I'd had time to get over my shock that Todd liked me and not her. That knowledge made me feel both invincible and sad. In the first few weeks I'd been having lunch at Madison's table, we had peacefully coexisted. She could've been nasty then, and she wasn't. She'd let me sit with her group when I had nowhere else to go. And this was how I repaid her. If I didn't owe her an apology for my comments last week, there was no question I owed her one now. I'd knowingly taken the boy she wanted. The fact that she'd never had a chance with him was beside the point.

I was so lost in these thoughts that I didn't notice the stares and giggles until I reached my locker. I didn't even feel trepidation when I saw the paper taped to the door—not until I got close enough to see the photo, my photo. It was blown up, in full living color. My heart galloped and my mouth went dry. I was naked from the waist up. I'd never seen myself quite that way. Of course I'd looked in mirrors, but a photo is something different. It's more than a representation of life, it's a retelling.

I can't explain why I did it. I didn't even let other girls see me in public change rooms. I'd always been shy about my body. I'd wait till the room was empty, or I'd duck into a toilet cubicle.

Todd and I had been texting for hours. It was close to one in the morning, barely seven hours ago, when he asked me to prove my feelings for him. What a stupid request. Really, I barely knew him, but at the time I didn't feel that way. I'd confided how I always felt like an outsider. He said he did too, that most of his friends couldn't be trusted. Everyone was always jockeying for status and position, looking to take each other down a peg. We could rely on each other, he said: the two of us against the world. I teased him for being so cliché; we were hardly Romeo and Juliet. He insisted on calling me Juliet for the next hour.

I pulled the paper off my locker and stuffed it in my backpack, as if that was going to change anything. I felt a thousand eyes burning into me from every direction. My face was so hot I'm surprised my head didn't burst into flames. It was all I could do to hold back the tears.

"Hey, Grace, nice tits! Who would have guessed?" I whirled around, expecting to see Todd, but it was a boy I barely knew.

"I don't know," said another boy. "From what I saw—and I saw EVERYTHING—I think she's going to need implants. What do you think, Grace? Time to go up a few cups?"

"She could earn money for the operation by stripping. She obviously enjoys it."

The comments came from all sides, a cacophony. I could no longer distinguish one voice from another. Laughter reverberated off the walls. It seemed like the entire school was there. I tried to push through the mass of bodies but they formed a wall, tight, impermeable. Then one voice rose above the others.

"I feel sorry for her. I always knew she was desperate, but I never realized she was quite that desperate. Imagine sending her photo to everyone. Why would she think any of us were even interested?"

Madison. She'd slithered through the same crowd that had prevented my escape and stood in front of me, her retinue behind her.

"Poor, pathetic *Gracie*," said Kelsey. "It's the only way she could get a boy to look at her."

Gracie? She'd never called me that before. In a flash it occurred to me that I had no idea who I'd been texting with all weekend. It might not have been Todd. Maybe it wasn't even a boy. I could see Todd now on the periphery of the crowd, smirking. Clearly he wasn't the sweet guy I'd been thinking, but there was no reason he'd single me out for this kind of humiliation.

Unlike Madison and her posse.

"It was you," I accused, though my voice was tentative. A part of me couldn't really believe she'd do it either.

"What was me?" demanded Madison.

"You were messaging me."

"I have no idea what you're talking about. All I know is that you're so desperate for attention that you sent your topless photo to the entire school. But I think you've had more than enough of our attention." With that, she collected her minions and the crowd parted to let her leave.

They closed in again before I could make an escape, but I'm not sure I would have been capable of it anyway. I was shaking so badly I felt in danger of collapsing on the spot. I turned my back to the crowd, opened my locker and just stood there, one hand gripping the top shelf for support. I leaned in, under the pretense of looking for books, and took deep breaths, trying to slow my racing heart. The barrage of comments continued but the buzzing in my own head was drowning them out. This couldn't be happening. I'd spent my entire life striving to go unnoticed. How could I have been so reckless?

After an eternity the bell rang and the crowd dissipated. When I was sure the last of them had cleared out, I sank to the floor next to my locker and tried to figure out what to do next. It wasn't like I had a lot of options. I was at the only interna-tional school in Mumbai with a North American curriculum. It briefly went through my mind that I could kill myself. Surely this was the kind of thing that drove girls over the edge. At the same time, a small voice of reason told me this would all blow over. I was certain I'd heard of other girls suffering things like this in the past. The fact that I couldn't bring any to mind was probably a good sign. I didn't realize I'd been hyperventilating until my breathing finally slowed to normal. No wonder I felt like I was going to pass out.

I got to my feet. I was going to get through this. The one silver lining was that at least my parents hadn't found out. I couldn't have borne it if they'd had this irrefutable confirmation that I was a loser who clearly didn't fit in to their perfect family. As bad as things were, at least that indignity had been avoided. I shouldered my backpack, closed the locker and made my way to the office for a late pass.

The secretary scrambled to her feet the second I walked through the door. It was odd behavior but I figured she was just keen to get me back to class.

"She's here!" she shrieked.

Something told me things were about to get worse.

7

Noor

I have a brother . . .

Shami arrived in the early evening of a drizzly monsoon day. The fruit-wallahs who lined our street were packing up their carts, giving way to the bars just starting to open. Men poured out of buses, mostly migrant workers eager to douse their loneliness in cheap liquor before spending their miserable earnings on gambling, or women like Ma. Ma was already inside with a jittery boy who'd been coaxed in by Binti-Ma'am herself.

We all knew Ma's time was close. Though Shami was still little more than a bump—Ma had carried him barely eight months—he'd already dropped low in her belly. Few men wanted her in this condition, but Binti-Ma'am insisted she continue to work.

"You should have got rid of it," Binti-Ma'am scolded. "Is it my fault that you chose to keep it? I'm not running a charity. You must pay for your bed like everyone else."

Ma didn't argue. Everyone knew that too many children was bad for business. One or two were acceptable, even encouraged. Young girls recently forced into sex work would often be forced to have children as well. The need to feed their own child was sometimes the only thing that broke their resistance to the work. Ma didn't state the obvious: she wanted a son. Binti-Ma'am knew as well as anyone. Everyone preferred boys. Why would Ma be any different?

And so it was that I found myself outside with Aamaal, perched on the step of the building next door to ours, which housed our local heroin den. The owner was one of a few in the neighborhood who would allow us to huddle in his doorway. He thought a couple of young girls out front would throw off any police who might be suspicious of his business. For a rupee I promised to tell him if I saw the cops coming, though the regular bribes he paid ensured that was unlikely.

My friend Parvati kept us company with her baby brother, Eka. He was fast asleep in her arms. Parvati could have left him at home under her mother's bed, but she'd heard there was a group of foreigners coming through our neighborhood. This happened periodically. There was a tour company that specialized in showing off the poor areas of Mumbai. My neighborhood, Kamathipura, was an especially popular destination. The tourists gawked at our mothers as if they were Madari monkeys performing for coins. They didn't look at us though, the children of Kamathipura. If they noticed us at all, they quickly turned away.

Parvati was determined to get money from these foreigners. She called it "only fair," though she knew they wouldn't share her sense of justice. It would take some trickery to squeeze it out of

them, which was why she'd brought Eka. It was common knowledge that foreigners couldn't resist babies. Professional beggars
would borrow or even rent babies to increase their earnings.

Parvati tried to enlist Aamaal as well. "When I spot them, you
must start crying, Aamaal, and clutch your tummy like you're
hungry."

"I am hungry," grumbled Aamaal. She was cranky because
she wanted to watch TV. Our small TV was in the room where
Ma and the aunties entertained customers. There would be no
TV for either of us that night, or any night. I wasn't allowed to
bring Aamaal inside until she was ready to drop from exhaustion so that she'd sleep peacefully under the bed without
disrupting business. Many aunties drugged their children at
night. Ma only did that when we were too sick to stay outside.

"That's even better," said Parvati. "If you're really hungry,
you should have no trouble convincing them. Remember to
grab the woman, if there is one, and don't let go until she gives
you something. If the amount is too small you must cry louder.
Money is nothing to them. They'll forget it in an instant. You,
if you're clever, can live off it for a week."

"I'm not so sure," I said. "I think they must love money very
much. It's never easy to get them to part with it."

"Perhaps we should undo her braids," said Parvati. "She looks
too clean."

"I spent half the morning picking out her lice and oiling her
hair. I certainly hope she looks clean."

"There they are!"

We all watched the group making its way toward us.

"Start crying now, Aamaal," urged Parvati. "It will look
more natural if your face is already red when they arrive."

"I don't want to," said Aamaal, though her lower lip trembled. Like me, she knew what Ma would do if she caught us begging.

Parvati sighed. "All right, watch me this time. You'll see how easy it is."

Dragging one foot, as if she were lame, Parvati hobbled out to the center of the street. She didn't even try to shelter Eka from the rain. He woke up and screamed his annoyance. Parvati ignored him as she focused intently on the approaching group. Cupping her hand and putting the tips of her fingers together, she gestured toward her mouth, making the motions of eating. She really did look pitiful.

There were six foreigners, three men and three women, with a local guide. A couple of them gave Parvati sidelong looks. The ones nearest shied away, almost tripping over each other in their determination to avoid her. Parvati limped after them.

"Just one rupee," she called out in her heavily accented English. I almost laughed. She would certainly not be satisfied if that was all they gave her.

The foreigners looked at their guide, who glared at Parvati. "Get away. Stop bothering them."

"Please, just one rupee. My brother is hungry." She singled out one of the women, catching up to her and grabbing her shirt. The woman gasped and pulled away, dragging Parvati and Eka with her. The guide raised his hand to Parvati threateningly but she stared him down. The guides were guests in our neighborhood as much as the foreigners. He wouldn't dare hit us. Snorting in disgust, he reached into his pocket, pulled out a small handful of coins and tossed them on the ground. They rolled into the muck at the side of the road. Parvati let go of the woman to dive for the change, leaving the group to hustle away.

Aamaal and I helped Parvati collect the scattered coins. Slime from rotting food, mixed with human and animal waste, coated our fingers by the time we'd collected every coin. There was barely enough for a couple of panipuri, but the vendor knew us. He added a third for free. We got spicy, but I reminded him to hold back on the onions as they gave Aamaal gas. Parvati divided the three small stuffed pastries equally, ripping a little piece off her own for Eka, though he had no teeth. He stopped whimpering as he sucked greedily on the fried dough, and we all settled back on the stoop to enjoy our treat.

We were just finishing when we heard loud voices from our own house next door. I heard my name called. My alarm was reflected on Aamaal's face as we leaped up and tore home. We slowed down as we entered, wary of coming upon Pran, who would surely beat us for coming inside so early.

Lali-didi, a recent addition to our house, practically plowed into us in the narrow hall. "Noor, thank goodness you came. I've been shouting for you. You must go down the street and fetch Sunita-Auntie. Your ma is having the baby right now." I didn't ask why Lali-didi hadn't gone herself. It would be years yet before she was allowed street privileges. She might have secured her freedom sooner if she'd had a baby of her own, but she was still a child herself.

I was happy to go back outside as I could hear Binti-Ma'am just around the corner in a loud argument with a customer. It sounded like the young boy who had gone with Ma.

I left Aamaal with Lali-didi, as she'd only slow me down, and ran as fast as I could to the house where Sunita-Auntie worked. Though she did the same work as Ma, she was no longer a live-in but had a room of her own in a building nearby.

She rented her bed only when she had a customer, and split her profits with her madam. She supplemented her income with her other skill, delivering babies. It was a dwindling business. Even in our community, women preferred to have their babies in a hospital.

I wove through the crowded streets, finally reaching Sunita's Auntie's brothel. Her madam snorted in disgust when I asked for her.

"If you find her, tell her not to bother coming here again. I've plenty of whores who can make better use of my beds."

"Please, Auntie," I said politely. "My ma's in a desperate way."

"Try the Elephant Café," she said, naming a gambling den that was as notorious for murders as for the large amounts of cash that changed hands each night.

I had strict instructions from Ma to stay away, but I was desperate so I continued on.

Half a block farther, I entered a long, narrow corridor not unlike the one at our house and followed the voices up a narrow staircase to the second floor. I didn't get farther than the top of the stairs when I was stopped by a large, muscular man.

"What's your business here, girl?" he said roughly.

"Please help me, Uncle. My ma is having a baby and needs the services of Sunita." I didn't give her last name. If he was from our community he wouldn't need it.

He examined my face, for what trickery I could only imagine. I looked at my feet to show him I understood his power and did not wish to offend.

"She's in there," he said finally, stepping back and gesturing to an open doorway farther down the hall. "But I'd think twice about having her deliver your ma's baby."

"Thank you, Uncle." I slipped past him and ran to the open door.

I heard Sunita-Auntie before I saw her. She was standing at one of the many round tables, arguing with another woman. They were fighting over a man who had a large pile of cash in front of him. The problem was as clear to me as any in my school Math book. In the next few moments they would come to blows if I didn't intervene. I rushed forward and grabbed Sunita-Auntie's arm. She was so absorbed in her dispute that she barely acknowledged me. I pulled at her with a desperation that finally got her attention. She was quick to follow when I explained the situation. Perhaps even she realized that the other woman, many years her junior, would inevitably win the wealthy customer, and give her a sound thrashing as well.

As soon as we got outside I could smell the liquor on her. Still, I was grateful that she followed me, however unsteadily. We tried to creep past Binti-Ma'am, who was now outside our door arguing with the same young man. He was demanding his money back, as I'd earlier suspected. It was impossible to hide from her.

"Tell your ma she owes me for this one," said Binti-Ma'am.

"You should be ashamed making Ashmita work in her condition, you greedy donkey!" snarled Sunita-Auntie.

Binti-Ma'am's chest puffed up as she prepared to explode. I shoved Sunita-Auntie through the open doorway. Sunita-Auntie's blood was still up from before. She was itching to let loose on someone. It wouldn't take much to ignite her long-standing feud with Binti-Ma'am. Many years ago they'd been friends, working alongside each other in the same house, but while Sunita-Auntie's unwillingness to train new girls had kept her forever at the bottom of the trade, Binti-Ma'am's innate viciousness had fueled her rise to the top.

Several aunties and their children waited anxiously in the hallway and directed us to where Ma was giving birth. We were too late to help. Shami was already squalling on Ma's chest when we arrived. It may have been fortunate he hadn't awaited Sunita-Auntie's arrival. In her current state, she may have cut more than his cord, though the scene we came upon was no less horrific.

Binti-Ma'am had sent Ma to the lockup to have her baby. The room itself made my heart race. Everyone who lived in our house had heard the screams from that room when new girls were broken in. Lali-didi had emerged from a prolonged confinement only three weeks ago and still bore the marks of her suffering.

It was more a wooden box than an actual room, standing four feet off the floor and accessed by a rickety stool. It was barely large enough for the single soiled mattress it contained, and the roof was so low it wasn't possible to stand upright, even for me, and I was small for my ten years. A bucket over-flowing with filthy rags and watery blood stood underneath the open door. Prita-Auntie, who shared our small four-bed room, stood sentry outside, giving orders to the other aunties to bring fresh water and clean clothes. A bucket arrived just as we did. Whatever rivalries might have existed between the aunties on a daily basis, they were family and would always help each other in a crisis.

"She's going to be fine," said Prita-Auntie. Her eyes told a different story.

I steeled myself to climb into the box. Sunita-Auntie made no move to follow. I didn't blame her. I glanced nervously at the bolt and huge padlock on the door. Binti-Ma'am would have no reason to lock us in, but I'd seen Pran's cruelty extend beyond reason, many times.

The room was stifling. Deepa-Auntie sat on the far side of the mattress, mopping Ma's face with a rag that looked little cleaner than the ones outside. Aamaal crouched beside her, rigid with fear. I tried to smile reassuringly at her. I'm sure it came out more like a grimace. Old Shushila, who'd long ago retired from the trade but stayed on at our house to help, was between Ma's legs trying her best to wash her. Light flickered from a single kerosene lantern that hung barely two feet above Shushila's hunched body. It cast ghastly shadows, making the scene look like a massacre and old Shushila a demon crone. I thought they must have cut the baby out and was surprised to see that Ma's exposed belly, covered in a film of sweat, was unmarked.

Ma looked relieved to see me. "Greet your brother, Shami."

I reached across her and took him in my arms.

"You need to get a box for him to sleep in. There should be some discarded fruit cartons at the garbage dump. Get the cleanest one you can find." Her voice was weak.

"I'll take care of it, Ma. Don't worry."

I was surprised by his lightness. He was much smaller than Aamaal had been. Even at birth she'd had round cheeks and a robust glow. Our brother was frail and wizened like an old man. His eyes fixed on me and his wails, which had reverberated off the walls since my arrival, subsided into a quiet snuffling. It was foolish to think anything of it. Babies couldn't see properly when they were this young. I kissed his forehead and held him close.

Ma fell asleep almost immediately. I took her hand. It felt as cold as death. I quickly dropped it. Shushila, who was continuing to gently bathe her, met my eyes and nodded toward the door. There was nothing more I could do. Aamaal lay down and rested her head in Deepa-Auntie's lap, closing her eyes as Deepa-Auntie stroked her hair. She would soon be asleep as well.

The quietness in the room, rank with the smell of blood, was oppressive. I scooted backwards toward the door and swung my legs out, carefully stepping down onto the footstool and then the floor. I knew Ma's bed would be empty for at least the next few hours. I wasn't ready yet to introduce Shami to our life. I wanted some time alone to get to know him, and privacy was scarce. The curtain around Ma's bed afforded our only hope. One of the aunties made a move to take him from me but I refused to give him up and the aunties seemed to understand. They returned their attention to guarding Ma and passing clean rags in to Shushila.

I was halfway up the ladder to our room, awkwardly holding Shami in one arm, when Sunita-Auntie stopped me with a hand on my thigh. I started and almost fell backwards. I didn't realize she'd followed me.

"Your ma's sick," said Sunita-Auntie.

"Just tired," I said.

"No," said Sunita-Auntie, with the certainty of one who had seen much sickness. "She has the virus, and so does the babe. You'd be doing everyone a favor by smothering him now." She turned away, placing a hand on the wall to steady herself before trudging off down the hall.

I waited until she'd rounded the corner and then looked into the milky, opaque eyes of my brother. "She's an old fool and a drunkard," I told him.

Shami didn't blink.

Grace

One thing I liked about the principal's office was that all his chairs were lined up in a straight row facing him, like he was about to deliver a speech and you were just there to listen. Most of the time I expect that's the way things went. He didn't count on my mom. I don't think she'd stopped talking in the fifteen minutes since she'd sat down. I felt sorry for him. Every so often he'd start to say something like *If I could interject here*, but she would barrel on. Sooner or later he'd realize she wasn't going to let him interject here, there or anywhere. I was grateful to be facing him and not her.

I was already in his office when my parents arrived, farthest seat from the door, closest to the open window. Are you having the same thought I was? In fact, I'd been sitting in that same chair for over an hour. I gathered that Mr. Smiley—that's his name; you can't make that stuff up—had called my parents even before I showed up. He was surprisingly calm about the whole thing. Maybe I wasn't his first student to "disseminate pornographic images to the student body." Yes, that is what he said. Technically, he didn't accuse me of disseminating to everyone, only those with a cellphone. Although apparently there were several images posted around the school, in addition to the one on my locker, so presumably the 1.2 percent of kids at Mumbai International without a cellphone were still exposed to my corrupting influence.

As luck would have it, disseminating pornographic images is an expellable offence. Personally, I think accusing a fifteen-year-old of being the likely culprit of her nude photo going viral should be an expellable offence, but that's just my opinion. Mr. Smiley did let me tell my side of the story, and he took copious notes. Then he had me write everything down and sign it.

I felt both panicked and vindicated when he asked his secretary to make an appointment for him to talk to Todd and Madison. I wasn't sure whether to bring up Madison's name. I didn't accuse her but I did say we'd had a disagreement about Todd the same day he started texting me. I genuinely wanted Mr. Smiley to draw his own conclusions. I didn't know what to think.

Dad was sitting in the seat closest to me. He didn't look at me, which was a relief and hurt at the same time. Only when we were well into the second thirty minutes of the interview did he reach over and take my hand. At that point, I was white-knuckling the hard plastic armrest. Mom had just started talking about getting a lawyer and suing the school.

Dad cleared his throat and Mom stopped talking. This wasn't a strategy they'd worked out ahead of time, unless you count the past twenty-two years as "ahead of time." Mom looked at Dad expectantly. I didn't need to see her expression to know it was a mixture of *Don't interrupt me* and *What took you so long?*

"I think it's obvious Grace has been the victim of a cruel if not criminal attack," said Dad. I couldn't help but notice Mr. Smiley was suddenly way more alert and not trying to interrupt. "She used bad judgment, but her error was a private one, which we'll address with her when we get home."

"I'm sorry, Mr. McClaren," said Smiley, who looked sorry and more than a little nervous. My dad runs a company with over two thousand employees; he can have that effect on people. "But even if Grace only sent the photo to the boy, she still sent a pornographic image to an underage student."

"Really," said Dad. "And have you identified that student?"

Mr. Smiley shifted uncomfortably. "Not as yet, no."

"Have you traced the cellphone number?"

"It doesn't match any we have on record, or the numbers of either of the two students Grace named as possible perpetrators."

"So, as far as we know, Grace could have been in communication with anyone, an adult even?"

"That's highly unlikely," Mr. Smiley objected. "The picture was sent to almost every student in the school."

"And how did that happen?"

"The image went viral. Students were passing it on. But your daughter was the first to send the image, obviously."

"We don't dispute that, but you can't produce a single student who received the image from my daughter, and she doesn't know who was play-acting as the teenage boy.

We're in complete agreement that Grace needs consequences for her actions, but the humiliation of having her
image disseminated is already a severe consequence. We'll take
her home for the rest of the day. It will give her time to reflect
on her actions and we'll talk to her. However, Grace cannot
afford to miss school. She'll be back in class tomorrow."

My father stood up. Mr. Smiley, no longer living up to his
name, stood as well. Mom and I followed suit.

"My colleagues and I will need to discuss appropriate sanc-
tions," said Mr. Smiley.

"We will not accept any consequence that jeopardizes her
education," said Dad firmly.

"At the very least she'll have to do community service to
atone for what she's done," said Mr. Smiley, equally firm.

"Grace already does community service as a requirement of
her International Baccalaureate diploma," said Dad. I could
tell he didn't like letting the school decide my punishment, but
he was wrong on the community service front. I wasn't involved
in anything. In fact, I'd invested considerable energy into dodging the community service requirement.

"According to our records, Grace is not yet involved in any
activity that will contribute to her required hours."

I stared at my feet.

"Thank you for letting us know," said Dad, without missing
a beat. "Of course, we support any effort to help Grace find a
suitable activity."

Dad held out his hand and Smiley shook it.

"I trust you'll keep us informed if you get any information
on who's responsible for this attack on my daughter." Dad
sounded every bit like the captain of industry that he was.

We walked out of the office. Dad only dropped my hand when it was necessary to pass through doors. He took it again when we were out of the building. I couldn't remember him ever holding my hand before. It felt nice, though weird. Mom stalked ahead of us to the parking lot.

"I'm sorry," I said quietly, daring to glance at Dad's face for the first time.

He gave me a wry smile. "Everyone makes mistakes, Gracie, but this sure was a doozy."

I couldn't help but grin. Only my dad would use a dorky word like *doozy*. Who says that anymore?

"I guess you were missing your brother," he said, as if he was trying to work it out for himself.

"And Tina," I said.

"But still."

"I know it was stupid but I never expected anything like this would happen."

We reached the car. Our driver, Vitu, opened the door for me. Mom was already in the front seat. She never sat there. Obviously, she didn't want to sit with me.

It was a silent ride home. She didn't speak in the elevator either, but I could feel the pressure rising with each passing floor. I tried to plan what I was going to say when we were finally alone. I felt mortified, apologetic, betrayed, frightened; I couldn't formulate a single sentence that would capture the depths of my regret. As it turned out, I didn't need to. The second we were inside the apartment Mom burst into tears and Dad wrapped his arms around her. No one acknowledged Bosco, who rushed to greet us and was jumping around, yipping with delight.

"Why don't you go to your room," said Dad. "We'll talk later."

"No," said Mom, pulling away from him. "We'll talk now. Grace, how could you do this?"

The abrupt shift from tears to anger left me speechless.

"You're a smart girl. How could you be so unbelievably stupid? Do you realize your image is out there in the public domain forever? Universities, future employers . . . someday your own children could see this. How are you going to explain to your own fifteen-year-old that you sent a topless photo of yourself to who knows how many people?"

"I didn't do it, Mom." I felt like I was going to throw up. As bad as I thought it was, it was so much worse. I hadn't even begun to think of all the ways this could come back to haunt me.

"Of course you did it, Grace!"

"She means she didn't send the picture to anyone but the one boy," said Dad. "Or whoever it was," he added under his breath.

"Exactly," Mom pounced. "She sent a photo to someone without even knowing who it was. What were you thinking, Grace?"

"This isn't getting us anywhere, Jen. What we need to do now is help Grace figure out how she can move on."

"She can't move on!" Mom roared. "This will never go away."

Dad frowned worriedly. Maybe he hadn't thought through the implications either.

"Go to your room, Gracie. Your mom and I need to talk."

I didn't need to be told twice. I scurried to my room, Bosco hot on my heels. Once inside, I shut my door, dropped my bag on the floor and threw myself on the bed, though I immediately had to get up again to lift Bosco up beside me.

I lay on my back, staring at the ceiling, clutching Bosco to my heaving chest. I'd wanted to be alone since I first saw the picture, so I could finally let the tears fall. Now that I was, I found myself dry-eyed. It was like I was wrapped in gauze; everything I'd done seemed like the actions of someone else. Maybe this was what people meant when they talked about being in shock. Certainly what I'd done was shocking, and the fallout was cataclysmic. But it didn't feel as though I was part of it. I could almost believe that I'd go to school tomorrow and be the same invisible nonentity I'd always been.

And then it occurred to me . . .

Trembling, I slid off the bed and walked over to my pack, knelt down and unzipped the front pouch where I kept my cellphone. It had already caused so much trouble. I would have been smart to smash it. Instead I pulled it out and brushed the screen. There, on the opening page, was my message icon showing fifty-two new messages.

Fifty-two.

I shouldn't have read them. I stopped after the first dozen or so.

Mom was right. This was so much bigger than I could ever have imagined, and the worst part was that I'd done it to myself. I wasn't the victim of random bullying. I was the one who'd sent my half-naked picture out into the world. The only thing Mom had wrong was saying I was a smart girl. She had it right when she told me I was stupid. I shuffled back to my bed and flopped down.

Dad popped his head in before he left for work.

"How are you doing?" he asked from the doorway.

"Is Mom still angry?"

"Give her some time, Gracie."

"Would you tell her I want to speak to her?"

"I think it's best to wait till she's ready. Why don't you message Tina?"

"I don't want to tell her what I did. I don't want anyone else to know. You haven't told Kyle, have you?"

"No, but you might consider telling him yourself. Your brother's always had your back."

"I just want to talk to Mom."

"I'm sure she'll come talk to you later in the day. She's getting ready to go out now. I think she's meeting some of her friends for lunch."

"Today?" I tried to hide the shock and hurt I felt that Mom could even think of going out when my whole world was falling apart.

Dad walked over to the bed and sat down next to me. I sat up and leaned into him. He put an arm around my shoulder. "I encouraged her to go. It will be good to take her mind off things. I'm sure she'll come back feeling much better, and then you two can talk this all through."

"Do you think she'll forgive me?"

"You will never do anything we can't forgive, Doodlebug."

"Dad, I'm fifteen! You have to stop calling me that." I was grinning though. My dad may be a dork but he's a smart dork. If he said Mom would forgive me, I was ready to believe him.

He kissed the top of my head and stood up. "Are you going to be okay here today? Have you got some work you can do?"

"Sure, I'll be fine." I wanted to ask him to spend the day with me. I knew he would if I asked, but as much as I loved my dad, my mom was the one I went to in a crisis.

I waited all day for her. I tried to do schoolwork but I couldn't concentrate. At least half the day I just paced the room. I checked my phone and Facebook a dozen times an hour. Each time there were new, hateful messages. I was only making myself feel worse, but it was like picking at a scab; I couldn't stop.

When Mom finally came home, she must have been deliberately quiet. Even though I'd been listening for her, I wouldn't have heard her if Bosco hadn't started yipping and jumping around on the bed. I lifted him down to the ground and opened the bedroom door so he could run to greet her. Leaving it slightly ajar, I hovered behind it. My plan was to dash to my computer when I heard her coming down the hall and pretend I'd been studiously doing homework.

She was murmuring to Bosco but I couldn't make out what she was saying. What I could hear was that her voice was getting fainter. She wasn't coming to my room. She was headed in the opposite direction.

As quietly as I could I pushed the door closed and walked over to my bed. I was trembling just as I had when I first saw the photo, as I had when Mom was shouting at me, as I had when I saw the hate messages. I lay down and stared at the ceiling. This wasn't going to get better. Mom wasn't going to forgive me.

I don't know how much time passed before I heard a light knock on the door. I was on my feet in seconds.

"Come in."

It had to be her. Please, let it be her.

Dad walked in carrying a tray, Bosco right behind him. "Vanita said you haven't eaten all day."

It's true. The few times our maid had stuck her head in the

door I'd shooed her away. I couldn't have gotten food past the knot in my stomach.

"It's tomato soup. I made it myself."

I attempted a smile. It was a joke between us. Dad was a hopeless cook. Canned soup was the extent of his expertise. He put the tray on my desk and stood uncertainly in the middle of the room. I too was still standing, my anxiety growing with each passing minute. Mom was the unseen presence between us. I waited for him to speak.

He cleared his throat. "Here's the thing, your mom feels it would be better if you two spoke in the morning. She's taking this pretty hard. She feels she's somehow responsible—"

"She's not!" I cut in, aghast. "How could she think that? This has nothing to do with her!"

"I know, but you have to see it from her perspective. She's invested so much of herself into raising you two. She gave up her career. She's always been so involved in your lives. She just needs some time to make sense of all this."

"Tell her I'm sorry," I said stiffly. I wanted him to leave so I could cry in private. I took a step back and sat on the bed so he'd take the hint.

"Eat something and try to get some sleep. Things will look brighter in the morning."

I leaned down and picked up Bosco, who was agitating to join me, and buried my face in his fur.

"Night, sweetie," Dad said from the door before shutting it quietly behind him.

I didn't know whether things would look brighter in the morning. I only knew that on the very worst day of my life, when I needed her the most, my mother couldn't even look at me. It's not like I blamed her. Mom had done everything right. What Dad had said was true. She had always been there for me, active at every school we'd gone to, home in the evenings every night, helping with my homework, making valiant efforts to get me to talk more. Before Tina, Mom had been my only friend. We did everything together, and still she was nothing but happy for me when Tina came along and I didn't want to hang out with her so much anymore.

I stood up and started pacing again. Nervous energy coursed through me. I felt as if I was going to explode. I reached for my phone; more new messages. I threw it at the wall. The sound was loud in the stillness, but it wasn't enough. I could still hear my mom calling me stupid. She'd never said anything like that before, to me or my brother. Mom wasn't a woman to toss words around. She'd been a successful lawyer before she had Kyle. If she said something, she meant it.

Stupid.

I could hear her voice saying it, the shock, the disappointment . . . the contempt.

STUPID.

The word went round and round in my head. It grew in volume. It reverberated off the walls.

I picked up a pen from the desk and took it to my bed, an idea already forming. I had to get rid of the word, but only after I'd taken control of it.

I dropped down, sitting cross-legged. Bosco immediately tried to crawl into my lap, but I pushed him away and hitched up my skirt, carefully choosing a spot on my inner thigh. I wrote the word, *STUPID*, pressing down until it hurt. Bosco whimpered. The imprint of black ink left angry welts. My leg ached.

It wasn't enough.

Tomorrow the ink would be washed away. A week from now, maybe sooner, the welts would disappear. The indictment of my stupidity would still exist. Outside of me, its power would only grow stronger. I needed to own it.

Taking the pen, I pressed down as hard as I could and went back and forth over the first letter. The pain was intense, yet strangely liberating. I felt only satisfaction when the first bubble of blood broke through my skin. As I set to work on the second letter, the intensity of my anxiety slowly drained away. Each letter brought with it more peace. By the end I felt calm. The pain of disappointing my mother was no longer an unbearable burden. It still hurt, but it had lost its power to consume me.

My scars, spanning the inside of my thigh, were my insurance that I'd never again be carelessly intimate with a stranger. My mother would never again have reason to call me stupid. I might not be able to take back what I'd done but I could contain it. All I needed to do, if my resolve ever weakened, was look at my scars. I was in control now, with my own private message to myself.

9

Noor

Devadasi is explained . . .

I was good at making up games. It was necessary in a life where there were always younger children who needed to be entertained, so they didn't get under the customers' feet. In school this earned me a reputation as lighthearted and creative. As my schoolmates and I milled around the schoolyard during breaks they would often turn to me. "What shall we play, Noor? Let's have some fun."

Toppling Towers was a game I invented one evening when Aamaal was being particularly difficult. She'd had an ear infection for days and Ma refused to buy medicine. A waste of money, said Ma, who had more faith in charms and homemade remedies. She was using both to treat Aamaal's infection. Like the many others she'd used before, they didn't work.

I finished flushing the ooze from Aamaal's ear for the third time that afternoon and slathered on Ma's concoction. I checked to make sure she still wore the amulet Ma had tied round her neck that morning. It was Ma's most precious possession, with a potency she swore could cure any ailment. Years ago Ma had made the dusty two-day journey to Saundatti, in northern Karnataka, to have it blessed at the Yallamma Gudi temple. The goddess Yallamma was revered by many women in our community, and Ma was no exception.

Aamaal complained that the amulet was too heavy. She'd removed it twice that day already—further proof of how sick she felt. Normally she loved Ma's charms, and though she was only five years old, she'd long coveted this one. Night was falling, but despite her discomfort I needed to take her outside and tire her before I could let her crawl under Ma's bed. I'd begged Ma to give Aamaal sleeping drugs but they also cost money, and since the birth of Shami we were always short.

Shami, now six months old, was constantly sick. Twice we thought we'd lost him to pneumonia but both times he pulled through. That night he'd sprouted sores all over his body. They'd appeared as simple scabies only a day before, but no sickness was ever simple with Shami. Disease courted him like a jealous lover, never far from his body and always fierce in its attentions. Ma covered him in charms to ward off the evil eye: a black string around his waist, black plastic bangles on each wrist and even black henna spots to mar his beautiful face.

Despite her efforts, Shami had suffered restlessly all day, so while other babies throughout Kamathipura were sleeping peacefully under beds, I wrapped Shami in a sari and hitched it over my shoulder. The warmth of our bodies pressed together should have irritated his rash further but, unlike my sister, he kept any misery he felt to himself, and even seemed comforted by our closeness. I took him outside, Aamaal grudgingly in tow.

"I don't want to go out," whined Aamaal.

I hardly heard her. My attention was drawn to the foot of our street where a noisy throng of men was spilling out of a bus, the night's customers arriving. I reached for Aamaal's hand. She resolutely stuck both behind her back.

"Stay close to me, Aamaal." I wanted to put some distance between us and the approaching mob. We couldn't go far. One of the aunties had asked me to watch her children that night and they were still loitering inside.

Someone hooted from within the ranks of men as they made their approach. I swallowed down my anxiety and stepped in front of Aamaal, blocking her from their view. The ones who came to Kamathipura regularly knew that the young girls roaming the streets were not part of the night's offerings, but every day there were men newly arrived from the villages. They didn't understand that the underage girls they desired were never allowed on the streets, where they might be rescued by the NGOs, private charities scattered throughout Kamathipura that attempted to prevent young girls from being forced into sex work. The determination of the NGO workers who patrolled our fifteen lanes looking for vulnerable girls was equaled only by the pimps.

Fortunately, just as I was thinking we would have to venture back inside in search of the other children, they tumbled out of the doorway, engaged in a spirited but good-natured fight. Adit, the older of the two, was dangling a paratha just out of reach of his brother, who had clambered onto his back. Bibek was clinging to Adit's neck with one hand, while trying to reach round and snatch the bread with the other.

"He's trying to kill me!" Nine-year-old Adit appealed for my help but couldn't hide his smirk. I took the paratha out of his hand and handed it to little Bibek.

"That was mine!" Adit objected.

"Not anymore."

I shrank back as several men reached our doorway and squeezed past us to go in. At the last minute one leaned toward me and squeezed my breast. I drew in a sharp breath.

Adit rounded on him. "Hey, don't touch what you haven't paid for!"

The man paused and stared at him, as if he couldn't figure out whether to be offended or amused. Suddenly he cuffed Adit on the side of the head, knocking him off balance.

Bibek launched himself at the man but I caught him in midair.

"Stop," I said. Grabbing a boy in each hand, I pushed them behind me as well.

"You need to teach those little bastards some respect," the man said. He raised his fist again, but one of his companions threw an arm around him and made a crude joke about the far greater entertainment awaiting them inside. They pushed past us, laughing.

Aamaal looked at me wide-eyed after they'd disappeared. She didn't say a word when I ordered her across the street.

"You should have let me fight him," said Adit, catching up.

"He would have killed you."

"Not before I got in a few good licks." Adit took out a tattered, hand-rolled cigarette to complete the picture of his bravado. His hands shook as he lit up.

The road was crowded, as it always was at this time of night. Snack carts and paan-sellers had rolled in, crowding into every inch of space on the sidewalk and lane that wasn't already inhabited by something more permanent. I yanked Aamaal back just in time as a bullock cart, laden with jerry cans of kerosene, rattled toward her.

"Pay attention, Aamaal," I said, though there were many things in our life I wished she were less aware of.

We crossed the road at an angle to give wide berth to Imran-Uncle, the old fruit-wallah. He used to let us pick from his spoiled fruit at the end of the day in return for the occasional favor from Ma, but after he began parking immediately across from our doorway Ma told us to avoid him. He still called to her whenever she came outside to talk to a customer. Ma acted like she didn't hear.

I wished she would let him be our father. I'd heard he had a small room a few streets away and lived there all alone. I couldn't imagine the luxury of a room just for our family and away from Ma's work. I knew the time was fast approaching when I'd be considered too old to sleep under her bed. Many children my age were already living on the streets. Each night they fought for patches of pavement. Parvati had been doing it for years.

Imran-Uncle's rheumy eyes followed us as we reached the curb on his side of the street. We paused so Aamaal could pet Lucky, her favorite goat. I caught Imran-Uncle's gaze and smiled. I was disobeying Ma's wishes, if not her direct orders, but I liked Imran-Uncle. He said he gave us only fruit he was going to throw away, but more than once lush strawberries and unblemished bananas had found their way into his offerings. I liked his appearance as well. His wizened skin and long white hair made him look more animal than man, not so different from Lucky, now nuzzling Aamaal's pockets looking for sweets. I imagined Imran-Uncle would be an undemanding father, content with Ma's attentions and not chasing after Aamaal and me as well. He might even let Ma stop working and look after all of us on his fruit earnings. It was a future almost too bright to contemplate.

Aamaal and Bibek were arguing over the half-paratha Bibek still had left.

"Lucky is hungry," Aamaal insisted. She gave Bibek an imploring look.

"Lucky is already too fat," I said seriously. Lucky was a huge beast. A full-grown man couldn't wrap his arms around the goat's middle, and he stood a good foot taller than Aamaal. Aamaal continued to plead with Bibek, who finally and very reluctantly gave in. No one could say no to Aamaal.

She carefully ripped the bread into bite-size pieces, despite the fact that we'd both seen Lucky eat entire shoes in one gulp. While she fed him, two more goats meandered over and tried to nose Lucky aside. Aamaal gave each of them a piece but reserved the bulk of it for Lucky. I looked on with mixed feelings. I was happy to see her distracted, but it wasn't wise to get attached to a goat. Lucky had been around as long as I could remember, but every Eid I feared would be his last. He could feed many families at the feast.

"I'm not sure it's such a good idea to fatten him up," I said quietly to Adit.

He took a last drag on his cigarette and flicked it to the side of the road. "Don't worry. The milk-wallah treats that goat better than his wife."

With the feeding finished, Aamaal's attention quickly returned to her sore ear. She cupped it with her hand.

"I want to go home, Noor-didi," she begged, her eyes filling with tears.

"I have a new game," I said. In that moment it wasn't true but I would think of one in the seconds it took to get them all a safe distance from the house. I nudged them to start walking again.

"What?" asked Adit eagerly.

Aamaal only sighed as she swiped her hand over her eyes.

"I can't explain it here. I have to show you."

"Come on, Aamaal," said Adit. "It will make you feel better."

Aamaal let me take her hand and we walked down the road to the nearest rubbish heap. I examined it hopefully. It often contained the equipment for some of my more inspired games. Discarded syringes, for example, were a versatile favorite. I briefly considered the piles of sheep and cattle dung. We'd created quite a blaze one night, setting those alight. Aamaal had loved it, but we'd got into trouble when flying sparks singed a passerby.

"We need to collect mango pits," I said, an idea forming, "the more the better."

As always, Adit and Bibek threw themselves into the task. "Be careful of needles and broken glass," I reminded them.

Aamaal stood by watching and I put my arm around her. It was unlike her not to join in. We waited for several minutes while the boys collected a large pile of pits. Some were still slimy and many covered in filth. I separated out the worst of them and divided the rest into two mounds, then explained the rules.

"Aamaal, Shami and I are one team and you two are on the other. We need to stand ten paces apart and stack our pits into towers, as high as we can get them. Each team keeps three pits back to use as missiles. When I say go, you throw your three and try to knock down our tower, and we do the same. As soon as we've thrown all the missiles we quickly rebuild. The first to rebuild their tower wins."

The most challenging part of the game turned out to be getting ten paces apart without having multiple obstacles between us. We lined up along the side of the road but the concept of roadside was fluid in Kamathipura, where sidewalks and roads alike brimmed with food stalls, livestock, vehicles and throngs of people. Lucky and his goat friends showed up and became particularly problematic as they were convinced we were throwing the pits for them and kept trying to eat them. Eventually, I got the idea to incorporate them into the game, and outrunning a goat to retrieve a pit earned extra points. Aamaal was reluctant to play at first, but by the time the goats had become a third team she was well into it and cheered gleefully every time the goats bested the boys. Shami fussed a couple of times when the game got too boisterous. I took periodic breaks, swaying my hips to rock him back to sleep.

It was late when the boys' mother finally stuck her head out the window and called them home to bed. I decided it would be a good time for me to slip in and put Aamaal and Shami to bed as well. We were all tired. Aamaal refused to go in until we gave awards to Lucky and his two accomplices, the clear champions of our new game. I dug through the stinking pile of refuse until I came up with a wilted flower for each of them. Aamaal presented them with great flourish and was delighted when the goats ate them. Then we all headed inside.

We skirted a pile of vomit just inside the door, the effects of Binti-Ma'am's homemade alcohol. The stench of urine in the hallway was particularly strong, as it always was in the evening. The customers rarely bothered to walk a few steps farther and use the latrine.

We approached the open doorway of the lounge, which buzzed with the loud voices of drunken men and the aunties trying to tempt them upstairs. Snack vendors calling out their wares as they circulated the room added to the din. Betel nuts were a particular favorite. Old Shushila would spend the next morning, as she always did, cleaning up the red spit that would coat the floor by night's end. By this point in the evening many aunties would be as drunk as the men, or high on drugs. I sped up, pushing my charges in front of me. We needed to pass quickly to avoid unwanted attention.

In my hurry, I didn't see the man coming out of the lounge until he was upon us. He bumped into Aamaal, grabbing her shoulder to steady himself.

"What have we here?" he said, pinching one of her soft round cheeks.

"Just the little ones going to bed," I said, prodding them forward. The boys slipped past but he still had hold of Aamaal, so I stayed where I was.

"You're a pretty one, and already with a baby."

I was relieved to see his attention diverted from Aamaal.

"I need to get them to bed," I repeated.

"How much do you charge?"

"I don't work, Uncle-ji." I deliberately used the term of respect. "I'm just a schoolgirl."

"I won't hurt you. We could have fun."

Aamaal whimpered.

"Go to bed, Aamaal. Tell Ma I'll be along soon." She stared at me with big eyes. I hoped she took my meaning. I untied the sari from my shoulder, gently shifting Shami into Aamaal's arms. The man let her pull away from him, his attention completely on me now. Aamaal ran, Shami's head bobbing on her shoulder as she rounded the corner.

"I'll make it worth your while," he said.

"I'm only eleven, Uncle."

"Don't be coy, girl. What's your price?" He put one hand on the wall behind my back and leaned toward me. I shrank away.

"Noor, what are you doing here?" It was the first time in my life I was happy to see Pran.

"I'm just going to bed," I said and tried to push past the man. He grabbed my arm.

"How much for the girl?" he demanded.

"She's not yet working."

"I'd pay a lot for a fresh girl."

"You don't want this one. She's too dark."

"I don't care. Name your price."

"Let go of my daughter!" Ma charged up behind Pran and stepped into the glow of the fluorescent lamp, grabbing my other arm.

The man laughed harshly. "She's your daughter? But you're a devadasi. Why delay the inevitable? How old were you when your parents sold you?"

"We'll sell her in good time." Pran put a hand on the man's shoulder and steered him back into the lounge. "Come, I'll show you a prettier one."

Ma and I stood alone in the hallway. Her face looked pale in the stark light, her cheeks deeply hollowed.

"What was he talking about, Ma? What does it mean to be a devadasi?"

"It's late, Noor. I need to get back to work, and you have school tomorrow."

I stood my ground. "Tell me."

She hesitated.

"It's the tradition of our community. It goes back hundreds of years. One daughter, usually the oldest, is dedicated to serve the temple."

"Serve in what way?"

Ma sighed.

"In what way, Ma?"

"In the old days we were courtesans to the priests and sometimes the wealthy landowners."

"And now?"

"The history has been lost. Now we're sold to the highest bidder. It's how we support our families. The practice has been outlawed but it remains our tradition."

"And I am also a Devadasi." I wanted her to disagree. There had to be a way out.

"No one can escape their fate, Noor."

I knocked her aside as I bolted past her, down the hallway, up the ladder, across our small, shared room and under her bed. Aamaal was already there. She was curled around a sleeping Shami but her eyes shone brightly from the shadows.

I pulled her into my arms with Shami sandwiched between us and massaged her knotted shoulders. "I'm all right, Aamaal. You did well."

Closing my eyes, I breathed in Shami's sour milk smell and the coconut oil I'd smeared on Aamaal's hair that morning. Gradually her coiled limbs relaxed and her breathing became deep and regular. When Ma came in I pretended I was asleep. All through the night I listened to the noises of her customers. They took on new meaning. For the first time I associated them with my own future. When the last one had finally departed I was still wide awake.

I crawled out from under the bed before dawn and spent longer than usual scrubbing myself in the washing room. I packed my schoolbag and went to school without speaking to anyone. Gajra was at the fence waiting for me when I arrived. Together we walked over to a cluster of girls from my class.

"It's not fair," said one. "The boys always have games at recess. They can play cricket and football. There's never anything fun for us. We just stand here on the sidelines watching."

"I have a game," I said, thinking quickly. "It's called Toppling Towers. You all need to get out your erasers, as many as you have, and perhaps pencil sharpeners as well, if they're flat and we can stack them."

"Trust you to think of something fun for us to do. I bet someday you'll be a games mistress at some posh girls' school."

"You forget she always takes first in Math and English," said Gajra, forever ready to point out my achievements. "Our Noor will become something far more important than a games mistress. A doctor is more likely, or perhaps an inventor."

"India's own Steve Jobs," crowed another girl. "What do you think, Noor? Will you one day be rich and famous?"

I forced a smile. "No one can escape their fate."

Grace

The ride to school was as silent as the trip home the day before. Dad held my hand again as we crossed the parking lot. Mom walked on the other side of me. I was grateful for the show of solidarity but it wasn't the same as forgiveness. Her back was rigid as we entered the school. Her eyes betrayed her anxiety, flitting from side to side as though she expected to see the walls plastered with my half-naked image. I wondered if she was thinking about her plan to run for school council president that year. Was it another disappointment I should apologize for?

When we reached the office, we were asked to take seats. We probably waited less than five minutes. It seemed much longer.

Mr. Smiley came out to greet us, shaking both of my parents' hands. They made some small talk about the heavy traffic as he ushered us into a large meeting room off his own office. I was alarmed to see not only the vice principal but my home-room teacher, the coordinator of the International Baccalaureate program, my community service advisor and the school coun-selor. For a fleeting moment, I registered horror that now *everyone* knew, which was silly when you think about it. Who on earth did I think *didn't* know?

As we took our seats, my parents insisted I sit between them. It made me feel marginally better to know that they were both claiming me as their own. Mr. Smiley looked as though he'd regained some of his trademark good humor. He opened the meeting by asking if we'd managed to talk things through as a family.

"We still have a few things to settle," said Dad.

Mom held the same tight expression she'd had yesterday in the elevator. I fervently hoped she didn't start bawling again.

"Well, we've had some very useful discussions on our end," said Mr. Smiley. "Mr. Donleavy, Grace's community service advisor, thinks he has the perfect program to help Grace make amends for what she's done and gain some insight into the risks of this kind of behavior."

"Well, let's hear it," said Mom in a voice that sounded like she wanted to do anything but.

"Mr. Donleavy, why don't you explain," said Mr. Smiley.

Mr. Donleavy immediately produced multiple copies of a package of information, which he slid across the table. He gave me an encouraging smile as I took mine and I did my best to smile back. Everyone liked Mr. Donleavy. If it's possible for a teacher to be hot—and let's be honest, some of them are—Mr. Donleavy was our school's number-one hottie. Before all this happened he'd even started to make me feel guilty because

I'd so resolutely vetoed his various suggestions for community involvement. I guess he got the last laugh.

I looked at the pamphlet clipped to the top of my pile. It had pictures of girls of various ages doing everything from yoga to studying. I really hoped he wasn't going to suggest I work with little kids. My single experience doing that was when I'd agreed to help one of my cousins babysit one summer. She left me alone on a beach with her three-year-old charge for ten minutes while she went back to the cottage to get us drinks. I got so distracted building the kid a sand castle that I didn't notice him wander away. We eventually found him, but after that my cousin and I both agreed I was not babysitter material.

"This is an NGO that works to prevent second-generation trafficking," said Mr. Donleavy. "They have a variety of programs for the girls, including after-school tutoring, life skills, sex education—"

"Wait a minute," Dad interrupted. "Who did you say these girls were?"

"The daughters of sex workers," said Mr. Donleavy, without a second's hesitation. The poor guy had no idea the beast he was about to awaken.

"SEX WORKERS!" Mom shrieked. "My daughter makes one tiny mistake and you think she's fit to work with sex workers?!"

"It's not a punishment—" started Mr. Donleavy.

"Well, actually—" cut in Mr. Smiley.

"She'd work with the daughters, not the actual—" the counselor interrupted, trying to bring things down a notch.

"She sure as hell won't!" said Mom, jumping to her feet. "I've heard enough. If you people can't come up with a better plan than this, this . . ." No one cut Mom off; she was just too angry to finish her sentence.

"What kind of work would it be?" I asked in a small voice.

Dad put a hand on Mom's arm. She sat down again.

"There are several activities, Grace," said Mr. Donleavy, "but I had a particular one in mind. If I may . . . ?" He looked at Mom, who gave a grudging grunt.

"The NGO wants to start a new teen-to-teen program. The girls would be a little younger than you, probably thirteen or fourteen. They'd like to pair students one by one, so you'd mentor one girl, sort of like a big sister."

"What would we do together?"

"Well, to some extent that would be up to you. You might help with homework. But, as you got to know each other better, you might plan outings. A lot of these girls never leave their own neighborhood, and it's a very poor neighborhood they live in."

"Will she know what I've done?"

"She'll know you're volunteering for school credit. What you tell her beyond that is up to you. But these girls grow up in brothels, Grace. I think you'll find they're pretty difficult to shock."

I nodded.

"I think I could do that. What do you think, Mom?" I was determined not to do anything else to disappoint her.

She gave me a long, steady look. Not taking her eyes off me, she answered, "I think any girl would be lucky to have Grace for a sister."

My relief was so intense tears sprang to my eyes. I didn't kid myself that my mom was over her anger but it was a start.

Mom and Dad left shortly after that and I spent another hour with the counselor talking about how to handle potential bullying at school. She made me promise to tell her if anyone gave me a hard time. All I had to do was show her my phone. Messages were coming in so fast I had to keep deleting them for fear they'd consume my message space. As tempting as it would have been to turn in my tormentors, I didn't know who they were. The last I'd heard, Todd and Madison were denying involvement, though I'd had a brief text exchange with Kyle, who confirmed his antipathy toward Todd. He refused to elaborate, just saying Todd had messed things up with him and Anoosha. Of course, I didn't tell him my own problem.

I walked into my third-period class feeling like everyone was whispering about me. It was probably the first and last time in my life I was happy to be in a Math class; the lesson was at least sufficiently challenging to hold everyone's attention. The class passed slowly but without incident.

The next period was lunch. I'd already resolved to spend that in the library and went back to my locker to drop my books.

I saw the word, scrawled on my locker, from ten feet away. I didn't let my steps falter, though other kids stopped walking to watch my reaction.

Conversations ground to a halt.

I unlocked my locker.

Someone tittered. It was an odd sound in the stillness, like birdsong at the scene of a crime. I piled my books onto the single shelf and shut the door.

"She doesn't even care," said a voice. I knew who it was. "She knows she's a slut."

I turned around and surveyed the group. It was a mix of

kids, some I knew better than others. I'd been in school with most of them for three years, shared classes with a few, worked on assignments with others, cheered alongside many at assemblies. I didn't cry or rage. I wouldn't give them that satisfaction. I just shook my head. Every one of them, whether bully or bystander, was enjoying my humiliation. They didn't care that I'd had thoughts of suicide, or felt so ashamed I'd carved into my own flesh. I was nothing more than a moment's entertainment. I'd never felt so alone.

"Who do you think you are?" asked Madison.

"Well, by all accounts . . ." I let the words trail off.

"You tried to blame me."

I didn't deny it.

"Why don't you just leave? No one wants you here."

Leaving was exactly what I wanted to do, but she and her group were only the front line in a thick circle of kids forming a solid ring around me. I was on the point of saying that when a ripple went through the crowd and it parted to let a boy step forward. Everyone in the school knew him, by reputation if nothing else. He had a following of his own, the school's beautiful people.

"Speak for yourself, darling," he said to Madison in a mocking tone. "I for one am positively delighted she's here. She's the first interesting person we've had at this school since, well, since I arrived."

Drop-dead-gorgeous VJ Patel, son of Bollywood icon Sanjay Patel and a rising film star himself, held out his hand.

"What do you say, Slut? Would you join me for lunch?" He shot me a saucy grin guaranteed to make any female not already in her grave swoon.

I'd never spoken to him before, and would have said he didn't know of my existence, but I did the only sensible thing I could do. I took his hand.

11

Noor

Sleeping on the street . . .

"It's easy," boasted Parvati when I told her I would have to join her sleeping on the street.

It had been two weeks since the man had tried to buy me, and Ma was a bundle of nerves. She acted like it was the first time a man had spoken to me in that way. Admittedly, I'd never told her about the bad things men said to me or the many times they'd tried to touch me, even her own customers. I always assumed she knew. In the same way I knew what men did to her. I thought it was our secret language. We kept our eyes open but our mouths sealed shut. After that night, I began to wonder.

She paced our small room for days. No one could calm her. Deepa-Auntie was the only one who dared try and Ma bit her head off. Prita-Auntie, who'd known Ma the longest and was the closest thing she had to a friend, made herself scarce. Lali-didi, who'd recently been moved into our room, sat nervously on her own bed, watching us both because suddenly we were always together. Ma wouldn't let me out of her sight. She even walked me to school and was waiting at the gate at the end of each day.

At first the novelty of her attention was gratifying. It was the first time I'd felt like I was more than a servant, perhaps even loved, but Ma's restless anger quickly wore on me. I created excuses to steal time away from her. One day I deliberately spoke out of turn in class to get kept after school. That was a mistake though. When my teacher finally let me go, Ma was a hissing cobra, barely able to contain herself until we got home, where she beat me.

I was the one who suggested I was too old to sleep in our house. "The men look at me differently now," I told her. "It will be safer if I sleep elsewhere."

I didn't say that men had looked at me this way as long as I could remember. Was there any other way for a man to look at a girl?

"But where will you sleep?" asked Ma.

It was a stupid question. How many people did we know who slept in the street every night? Did she think I could give her the coordinates of the patch of pavement I would claim as my own?

"I'll go with Parvati," I said. "She knows someone with a small room we can share."

This was a lie and Ma knew it. If she'd believed me she would have asked for more details. To have a room was sufficiently extraordinary that it bore investigation. Perhaps there would be space for Aamaal and Shami as well. But Ma said nothing.

She crinkled her already deeply lined brow and gave me a hollow-eyed stare. It went through my head that she used to be pretty and I wondered if her horror that men were noticing me was in part because she struggled now to get their attention. What would happen if men no longer paid to be with her? How would she support us? I didn't know how old Ma was. Like most people, myself included, her birth wasn't registered and the date was long forgotten. She didn't even have a fake birth certificate, like the one I got to register for school. She'd once said she was barely in her teens when she had me, so she had to be in her twenties still, but time moved faster in our community. Many women, their bodies wasted by disease and addiction, didn't live to see thirty.

"I don't want you begging," Ma said. "I don't send you to school to have you end up a beggar."

I wanted to ask why she did send me to school. What was her plan for me? Did she have one? "I'll only sleep with Parvati. That's all."

She sighed and sank down on the edge of Lali-didi's bed. Lali-didi practically left behind her own skin in her haste to scuttle away.

"I don't like Parvati. She's a bad influence."

I suppressed a smile. As if anyone could be a bad influence in our neighborhood. What did she think I might learn from Parvati that I didn't already know?

"She doesn't even go to school," Ma continued.

"That's not Parvati's choice," I said indignantly, though Parvati always pretended she was glad she didn't have to go to school. "Her ma won't pay for the uniform and books."

"You'll need to be back first thing to wash the dishes. You know what Pran will do if he wakes up and finds the dishes haven't been cleared up."

I nodded, though no one ever knew what Pran would do.

I stood outside our building that evening, discussing sleeping options with Parvati. Although it was late, I still had Shami strapped to my back. He had a cough that made it hard for him to sleep lying flat. Sticky yellow goo collected in his lungs so he woke up gasping for breath. It was another reason I didn't mind sleeping outside. Keeping him quiet and breathing at the same time was becoming an impossible task. He would breathe easier if I could keep him upright.

"I told Hussein there would only be two of us," said Parvati for at least the third time. "Why can't you leave Shami with your ma? Aamaal can watch him."

I looked across the street to where a fight was brewing between two men outside a bar. We needed to get moving. It wasn't safe for us to be hanging around this time of night.

"We can sleep under the bridge," I said.

Parvati often worked with the beggars who'd built a shanty community under the railway bridge near Grant Road Station. It wasn't far from Kamathipura. We could make it there on foot in thirty minutes. I'd suggested it earlier but Parvati refused. I couldn't figure out why. I thought the beggars were her friends.

Parvati put her hands on her hips and gave me a look, like I was being unreasonable. Maybe she wanted to show off her "boyfriend," Hussein, who sold T-shirts outside Central Station. He claimed he owned the stall where he worked and we could sleep under the table when he shut down for the night. I had my doubts on both counts. He was too young to own a stall, and I didn't want to risk being discovered by his boss and chased away in the middle of the night. If it had been closer I might have agreed to try it out, but it was more than an hour's walk.

"Why would he let us sleep there for nothing?" The boy's ulterior motive was the other thing worrying me. We couldn't afford to pay him, not in cash anyway, and I didn't want to contemplate what other form of payment he might expect.

Parvati shrugged. "He said he loves me. He gave me this T-shirt and he didn't ask for anything." She puffed out her chest in case I'd failed to notice she was wearing a T-shirt emblazoned with *I'm a Princess* in gold lettering. She was also wearing new blue jeans. It was the first time I'd seen her out of traditional clothes. The difference was startling, as if she were one of those girls who advertised toothpaste on television, with a life as perfect as her teeth.

"Did he give you the jeans too?"

"No, I bought them myself." She looked way too smug.

I suspected she'd stolen them. I just hoped she'd been smart enough not to steal from a stall near the T-shirt shop. The vendor was bound to notice if she sashayed past wearing them. Parvati scared me sometimes. She was much too bold for a girl. It would get her into trouble one day.

Two men walked by and gave us a speculative look. Even after they were beyond us, they turned back for a last gawk. Parvati winked at me.

"Those clothes reveal too much," I said, grateful Ma had already been inside with a customer when Parvati showed up.

"You're just jealous." Parvati arched her back and squeezed her arms on either side of her tiny boobs.

"You can't make melons out of cherries," I said grumpily.

Parvati sighed. "When I get rich I'm going to buy boobs the size of melons!"

"They'll grow on their own, Paru," I relented. "Your ma has the biggest boobs on the street."

Parvati smiled happily. "That's true, isn't it? But I'm a teenager. They should be bigger by now."

"You're twelve. That's not a teenager."

"You don't know how old I am."

"Neither do you."

"That's the problem with being the oldest. Do you remember the exact date Aamaal and Shami were born?"

"Of course."

"Never forget that. When Eka starts school he won't have a fake date on his birth certificate like you and I did. My ma couldn't tell you when he was born but I remember."

"Your ma didn't register his birth so you'll still have to fake the certificate." I didn't have to ask why she knew her ma would let Eka go to school when she'd pulled Parvati out after third standard. Even a goat knew education was more important for boys than for girls. I also didn't suggest that Eka might not be the best candidate for school. Parvati's ma had a serious drug problem. It didn't seem to have affected Parvati but I wasn't so sure about Eka. He wasn't sick as often as Shami, but Shami was already talking, while Eka, though eight months older, was still babbling.

"It's getting late, Paru. We need to decide where we're going."

"Fine," she huffed, "let's go to Grant Road. But leave Shami at home tomorrow night."

I started walking. Parvati fell in step, taking my hand. We both knew that tomorrow night I'd show up again with Shami. We'd have the same argument, and Shami would come along. Parvati may not have loved Shami as much as I did but she did love him, the same way I loved Eka. They were family. And Parvati understood that in the nearly two years since Shami's birth he'd become a vital part of me. I was so used to looking after him that sometimes at school I felt his absence as if the air had been emptied of oxygen and I couldn't breathe. All I could think about was rushing home to make sure he was still okay.

As if he knew what I was thinking, Shami stirred and wrapped his fingers around a strand of my hair. I craned my face around and kissed his tiny fist.

"Do you want me to carry him for a bit?" asked Parvati.

"No, he's not heavy." The truth of that statement made my stomach twist.

"He'll grow, Noor. He's like my boobs. We're late bloomers, right, Shami?" She briefly dropped my hand to reach up and ruffle his hair.

"Right, Shami," agreed Shami.

We laughed.

Leaving our crowded street, we hit the bright lights of Bapty Road. Food stalls on carts gave way to proper restaurants, open at the front so their fluorescent lighting lit up the whole street. You could tell we were coming into a richer neighborhood because bright lights shone from upstairs windows as well, as if the whole street were one big carnival. In our neighborhood, electricity was scarce and not so frivolously wasted.

"Are you hungry?" asked Parvati. She always seemed to have money these days. That also worried me.

"Are you buying?"

"Sure, why not?"

I almost asked her where the money came from but she beamed at me so full of pride that the words shriveled on my tongue and I swallowed them down again. "I'm not hungry," I lied, and immediately felt guilty. Even if I didn't want to take her money, I couldn't deny Shami. "Maybe just a samosa for Shami."

"We'll all have samosas," she said magnanimously, like an NGO worker who could produce food as easily as spit.

We stopped at a café that had tables spilling onto the sidewalk. That was another thing you didn't find in our neighborhood: space was too precious to waste it on the luxury of tables and chairs on sidewalks. People ate as they walked along or took their food home. We approached the counter. There was already a crowd of men waiting to be served but Parvati pushed her way to the front and shouted her order. The server tried to ignore her, looking over her head to the men who now engulfed her. She put her hands on the countertop, which was almost as high as her shoulders, and peered over the top, continuing to bellow. I chuckled at the foolish man who thought Parvati could be ignored. Giving her a foul look, he took her order, snatched the cash she held up and practically threw a bag of samosas at her.

Parvati returned, grinning all over her face. She handed me one samosa and broke off a small piece from another, holding it up to Shami. I felt rather than saw him turn his head away.

"Keep trying," I said. "He'll take it eventually."

We started walking again and Parvati did her best to get Shami to eat, in between tucking into her own samosa. In the end he didn't have more than a few bites but I still felt a measure of satisfaction. Every bit of food that went into him felt like a victory.

It was close to midnight by the time we reached the shanties under the bridge. I was ready to drop from exhaustion and wondered if we were really going to have to make this trek every night. Lots of girls didn't. They just slept in doorways or on the sidewalk in our own neighborhood. Lots of them got attacked as well though. It was worth the walk to sleep surrounded by people we knew, even if they were Parvati's friends more than mine.

Several people greeted her as we wove our way through the corrugated metal and tarpaulin structures looking for a few feet of empty pavement. Finally we came to a patch large enough for all three of us to stretch out. Parvati helped me ease Shami off my back. He'd fallen asleep after his small meal and we didn't want to wake him. She held him while I spread the sari on the ground and then gently laid him on it. Without discussion, we settled ourselves on either side.

Kidnapping was another hazard of life on the street, though baby girls were more often stolen than boys. Boys could be sold to beggars, who used them as props to get bigger handouts, but girls could be sold to brothels. They were far more lucrative. Babies sometimes disappeared from the brothels themselves. No baby had ever been stolen from our home but I knew several aunties whose babies had gone missing. Everyone knew it was the brothel owners. They sold them to traffickers who resold them in distant cities far from the protection of their families. The brothel owners made money, and it was a powerful way to punish mothers who'd resisted allowing their children to follow them into the trade.

I was almost asleep when I was aroused by a thud, quickly followed by a shriek. I sat up to discover Parvati rubbing her shoulder and recoiling from the raised foot of a young man.

The stubble on his face was as patchy as grass in the dry season. He couldn't have been more than sixteen.

"Get up, thief," he snarled.

Parvati scrambled to her feet, planting herself firmly between the boy and Shami. I jumped up too and reached down to pick up Shami, taking in our situation at the same time. There were half a dozen of them. The boy who kicked her was the oldest. The youngest looked to be about Adit's age. I stepped closer to Parvati so our bodies were touching.

"Where's my money," demanded their leader. He seemed genuinely furious, but that didn't impress me. From what I'd seen of life many people spent every moment of every day simmering with anger.

"I haven't been working." Parvati glared back at him defiantly.

Parvati never understood the value of pretending humility. I cast my eyes downward, trying to communicate my own respect.

He backhanded her across the face. Her head cracked sideways with the force of the blow. Blood spurted from her lip and hit my cheek. I caught her as she staggered into me, but she righted herself quickly and again met his gaze.

"Have you seen me begging?" she demanded. "I haven't been working."

I silently willed her to be quiet.

"We've all seen you throwing your money around. If you're not begging for it, you must be stealing. Either way, you owe me my cut."

What had Parvati done? Surely she wouldn't steal from her fellow beggars. There was a hierarchy in every begging community, just as there was for sex workers. Beggars worked in teams under the supervision of middle-level lieutenants who reported to gang lords. Whatever beggars earned on the street had to be turned over to those they worked for. Parvati knew that. It suddenly occurred to me that maybe she had bought her jeans. Was that the meaning of her sly smile?

"What if I do have money? What's it to you? I didn't earn it begging. You have no claim to it."

Why couldn't she have just lied?

"I own you. That means I own everything you earn. What do I care how you earned it? It's still mine. In fact, you should be grateful your money is all I take from you."

"You would have to force a girl, wouldn't you, Suresh? No girl would let you touch her voluntarily."

We reached for her at the same time, me to pull her back and him perhaps to kill her. We met halfway and he knocked Shami from my arms. I leaned over to pick up Shami, who was already struggling to his feet, stunned.

Parvati dove for the boy's neck, wrapping her hands around it. Shami headed unsteadily toward them but I caught him and wrapped my arms around him. Several more boys joined the fray. Parvati was knocked to the ground. I left Shami to go to her. Kicks connected with my back and sides as I shielded her. Suddenly Shami was beside me, taking blows meant for me. Tears streamed down my face as I beseeched them all to stop.

When we were all three on the ground bleeding and inert, they stood back to savor their victory.

Suresh leaned down to Parvati, shoving his hands into every one of her pockets until he found her money.

"Don't ever try to cheat me again," he warned.

Parvati's unflinching stare said it all. He laughed, but it was a reed-thin imitation.

We were silent after they left. I carefully examined every inch of Shami. He'd have some bruises in the morning but there was nothing broken and only minor cuts. It was still agony to see him hurt. He winced when I held him close and buried my face in his hair.

Parvati reached over and stroked Shami's head. "Don't worry, Noor. One day I will make Suresh pay for that beating." Her beautiful new T-shirt was smeared with dirt, the *I'm a Princess* obscured.

If anyone else had made the threat, I would have put it down to bravado, but it was Parvati. I didn't doubt her.

"Be careful, Paru. Suresh is protected. If you defy him, he'll only do worse to you."

Neither of us knew how right I was.

12

Grace

I didn't know where VJ normally sat, but I noticed that he chose a table in the epicenter of the cafeteria, guaranteed to ensure we could be seen from every direction.

"Can you give us a moment?" He looked around at the girls who'd followed him in. "Grace and I need to have a private talk."

A couple of the girls shot me hostile looks but they melted away at his request.

"What do you want to eat? I'm buying."

Still reeling from the last five minutes of my life, I had no idea what to say. I'd never spoken to this boy before and he was offering to buy me lunch. Would it be more rude to refuse or accept?

"Chips?" I suggested hesitantly.

"Not going to happen, my nubile nymph." He pursed lips that any girl would kill to have—kissing her, or just stuck on her own face. "I'm not going to be the one to destroy your perfect feline physique, so let me rephrase: Do you want a veggie wrap or a salad?"

"Salad?"

"Perfect choice! Aren't you clever." With that he sauntered off, pausing at least a half dozen times on his way to the food line to chat with people, all of who seemed utterly charmed by him.

As surreal as the last twenty-four hours of my life had been, this took bizarre to a whole new level. VJ Patel was the local version of royalty. There wasn't anyone in the school richer or more famous. Everyone knew he drove around in an armored car with a personal bodyguard, though apparently school regulations required the bodyguard to wait in the parking lot. The stories of his lavish parties and excessive drinking were legendary. In fact, legendary pretty much summed up VJ Patel. So . . . what was he doing with me?

It was possible he felt sorry for me, but I wouldn't have pegged him for a particularly altruistic guy. The numerous times I'd seen him on the front of the lifestyle section of the newspaper it was never in connection with anything charitable, unless he was attending a fundraising art auction or gala.

I wasn't thrilled about being his latest charity until a more hideous thought occurred to me. He was concerned about me gaining weight. A wave of nausea swept over me. Did he believe the hype that I was a slut? Given the photographic evidence, it was hardly surprising. The only question was, did he want me for himself or was he planning to follow his dad into the film industry, perhaps starting with a porn flick? As shocking as my behavior was to the average westerner, it had to seem worse to the Indian students. Their own films had only recently allowed kissing. Even imported western films were heavily censored.

VJ appeared with a large Greek salad, placed it in front of me and dropped into the chair across the table. I stared at the salad. With the knot in my stomach I wouldn't be able to force down a single bite. I cleared my throat. He grinned.

"What's on your mind?" he said. "Spit it out."

I tried to think of a tactful opener. "I really appreciate you rescuing me," I started. "But, you should know I'm not . . . I'm not . . ."

He arched his perfectly shaped brow. He was so good-looking he was pretty. "You're not what?" he prompted.

"Available."

"Available for what?"

I blinked and made the mistake of shoving a forkful of salad into my mouth with the hope that it would give me time to think.

"Sex?" he asked, leaning forward across the table. "Are we not going to have sex?"

I couldn't chew. His face was inches from my own and he was talking about sex. My face was suffused with heat.

VJ leaned back in his chair and sighed heavily. I quickly chewed, swallowed and resolved to give up vegetables for the foreseeable future.

"Well, Gracie," he said, "I'm going to tell you something, but you have to swear it won't go any further."

"Who would I tell? Everyone hates me."

"This secret you could probably sell to the press."

"The last thing I want is more attention."

His tone was so dramatically earnest that I wasn't sure if he was serious, but his dark eyes searched my face as though he really was trying to decide if he could trust me.

"Okay." He took a deep breath. "I like boys, Gracie. That's the truth of it. I like you too, obviously. As a person, I think you're very interesting . . . but not in *that* way."

My mind was reeling. In all the stories I'd read and heard, not one said VJ Patel was gay. I was never obsessed with him or anything, but I was a major Bollywood film fan. I felt this was something I should have known. I'd seen him in at least three films playing a teen heartthrob, and I'd read countless articles detailing his latest romances. I had to hand it to him: if he was telling me the truth he was a better actor than I'd given him credit for. At another time I might have been disappointed—like every other girl in the school, I'd harbored a small crush on him—but recent events had decidedly dampened my romantic inclinations.

Still, it was hard to reconcile the boy before me, claiming his lack of interest in girls, with all the stories. "I don't understand," I said.

"You don't understand?" A smile played about his lips. "How shall I explain?" He thought for a moment. "As much as I hope we can be friends, at no point are you going to get any. I hope you're not too disappointed."

I laughed.

VJ frowned. "That's a little harsh, pet."

"I'm sorry." I tried to stop grinning but I couldn't help it. I was just so massively relieved. "So, if you aren't interested in me, why'd you bail me out?"

"Who said I wasn't interested in you? You're the school slut. I think that's positively delicious."

"I'm not really a slut."

"Don't be so quick to give away your power. Remember, there's no such thing as bad press."

"Look at that, she's already got her claws into another guy." Madison's voice rose above the usual cafeteria babble. I looked over to discover that she wasn't at her usual table. She, too, had chosen to sit in a central spot. But it was who she was with that took my breath away. Flanked by her usual entourage, she sat directly across the table from none other than Todd.

"I don't believe it," I said, more to myself than to VJ.

He followed my gaze. "Ah, an alliance of your enemies. What can it mean? The intrigue of it all! This just keeps getting better!"

I gave him a cool look. "I'm glad you find my life so entertaining."

"Of course I do. I wouldn't hang out with you otherwise."

"Is nothing serious with you?" I knew I didn't have enough friends to risk losing the only person willing to speak to me, but I was starting to wonder if VJ was really friend material.

He straightened his face and looked so determinedly solemn that I found myself smiling.

"There are many things I find serious. Declining achievement levels in rural schools, female infanticide and my mother's suicide attempt after my father's affair are all things I consider very serious. A bunch of children displaying their pack mentality by attacking a vulnerable girl is distasteful but hardly catastrophic."

"Did you say your mother's suicide attempt?"

"I shouldn't have said that. I don't want to talk about it."

"I'm sorry."

"Me too. It destroyed my family. But it also put a lot of things in perspective."

"So what I did, you don't think that's serious?"

"You showed off your boobs. I'm no connoisseur but it didn't seem to me you have anything to be ashamed of. You're very thin but you know what they say about wealth and thinness."

"Don't you think my behavior was a little . . ." I found I couldn't bring myself to say the word, though I'd been called it so many times in the past twenty-four hours I was surprised it still stung.

"Avant-garde, bold, even, gasp, sexy?"

"Slutty. You have to admit, what I did was slutty."

"Grace," said VJ, looking me straight in the eye without a hint of humor. "My forty-two-year-old father encouraging every young ingénue in Mumbai to think sex with him will further her career is slutty. What you did may not have been your wisest decision, but it wasn't slutty. In fact, it was so naive it was kind of sweet. Seriously, Grace, didn't your parents teach you anything?"

"Apparently not," I said wryly.

"Well, Bambi, you've come to the right place. As someone who's spent a lifetime in the public eye, who's had his every debacle documented, I'm going to teach you how to deal with the hunters."

"If you've had every debacle documented, are you sure you're the best person to advise me? It doesn't sound like you know how to avoid publicity."

"Avoid it?" VJ made big eyes. "Baby, why would you want to avoid it? What you want to do is control it."

"Like you do?" I didn't even try to hide my skepticism.

"Absolutely. Let me ask you one question. Did you know I was gay?"

I paused. He had me there. Everything I'd ever read about him told the same story. He was a womanizing bad boy, in sharp contrast to his father, invariably portrayed as a dignified family man. How could the press have got it so backwards?

"Exactly." VJ read my mind. "The trick is to take control of your image. Don't let it control you. Now finish your salad. You're going to need your strength for the days ahead."

"Why do you even want to help me?"

"Did your brother Kyle ever mention me?"

"No, I don't think so."

"He was on my cricket team. Last year we played a tournament in Singapore. He never mentioned that?"

"I knew he went, but so what?"

"I met someone at the tournament. It was the first and last time I've had the freedom to act on my feelings. We got a little physical and your brother walked in on us. He never told you about that?"

"No, he didn't say a thing."

"I'm not surprised. He never told anyone. He could have destroyed me, but he didn't, and he never made me feel awkward about it either. He didn't treat me any differently than before."

"You know it really isn't a big deal, right? It's perfectly normal."

"Not in my world. If the press got wind of my inclinations, my career would be over. It's not okay for a regular Indian boy to be gay, much less a teen idol. And take a good look at my friends, wannabe starlets and sycophants. Not one of them would stick by me if my star plummeted."

"You don't know that. Maybe you just need to give people a chance." I suddenly realized I'd just parroted the same advice Kyle had given me not so long ago.

"Has that been your experience, Grace?"

My silence was sufficient response.

"Do your parents know?" I couldn't imagine how hard it would be to keep a secret like that.

"I told my mother last year. She slapped me and said we wouldn't speak of it again." He kept his voice level but his eyes clouded at the memory.

"What are you going to do?"

"I'll do what my parents expect of me—get married, produce at least one child, ideally a boy, and never under any circumstances let anyone outside the family find out what I am."

I only had time for one more bite of my salad before the bell rang, but it wasn't going down so well anyway. As I picked up what was left of it and headed for the bin, I found myself worrying about the most popular guy in school, which probably explains why I didn't see her coming. She crashed into me, tipping salad down my shirt. The whole oily mess crashed to the floor. A crowd quickly formed, her minions already on the scene.

"Get your cameras ready, boys. She's probably going to whip off her shirt and start rubbing that oil on herself."

I stared at the mess on the floor. "Why don't you give it a rest, Madison?" I was more sad than angry.

"Why, what are you going to do about it?"

"Oh, good!" exclaimed VJ. I didn't realize he'd pushed his

way through the crowd to stand beside me. "Look, Grace, it's the wicked witch and her flying monkeys!"

Madison glowered, but even surrounded by her supporters she didn't have the nerve to take on the famous VJ Patel.

"You drag me into your sordid little drama again and you're dead," she snarled, but she scuttled away before I could respond.

"Hey, man, what are you doing?" asked Todd, perhaps emboldened by his own role in my downfall. "You can do better than her."

"Actually, *man*, I've convinced Grace that she can do better than you. Strangely enough, that wasn't hard."

There were a few giggles from the crowd.

"I'd certainly take VJ over Todd," said a senior I didn't know but instantly liked. This was followed by general murmurs of assent.

Todd looked around at his faithless friends.

"Do you know what I can't figure out, McClaren?" Todd demanded. "How you could have believed even for a minute that I'd be interested in you. Don't you know what a total loser you are?"

VJ stepped up to Todd so their faces were inches apart. "You're the only loser I see."

"Whatever, man." Todd shot me a final contemptuous look before stalking off.

I waited for the crowd to disperse before I turned to VJ. "Are you sure you want to hang out with me? People are going to wonder why you're sticking up for me. They might even think we're a couple."

"Exactly, darling. Now you're getting the hang of it."

13

Noor

The doctor . . .

I rehearsed what I was going to say when my name was called.
I'd tell them Ma was too sick to come but gave me permission
to bring my brother. I'd admit he'd been coughing for several
weeks but I'd lie about the blood in his spit, claiming it was a
new symptom. To admit the truth would have raised questions
I didn't want to answer.

We took two buses across town to visit a hospital where we
weren't known. I hoped there wasn't a central registry of hospital visits. We'd been to more than a dozen throughout the
city. Ma had no idea we'd visited any. She would have beaten
me senseless if she'd known.

It was the only way I could get enough medicine for Shami.
Each new clinic would give him only a single injection and
medicine for a week or two at most. I was handed prescriptions
for the rest, which I hadn't the money to fill. Traveling to a
new clinic was half the cost of filling the prescription and had

the added benefit that if his condition worsened, a doctor would catch it.

Each new doctor had given me a stern lecture on how to administer the drugs, writing it all down so I could pass the information to my mother. Each time, I'd listened intently, folded the instructions and made a show of zipping them into my bag. Never once did I say my mother couldn't read or that she believed doctors were tricksters and thieves. Ma said free clinics were like the fruit-wallah who gave you a slice of mango and then tried to sell you a whole one at twice its value.

Fortunately, like every other morning, Ma was sleeping off the effects of alcohol and her night's work. If things went according to plan, I'd have Shami back under her bed before she noticed he was missing, with another dose of drugs in his system and a small supply to keep him going.

That day, the trip to the clinic had taken longer than I'd expected and it was already full of people when we arrived. I checked in at the front counter and was given a number in the hundreds. I could only hope that they didn't start with number one each day but carried numbers over from one day to the next.

The clinic was in a small section of a much larger hospital. The designated waiting area, on the second floor, was little more than a widening of the corridor with several dozen hard, molded chairs bolted together and to the floor. Every one of them was already filled, as was most of the available floor space. In some cases whole families were camped out. It was a roll call of diseases, every one present and accounted for. Running noses and hacking coughs were the most obvious symptoms, but Shami wasn't the only child with a glassy-eyed stare.

He'd fussed on the trip over, trying to convince me with his few words not to take him. Barely two years old, he knew where we were bound whenever we boarded a bus in the early hours of the morning. The excitement of the first time had long since passed. For him it meant poking and prodding, a painful injection and foul-tasting medicine. He didn't understand that it was to make him better, and truthfully I was losing faith in that myself. This bout of bloody coughing was only his latest affliction. He was visited by one symptom after another, each gnawing at him, stealing the light from his eyes, so it seemed as he got older that he'd skipped childhood altogether and gone straight to old age.

"Shami want 'nana," said Shami. I held him in one arm with his own draped around my neck. He watched me as I scanned the room for a place to sit down.

I turned my attention to him skeptically. Shami rarely expressed hunger, even less so in the past weeks. The cough had drained his desire for food, along with the energy to eat it.

"If we leave, we'll lose our place."

"Shami want 'nana," he repeated earnestly.

I spotted a corner for us at the end of the waiting area farthest from the doctor's office. I took him over and settled us on the floor. I laid Shami out beside me with his head in my lap and stroked his hair. It was a relief to sit down, though I kept a vigilant eye on the doctor's door. Shami fell into a fitful sleep despite his frequent fits of coughing.

Two hours passed with fewer than a dozen people going in and out of the office. I looked at the other invalids and was reminded of the herd of goats that filled our street every Eid. They were petted and overfed, yet their darting eyes showed too much white. Somehow they understood death was upon them. How many of these patients knew they would never recover? A doctor's visit was just one more item crossed off their list of chores and had less purpose than cleaning a toilet.

Shami started another deep bout of coughing. My rag was already wet with his blood but I held it to his lips anyway so it didn't splatter on the floor. It oozed between my fingers. I rummaged in my bag for our water carafe with my free hand. When his coughing slowed, I held it to his lips.

"Take him outside before he makes us all sick," scolded a woman who was seated on the floor a short distance away.

She was round like a tomato, as were her husband and even her two young children. I wasn't surprised at her order, though she knew very well I wouldn't obey. Picking fights made the waiting pass more quickly. A schoolgirl alone with her baby brother was an easy target. Who would speak up for me? I looked at her gold necklace. It was only gold-plated, and the inlaid jewels were fake. Did she think she was fooling anyone?

"So sorry, Auntie, but I must let the doctor see him. My mother is also sick or she would have come." I kept my eyes down, my tone respectful. There was nothing to be gained by fighting. She was a married woman, a mother and wife. Shami and I were nothing, less than nothing. Whether she'd started it or not, if I allowed myself to get drawn in, we would be the ones tossed out on the street like trash.

"Go sit farther away." She didn't sound any friendlier but she was no longer demanding we leave. I looked around us. Every inch of space was taken.

"Shami want 'nana." Shami regarded the woman hopefully.

"I'll get you a banana after we see the doctor," I said hastily. Shami sighed.

The woman murmured something to her husband and he handed her a large bag. She opened it up and rifled through, pulling out a metal tiffin box. Shami watched in fascination. She opened the top level, revealing a dish of fresh-cut fruit— mangoes, papaya and pineapple. She handed the dish to Shami, who snatched it greedily and began tucking in. Since Ma's brief affair with the fruit-wallah ended, we rarely got fresh fruit.

"Thank you, Auntie," I said.

"Your mother should be here," she said gruffly, watching the fruit rapidly disappearing into Shami as though he was worried she might snatch it back if he weren't quick.

In my head I made a promise that I would talk to Ma about giving Shami more fruit. In school they taught us about eating a balanced diet. But they never taught us how to do that when you lived in a house with two dozen other families and everyone, all the mothers and children, shared a tiny kitchen with a single element for cooking. Like most residents of Kamathipura, we lived on street food, fried dough, sometimes stuffed with potatoes and onions. The closest we came to fresh fruit was the occasional dollop of tamarind chutney.

I'd have to make up a story about why I thought it likely Shami would even eat fruit. That didn't worry me. Most of what I said to Ma was lies or half-truths, as was most of what she said to me. Sometimes, if Ma lied hard enough, I could make myself believe her. I don't think Ma ever believed my lies, though. I think when you get bigger your imagination gets smaller, or maybe Ma just didn't have the energy for pretending.

Shami finished the dish and began noisily sucking juice

off his fingers. I handed the dish back to Fat-auntie. Shami smiled at her. She fought a losing battle to hold back her own smile, which flooded her face like a monsoon rain.

"He's a beautiful child," she said.

"Yes," I agreed without embarrassment, because it was true, yet counted for so little. A boy needed only to be strong, and Shami wasn't that.

"Shami strong," said Shami, reading my thoughts as he so often did.

"Of course you are," said the woman, exchanging a look with me.

"Shami strong," Shami repeated firmly.

"Do you know what time it is, Auntie?"

She nodded to a clock on the wall.

It was later than I'd hoped. Ma rarely got up before one, but when she did, she'd expect to find Shami at home, either asleep under the bed or playing with Deepa-Auntie. No matter where Shami and I spent the night, I always took him home before leaving for school. I'd told Deepa-Auntie where we were going. I gave her instructions to tell Ma I'd taken Shami for a walk because his cough had made him restless. Ma would see through the deception in an instant. I would never willingly miss school. If we weren't back by one she'd try her best to beat the truth out of me. She wouldn't succeed. It had worked when I was a child but I was more stubborn now.

Parvati had agreed to walk Aamaal to school, which was kind of her, considering we'd both had another restless night. She had a new boyfriend who pumped gas at a station not far from our street. He'd told us we could sleep behind the station building, but halfway through the night his supervisor, alerted by Shami's coughing, had discovered us and chased us off. It was getting harder and harder to find a safe place. If Shami were not so sick I'd have asked Ma for money to rent space in a room. Lots of families did that, several families together in a room not ten feet square. The rooms were cramped and unventilated but it was better than sleeping on the street. Instead I hoarded every rupee I could squeeze out of her for trips to the doctor and herb-filled poultices for his chest. Ma didn't even seem to care about him anymore. She never suggested he stay with her at night. Aamaal was the only one she noticed.

"Shami pee pee," said Shami, interrupting my thoughts.

"All right." I'd seen a washroom near the entrance downstairs. I stood up and took his hand. Just then a nurse poked her head out of the office door and called our number.

"It will have to wait, baby. Can you hold it in?"

Shami furrowed his brow. I took that for an affirmative and led him through the crowd to the doctor's office. We entered a tiny waiting room with two vinyl-cushioned chairs and one metal-and-plastic one. The nurse sat in the metal chair and reached for a clipboard. She directed us to sit as well. I pulled Shami onto my lap but he wiggled off and climbed onto his own chair. It was covered in bright red fabric that looked like leather but wasn't. Shami pressed his finger into the cushion and giggled in wonderment when it regained its shape.

"Why are you here?" asked the nurse.

As if on cue, Shami started to cough violently. The nurse looked alarmed, though she must have dealt with this kind of sickness many times.

"How old is he?" she asked.

"Two and four months."

She looked surprised. "He looks younger. I thought under a year. And what is the patient's name?"

"Shami," said Shami.

I added our family name and answered her other questions with the lies I'd rehearsed.

She had him stand on a scale and weighed him. His weight had dropped since our last visit to a doctor two weeks ago. I bowed my head in shame, though the nurse couldn't have known. Finally she told us to wait and disappeared through an inner door, where I knew from experience the doctor would be finishing up with another patient.

Ten minutes later the nurse reappeared and ushered us into the examining room. The doctor was a woman. She looked around the same age as Ma but years younger at the same time. Her glossy black hair hung loose around her shoulders. Her back was straight, her eyes clear. The first time I'd encountered a woman doctor, I was surprised to discover women could be doctors, but now I knew they were as common as men, at least at the free clinics.

Familiar with the routine, I lifted Shami onto her examination table and took the wooden chair next to it. She sat on a rolling chair that allowed her to roam the empty space between her desk on the far wall and us. She slid up next to me and grinned. It made me nervous to have her so close.

"So, who have we here?" she asked, reading the chart.

"This is Shami. He has a cough with blood. My name is Noor. I'm his sister." While she'd asked her question in Hindi, I'd answered her in English, for the same reason I'd put on my school uniform that day. She might know my caste from my family name, if not my too-dark skin, but I would do everything I could to give her the impression I was from a respectable family.

"Where are your parents, Noor?"

"My father is dead. My mother is sick. She wanted to come today but she was too weak."

"I'm sorry to hear that. When did your father die?"

I didn't hesitate. I'd told this lie many times. "Three years ago. He had a heart attack."

"I see. And what's wrong with your mother?"

"She has a fever. It's probably just a virus." I blanched, realizing what I'd just said. In our neighborhood a virus meant only one thing. "Like the flu," I added, "or a bacterial infection."

"A bacterial infection?" She had a mischievous gleam in her eye. It made me feel even more jittery. "Or a virus. Well, that covers it, doesn't it? How old are you, Noor?"

"Fifteen," I lied again. I'm not even sure why I told that lie. Fifteen was no better than my real age, twelve and a half. Either way, I was still a minor with no right to make any decisions for myself, much less my brother.

"And you go to school. What standard?"

"Nine." This was only a minor lie. I was in eight, which was correct for my real age. I couldn't say that though because nine was already a year behind for my fake age.

The doctor gave me an appraising look. "Your English is very good. You must study hard."

I didn't know how to answer this as my lie suggested the opposite.

"I'm trying to catch up," I finally said. "I got sick last year and had to repeat."

"Hmmm, a lot of sickness in your family. What were you sick with?"

I stalled again. She asked more questions than most free clinic doctors. Usually they were too busy. No wonder she had such a crowd waiting outside. I considered pointing that out.

"Pneumonia." Shami had had pneumonia several times, so I was familiar with the symptoms. If she wanted to continue the interrogation, I was well prepared.

She just gave me a long look before standing up and moving over to Shami.

Taking the stethoscope from around her neck, she began the all-too familiar routine of checking him out. Even Shami knew what to do, taking deep breaths, which brought on another fit of coughing, leaning forward and back, opening his mouth, tilting his head. He followed every instruction almost before she asked.

She turned to me. "How long did you say he's been coughing up blood?"

"It started yesterday."

She pinned me with penetrating eyes. I felt myself sweat. I reassured myself that my anxiety didn't show on my face. I was a master at hiding my feelings. Her loud exhale told me she knew I was lying. My gaze didn't waver.

"He's significantly underweight," she said.

"He's a picky eater." I felt guilty, remembering the fruit.

"Is that true, Shami?" she asked in Hindi. Her voice was light but I saw through her act. "Don't you like to eat?"

"Shami eat manga an' napple," said Shami.

"Oh, I love manga an' napple!" the doctor exclaimed.

"Shami like 'nana," said Shami.

"Me too!" said the doctor. "You and I must go out for lunch sometime, Shami. I can see we have the same culinary tastes. You relax now. I'm going to talk to Noor."

"Where do you live?" She sat down again and picked up the chart and her pen.

"I told the nurse."

"It says here you live in Bandra." She named the upper-middle-class neighborhood I'd laid claim to. It was nowhere near Kamathipura, but familiar to everyone in the city for the number of Bollywood stars who lived there. It was also close to this clinic. I didn't want to raise the slightest suspicion that I'd traveled halfway across town because I'd already been to every free clinic near my own neighborhood.

Her pencil stayed poised above the chart. "You live in Bandra?" Her distrust was badly concealed. The rich were so often poor liars. It made me wonder how they were so successful.

Though I was lying, I felt angry to be disbelieved. I didn't answer. She glanced up. Her lips twitched as she tried to maintain a serious expression. Suddenly I was reminded of Parvati.

"Reclamation," I amended my story. It was a mixed neighborhood on the edge of Bandra, mostly squatters' shacks. I could have lived there. Despite my worn, too-tight uniform and scuffed shoes, I was still a school-going girl.

She put down the pen. What did she think she knew? Was my mother's profession printed on my forehead? It wasn't her business anyway. Her job was to give me the medicine. No wonder her line of patients moved so slowly. Did she think we had all day to pour out our life stories so she could spice up her boring life with our desperation?

"And you're fifteen, you said?"

I stared at my feet. I could feel her watching me with the intensity of a raven, as if my words were morsels of food and she was just waiting for me to drop one. I hoped I looked humble, like a beggar. I didn't want her to see the tiger inside me.

There was a long pause as she waited for me to say something.

"What do you say we try this again, Noor," she said gently.

I didn't know if it was her tone, or the stress of too many doctors, too many close calls with Shami's life. A tear slid down my nose and dropped on my knee, and then another. I wiped them away as quickly as they fell but they wouldn't stop coming. It was not worth it, all this trouble for a few days' worth of medicine. I was so tired of it all. Shami's sickness consumed us both. I could have no life while I watched his slip away.

I heard her chair roll toward me and suddenly her arms were around me, hugging me tight. The shock of it made me freeze; my belly seized, trapping my breath inside.

"Let's see if we can't help Shami together," she said. Her face was close to my hair. I'd oiled it only yesterday but still I feared lice would leap from my head to hers. She rubbed my back and gradually my breath returned.

"I don't know how to help him," I said truthfully.

She slid back and lifted my chin so she could see my face. "An accurate medical history is a good place to start. How long has he been sick?"

I swiped my hand across my eyes and took a deep breath, trying to regain control. A million lies flooded my brain. I could have told any one of them.

"From the day he was born."

We talked for a long time after that. I told her everything, or most things, anyway. I didn't tell her about Parvati, or my dream of becoming a doctor myself, or being a Devadasi. But I told her what Ma did. She asked many questions about Shami's birth. I said only that it was a home birth but I did my best to remember every illness he'd had since then and gave a faithful account. I told her we didn't have any place to cook proper meals. I was grateful when she accepted that and didn't ask for details. I told her Shami slept on the floor and let her figure out the significance of that. I'm not sure she could have imagined it, even if I'd explained. I didn't tell her we slept on the street, wherever I could find a place. I think she knew. Her raven eyes glistened with unshed tears. She seemed shocked by what I told her, as if she didn't live in Mumbai and drive by people living under bridges every day and see others digging through garbage to survive. She was like the people who took guided tours through our neighborhood, capturing our images with their cameras while failing to actually see us. We were no more real than a Bollywood film. Still, I was amazed by how stupid smart people could be.

Finally, she asked if she could test Shami's blood. I knew what she wanted to test it for. I told her what I'd told all the previous doctors: I had no money for the test, and it wouldn't matter anyway because we couldn't afford the drugs. She said there were ways to cover the cost if Shami was registered with an NGO. I'd heard about these NGOs that took children like Shami away from their families. They shoved all the sick children in big homes together, separated from everyone who loved them. How was that a better life for my brother? I agreed to talk it over with my mother. It was yet another lie.

I was on the point of leaving when a male doctor poked his head in the door. It startled me, not just because of the intrusion. I had the unsettling feeling that I knew him. I kept my back to him and crossed my arms over my chest so he couldn't see the school crest on my shirt. Was it possible I'd taken Shami to him in the past?

"Are you just about done here, Karuna? Our meeting has started."

"I'll be along shortly. You're on the board of Mercy House, aren't you? Do you know if there's any space for a new admission?"

I felt the doctor's eyes on my back but didn't turn.

"How old is he?" There was a pause. The question was directed at me.

"Almost two and a half," said the lady doctor.

"I'll look into it."

They were discussing putting Shami away as if it were as routine as prescribing a pill. The male doctor left, but a yawning gorge had opened inside me. The lady doctor and I were not on the same side.

She gave me another hug and for an instant I allowed myself to picture a life totally different from my own. But it wasn't my life.

As I stepped out into the heat and bustle of the swarming masses and joined a sweaty crush of people shoving each other for space on a bus, I was already planning which hospital we'd go to the next time Shami needed drugs.

Grace

I was not a maverick.

Whatever VJ thought, no amount of telling me it was good to be different could change nearly sixteen years of wanting to fit in. Alone in my bedroom that night I couldn't get Todd's comment out of my head. As much as I didn't like being called a slut, being called a loser was so much worse. *Slut* only described my recent behavior; it didn't define me. *Loser* was something else again. A loser was a person who couldn't make friends. Losers screwed up all the time and hurt those around them.

Until Todd said it, I'd never realized that, as insecure as I was, I didn't think of myself that way. I knew I was shy and had trouble making friends, was lousy at sports and was just an average student. But lots of kids are like that. Even my recent debacle had seemed like poor judgment, not a defining moment. I'd already taken steps to make sure I didn't screw up like that again.

So why was the word *loser* going around and around in my head? My nerves jangled as I stood up and walked to the window. I stared at the world below without seeing it. Was that what everyone thought of me? It had the ring of truth. I was the main reason my parents had stopped moving around. Kyle flourished no matter where we went. It was my social isolation they worried about.

I sat down on my bed and pulled up my leg to look at the word I'd carved into it the day before. I remembered the peace I'd felt when the task was finished. Though the wound still hurt, the word itself had lost a lot of its power. It didn't change Mom's disappointment in me, or my disappointment in myself, but it did make me feel more in control. I didn't want to do it again though—that would be crazy. Nevertheless my body vibrated with the effort of keeping still.

I pulled up my legs and wrapped my arms tightly around them, willing myself to calm down. Suddenly my phone beeped. I tried to ignore it. It had to be another hater. There was nothing to be gained from reading another cruel message but not reading it only made me dwell on it even more.

Finally, curiosity got the best of me. I got up to fetch my phone, hoping that at the very least, it would take my mind off cutting. I flipped to the message as I walked back to the bed.

U been quiet lately. Everything ok?

It was my brother.

I sat back down. Why was he texting me now? Had Dad told Kyle what I did?

U there grace?

Dad said you were having friend problems.

I knew it! I seethed.

Bosco stood up on the bed madly wagging his tail.

"How did you know it was Kyle?" I demanded. "I know you miss him but you're going to have to get used to the fact that it's just you and me now. He deserted us." It was an unfair thing to say. I felt guilty when Bosco sat down and cocked his head like he'd actually understood.

"I'm sure he's missing you too, Bosco," I said, scratching his ear before turning my attention back to the phone.

Im fine, I texted. Was asleep. Will call u tomorrow.

Would I call him tomorrow? And say what? If I told him about what was happening to me, I'd have to tell him what I'd done to provoke it. There was no way I could tell him that.

Ok, call anytime. Luv u sis.

I furiously wiped away the tears that had started streaming down my face. I'd managed not to cry today, up till now. I knew Kyle was just trying to be supportive, but reminding me how much I missed him wasn't helpful. If he'd been here maybe I would have found the courage to tell him everything. Though if he'd been here, probably none of this would have happened. I might have had a lot of years of feeling lonely and different but I'd never been bullied before, because no one would have dared mess with Kyle McClaren's little sister. Who knew how many kids over the years had wanted to tell me I was a loser but had only been deterred because of my perfect brother? Even VJ had said he was only being my friend to pay back Kyle's kindness. If it wasn't for Kyle, I would have been labeled a loser years ago. Kyle had been the only thing standing between me and the truth. I really was a loser.

I got up and went down the hall to the kitchen. Vanita was there doing the dishes. She eyed me curiously when I went straight to the cutlery drawer and pulled out the sharpest knife I could find.

"What are you looking for?" She came and stood next to me. "Do you want me to cut some fruit for you?"

"No, thanks." I liked Vanita but, like everyone, she treated me as if I were helpless. "I'm just working on a school project."

I returned to my bedroom and closed the door behind me. Bosco was sitting up on my bed giving me "the stare." It usually meant he wanted food, but if I didn't know better I'd have sworn he knew what I was planning.

"You can stare all you want but you're not going to stop me," I told him firmly. "I have to do this, Bosco. I promise it will be the last time."

He looked at the knife.

"I know what I'm doing. It will make me feel better."

The minute I sat on the bed and crossed my legs he leaped into my lap.

"Stop it, Bosco!"

I pushed him off and lined the knife up neatly under the first word. Bosco knocked the knife out of my hand as he clambered into my lap again.

"NO! Bad dog! I could have hurt you."

I got off the bed and fetched the knife from the floor. Dropping down to sit there, I was for once grateful that Bosco was too cowardly to jump down from the bed by himself. I felt the same sense of relief when I made the first cut. I owned the word now. It didn't own me.

When I was finished, I lay down on the bed and pulled Bosco into my arms, closing my eyes. Like meditative chanting, my leg throbbed with every beat of my heart. I fell asleep to the steady pulse of my own blood.

The next morning, I arrived at school to find a fresh coat of paint on my locker. Where *SLUT* had been the day before was a bright orange Post-it note telling me to go to Mr. Donleavy's room. I sighed as I pulled off the note and shoved it in my jeans pocket. I liked Mr. Donleavy, and I did want a chance to redeem myself, but I was the school loser. Did he really think I could provide any guidance to a younger girl?

Mr. Donleavy was standing at his whiteboard writing his quote for the day. He was that kind of teacher. You could tell he didn't teach because it was the only thing he could do. He really believed he was inspiring the world's future leaders.

Today his quote was: "Everyone thinks of changing the world, but no one thinks of changing himself." He added the author's name, Leo Tolstoy.

"Did you choose that one just for me, Mr. Donleavy?"

"Grace!" He gave me a huge smile. "Trust me, there are plenty of people who need to remember Tolstoy's wisdom, myself included. Have a seat and let's go over our plan for today."

I was pretty sure *our* plan meant *his* plan, but I was in no position to claim that I didn't need help in the planning department. The desks in Mr. Donleavy's classroom were arranged in a semicircle. I sat where I always did, nearest the door. Mr. Donleavy came over and perched on a desk nearby.

"I've made arrangements for us to go to the NGO this afternoon."

My heart started to pound. "That fast?"

"We're already almost four weeks into the term, Grace, and you still haven't earned any community service hours."

Fair point.

"Your parents have agreed that I'll take you today after school. I've had another student volunteer so you'll have some company. You need to be in the east parking lot by three forty-five."

There wasn't much left to say so I headed to class wondering who else had been roped into volunteering.

The rest of the day was relatively uneventful. I had only a few new hate messages on my phone, no doubt because I'd blocked virtually everyone. Unfortunately, it was a small school, and Madison was in most of my classes. I kept a low profile, something I used to be good at. Once, I accidentally caught her eye when I was leaving a class. She gave me a contemptuous look and whispered something to the girl next to her, but I kept walking as their laughter followed me.

In English, our teacher told us to get into groups to discuss a novel. As desks were shuffled and groups formed I found myself facing closed circles. It wasn't the first time I'd been left out that year, but it was the first time it felt deliberate. The teacher, perhaps because she knew about my problems with Madison and Kelsey, directed me to join three boys. This occasioned a round of "slut" coughing. I'm not sure which one of us was most embarrassed. In any case, the boys ignored me and I stared out the window. I spent some time wondering how everyone would react if they came to school the next day to discover I'd killed myself. No matter how hard I tried, I couldn't imagine anyone would care.

VJ turned up at my locker at the beginning of the lunch period. He was definitely committed to the ruse that we were a couple, though he spent the next forty minutes talking about Luca D'Silva, the hottest boy in school if you took VJ out of the running. I must have repeated one hundred times that I didn't think Luca was gay but, as VJ pointed out, I would have said the same thing about him not so long ago.

As the end of the day approached I felt more and more apprehensive. I wasn't good with new people at the best of times. The idea of going into the red-light district of Mumbai and trying to make friends with kids whose life experiences were beyond my imagination was terrifying. The fact that our only common link was that their mothers took their shirts off for money and I did it because I was spectacularly stupid seemed like a tenuous basis for a friendship. By the time I'd loaded my books into my locker, I'd concocted so many reasons why this was a bad idea that I actually felt ill.

I dragged myself to the back of the school, walking as slowly as I possibly could. I didn't think Mr. Donleavy would leave without me but it was worth a try. When I reached the parking lot he was waiting for me. I was only mildly surprised by the person he was with.

"Gracie," VJ called out, "what kept you?"

I didn't like to admit to myself how relieved I was to see him. I smiled.

"The stars must be aligned." VJ beamed back warmly. "She's smiling!"

"All right, troops, let's saddle up," said Mr. Donleavy.

"I'm sorry, Mr. D.," said VJ, mock-serious, "this just isn't going to work if you're going to impose your imperialist American culture. We are not conquering the Wild West but the Wild East!"

"VJ, don't make me regret letting you tag along."

"Not a chance, sir. I'm the only one who speaks Hindi and

Marathi, not to mention a bit of Kannada and Gujarati. You people would be lost without me. And I have an armed guard . . ."

"Who we agreed will follow in his own car."

"I wouldn't have it any other way. When the tires get slashed on this heap, we're going to need my ride."

Mr. Donleavy climbed into the front of the van, next to the driver, while VJ and I sat behind. The drive took close to an hour but VJ had no trouble keeping us entertained the entire trip with Bollywood gossip.

I wouldn't have noticed when we left the wide streets behind and entered the narrow laneways of Kamathipura except that we had to slow down to a crawl. There were so many motorcycles, beat-up old cars, snack carts, bullock carts, various huge wooden wagons, and such an assortment of cows, goats and the ubiquitous stray dogs and cats—not to mention people—filling every inch of space that we had to force them aside with our vehicle. At times we were defeated and we were the ones standing still, waiting for some room to inch into. Finally, the driver decided he'd driven us as close as we were going to get and pulled off to one side. In any other part of the city people would have honked at him. Where I lived the van might even have been towed. But in that neighborhood it was now just one more obstacle in a lane that was full of them.

The first thing that assaulted me on stepping out of the car was the awful smell. Though the source wasn't immediately clear, an open sewage canal on one side of the road could certainly have been part of it. Equally possible was the garbage strewed everywhere, and the occasional piles of goat and cow dung. We hadn't been walking two minutes before I noticed a child squatting at the side of the road relieving himself.

Mr. Donleavy must have caught the look on my face. "A lot of these people are homeless. They have no access to running water, electricity or toilets. Some of the girls you meet today will sleep on the street tonight."

"It's so congested. Why's it more crowded than the rest of Mumbai?"

"Kamathipura's a draw for the most impoverished. Migrant workers, beggars, thieves, drug addicts, gamblers, sex workers all make a home here and are accepted in a way they might not be in other parts of the city."

I looked around and for the first time noticed how many people had stopped what they were doing to stare at us. It must have been hard for them to be confronted by our evident wealth. How could they not feel resentful? I was glad I'd followed Mr. Donleavy's advice and left my schoolbag and phone in the car; though, come to think of it, if my phone got ripped off it wouldn't be a disaster.

Mr. Donleavy was already weaving his way around a cart selling some kind of greasy fried dough and heading for an open doorway.

"Ready?" I asked VJ.

"Always," he said.

15

Noor

Crocodile arms . . .

I waited for Parvati for over an hour outside our usual café at the train station. I'd come late and was worried I'd missed her. Our house was in an uproar because Lali-didi had disappeared. The night trade had just started and, as usual, Lali-didi was in great demand. Every night she had enough regular customers to meet her quota, but Pran forced her to take as many as turned up. They waited their turn in the lounge like passengers waiting for a train. No one knew how many customers she had each night. Only Binti-Ma'am saw the money that changed hands. She promised Lali-didi that one day soon her debt would be cleared, but everyone knew Binti-Ma'am was a liar. No one in our house cleared their debt while they were still young enough to fetch a high price.

Everyone in the house said Lali-didi was too young for the work. Prita-Auntie was particularly vocal. Lali-didi herself said little. Ma said she was resigned to her situation but I wasn't so sure. I saw the scars that snaked up her arm, horizontal lines, like the belly of a crocodile, and only on her left arm. Lali-didi was right-handed.

Her last day with us had seemed no different from the others. I'd been at school, so I didn't see her until the early evening. She sat on her bed making preparations for the night, lining her eyes with kohl and painting her lips. As always I felt a stab of anxiety as I watched the transformation from the girl that she was, little older than me, to the object that she became. For weeks I'd seen something die in her each time she went through this process, and every day less of her returned. She rarely spoke, never laughed; it was as if she was dead already.

Pran discovered her bed empty only when he was ushering in yet another man. They'd passed Shami and me in the downstairs hallway as we were leaving for the night. Pran's outcry drew me back. Her few possessions were in their usual place, as if she'd just stepped out to the latrine. Lali-didi didn't have the freedom to step out anywhere—and yet she had. Like a bird slipping through the bars of her cage, Lali-didi was gone without so much as a whisper. Of course, someone must have helped her. That much was undeniable, though no one was admitting to it.

Pran flew into a rage. Deepa-Auntie was his first suspect, not because she was the most likely but because he wanted her to be guilty. "I'll kill you!" he screamed, beating her until she was no longer able to rise from the ground. "Tell me where she's gone!"

Ma ordered me out of the house. I wanted to leave—I didn't want to witness any more—but I couldn't. I feared Pran would kill Deepa-Auntie. Finally Ma gave up trying to shoo me out and turned on Pran.

"Stop it, Pran," Ma commanded.

He raised his fist to her too but she didn't quail.

"That's enough," she said. "Deepa's too stupid to have planned a betrayal like this. What do you think she did, squeeze Lali through the window bars? Deepa was with a customer. She couldn't have helped."

"Keep out of it, Ashmita. This is none of your business."

"Isn't it? How do you know I didn't do it?"

"Because you're not a fool. You understand how things work, and you have too much to lose. You're already splitting your profits with my mother. In another year or two you'll have enough money to rent a room for your family."

"If I live that long," said Ma, giving him a steely look.

Ma talked more and more of her own death these days. I wished she would stop. She ate little, even when I skipped my own dinner so I could afford her favorite biryani.

"Deepa knows something," Pran insisted.

"She would have told you if she did. She's little more than a child. Do you really think she could hold out against a man like you?"

I almost laughed. Behind his back, Ma called Pran "the little brown monkey" because he danced to Binti-Ma'am's bidding.

"There will be trouble from this," Pran threatened.

He didn't say that the worst trouble would be for him. His ma was the brothel-keeper but they both worked for another man. Nishikar-Sir, the owner of our brothel, was the overlord of our world. Some say he owned twenty brothels in Kamathipura. We rarely saw him. The arrival of his black Mercedes was an event greeted with equal measures of awe and dread. Stories of his temper were exceeded only by those of his violence. He wouldn't let the loss of one of his most valuable girls go unpunished. As the enforcer in our home, Pran would be held accountable. I felt a shiver of anticipation and hoped I was around when the confrontation took place.

"Look what you've done to her face," said Ma, gesturing to Deepa-Auntie, who was lying on the floor quietly moaning. "How is it going to help you to damage the girl who is now your top earner?" Ma must have been really frightened for Deepa-Auntie. Otherwise she'd never have admitted Deepa-Auntie was more desired than herself.

"Clean her up and get her back to work," Pran snarled. "Everyone meets their quota tonight." He turned on his heel and disappeared down the ladder.

Ma and I rushed to Deepa-Auntie, who was struggling to sit up.

"Help her wash," ordered Ma.

"But what happened to Lali-didi?" I asked.

"Who can say?" said Ma, but a look passed between her and Deepa-Auntie. "The girl wouldn't have lasted much longer. We're well rid of her."

Deepa-Auntie leaned heavily on me as I got her to her feet and over to the ladder. I went down ahead of her and was relieved to find Shami exactly where I'd left him, sitting against the wall near the bottom rung. Deepa-Auntie moved slowly. She was favoring one foot and hunched over, cradling her chest. I hoped nothing was broken. I helped her hobble to the washroom.

As soon as the door was closed she quickly filled me in on the basics. "The customer I was with had really come to rescue

Lali. He's fallen in love with her and agreed to help her escape. She's going to live with him now."

"Did Ma help?" I was incredulous.

"Your ma planned the whole thing, Noor-baby. Lali wasn't strong enough for this life."

I helped her wash as quickly as I could but her pain was extreme. She must have had cracked ribs at the very least. I begged her to let me take her to a hospital but she refused. Her fear of Pran was far greater than her fear of a rib puncturing her lungs. It was more than an hour later before Shami and I were on our way again.

Standing outside the café, waiting for Parvati, I felt spent. The nervous energy that had seen me through the last hour had left me feeling hollow and weak. I just wanted to sleep but I didn't want to bed down without Parvati. Pran's recent viciousness was still vivid in my mind. The streets felt even more dangerous than usual. Without Parvati's reassuring bravado I felt exposed and vulnerable. I tried to think where she might have gone. We'd recently found a quiet spot behind the train station but I'd checked there before I came to the café. There was no sign of her.

"What do you think, Shami?" I looked down at Shami, who was sitting on the pavement at my feet. He was too little to have an opinion but his presence comforted me. "Where's Parvati? Should we try the bridge?"

"I want Par-di," said Shami.

"Me too," I said.

I hitched him up on my hip. His arms circled my neck and he rested his head against my chest. It didn't make sense to me that she'd go back to the shantytown where we were attacked, but it was the only place, other than our own street, where I knew she had friends. I was on the point of setting off when I heard a noise that froze me in place.

"Did you hear that, Shami?"

He cocked his head, his face scrunched with the effort of listening.

"Paru," he confirmed.

It certainly sounded like someone calling my name, but the sound was so faint it might have been buzzing from the fluorescent streetlamp above us.

"Noor," called the voice again. That time it was unmistakable.

I looked past the café to the narrow alley that separated it from the pawnshop next door. I wanted to run but my legs had gained twenty pounds in an instant. I was terrified of what I'd find. I put Shami down and took his hand. We followed the sound, running as quickly as we could. It felt as if we were moving in slow motion.

Rounding the corner of the building, we stepped into a dimly lit passageway. It was barely wide enough for the two of us to walk side by side, and it got darker with every step. Broken glass crunched under my sandals, and I almost slid on something with the distinctly foul smell of human waste. We moved cautiously, jumping at every shadow. Finally, we saw a mound on the ground that moved ever so slightly. We'd found her.

I cursed the darkness as I knelt beside her and tried to assess the damage. Curled up on her side, she raised one hand and touched my face, feeling my features like a blind person. That terrified me. Her blouse was ripped, exposing one shoulder. She had no other clothes on. I gagged at the metallic smell of blood.

"Noor." Her voice cracked. I could hear rather than see that she was crying. I took her hand and held it.

"Paru," I said. "Were you . . . ?" I couldn't finish my question. I didn't want to hear her answer.

"Yes. It was Suresh," she said. "And he wasn't alone."

"We need to get you to a doctor."

"No."

For just a moment I felt a searing flash of anger toward Lali. If I hadn't been delayed by her escape, I would have been on time to meet Parvati and this wouldn't have happened. Deepa-Auntie and now Parvati; how many more victims would Lali claim with her selfish flight? I immediately felt guilty. Lali couldn't have lasted much longer. But what could I do now for Parvati?

I pulled Parvati's head and shoulders onto my lap and scanned the dark alley for her clothes. I could see a pile of something some distance off.

Shami crouched beside me and touched Parvati's face.

"Is Par-di sick?" asked Shami, his voice etched with worry.

"She'll be fine," I said. "Go find her clothes, Shami."

He set off with the resolve of a three-year-old on a mission. He crouched down at the pile then straightened up and kept going. My heart stopped for a minute when he disappeared around a huge heap of refuse. Seconds later he reappeared with something in his hands and ran back to us.

"Don't run," I scolded. The damp, uneven ground was littered with all manner of dangerous things. I felt a surge of hatred for Parvati's attackers, who had discarded her in a dumping ground.

Shami handed me her clothing. Her pants were ripped as well. I wasn't sure they would cover her. For the moment I laid them on top of her. She moaned at even that light pressure. Shami crouched down beside us and patted Parvati's hair.

"It's okay, Par-di. Me and Noor-di are here."

She closed her eyes and gave the smallest of smiles, wincing with the effort.

"I know, baby," she said. "I'm okay now. Don't worry."

After a time her breathing became deep and regular and I realized she'd fallen asleep. Only then did Shami settle himself on the other side of me, curling against my side, with one arm draped around my waist. He too fell asleep. If I'd only had Aamaal, my world would have been complete, surrounded by the people I loved. Then I thought of Ma and felt bad because I'd so easily forgotten her. And what of Deepa-Auntie?

Though it was now the early hours of the morning, the noise from the street beyond our alley still echoed inside our narrow refuge—a refuge where my best friend had been thrown away like trash. In my head, I made a list of all the people I would take with me if I could disappear like Lali had. I'd start over someplace clean and safe, where young girls slept without fear, and children never went hungry or were wasted by sickness.

Finally the events of the night caught up with me. My determination to remain on guard faltered. I too gave in to sleep.

Not many hours later I awoke to the coldness of Parvati's absence. She hadn't gone far. She'd pulled on her pants and was several feet away, near the garbage where Shami had found them. She didn't notice I was awake, too intent on what she was doing. It was seconds before I realized what that was.

I leaped to my feet, startling Shami awake, and ran down the passageway, dropping to the ground beside her. I grabbed the fist that was doing the slashing and wrenched the broken glass from her hand. There was so much blood it was hard to tell how many gashes she'd already made.

She gaped at me wordlessly as if she shared my horror at her handiwork.

"No, Paru," I sobbed. I took off my dupatta and wrapped it tightly around her crocodile arm.

Grace

We entered the open doorway of a narrow, nondescript, two-story wooden building. The single thing that set it apart was a small hand-painted sign above the door that read "Sisters Helping Sisters." I was glad to leave behind the heat and chaos of the street outside, until I discovered the temperature inside was easily several degrees hotter, and the cacophony of voices was ear splitting. Even more overwhelming was being immediately swallowed up by a pack of street urchins.

Altogether, there were perhaps thirty children. From their clothes, I thought they were all girls, though it was hard to tell. Several had shaved heads. Most of them were dressed in salwar kameez, though a few wore bright frilly frocks and still others were in school uniform. Their clothes looked worn but relatively clean. They ranged in age from three or four years old to perhaps ten or eleven. They were desperately thin in the arms and legs; many had protruding bellies. I knew enough to understand this was a sign of malnutrition and not good health. It took me several minutes to realize that, amid the cacophony, several were shouting in English: *How are you?* and *What is your name?* I glanced at VJ, who was removing his shoes while carrying on multiple conversations at the same time. I recognized a bit of the Hindi, but he must have been speaking other languages as well because sometimes I couldn't pick up a single word. Mr. Donleavy, who'd preceded us inside, was nowhere to be seen.

VJ carried his shoes to a large pile of sandals, mostly little ones, on one side of the entrance, so I took off my own sandals and did the same. We walked farther into the room, dimly lit by a single fluorescent bulb, and paused to allow our eyes time to adjust. There wasn't a single window or any source of ventilation but the open doorway.

The children led, or more accurately dragged, us over to a metal ladder that went straight up to an open hatch in the ceiling. Since it was the only place Mr. Donleavy could have gone, we started climbing. I went first, eager to get away from the noise. I hoped the children wouldn't follow. I already felt overwhelmed.

I saw Mr. Donleavy as soon as I emerged through the hatch. He was sitting on a chair, talking to three women, all Indian, in a tiny office partitioned off from the rest of the room by a half-wall. One of the women was sitting in the only other chair. The other two were awkwardly hunched over behind her. The ceiling was too low for them to stand upright.

"Grace, there you are," said Mr. Donleavy.

I stepped through the hatch and kept moving to allow VJ to follow. I was dismayed to see he wasn't alone; the children were right behind him. The upstairs room quickly became even more crowded than the downstairs had been.

Since the only other option was crouching, VJ and I plopped down on the cement floor in the room outside the office. Though the floor was stained, it was spotlessly swept. The children seemed to have some sense of what was happening. After much shoving to establish who would have the privilege of sitting next to us, they all sat down as well. I had one on either side, and they pressed up against me, even though there was room for them to have a bit of space. One grabbed my hand and held on to it. The other reached up and stroked my ponytail. My hair has always been a mousy brown, definitely not worthy of the admiration she was according it.

The upstairs room was at least ten degrees hotter than it had been downstairs, and again there was no ventilation. The sweat poured off me. VJ, on the other hand, was as fresh and dry as when we'd arrived, and happily chatting with the children.

"I wouldn't have pegged you for a kid-lover," I said, trying not to sound as jealous as I was feeling.

"Come on, Gracie, in a world full of conspiracies, malice and deceit, how can you possibly not like children? They're the only honest creatures on the planet."

I had to admit I'd never thought about it that way. I gave the little girls now leaning against me a tentative smile and was rewarded with two exuberant gap-toothed grins in return.

Mr. Donleavy came out of the office with the women and they joined us on the floor. I wouldn't have believed there was space for close to thirty children, two teenagers and four adults.

"This is Miss Chanda," said Mr. Donleavy, introducing one

of the women. "She's going to tell us a little bit about their concept for the program."

Miss Chanda didn't look much older than a teenager. She wasn't beautiful, but every time she smiled, every single kid in the room smiled back. You could tell they worshiped her.

"I want to thank you so much for volunteering," she began. "I'd like to introduce you to one of the girls who will explain what we do." She looked across the room at an older girl. "Fatima, can you tell us a little bit about yourself?"

"My name is Fatima," said the girl, and laughed nervously when she realized she'd just told us the one thing we already knew. "I'm fourteen years old and I like school very much." I was shocked to discover she was that old, and I looked more closely at the other girls. They were all so small. Perhaps I'd misjudged their ages.

"My mother says I should be going to school but sometimes we don't have money for books and . . ." She hesitated and looked at Miss Chanda, as though she wasn't sure how much detail she should go into. I was willing to bet the list of what her family didn't have money for was a long one.

"One of the things we provide here is funds to cover any school-related costs the girls have, as well as meals and some- times night shelter," said Miss Chanda. "Why don't you tell them how long you've been coming to SHS?"

"I am coming to Sisters Helping Sisters since I am three years old. My mother didn't to let me sleeping in the . . . the . . ." She looked at Miss Chanda again.

I was shocked at how good her English was, though I sus- pected that was why she'd been chosen to be spokesperson.

"Do all the children speak English?" I asked Miss Chanda.

"They all speak a little. Some, like Fatima, study in English-language schools, so they speak more. We'll only match you up with girls you can communicate with." She gave VJ a worried look. "I'm afraid we won't be able to give you a girl to mentor. Many of our girls have already been molested, so we're careful not to put them in vulnerable situations. But you're more than welcome to work here at the center in our after-school tutoring program."

"I'd be happy to do that," said VJ smoothly, not mentioning that the girls were in no danger of sexual advances from him. "If it's all right, I can help Grace with whoever she's paired with."

Miss Chanda looked relieved to have that settled. "Great. Then let's talk about how this will be structured. Today I'm going to introduce you to a few girls and give you a chance to get to know each other. At the end of the session, I'll ask you if there was a particular girl you felt you could help."

"This sounds just like speed dating," said VJ. "What fun! I've always wanted to try that!"

Miss Chanda gave him a stern look. "We're going to get out some paper and pencils. Our girls love to draw. It will help them relax and give you a chance to chat at the same time."

"What happens when we've found the girl we want to be paired with?" I asked.

"We ask for a minimum of two hours a week. Our girls have had little experience of life outside the brothel. Most of their mothers were sold against their will, and in spite of that, many have been disowned by their families. For the girls who grow up here, the brothel life is all they know, and there's often pressure to follow their mothers into the trade."

I looked at the sweet faces of the girls surrounding me. I

could tell Mr. Donleavy was watching me carefully. If he was wondering whether it had been a good idea to bring me here, he had reason to be concerned. There was no question these girls and their mothers needed help, but what could VJ and I do? We were just kids ourselves.

"Well, I don't know about the rest of you," said VJ, "but I can't wait to get started. Where are the art supplies?"

Noor

Coming first . . .

In the months after Parvati's rape I threw myself into my studies. Only at school could I pretend everything was the way it had been before. Parvati had become a ghost. Suresh hadn't stopped with the single rape; he took her every night he could find her. Together we hid from him, constantly changing where we slept. Still, there were days I got home from school and Parvati was nowhere to be found. On those days, I knew he'd found her first.

In the middle of September every year, regular classes ceased and we wrote our first-semester exams. Just before we broke for the holiday, the grades were posted. My friends and I always met at school to look at our grades together. For many children, this was a time of great anxiety and disappointment. For me, it was a rare time when I didn't feel like a fake. I always took firsts in English, Math, and Biology. Several times I'd taken firsts in Chemistry as well.

None of my schoolmates knew where I came from. Over the years I'd created a family history of such complexity, with so many embellishments, that to them it had the familiarity of truth. I retold the lies so often that at times I almost believed them myself. My classmates knew all about my father, the mid-level civil servant, my mother, the former actress who gave up fame to marry him, and of course my siblings. It was my one disappointment that I couldn't enhance their attributes, but Aamaal already went to the same school, and I had every hope that someday Shami would as well. Aamaal had been coached to maintain our fiction. With her sweet face and enormous, thickly fringed eyes, people were always inclined to believe her. They never suspected that in addition to being beautiful she was a skilled liar.

The one time I felt closest to my fictionalized self was when I looked at my exam results. No one would have believed that the girl who was awarded so many prizes came from a brothel in Kamathipura. Even I found it hard to reconcile. My two selves—the school-going girl and the daughter of a sex worker—felt like two separate people, awkwardly inhabiting one body. I was like a *hijra*, not one thing and not the other, but a third thing entirely, unique and not happily so.

Gajra and I stood with a group of our friends near the school gate discussing our results.

"I knew you'd sweep the awards," said Gajra, squeezing my arm excitedly. Her pleasure was so complete you might have thought she'd achieved the results herself. Gajra had never taken a first in anything in her life, though her kindness outshone all my achievements. I could never understand why being a truly good person was overlooked when it came to handing out medals. It seemed to me it must be much more challenging, considering how few people managed it.

"Of course she did well," said Sapna, whose scores were never far behind mine. "Her father does nothing but sit at home and coach her. My father's a doctor. He can't be spending every minute helping me."

"Which is why you have hours of paid tutoring every evening," said Kiran, Sapna's best friend and fiercest competitor. I actually think their friendship survived only because I so often snatched the wins from both of them.

"Well, it appears to have paid off. You beat me in only one subject this year," said Sapna.

"The year's not over yet," Gajra intervened. "There's still plenty of time for everyone to get good results. The important thing is to improve our own scores."

"Tell that to my father," said Sapna darkly.

"I think you're going to have to tell him yourself," said Kiran, forgetting their recent fight and slinging her arm around Sapna's shoulder. She nodded to the other side of the street, where Sapna's father was just emerging from a parked car.

I recognized him the minute I saw him, though it had been well over a year since he'd come into Shami's examining room. That was why he'd looked so familiar. It wasn't because I'd already taken Shami to him before.

I looked away, hoping he hadn't noticed me. The danger of my identity being discovered was far worse than just being caught in a lie. Ours was a fee-paying school, and a good one. I would be expelled if it was discovered that my mother was a sex worker. If he remembered that I had an HIV-infected baby brother he'd make the connection in an instant, especially considering we were only blocks from my red-light neighbor-hood. I said a fervent prayer that he wouldn't recognize me in my school uniform. Then it occurred to me that I'd been in uniform the last time he'd seen me. I started to sweat.

"Come on, Gaj. Let's see if any of our teachers are in their classrooms so we can wish them a happy midyear break." I took Gajra's hand.

"Okay, but we must say hello to Sapna's father first," she said.

I reluctantly let her hold me back. It would have drawn more attention if I'd insisted on rushing off, now that she'd made the point that we must greet him.

I toyed with the books I was holding and told myself I was being ridiculous. To the best of my knowledge I'd never spoken to Sapna's father before, or since, the hospital visit. He must have seen hundreds, even thousands of kids like Shami and me. But how many of them went to his daughter's school?

I knew from Sapna that her parents' expectations of her were high. They came from more modest backgrounds than many of the girls at our school. Ironically, her real-life story wasn't so different from the fake life I'd created. Her father had raised her family's status through his own determination and hard work, but it had taken them only so far. His greatest ambition was to see his children marry into the wealthy, more established families who were happy to call on him when their health was poor but would never welcome him at their dinner tables. Getting his children into the top universities was his only hope of further elevating their status.

"Darling," he shouted grandly when he was still several feet from the gate. "How did you do? How many firsts?"

I feigned absorption in my Biology text. For once, I felt sorry for Sapna. She wasn't the nicest girl, often bossy and opinionated, but it couldn't have been easy living up to such high expectations. Being fatherless had its advantages. At least there was no one to embarrass me in front of my friends.

Sapna didn't answer. I snuck a peek at her and was horrified to see she was hanging her head, close to tears. Kiran had both arms around her now and Gajra had stepped closer, supporting her from the other side.

I tried to think of something I could say that would take the spotlight off her, though the last thing I wanted was to draw attention to myself. I felt a pang of guilt at my own role in her humiliation and scowled at the ground, willing her father to go away. He stood on his side of the gate, waiting for her reply.

"I only took first in Geography," Sapna mumbled, her voice so low I wouldn't have been able to understand her if I hadn't already known her results.

"What was that? Speak up, Sapna."

I shot her a sympathetic look.

"You didn't get firsts in any of the sciences? After all the money we spent on tutors?" She didn't answer. What could she say?

"Aniket Bihar took the first in Physics," I said, louder than I'd intended. "His father is Dilip Bihar. Perhaps you've heard of him?" I added the last comment knowing full well it was provocative. Aniket came from probably the richest family in our school, just the kind of connection Sapna's father hoped to secure.

"I see." He scrutinized me as he might a perplexing rash. "I've forgotten your name."

"Noor Benkatti."

"And how well did you do, Noor Benkatti?"

Was it only my imagination that his tone held a subtle threat? My heart pounded, certain I'd been found out.

"She took firsts in everything," said Sapna. I understood that, though she was exaggerating, she wasn't trying to make things worse. In the subjects that mattered to her father, I had taken firsts.

"Ah," said her father. He unhooked the gate and stepped through. There was now less than a foot separating us. My stomach roiled.

"I believe we've met." He let that sink in before he continued. "I believe your mother works in the neighborhood, isn't that correct?"

My skin went hot and cold in quick succession as bile gushed up my throat. It was as bad as I'd feared. The lady doctor had told him everything.

"No, sir," I said, "you've mistaken me for someone else. My mother is a housewife."

"You have a little brother," he continued, ignoring my denial. "He's very sick."

I turned away just in time to fall to my knees and vomit in a patch of grass. I was surrounded immediately by solicitous friends. I was fortunate that they liked nothing better than a bit of drama, and I was certainly giving it to them. Hands reached for me and practically lifted me off the ground. I was relieved to see Sapna's father had stepped back. He watched through narrowed eyes as I was hustled away. We were almost at the school building before I realized it was not just Gajra but Sapna supporting me.

"Thanks." She smiled. "That was a tad dramatic. Still, if you're ever in a jam, I promise I'll do my best to fake an emergency to get you out of it."

I gave her a weak grin. "Anything for a friend."

The next hour was a blur. I was taken to the nurse's office. She tried to make me lie down but I was more jittery than I'd ever been on exam day. I knew who he was and he knew me. The only question was what he would do about it. I tried to calm myself with the idea that he was a doctor. Surely, he wouldn't be so unkind as to get me expelled. But Sapna had made no secret of her father's ambitions. He'd clawed his way out of the muck and demanded only the best for his children and from them. The last thing he'd want was to have his daughter associating with the low-caste daughter of a sex worker. The fact that I also surpassed her academically only added to my peril.

I walked home on shaky legs. As soon as I reached my street I went looking for Parvati. It never occurred to me to talk to Ma. I knew that somehow she'd blame me, and there was always the chance she'd pull me out of school. My fear that my school days were numbered had intensified since Parvati had fallen under Suresh's control. So many of my neighborhood friends were already doing sex work; how could I be far behind?

I didn't even bother to change out of my uniform. I searched for close to an hour. Other than hearing multiple reports that she'd last been seen heading for Bhatti Road, no one had a clue where she was.

Tired and grimy, I finally went home. I wasn't looking forward to the fight I was bound to have. I was late for my chores and Ma would be furious I hadn't at least come home to change out of my school clothes. Her pride in my uniform, visible proof of which school I attended, was almost as great as her pride in my medals. I reluctantly clambered up the ladder to our room, only to find Ma wasn't there. Deepa-Auntie was sitting on her bed braiding Aamaal's hair. Prita-Auntie was asleep on her own bed, an open movie magazine draped over her face. The small black-and-white TV, perched on a high shelf in one corner of the room, was on as usual, though no one was watching it. Shami played in the corner with Deepa-Auntie's basket of hair clips.

"Where's Ma?" I whispered, after greeting Deepa-Auntie and giving my siblings a hug. Prita-Auntie could get riled up almost as fast as Ma if you disturbed her "beauty rest," as she called it, though she was about as beautiful as a plucked chicken, even on her best day.

"She got called to your school," said Deepa-Auntie. A worried frown creased her unlined face. "Did something happen today? Weren't you getting your exam results?"

My heart plummeted as I sank down on Ma's bed. I didn't know what to say. I wanted to tell her the whole story so she could reassure me there was nothing to worry about but I knew that wasn't true. The coincidence was too great. What other possible reason could Ma have for going to the school if it wasn't provoked by Sapna's horrible father? Ma never went to my school, not when I won medals, not when there were parent meetings, not ever.

"Did she say why she was going to school?" I asked.

Deepa-Auntie shook her head. "Do you know why?"

I nodded and told her the whole story.

"We can't be certain. Maybe your ma went to school for another reason," said Deep-Auntie.

Prita-Auntie rolled over. Her dupatta slid to the floor as she fastened me with a death stare.

"Aamaal, go get Prita-Auntie some tea," I ordered quickly, pulling some coins from my pocket.

Deepa-Auntie had only finished one braid but Aamaal scrambled off the bed. She had no more desire to see Prita-Auntie's temper than we did.

"Wait," growled Prita-Auntie before Aamaal could make it to the hatch. "Take some money out of my box and buy me some masala kheema. Make sure you get it from Basheer on the corner, the old Muslim. Don't buy it from that young donkey that's set up next to him. He'd cheat you as soon as look at you, and he drips his snotty nose right in his mix. You can tell him I said that."

She barked out a few more directives as Aamaal crawled under her bed to rummage in the tin box where Prita-Auntie kept all her worldly possessions, and at least one dead baby, if local gossip was to be believed. Finally Aamaal emerged, triumphantly clutching a hundred-rupee note.

"Make sure you bring back the change" was Prita-Auntie's parting shot.

"Now, what's this nonsense I'm hearing about Ashmita being called in to school?" Prita-Auntie moved to the head of her bed and heaved her bulk heavily into a sitting position, leaning back against the wall. She closed her eyes again. "I can feel you staring at me, mutton-breath. When you've done this work for as many years as I have, you'll enjoy a drink or two as well, even if you do suffer for it the next day."

It wasn't clear if she was talking to Deepa-Auntie or me. We exchanged nervous looks.

"Noor-baby has run into some problems with a doctor she met on one of Shami's hospital visits," said Deepa-Auntie. "He may have told the school who she is. Ashmita's been called in to speak with the principal. We don't know for sure that was why they called her in though."

"Of course the doctor has told on her, turnip-brain. She's a bright child, a good deal brighter than his own children, I'll wager. He won't be able to stand it. A prostitute's daughter, and a dark one at that. It's against the whole order of the universe." She opened her eyes and fixed her glare on Deepa-Auntie. "Get me a drink, a real drink. I need to figure this out."

"But we don't know yet what the school will do, Prita-ji," said Deepa-Auntie.

Prita-Auntie snorted in disgust. "How long have you lived in this country, Deepa? And you still haven't figured out the first thing about it! A rich doctor exposes the school's top student as the daughter of a sex worker. What do think the school is going to do? If Noor were a stupid child she might have some hope of being allowed to stay. All those rich parents would smile their pitying smiles and pat themselves on the back for being so broad-minded. But our Noor is the top student. They won't be able to get rid of her fast enough."

Deepa-Auntie hung her head. I hopped off Ma's bed and went over to sit with her on hers. Shami, catching the mood of the room, came over and crawled into my lap.

"They'll ask Noor to leave school," predicted Prita-Auntie. "Just you wait."

"Isn't there something we can do?" asked Deepa-Auntie.

"There's nothing you can do. You're not even from this country," said Prita-Auntie sternly. Though she didn't mean to be unkind, Deepa-Auntie looked stricken. "I will take care of it. You can be sure our Noor isn't going to get kicked out of school until her mother decides it's time for her to leave."

With that, she resolutely stood up and reached for her kurta, pulling it over her head. "Get up, Noor, you're coming with me."

"Should I could come too?" asked Deepa-Auntie hopefully.

"Just because you're allowed out of the house now, that doesn't mean you're of any use to us," said Prita-Auntie. "Stay with the children."

"Good luck, Noor," Deepa-Auntie said as I followed Prita-Auntie to the hatch.

I waited while Prita-Auntie lowered herself through. If she'd been out of earshot, I would have reminded Deepa-Auntie that being Nepali hadn't stopped her from helping Lali-didi escape. She was far from the useless creature everyone made her out to be. Then it occurred to me that being thought useless was probably the only thing that had stopped Pran from killing her.

I ran back and gave her a quick hug before leaving.

18

Grace

I don't know what we would have done without VJ. I tried to talk to the few girls who spoke English but the conversation remained stilted and limited. I wasn't sure if it was the cultural difference or the language. I just knew they didn't want to speak to me. With him they were voluble and uninhibited. It surprised me, given what Miss Chanda had said about their bad experiences with men. Clearly they could overcome that in the presence of a cute, not to mention famous, boy.

Mr. Donleavy had just told us our time was almost up when we heard loud voices from the floor below. Someone sounded angry. Too late, it occurred to me that we were trapped in that tiny windowless room, in a neighborhood that most Mumbaikars would never dare venture into.

Miss Chanda crouch-walked double time to the ladder. All of the other adults, including Mr. Donleavy, followed.

"Do you think we should stay up here?" I asked VJ.

"If there's trouble, we'd be safer down there, where we can slip out the door."

He went first and I followed, though a couple of kids squeezed in ahead of me.

The room at the bottom of the ladder was packed. I had to push myself between several unfamiliar women to get off the ladder.

A fleshy woman with a fierce look about her was shouting loudly at one of the NGO staff. There was a palpable feeling of discontent among the audience she'd brought with her. The NGO staff were looking nervous. I almost didn't notice the young girl standing next to her. She was making every effort to back away from the argument, but there was nowhere for her to go. Her obvious desire to melt into the background was such a familiar emotion that I felt immediate empathy. In fact, her look of embarrassment and distress was so painfully reminiscent of the way I'd been feeling almost constantly for the past few days that I wanted to go to her. Slowly I worked my way through the crowd.

I couldn't understand what the argument was about. They weren't speaking English. The big woman was doing most of the talking. She seemed to be demanding something that Miss Chanda wouldn't agree to.

I reached the girl and tried to catch her eye. She was staring resolutely at her feet. I doubted she spoke English, but she was in a school uniform and looked a little older than most of the girls upstairs, so I figured it was worth a try.

"Is that your mom?" I asked.

She looked up in surprise.

"No," she said gruffly, and looked down again. Though it

wasn't a response that encouraged conversation, I'd just spent the past hour feeling expendable, and here was a girl who seemed as uncomfortable as I was.

"What's she shouting about?" I persisted.

She glanced up again and away. I wasn't sure if she was considering her answer or ignoring me. She was very thin, like most of the girls, with watchful, intelligent eyes.

"Why are you here?" she finally asked.

It was my turn to hesitate. The truth was, I wasn't sure myself. The past hour had reinforced my skepticism that I could be helpful to these girls. While the little ones were friendly, the older ones, the girls I was supposed to connect with, had no interest in talking to me. I couldn't imagine mentoring any of them.

"I have no idea," I said honestly.

She smiled sympathetically and nodded in the direction of the angry woman. "She is asking them to help me stay in school."

"Well, I guess we have that in common." I smiled back.

"Your school is saying you must leave? What did you do?" She sounded genuinely intrigued.

Having started down this path of honesty, I found myself stuck. As much as I didn't want to admit the truth, I didn't want to lie to her.

"I took a picture of myself without my shirt on and sent it to someone I thought was a boy I knew, and he, or someone, sent it to every kid in the school. They even printed up a few hard copies and posted them around the halls."

She giggled.

"It really wasn't funny."

She giggled again.

"Still not funny." I tried to sound stern but fell short, mainly because I was shocked to discover my own spirits had lifted at her reaction. Maybe someday even I would see the humor in what I'd done.

"Okay," I said, "fair is fair. I told you mine. Now you have to tell me what you did."

"I got first in all my subjects."

"Wow, your school is tough. In my school, the worst you'd get for good grades is a suspension."

She laughed outright. Her English was excellent and I'd made her laugh. My spirits rose higher.

Together, we watched the adults for a few minutes. Their discussion wasn't showing any signs of calming down. The angry woman was practically spitting she was so mad, and several of her friends were throwing in their own comments. I was worried for Miss Chanda.

"What did you really do?" I asked.

"My ma is a sex worker."

"I figured that."

She looked offended.

"Only because you're here," I said quickly.

She nodded. "The school found out about my ma."

"So?"

"They do not want the daughter of a sex worker in their school."

"Too bad. Just refuse to leave."

"It is not like that. They can make trouble. My ma does not have an identity card. She does not have a birth certificate. And my birth certificate is fake. I have no right to be in the school."

"That's crazy."

She shrugged.

"Well, then the rules need to change," I said stoutly.

She gave me a look like I'd just suggested we should throw up a high-rise across the road to solve homelessness.

"Hello," said VJ, suddenly materializing beside us. He extended his hand to the girl. "I'm VJ Patel. Yes, that VJ Patel. And who might you be?" He gave her his best magazine-cover smile.

I thought, even in her current circumstances, her heart must have skipped just a little. If so, she hid it well. In fact, she looked at his hand as if it were a dead rat. After a delay that would have embarrassed most people, though it did nothing to shake VJ's confidence, she took it for about a second.

"Noor," she said. She added her surname after an extended deliberation. "Benkatti."

"Noor Benkatti," said VJ warmly. "It's a pleasure to meet you!"

"So why have you come to Sisters Helping Sisters?" I asked when it was clear that Noor wasn't going to respond to VJ. "Are you a member?"

She cut a look at VJ and crossed her arms. I wished he'd leave us alone. Instead, he shot her another winning smile. She glowered back but finally answered.

"I am not a member, but sometimes the NGOs can stop the schools from making us leave."

"Her school's going to kick her out," I explained to VJ.

"Really?" exclaimed VJ cheerfully. "I go for years not meeting a single interesting person and then I meet two rebels in one week. Isn't life unexpected?"

"So, if the NGO speaks to the school they'll let you stay?" I asked, elbowing VJ in the ribs.

"I said *sometimes*."

"We don't need the NGO," said VJ. "Just tell me who to pay off."

"My ma does not know I am here," said Noor.

I could tell by the way she said this that it was significant information. I'd actually forgotten that the woman with her wasn't her mom.

"Is your mom sick?" I asked hesitantly.

"I could pay the medical bills as well," said VJ.

"My ma hates the NGOs," said Noor.

"Oh." I didn't really understand. Even if her mom didn't like NGOs, surely she'd make use of them under the circumstances. "So . . . ?" I prompted.

"The NGO lady says they cannot help me because I am not in their program."

"Can't you join?"

"My ma would never allow it. Prita-Auntie, the lady who brought me, wants the NGO to talk to my school anyway."

"Do you want to be in the program?" asked VJ. I could tell he was hatching something.

"I want to be in school. If I have to be in a program for them to talk to my school . . ." She trailed off. "Ma will never agree. She will take me out of school before she will allow me to come here. Ma says the NGOs think they are better than us. They waste our time teaching useless things like sewing and Mehndi."

"Mehndi?" I asked.

"Henna design," said VJ. "Noor, if you take Mehndi, can I sign up with you?" he added.

I glared at him, while Noor looked at him curiously. Even I knew that only girls did Mehndi.

"Ma is proud," Noor continued, as if she was explaining to herself as much as me. "She comes from a tradition where sex work was part of a religious duty."

I tried not to let the shock show on my face but that had to be one of the strangest things I'd ever heard. "Religious?"

"Devadasi," said VJ. "I'll explain it to you later. It's positively medieval."

Noor scowled at VJ. "It goes back a long time to when women like my ma were given to the temple to serve the priest. At that time, it was not only for sex. Devadasi women had many talents. Ma is not proud of being a sex worker but she is not ashamed."

"So, let's just recap, if I may," said VJ, holding up his fingers as he itemized his points. "Noor has to join the program but can't actually darken the door of this building as someone in the neighborhood is bound to see her and spill the beans. Gracie has to find a teen she can mentor, which isn't going to be easy since the girls here aren't keen on her."

I started to object but he raised his hand and continued. "Sorry, darling, but you know it's true. So, I have the solution."

VJ stepped away from us and raised both hands in the air. "Ladies, attention, please," he shouted over the babble of voices. "We've solved the problem."

Shockingly, everyone actually did quiet down.

"Grace and Noor have discovered a budding kinship. They give true meaning to the idea of sisters helping sisters . . ."

"Get to the point," I groused.

He gave me a wounded look before continuing. "They're going to meet at least once a week, for the requisite bonding experiences, but they will never meet here, so there's no need to get Noor's mom's permission. Should anyone ask, we say only that Grace is Noor's new friend. Are we all in agreement? Can I have a show of hands?"

There were several minutes of stunned silence. VJ repeated his suggestion in Hindi.

"Is this what you want to do, Grace?" asked Mr. Donleavy.

I didn't even have to think about it. "If Noor agrees."

I looked down in surprise when I felt Noor slip her hand into mine.

19

Noor

The foreigners . . .

Parvati and I waited on the corner, at the end of our lane, for the foreigners. Shami was asleep in my arms. As usual he had a fever. It wasn't too high, though his breathing was raspy and labored. I'd stolen some of Binti-Ma'am's alcohol that morning. An alcohol-soaked rag was wrapped tightly around his chest.

Aamaal picked through a rubbish heap across the street from us. I scolded her whenever she accidentally picked up broken glass or syringes, though she rarely did. Aamaal had learned quickly how to avoid the dangers of our world. Most days she amassed a small bag of recyclables, carefully sorted, to sell to the rag picker when his cart rattled by. I let her keep what she earned. We could have used the money but she wouldn't have stuck with it if she'd had to share. It was worth it just to keep her busy.

"Are you sure they can be trusted?" asked Parvati, for perhaps the tenth time.

A lot had changed in the months since Parvati's rape, not the least of which was Parvati herself. She'd always been distrustful of strangers; that was just common sense in a community where most of the girls and women we knew had been forced into sex work. But her spark of mischief had withered.

"You can't count on them to help you. Foreigners are as different from us as elephants." Parvati rhythmically thumped Shami's back as she talked. She was as familiar with the tricks for loosening the mucus in his lungs as I was. "Elephants act tame for years and then one day they crush their masters to death. People think the attacks are unprovoked but elephants have long memories. They take revenge for things that happened long ago, sometimes in a previous life. Foreigners are like that—unpredictable."

I squeezed Parvati's shoulder. I knew what was really troubling her. "We'll find a way to get you away from Suresh. We don't need the foreigners for that."

Parvati self-consciously put her left arm behind her back, as if I hadn't already noticed the fresh cuts. I had tried to talk Parvati into asking Chanda-Teacher for help but I couldn't convince her she wouldn't be arrested for prostitution. We'd both heard stories about the prisons where they incarcerated underage sex workers who'd been "rescued." The conditions were so bad that only last year a group of girls had scaled the thirty-foot fence surrounding their "rescue home" and broken their legs in the long, desperate drop to freedom.

"What if the foreigners try to kidnap you?" asked Parvati.

I had explained the deal I'd struck with the NGO, but Parvati refused to believe that friendship with a foreigner was necessary to prevent my being expelled from my own school. I still felt raw when I thought of the teachers I'd loved who'd tried to get rid of me. I wondered if any of them had argued to let me stay before Chanda-Teacher spoke to them.

Chanda-Teacher tried to comfort me by saying that many of my teachers were even more impressed with my academic success when they learned of my background, but that made me feel worse. It was like everyone expected me to be stupid or lazy just because my mother was a sex worker. Didn't they know it was because of my mother that I studied so hard? Ma suffered to send me to school. The teachers had things completely backwards.

"I have to do this, Paru."

"I still don't understand what the foreigners want."

I didn't have time to answer as just then a gleaming silver SUV turned into our lane and stopped. I glanced back at our house to where Adit was leaning on the wall out front. He'd followed me outside. In the old days I would have invited him along but we weren't friends anymore. Adit said he had no time to waste with girls. I'd heard he was working in one of the gambling houses, running errands. I prayed he wouldn't tell Ma what I was up to. It made me nervous, the way he watched me.

"I'll let you do the talking," said Parvati.

I hid a smile. I doubted Parvati's English would have been up to doing the talking and it was me the foreigners were coming to meet, not her.

"If I nudge you," she continued, "it means there's something suspicious going on and we must make an excuse and leave."

I gave her a solemn nod. I couldn't admit that secretly I hoped the white girl was serious about being my friend. Parvati would have said I was foolish. Even worse would have been to share my hope that perhaps the foreigner understood, even more than Parvati, that my too-dark skin and my mother's work weren't the whole story of who I was. The white girl didn't come from a world where people were judged by the caste they were born into.

The car doors opened and suddenly she was there in front of me. Vijender Patel climbed out on the other side. Parvati gasped. I hadn't told her about Vijender. There was no way she would have agreed to spend the day with him. The only people Parvati mistrusted more than foreigners were film stars. Every once in a while they showed up in our neighborhood, taking photos of themselves handing out cheap toys to the poor children, which was us. They always promised they were going to make our lives better but the promises were broken as quickly as the toys.

Vijender came round the car and again held out his hand to me. This time I didn't let my nerves show. I shook it and politely introduced him to Parvati.

"Pleased to meet you, Parvati," he said. "Will you be joining us today?"

I wasn't sure what he meant by *joining him*, since we were just going to sit in a local café.

"Hi, Noor," said Grace. "It's nice to see you again."

I was reassured to have the same good feeling about her as before.

Aamaal raced over from the rubbish heap and leaped on VJ Patel. She must have recognized him from billboards or TV commercials. I would have smacked her for her boldness if we'd been alone.

"Hello," laughed VJ, pretending he liked nothing better

than little girls leaping onto his back. He pranced around in a circle for a moment and whinnied like a horse. It was funny and got us through the awkwardness, but she was still going to get a scolding later.

"And who might you be, young sir?" asked VJ, speaking in Hindi to Shami, who had just woken up.

"Shami," said Shami. He wasn't impressed by film stars.

"Would you like to climb aboard as well?" asked VJ, leaning toward us.

Shami shook his head and stuck his thumb in his mouth. I pulled it out and kept hold of his hand as I knew he'd just stick it back in.

"So, shall we be off?" VJ gestured toward the gleaming car.

"Off where?" asked Parvati suspiciously.

"Bollywood, of course. We were told to expose Noor to new experiences, so what better place to start than the epicenter of this great city of ours?"

"He wants to show you where his dad works," said Grace. "Don't worry. If it's boring we'll do something else."

"Of course," agreed VJ grandly. "Your wishes are my command."

"I cannot go," I said. "I must look after my brother and sister."

"Bring them along. Don't tell me they wouldn't like to see a real Bollywood soundstage."

"I want to go to Bollywood," said Aamaal, pounding VJ on the back.

"Feisty," said VJ. "I like that in a girl."

I gave him a look, which meant *Don't try anything with my sister*. He smiled innocently. Normally that would only have deepened my suspicions, but I felt strangely reassured. VJ might be a foolish boy but he didn't look at us the way I was used to men staring in Kamathipura, like they wanted to eat us up.

"We could go, Noor," said Parvati in Kannada, so even Vijender was excluded from our discussion. "Your ma won't miss you for hours."

I tried to hide my surprise. It was the first thing she'd shown interest in since the attack.

"Someone might tell." I glanced down the street. Adit was still watching. If he told Ma I'd gone off with foreigners there'd be no end of trouble.

Parvati looked away, but I caught the flash of disappointment.

"Can you meet us on Bhatti Road?" I asked Vijender. The main road was far enough away that at least Adit wouldn't see us getting into the car.

"No problem," he said.

The car was cold when we climbed in a few minutes later. I pulled Shami onto my lap, though there was space for him to have his own seat, and wrapped my arms around him. He seemed more tired these days. He was often asleep when I got home from school and had no interest in playing. Every evening, he fell asleep right after dinner and rarely stirred till morning, even if I was having a disrupted night finding us a safe place to sleep. Sometimes, when I was holding him like this, it felt as though his chest wasn't rising at all. At times like that I squeezed him hard, until he squirmed, so I could go back to knowing he was alive.

At every traffic light, beggars tapped at our windows. For the first few lights I looked closely to see if it was someone I knew. After a while I realized we were too far from Kamathipura, so I did what the foreigners did and tried not to look at them at all. I still heard them though—*tap, tap, tap*. They must have thought I was rich, riding in a car like that. I wanted to lower my window and explain. I had a few rupees in my pocket for lunch. I was tempted to hand it over, which would have been foolish. It would only have gone to their gang boss, and then how would I have fed Shami and Aamaal? The foreigners talked the whole trip, as if the beggars were just part of the landscape, like garbage and stray dogs.

Gradually, we left the heavily populated part of the city and entered an area that was a mix of small settlements and open spaces. Whistling Wind Studios was on the very edge of Mumbai, in the forested foothills. As we passed through ornate iron gates and headed down a long, winding road, I watched intently for leopards and monkeys. All I saw was what must have been movie sets. There were huge mansions, covered in scaffolding and plat-forms; a town that was only storefronts; an arid patch of sand, with a few bristly plants that had arm-like branches sticking straight up. Scattered throughout were large, square, windowless buildings pasted with gigantic movie posters. It was interesting, but I would have preferred to see a leopard.

We pulled up to another gate and were waved through by a guard. He saluted to us, as if we were important. Parvati clutched my arm. I think she was regretting our decision to come.

We stopped outside a long, two-story, sparkling white build-ing. It didn't have any paint missing at all, and there were lots of windows with glass in them and no shutters or metal bars. The windows were so clean and so much light poured into the building that you could see the people inside going about their business.

Shami slept during the drive but woke up when I lifted him out of the car. Two women were standing in front of the build-ing. They rushed forward and hugged VJ. One called him

"Darling." He put his arm around her but his eyes were cold when he turned to us and introduced her.

"You all recognize Vanita Kapoor, don't you? Rising starlet and the leading lady in my father's new movie."

"Not the leading lady, darling," she purred in a sex-me voice that sounded as false as any I'd heard at home. "Your wicked father only gave me a tiny part."

We heard the approach of VJ's father even before he came into view. Sanjay Patel was surrounded by a crowd of people, all competing to be noticed, yet he strode along as though he didn't even see them. It was the same way the foreigners had acted with the beggars outside the car window. I wondered if rich people all had this ability of not seeing.

VJ's father had his eyes fixed on the beautiful young film star clinging to his son. He seemed far more interested in her than VJ, who stood rigidly, making no pretense of enjoying her attention. I wondered if it was just this girl VJ didn't like, despite her beauty, or if perhaps girls were not his preference.

There were plenty of boys in our neighborhood, working alongside Ma and the Aunties, who served the men who preferred other men. VJ had been friendly to us, without being the least bit aggressive, just like these boys always were. It would be rash to let down my guard but I didn't feel threatened around VJ like I did around most boys.

"Welcome, welcome," he said, clapping one hand on VJ's shoulder and the other on the starlet's back. "On the set barely a minute and already he's in the arms of a beautiful woman. Be careful of him, girls. My boy's a heartbreaker."

"You've broken more than a few hearts yourself," said VJ.

20

Grace

VJ's father loaded all of us, including the starlet, into a bus, saying he had a surprise waiting on a neighboring set. VJ was uncharacteristically grim-faced and subdued. He clearly wasn't a fan of his father's surprises.

We drove a few minutes back down the road and turned into a parking lot in front of a building that looked every bit like a palace out of the Raj era. A dozen or so people waiting in the lot surged forward, surrounding us the second we alighted from the bus.

"Stop," said VJ's father. "I haven't told them the surprise yet." He turned to us. "You're all going to be in my movie. These people will take you to costume and makeup."

He paused for a response. I glanced nervously at Noor, not sure how she'd feel about all this attention.

"They're a little shy," said VJ. "Being in a movie is a bit much for their first outing."

"Nonsense," said his father. "Wait till they see the costumes." He said something in Hindi to Noor and Parvati.

It was Aamaal who answered. I wasn't sure what she said but everyone laughed.

"I guess we're making a movie, then," said VJ, ruffling Aamaal's hair. Noor immediately stepped between them and put a hand on Aamaal's shoulder.

We were led away by a group of women to a large dressing room. There was a rack of gowns in the center, couches along one wall and mirrored dressing tables along the other. One of our entourage directed us to the couches while they searched for our sizes.

I sat next to Noor, with the little ones on her other side and Parvati at the far end. A woman approached with a shimmering length of fabric over her arm and a gold-sequined blouse.

"This would be perfect for you, darling," she said, holding it out to me. "We just need to get you out of those clothes."

I was so busy sweating over the possibility that we might be required to say lines that getting undressed hadn't even occurred to me. I felt as though my wounds were suddenly giving off heat. I cupped one hand over my thigh.

"Thanks," I said, my voice barely more than a whisper, "but I'd rather just watch."

"We can't have that," said the woman firmly. "Mr. Patel will be disappointed."

"I don't want to," I said more forcefully.

"Don't be shy. We're all girls here."

"I'll try it." Noor stood up and reached for the blouse.

"It's too big for you," said the woman, holding the ensemble just out of Noor's reach.

She didn't count on Parvati, who leaped up and snatched it out of her hands. The woman made a dive to retrieve it but she was no match for Parvati, who easily ducked away, a triumphant gleam in her eye.

"Grace is feeling sick," Noor said firmly.

She couldn't have known how accurate her assertion was.

Costumes were brought for the others, including the cutest little maharaja suit for Shami, complete with turban and golden dagger.

Makeup followed. Only Aamaal reveled in the attention, insisting on false eyelashes in addition to the mascara and eyeliner. She chortled with delight at sparkly green eye shadow and everyone joined in when she demanded Shami must wear it as well.

"She's going to be a star when she grows up," commented one of the makeup artists, admiring Aamaal in the mirror as she brushed her hair.

"Is your mum a model, hon?" asked the makeup artist who was working on Noor. Obviously, VJ's father hadn't told them anything.

"She's a housewife," Noor said, "but she's also a great beauty."

"You should tell her to get a screen test for your sister."

Finally they brought out the jewelry. The chief costume lady held up an ornate necklace that she said had been designed by a famous jeweler to match a genuine period piece. Though the emeralds and rubies were fake and it was only gold plate, she claimed it had cost well over eight hundred dollars to commission and would sell for a good deal more. Parvati, who'd shown little interest in the clothing and makeup, perked up considerably at the sight of the necklace and listened carefully as the woman described its value. She squabbled with Aamaal over which of them should wear it. Noor stepped in and decided in Parvati's favor.

In the end, with all the preparations complete, the four of them looked as though they'd fit right into a maharaja's court. I followed as they walked confidently down the long hall, built to look like a throne room. Mr. Patel, sumptuously costumed, was seated on a throne at the far end. VJ stood off to one side looking decidedly out of place. It wasn't just that he was still in his jeans and T-shirt, it was his angry expression as he watched his father chat with a gaggle of women simpering around him. He raced over as soon as he caught sight of us and scooped Shami up into his arms.

"You look great, little man," he said. "He should have come in riding a horse though. Where are the horses, Papa?" he shouted back to his father.

His father got up and came over to join us. "They're tethered out back where they always are. When VJ was little he always begged to come to work with me. I was never sure if it was me or the horses he really loved." He chuckled as he clapped a hand on VJ's shoulder. VJ casually slipped out of his grasp and walked away, carrying Shami.

Mr. Patel watched his son take Shami to the throne and set him down. "He was always a kind little boy," he said. A look of infinite sadness crossed his face. He quickly replaced it with a mask of good humor.

"So, let's get started, shall we?" VJ's father said. "My word." He bent down to Aamaal. "Don't you look lovely."

A director materialized and the next hour sped by as they shot several takes of a crowd scene. Aamaal loved all the pageantry, and her excitement was infectious. Shami made everyone laugh as he trundled around in his finery earnestly saying the lines he was fed. He was, without a doubt, the best-natured four-year-old I'd ever met. I was almost sorry when the director called a wrap and we headed back to the dressing room.

After they changed, VJ took us to the stable behind the "palace." He harnessed a huge, sleek horse and brought it out to where we waited in a dusty paddock. Effortlessly, he mounted it bareback and reached down for Shami.

Noor pushed Shami behind her back. "He can't go up there. It's too dangerous."

"I want to go," said Aamaal.

"No," said Noor.

Shami tugged at Noor's shirt and said something in their language, giving her a pleading look.

Noor sighed. "Hold them tightly," she said sternly. "None of your fooling around."

VJ gave her a solemn nod, though his eyes sparkled.

Noor handed Shami up first, rattling off extensive instructions for both boys. Shami clutched the arm that VJ wrapped round his stomach.

Parvati handed Aamaal up, who settled in front of Shami and leaned forward to pet the horse.

VJ clicked his tongue and they were off at a leisurely walk, kicking up dust, which stopped me from following but didn't deter Noor or Parvati. VJ did three tours around the enclosure before lifting the children down.

"Next time I bring Eka," said Parvati.

Noor didn't comment as she was too busy dusting off Shami while simultaneously barking orders at Aamaal to stay away from the horse. Aamaal ignored her and cooed at the horse, kissing its face. It nuzzled Aamaal's stomach, almost knocking her over. VJ stayed close, ready to catch her, but had the good sense not to provoke Noor further by touching Aamaal unnecessarily.

After a minor battle to separate Aamaal from her new pet, we left the stable and headed to the parking lot. VJ texted his dad that we were on our way, so Sanjay Patel was waiting for us at the bus. He insisted we go back to the first building, where he had lunch waiting for us. We were on the point of leaving when the costume woman came running out of the palace, shouting.

"One of them took the necklace!" Her chest was heaving as she reached us.

"What necklace?" asked VJ's father, calmly.

"The Jindan Kaur. She was wearing it." She glared at Parvati. We all turned to Parvati.

"I am giving you. You are putting in box," said Parvati indignantly.

"That's true," I said. "I saw you put it in a box."

"It's not there now," insisted the woman.

"I'm sure it will turn up, Sheetal," said VJ.

"It will not turn up," she said heatedly. "I am not so careless that I misplace expensive jewelry."

"Now, now, calm down," said Mr. Patel. "One necklace is not serious. Surely we can replace it."

"It took weeks to have it made. It's a perfect copy of the original."

My attention was diverted by Noor and Parvati. They'd walked away from the group and were having their own discussion. Only because I was watching carefully did I notice Parvati slip something into Noor's hand. I casually moved closer and reached out to Noor. When I felt the necklace in my grasp I stepped away from them.

"I was going to give it back," I said, holding out the necklace. "I just wanted to try it on, since I didn't get a chance to dress up."

"You refused to dress up!" exploded the costume lady, snatching the necklace and giving me a foul look.

"No harm done," said VJ, taking my arm and steering me hurriedly in the direction of the bus. "Now, who's ready for lunch?"

We left the lady still sputtering as we piled in.

"I always love a happy ending, don't you?" said VJ's father, settling into the seat beside his son and giving him a warm look.

VJ turned away and stared out the window. Film star Sanjay Patel brushed a hand across his eyes as he failed yet again to win over the only fan he really cared about.

Grace

She doesn't do it for money she does it because she LIKES it!

I contemplated the message. This was my life, my new normal. Every morning, with the obsessiveness of an ingénue reading her reviews, I dumped my books in my locker, grabbed what I needed for the day, and trudged upstairs to the sixth floor girls' bathroom. In the fourth cubicle, the farthest from the door, I read the latest messages on a Hater Wall devoted entirely to me.

I knew it was stupid, if not masochistic. Who cared what a few bored girls wrote about me on a bathroom stall? In the past three weeks I'd been befriended by the hottest guy in school—the fact that he was gay only made it more perfect— and I was possibly making a new friend in Noor. The previous weekend, when I hadn't wanted to get undressed for our Bollywood debut, she'd somehow understood, and I know she appreciated me taking the heat for the stolen necklace.

She'd even suggested we get together this coming week.

But somehow these small wins couldn't outweigh the losses. I missed my brother and Tina. I missed having someone I could have a completely honest conversation with. Maybe I spent too much time alone in my room thinking about what I did. Things were still strained with my mom. It didn't help that I found myself constantly lying to her. I couldn't bear for her to know that I really had screwed up my life as badly as she'd predicted. I wanted her to think everyone at school had moved on, so maybe she would too. I claimed I had friends, never mentioned the bullying, and hid my wounds both inside and out.

I was basically shunned at school, but at least the snide remarks and crude messages on my phone and Facebook had dwindled to almost nothing. At times I could almost believe that my humiliation was forgotten, except for this, a wall full of comments. There were hundreds of them. Okay, if I'm being completely honest, as of that morning there were fifty-three. Yes, I counted. Who wouldn't?

They weren't all bad.

Seventeen of them were at worst neutral, girls asking stupid questions, like, *Does she really charge for it?*

Eight were positive. My favorite said, *Why don't you people get a life?* Though, arguably, that one could have been directed at me. It was exactly what VJ would have said if I'd told him about the wall. I preferred that he think—like my parents— that things had blown over. He expected me to be strong and fearless like him. If he'd known about the wall, he would have laughed it off and been disappointed in me that I couldn't do the same.

I read through the new comments, repeating the few positive ones in my head, trying to commit them to memory. It was a challenge I set myself every morning, and every morning, I failed. Hours and days later I could recall every cruel word while the kind ones always eluded me. Many of the comments were petty and mean-spirited. They said far more about the writer than they said about me, yet a part of me agreed with them.

They were substantively inaccurate: I wasn't giving BJs behind the equipment house at the pool, and I hadn't had sex with any of the many guys listed. I hadn't had sex with anyone, but I had been intimate. With a complete, still unknown stranger, I'd exposed my self and not just my body. I'd revealed my innermost thoughts, my fears and hopes. I'd treated my own soul like a commodity at a fire sale that I couldn't unload fast enough. As much as these girls hated me, they couldn't come close to how much I hated myself.

I jumped when I heard the bathroom door open and was glad I'd had the foresight to lock the stall. It was unusual for anyone to come in at that time of day. Being on the top floor, far from the lockers and cafeteria, this bathroom wasn't convenient.

"We were just talking. I asked him what he was doing this weekend."

The voice was familiar but I couldn't place it immediately.

"And how are my boyfriend's weekend plans any of your business?"

That voice I knew.

The only thing worse than sitting in a bathroom stall eavesdropping on someone else's conversation was realizing that

the two someones were Madison and Kelsey. There was nothing I could say that would convince them I'd just happened to
overhear by accident. And this almost definitely confirmed
that they were contributors to my Hater Wall—not that I was
ever in doubt.

"I was just making conversation," said Kelsey.

"Liar. I've seen the way you get all giggly around him."

"You're paranoid because of what Grace did. I'm not a slut
like her."

Hang on. How did I get drawn into it?

"From where I was sitting you didn't look much better!"

Whoa! Madison was out for blood.

"Excuse me?" Kelsey sounded every bit as angry as Madison
now. "You think I'd send naked photos of myself to a guy?"

"She didn't send them to a guy. She sent them to you!"

I held my breath. Was this the moment I'd finally find out
what really happened?

"She didn't know that." Without even seeing her I could
hear the smug pleasure in Kelsey's voice.

"Just stay away from my boyfriend," snapped Madison.

There was a shuffling and the sound of the door opening
and closing. I gave myself a few seconds to calm my breathing
before emerging from my hiding place. I walked past the stalls
to the sinks and practically jumped out of my skin when I came
upon Kelsey in front of the mirror, reapplying her mascara.

"You were listening?" she accused, rounding on me angrily.

I met her gaze. "You were the one who did it?"

I didn't have to say what "it" was. Her guilty look said it all.

"Not everything," she said, as if that should make all the
difference. "I was the one you were texting with but it was

Madison's idea. She was the one who sent your photo to the entire school and pasted one to your locker."

"Why?"

She shrugged. "I guess she was jealous of you."

I didn't waste time challenging the ridiculousness of that assertion. "I'm not asking about her. Why did *you* do it?"

Her eyes cut to the door. I was blocking her way, but if she'd tried to get past me I would have let her. I had an overwhelming desire to burst into tears and I did not want to cry in front of her.

Kelsey beat me to it.

"I'm sorry," she sobbed. "I don't know why I go along with her. I just want her to like me."

I stepped forward and patted her on the back. Despite everything, I felt sorry for her. I knew exactly what she meant about trying to curry favor with Madison. I didn't think I'd ever stoop as far as Kelsey but I'd done my own share of sucking up. Madison may have been a mean girl, but she was the one who had to be placated if you wanted to fit into their group.

"Are you going to tell?" asked Kelsey.

I thought about it for a minute. "No, I just want everyone to forget about this."

"You're a lot nicer than Madison."

"That's setting the bar a little low, but thanks."

"You're kind of pretty too. At least you would be if you made more of an effort."

"We'd better get to class." I didn't wait to see if she was following as I walked out the door and headed downstairs.

It was an hour into second period when a messenger showed up at the classroom door with a note for me to report to the principal's office. I felt a rush of anxiety.

The first thing I heard when I stepped into the outer waiting room was Madison's voice. Twice in one day was twice more than I wanted. I couldn't imagine how this could end well for me.

"She's lying," she howled loudly.

The response was inaudible.

"Sit down there for a minute, Grace," said the receptionist.

Madison's crying got even louder as a door opened somewhere in the warren of offices. Mr. Smiley rounded a corner and beamed at me.

"Grace, how are you?"

"Fine," I said cautiously. Something told me that was about to change.

"Wonderful! Would you like to come with me?"

I got heavily to my feet and shuffled after him down the hall. I could see we were heading to the conference room, which was all too familiar. Madison's voice got louder with every step.

For some reason I didn't expect the room to be full. You'd think I would have learned from the last time. Both my parents, Mr. Donleavy, the school counselor, my homeroom teacher, another teacher who must have been Madison's homeroom teacher, Madison herself, and her parents all looked at me expectantly. If Mr. Smiley hadn't been directly behind me I would have turned right around and fled.

"Why don't you sit here with your parents, Grace?"

I slumped into the chair next to my mom and tried to make myself as small as possible.

"Madison, would you like to start?" asked Mr. Smiley.

"She's a liar," said Madison.

I was pretty sure she wasn't supposed to say that. I shot a look at Mr. Smiley, who was giving Madison a disappointed look.

"There's no proof she did it," said Madison's father.

Did what?

"Two other students brought this to my attention just today," said Mr. Smiley firmly. "And Madison has already admitted that she said mean things to Grace."

Madison glared at me.

"The sooner you apologize, the sooner we can move on," said Mr. Smiley to Madison.

"What will the consequences be if she admits it?" asked her father.

"We'll discuss that at a later time. First, Madison needs to apologize."

There was a long pause.

"I'm sorry," said Madison.

I was completely confused. What was she apologizing for, exactly? Kelsey had admitted to me that she was the one texting me. We only had her word so far that Madison had anything to do with any of it.

"That's okay," I said. I'd have apologized myself if it would have got us out of the room faster.

Mr. Smiley practically glowed, and there were a few sighs of relief around the table.

Mr. Donleavy didn't seem to be buying it though. "So, you're admitting you did all this, Madison?" he asked gently. "The texting, and sharing the photograph?" I was a little annoyed that he was being so nice to her, but it was a fair question.

"Sure," she said, which wasn't the same as saying yes, though only Mr. Donleavy and I seemed to notice.

"Well, that's it then," said Mr. Smiley. "Thank you all for

coming. Grace, you can go back to class. I hope we can all put this behind us now."

My parents and I stood up and filed out. They gave me hugs and congratulations, neither of which felt deserved. I still had a knot in my stomach. I knew for a fact that Madison was taking the fall for Kelsey on the texting. And none of this explained why Todd had been such a jerk the other day. For someone with no part in this at all, he'd certainly seemed eager to humiliate me.

I couldn't ask Kyle if Todd might have a reason to hurt me, since he still didn't know what I'd done, but there was nothing to lose by asking his former girlfriend, Anoosha Kapur. Kyle had told me that Todd had ruined their relationship. Maybe that was a clue.

I looked for Anoosha as soon as I reached the cafeteria at lunch. I was disappointed but not surprised to see her in a large group of popular girls. If I hadn't been so desperate, there's no way I would have gone up to them.

"Grace, I've been meaning to talk to you," Anoosha said as I approached. "How are you doing?" Her voice was full of concern. "Sit down."

"Could we talk in private?" I asked, avoiding the stares of the other girls.

"Sure." She stood up. "Watch my things," she said to her friends, and she followed me out of the cafeteria and down the stairs to the school's reception area. We sat down on one of the two couches.

"So, how are you really?" she asked.

"I've been better. I'm still trying to work out how all this happened. It's a little confusing. I was wondering if you know anything about Todd's involvement."

"Probably no more than you do. He came to school bragging you'd sent him a topless photo. No one believed him at first, till he forwarded it to a bunch of people."

"Wow! That's already more than I knew. So Todd thinks it was me who sent him the photo?"

"He did at first, but then we all heard about the sexting and realized someone had been leading you on. I'm sorry you got tricked like that."

"So Todd passed my photo on just to show off?"

"Partly, but he also hates your brother. You gave him a perfect opportunity for revenge. He had a crush on me last year and did everything he could to break Kyle and me up. One night at a party, I was drunk and I let him kiss me. I made a mistake, and Todd finally got what he wanted. Your brother dumped me. But even after we broke up I wouldn't go out with Todd. He's a bad guy, Grace."

There wasn't much left to say. Kelsey was the one doing the sexting, and Todd had sent my photo to the entire school to get back at my brother by humiliating me. Kelsey said it was Madison's idea, but she'd lied about Madison sending my photo to everyone, so maybe Madison wasn't involved at all. Mr. Smiley said two students had squealed on Madison. After Kelsey had admitted her involvement to me this morning she might have panicked that I'd change my mind about turning her in and decided to give Smiley someone else to blame. Todd was a slime for going along with her but, given what Anoosha said, it wasn't hard to believe he'd pin everything on Madison to save his own skin. With college applications looming, they both had a lot riding on maintaining clean records.

I followed Anoosha back to the cafeteria and took a seat at

my usual table. I was glad VJ wasn't there yet. I needed some time to think.

I felt Madison's presence before I saw her. She came up behind me and slammed one hand on the table, leaning in so our faces were inches apart.

"I know you're the one who told on me. Smiley wouldn't say who it was but I *know!*"

I was so shocked by the accusation that I didn't know what to say.

"First you try to steal the boy I like by sending him a boob shot, as if your flat chest would attract any guy, and then you accuse me of being behind it all. Do you really think a hag like you is a threat to someone like me? Why would I bother to take you down? You're already beneath me."

"Look, I know Kelsey was the one sexting me. Why don't we go tell Smiley together? You shouldn't be taking all the blame for this."

"Just because you're a rat doesn't mean I am."

"I didn't tell him you did it, Madison."

"Yeah, right, who else would do it?"

"Smiley said two students came forward, so it couldn't have been me. Maybe it was Kelsey and Todd."

"You really expect me to believe that? You tried to steal the boy you knew I liked, and now you try to drive a wedge between me and my best friend. You just don't give up, do you?"

"Ladies!" VJ arrived at the table, shouldered Madison out of the way and took the seat opposite me. "Are you joining us today, Maddy dear? Do say you are. I haven't seen a good catfight in weeks."

Madison barely noticed him she was so focused on me. "Do you know you got me suspended for three days? It's going on my permanent record."

She didn't deserve that. It was a serious consequence for something we both knew she didn't do.

"Well, maybe next time you'll think twice before being such a colossal bitch," said VJ.

Madison flinched. I felt a pang of sympathy as she turned and walked stiffly away. I was pretty sure she was trying not to cry, and I knew what that was like.

"She didn't do it," I said. "I think I should go to Smiley."

"Stay out of it," said VJ. "It's karma. She's done plenty to deserve retribution. You're too soft. You need to toughen up."

I nodded, but I wasn't sure I agreed. Maybe I needed to be tougher, but that didn't mean it was okay to jeopardize Madison's future for something she didn't do. I looked around for Kelsey and wasn't surprised to find her sitting with Todd, giggling. Had that been her endgame all along?

"Madison's taking the fall for Kelsey, and she thinks I'm the one who told Smiley it was her."

"Good. Maybe now she'll realize you're not someone she can push around."

He couldn't have been more wrong.

22

Noor

Equal chances . . .

If she'd been old enough I would have sent Aamaal to school alone the first day back from midterm break. I didn't want her with me when I encountered my friends. I knew the stain of who I was couldn't be washed away by medals, or even years of friendship. I only hoped the parents of Aamaal's friends would spare their young children the knowledge that a cherished playmate was the daughter of a prostitute.

Only Gajra was waiting at the gate when we arrived. That was unusual but not unheard of. Particularly after a break, the other girls were often swept up in the excitement of sharing details about their recent vacations. I cringed to remember the fantastical stories I'd told them myself over the years. Would they realize that every word was a lie?

Gajra opened the gate for me and hugged me as soon as I stepped through. Then she bent down and hugged Aamaal as well. Aamaal was startled but hugged her back. It was as if

Gajra were consoling us for a death in the family, which in a way I suppose she was. The family that I'd created, the one I desperately wanted to be true, was gone forever. Stripped of my past, I had no idea who I would be in this new future. I clung to the only thing I was sure of, Gajra's affection.

"Thank you," I said.

"For what, Noor?" She linked her arm in mine, as Aamaal raced off to find her friends. I watched her go and was relieved to see she was quickly absorbed into a game of chase.

"Shall we go see how everyone's holiday was?" asked Gajra.

It was the last thing I wanted to do, but there was no point delaying the inevitable. Arm in arm, we walked toward a cluster of my former friends. They pressed together at our approach like a flock of skittish pigeons.

"My father says it's improper for a girl like her to go to school with girls like us." Sapna kept her back to me but spoke loudly so I was certain to hear.

"My father says it doesn't matter where you come from, it only matters what you do with your life," said Gajra. "What is it your father objects to, Sapna—the fact that Noor bests you in almost every subject, year after year?"

"I'm the daughter of a doctor!" Sapna rounded angrily on Gajra, her hands balled into fists. "She's just a . . . a . . ." Poor Sapna was trapped by her own snobbiness. It would be unthinkable for a well-brought-up girl to even say the word "prostitute."

"She's just a what?" Gajra demanded fiercely. "A straight-A student? Our future valedictorian? Our future prime minister, perhaps? What is it you're trying to say?"

"Why do you defend her, Gajra? She's not one of us."

"You're right. She's smarter and works far harder than any of us. But who knows, if we're lucky maybe some of her perseverance will rub off. Didn't your father also come from modest beginnings, Sapna?"

Sapna turned crimson.

"What was your grandfather?" Gajra continued, "A taxi-wallah, isn't it?"

"That's a respectable job."

"Of course it is, and wasn't he lucky to be born a boy so every career option was open to him. Wouldn't it be wonderful if girls had the same opportunities?"

"Her mother could have been a maid, or a street-sweeper. There are other jobs for low-born women."

"Yet you only have to look outside the gates of our school to see whole families living on the street. Work is not easy to come by. Don't you listen to what our teachers tell us? Seventy percent of our population lives in slums, a quarter lives in absolute poverty. Would you really judge a mother harshly because she would do anything to provide for her children?"

"Perhaps you're the one who will be our future prime minister, Gaj," I teased, trying to lighten the mood. "You can certainly argue like a politician."

We all laughed—all but Sapna, who continued to glower at Gajra.

Gajra stared her down. "I want to live in an India that isn't held back by the prejudices of caste and color. Don't you, Sapna?"

Sapna looked from Gajra to the other girls. It was clear which one of them had won the day. She gave a grudging nod.

"All this talk of politics is making me bored," said Kiran. She sighed dramatically. "Come on, Noor, haven't you got a game for us?"

"I'm sure I can think of something." I looked around at the faces that had become so dear to me over the past eight years. For the first time they were looking back at me, the *real* me. They waited eagerly as I decided what we should play.

The rest of the day was like my first day of school. I entered every class, each new cluster of schoolmates, frightened of rejection. I needn't have worried. My friends cocooned me with their laughter, and most teachers went to great pains to congratulate me on my recent medals. There were a few who were awkward around me, but none mentioned the revelation of my origin. I collected Aamaal at the end of the day, confident we'd weathered the worst. She too had had an uneventful day and was full of stories of one of her friend's rabbits. It had had babies over the break, and Aamaal pestered me all the way home to let her have one.

When we entered our street I managed to distract her by giving her a few rupees to buy some greens for Lucky the goat. While she was suitably distracted I went inside to pick up Shami. The house was just waking up, but Deepa-Auntie already had Shami bathed and fed and was playing catch with him in the lounge. I was pleased to see Shami chasing a tightly balled sari. He was having one of his good days. The labored breathing that had hung on for weeks was finally responding to a new antibiotic.

I no longer took Shami to doctors. It was easier, not to mention cheaper, just to ask advice from the other aunties and buy what they recommended. I was pretty certain Shami had tuberculosis, and I knew he had the virus. I was determined he'd be one of the lucky ones who survived. He just needed to hang on a few more years. As soon as I got my school-leaving certificate, I'd get a job so I could afford the medicine and look after him properly. Three more years was all I needed. I knew lots of people with the virus who'd hung on longer than that, my ma included.

Shami squealed with delight when he caught sight of me. "Noor-di, Noor-di!" He hurled himself into my arms. I caught him mid-flight and swung him up onto my hip. I had a flash of anxiety that at four he was still tiny enough that I could easily support him with one arm.

I gave Deepa-Auntie a questioning look. "He's had a good day," she confirmed. "He took only a short nap today, so you might get him to bed early."

"Ma?" I asked.

"Still sleeping."

I set Shami down. Ma was getting harder and harder to rouse these days. Even Prita-Auntie had tried to talk to her about her drinking, and everyone knew Prita-Auntie was one of the biggest drunks on the lane.

"I'll be back in just a minute, Shami. You play with Deepa-Auntie."

"I want to come. I want to see Ma."

"She needs her tea first, Shami. You know she'll be happy to see you once she's had her tea." I hoped this was true, but Ma's moods had become as uncontrolled as her drinking. Even Aamaal, her clear favorite, could never be sure whether she was going to get a kiss or a smack. She'd taken to avoiding Ma altogether. She refused to even come inside to change her clothes after school until I told her it was safe. Often I had to bring her clothes down to her and she changed in the washing room, not greeting Ma at all.

I left Shami in the lounge and walked down the hall, careful to listen for Pran. I could hear some of the other aunties in the downstairs room that was just below ours. I poked my head in their door to greet them as I passed. A large rat scuttled toward me. It noticed me at the last minute, turned tail and disappeared down the corridor back to the kitchen. I paused at the bottom of the ladder. There wasn't the slightest noise from above. I should have asked if Prita-Auntie was still passed out as well. I quietly climbed the ladder and breathed a sigh of relief when I popped my head through the hatch. Prita-Auntie's bed was empty.

I scrambled up the rest of the way and walked over to Ma, who didn't stir, and watched her for a moment. Even in sleep the lines around her once-beautiful face drew her mouth into a perpetual frown. Several locks of lank, greasy hair had escaped from her braid and fell across her folded arm. Her body under the threadbare sari was little more than bones. It was hard to remember the way she used to be, so full of energy and determination. I used to pride myself on being like her.

Silently, I vowed that in three years I'd take her away from this life as well. I hoped it wouldn't be too late for her to regain some measure of who she used to be. At least she could live her final years in peace and comfort. We wouldn't need much, just a small room we could call our own, a kerosene cooker and, if we were lucky, running water and electricity. I'd seen rooms like that in Kamathipura, but my mother was not going to end her days among the men who had used her. I would take us as far from these fifteen lanes as it was possible to go. As Gajra had so recently pointed out, India had no shortage of slums. We'd make our home where no one knew us.

I reached under the bed for our stash of food and pulled out the tea, powdered milk and spices. I took her mug and our single pot from her bedside stand and returned to the ladder.

Ten minutes later I was back at her bedside holding a steaming brew of masala chai. Cinnamon scented the air, briefly overwhelming the usual, less pleasant odors.

"Ma." I gently shook her shoulder. It felt as if the bones rattled under my touch. She, on the other hand, didn't move at all.

"Ma," I said more loudly.

Her eyes peeped open. "Leave me alone," she groaned. "What time is it?"

"It's late, Ma, almost five. The men will be coming soon. Deepa-Auntie has already turned one away."

This was a lie but it had the desired effect. Ma hastily dragged herself into a sitting position, resting her back against the wall. "You haven't let her steal any of my regulars, have you?"

"Of course not, Ma, I would never do that." There was no point trying to defend Deepa-Auntie, who had never once accepted one of Ma's regulars, though many had approached her. Ma's mind traveled in deep grooves like a train, impossible to derail.

I knelt down and pulled out the box that stored our clothes and took out a salwar kameez for Aamaal. "Shami's doing well today, Ma. He's running around downstairs."

"I went to the temple last week. It's already working. Have you been this week, Noor?"

"Yes, Ma. Shall I go again?"

"Yes, go tonight. We must give thanks. Have you done your homework?"

"I'll do it now. I just need to feed the children first." I didn't tell her I was meeting up with Grace and Parvati, both of who were eager to hear about my first day back at school. Ma still didn't know about Grace, or why the school had decided not to expel me. She thought it was her own appeal that had convinced the principal to let me stay.

"Don't neglect your studies. You mustn't give them any excuse to try to get rid of you again."

I picked up the cup of tea she'd drained. "Would you like anything before I go, Ma? I could brush your hair or massage your feet."

"No, just send Aamaal up. I never see that child anymore."

I nodded, then leaned over and gave her a quick hug. She brushed me away.

I picked up Shami on my way out and found Aamaal, where I knew she'd be, still playing with Lucky. That goat was a better childminder than I'd ever be.

"Go inside and change, Aamaal. You can put your uniform away and give Ma a hug."

"Is Ma okay today?"

"Yes, I wouldn't have told you to go to her otherwise. Don't ask stupid questions."

She ran off and I immediately regretted my harsh words. It was my jealousy rearing up. The sight of Aamaal would cheer Ma in a way that I never could. I sometimes wondered if Ma actually knew Aamaal's father, maybe even loved him. I'd never known Ma to have a serious boyfriend the way many of the aunties did. She said a boyfriend was just one more man stealing your cash, which was true. Most aunties ended up supporting their boyfriends, even if the relationships didn't start out that way.

One thing was certain. Ma never loved my father, black dung beetle that he must have been. Whatever Gajra said about the new India, my too-dark skin, several shades darker than Ma's own, couldn't help but disappoint her. It was no wonder she preferred Aamaal.

When Aamaal returned, we headed for the café where Parvati and I had agreed to meet Grace. Parvati was supposed to be waiting for us in an alley just one lane over from our house. She wasn't at our meeting place, but I'd told her to go on ahead if Suresh was already on the hunt for her. I could only hope that was what she'd done.

The café we'd chosen was a long walk from Kamathipura. It was part of a large, modern chain, so a safe place for the foreigners to wait and the last place Suresh would think to look for Parvati. A single coffee there cost more than three times what a man would pay for our mothers. I wouldn't be wasting any of Ma's earnings on refreshments, so I bought Aamaal and Shami a couple of vada paav at a street stall on the way. The potato fritter in a bun wasn't a favorite of either of my siblings but at only ten rupees it was a regular standby.

I was disappointed, thirty minutes later, when we finally walked through the door, sweaty and tired, to find Grace sitting by herself. No Parvati.

"You came alone?" I said, glad she'd left VJ Patel behind.

She was at a table with four chairs. Aamaal immediately plopped herself down in one and looked around with interest. This wasn't the kind of place any of us was used to. I'd been carrying Shami on the long walk over, so I was happy to drop him in his own chair. Only when I'd sat as well did I notice other patrons eyeing us strangely. Most of them were in western dress. The few in salwar kameez wore the plain, tailored, high-fashion kind that I'd usually seen only on billboards, so unlike the boldly colored, ill-fitting, street-stall kind Aamaal and I wore.

"My mom doesn't know I came alone," said Grace. "I had to take a taxi because I told her VJ's driver was bringing us."

"He didn't want to come?"

"I didn't tell him." She smiled conspiratorially, but there was something forced about her smile.

I remembered VJ hadn't been paying attention when we'd made plans to meet. It had been at the end of the day, after we'd visited his father's studio. VJ had been lost in his own thoughts. It was obvious there was something wrong between he and his father. He seemed to resent it when his father showed off his studio, but VJ was the one who took us there, so he must have been proud of his father in some way. He'd seemed particularly angry when his father flirted with the young film star. I didn't understand why that upset him. His father showed far more restraint than I was used to seeing from men. Still, I knew what it felt like to be ashamed of a parent and proud of them at the same time.

"Where's Parvati?" asked Grace.

I hesitated. She didn't really know Parvati. I'd done most of the talking when we were all together. Parvati's English was good enough for scrounging a few rupees off foreigners on the street but not really up to serious conversation. Even if she'd had the words, Parvati would never have told them about Suresh.

"Perhaps she forgot."

Aamaal reached for the small menu that was wedged between the condiments in the center of the table. I snatched it out of her hands and replaced it where it had been. Grace took a sip of her drink. It looked like coffee but it was in a tall plastic glass with ice and a straw.

"Do you want one?" she asked. "My treat."

Aamaal and I said yes and no at exactly the same time. I repeated no and gave Aamaal a *watch out or I'll hit you* look.

"Shami wants that," said Shami. He pointed to a white frothy drink that was just passing our table in the hand of a chubby boy. But he spoke in Kannada. I was relieved that Grace wouldn't understand.

"You want a vanilla Frappuccino, Shami?" she asked, to my surprise.

Aamaal and I said yes and no at exactly the same time again. Grace laughed and stood up. I stood too.

"They just had dinner," I said. "They'll be sick if you give them anything else."

"I'll take that chance," said Grace, and she walked toward the counter.

I thought about chasing after her. Now that she was gone, the other customers were openly staring at us. I sat down and scolded both children until Grace returned. I was dismayed to see she was carrying two of the white mixtures and a third drink that looked like her own. She set that one in front of me and the white drinks in front of Shami and Aamaal.

I flushed with embarrassment. "I'm not thirsty."

Grace looked disappointed. "I've paid for it, so no point letting it go to waste."

I stared at the drink that cost many times the price of my mother, or as much as a month of medicine for Shami. Grace was right about one thing; I couldn't waste it. I took one sip. After the long, hot walk, the drink was like cool rain on a sweltering night. I took another.

23

Grace

I realized too late that I'd offended Noor by buying her the drink. I wasn't sure what I should have done. I couldn't very well have sat there drinking alone, especially with Shami and Aamaal looking on longingly. I tried to come up with something I could say to lighten the mood. I was sorry she hadn't brought Parvati and wondered if I'd done something to offend her as well. It was bad enough that everyone at school hated me; I wasn't sure I could bear it if Noor and Parvati didn't like me either. Maybe I should have brought VJ. Everyone liked him.

It was selfishness that had made me come alone. I needed a friend, a real friend I could talk to. I had to tell someone about the cutting. I wanted to stop but I wasn't sure I could do it on my own. The desire, ever since Madison had called me a hag, was almost overwhelming. I just couldn't get the word out of my head, and cutting had helped the last time. Maybe I wouldn't even have to tell Noor about the cutting. Maybe I could just tell her what Madison had said, and that would be enough to get it out of my system.

I'd tried to talk to VJ about it. He'd said that Madison was just lashing out and it was ridiculous to let it bother me. But VJ had never been anything but beautiful and popular. Madison may have been lashing out, but she'd voiced my deepest insecurities. Was I ugly? Was that why no boy had ever shown an interest in me? Her words had festered like an infected cut, far more painful than the ones I'd inflicted on myself. It had taken all my resolve not to add *ugly hag* to my previous inscriptions, but I wasn't out of the woods yet. Even as I sat looking at Noor across the table, the desire to cut was a time bomb ticking inside me.

"How is Parvati?" I asked.

"She is well, thank you."

Perhaps it was just her school-taught English, but the formality of Noor's reply seemed designed to keep me at a distance. She wasn't looking at me either, as she fidgeted with her straw. Parvati was definitely an uncomfortable topic of conversation. Maybe she'd told Noor she didn't like me. Noor had to meet me as part of her deal with Miss Chanda, but Parvati didn't. I suddenly felt embarrassed to have forced Noor into being my friend.

"How did your first day back at school go?" I asked, hoping she hadn't also been bullied. It couldn't have been easy walking into school with all her longtime friends knowing the truth about her for the very first time.

"It went well, thank you."

Another formal response. I looked around the café, trying to think of something else I could ask.

"Asmi is having rabbit with six babies. Asmi is wanting give me baby," said Aamaal.

"Really?" I could have hugged her I was so grateful someone wanted to talk to me. "That's really wonderful."

Aamaal gave her sister a triumphant look. "Noor say no."

I grimaced at Noor. "Sorry, I didn't know."

"We have no place to keep it." She hissed something at Aamaal in their language. Aamaal stuck out her lip. Her eyes filled with tears.

This just kept getting worse. How could I have been so stupid as to think Noor might like me when I couldn't even connect with kids from my own culture?

Shami said something to Noor in their language. Whatever it was, it didn't help. She responded, clearly annoyed at him as well.

"What did he say?" I asked, not really expecting she would tell me.

"He also wants a rabbit."

I wished I hadn't asked.

"I got called to the principal's office yesterday," I blurted, though the hope that I could confide everything was dying fast. "They think they figured out who pretended to be a boy and sent my naked picture all over the school, but they've got the wrong girl. Madison, the girl they've accused, didn't do it. It was her best friend texting me. And now the friend is making a play for Madison's boyfriend."

Noor cocked her head. I wasn't sure if she'd understood. Her English was really good but I'd been speaking quickly. I gave her a few minutes to respond. I don't even know why I continued when she didn't.

"I overheard the two girls talking when I was checking out my Hater Wall. It's this wall where everyone who hates me writes about how much they hate me. I think these girls are the ones who started it."

I paused. I couldn't believe I'd told her all that. What possible interest could she have in my pathetic little problems?

"I'm sorry," I said. "I don't have anyone to talk to." I blinked back tears and hung my head. It was mortifying.

Suddenly a tiny pair of feet were next to mine. I looked up and was eye level with Shami's unwavering gaze. He clambered into my lap and rested his head on my chest. I glanced at Noor. She smiled sympathetically, which only made me want to cry more. As usual, I'd messed everything up. I was supposed to be the one helping her, not the other way around. I put my arms around Shami.

"Can I ask you a question?" I asked.

Noor immediately looked wary. "What?"

"Did I do something to upset Parvati?"

"No." She shook her head. "Why do you ask?"

"I expected her to be with you. Why didn't she come?"

Noor took a napkin out of the holder in the center of the table and leaned over to wipe Shami's face. She took away the straw he was blowing through. Spitting on the napkin, she used it to wipe his sticky hands as well. She kept up a running commentary to him the entire time. Even without the translation I knew she was telling him off, but her voice was gentle, and he watched her as though she was the center of his universe. When she finished he slid off me, crawled onto her lap, put his thumb in his mouth and closed his eyes. I could still feel the warmth of him on my empty lap and couldn't help but feel envious. There wasn't a person in the world who would choose me first if they had other choices. I wasn't being self-pitying, it was simply the truth. Even my parents would have chosen my charming, successful brother if they'd had to choose just one of us. Heck, I'd have chosen him over me. I didn't blame them.

"It's not you," she said, returning to our conversation. "Parvati has a problem so she could not come today."

"Is it something I can help with?"

"It is a big problem. I am telling Parvati to speak to Chanda-Teacher but she will not. She also will not like it if I tell you."

I tried not to feel hurt. "Is it a secret?"

"Yes, it is *her* secret. If she wants you to know, she must tell you. I think perhaps you also keep secrets for your friends."

"I would, if I had any friends."

"I think you have a secret with Vijender Patel?"

"He's more of an acquaintance. He's nice, but we're not that close." I suddenly realized what she was getting at. Of course I was keeping a very big secret for VJ.

"Would you tell me what really happened when you returned to school?" I asked. "I've been worrying about you."

"Everyone was kind to me. My best friend Gajra told everyone we must treat each other the same. It does not matter who your parents are, or what caste you're from."

"Can I ask you something else?"

"You may ask. I may not answer."

I scanned the café and noticed several people watching us. It confirmed the suspicion that had been growing in me. "Why did you choose this café? It's a long way from where you live and it doesn't seem like . . . your kind of place."

Noor gave me an appraising look. She also glanced at the nearby tables. You could almost see the other patrons leaning in, trying to eavesdrop. We were the definition of colliding worlds: not east and west, but rich and poor. This café was a bastion of the rich. The people in here may have shared nation-hood with Noor, but they were my people.

Noor stood up, shifting Shami onto her hip. "Do you want to see my home?"

"I thought you'd never ask." I jumped to my feet. "Time to go home, sweetie." I extended my hand to Aamaal, who took it as though holding my hand was the most natural thing in the world.

When we got out on the street my first impulse was to flag a taxi. I stopped myself just in time. Noor was showing me her world, so we'd do it her way.

Twenty minutes later I was seriously regretting my decision. Not taking a cab in brutal heat, when you have more than enough cash in your pocket, is just stupid. It had to be worse for Noor. She hadn't put Shami down once. Nor had she shown any of the annoyance I'd felt on the multiple occasions we'd had to walk in the street because everything from livestock to makeshift stalls had taken over the sidewalk. Several times I'd had to stop walk-ing and jump out of the way to avoid becoming roadkill.

"Are we almost there?" I asked for the third time.

"We are close," said Noor, as she had the previous two times.

Finally we turned into a quieter lane, though that was mainly because it was so congested with people and animals that the cars could only inch along. I walked carefully, watching the ground, but had to look up occasionally to avoid collisions.

There was filth everywhere. Even the walls of the crumbling cement buildings were cloaked in a layer of grime. I knew, from my previous visit, that we'd entered one of the narrow lanes of Kamathipura, though being later in the evening it was busier and somehow different from before.

Though it was teeming with people, women were scarce. A few burqa-clad women fluttered quickly from stall to stall making their purchases before racing off. In contrast, the other women, in neon-bright saris, with fake jewels sparkling in their noses and ears, lounged in doorways or strolled slowly up and down the lane shouting out to passing men.

Many women greeted Noor, and she paused each time to exchange a few words. Her whole demeanor changed as she wove her way down the lane. Gone was the girl who'd perched uncomfortably on the edge of her seat in the coffee shop. Noor was at ease here. It was home.

At first I wasn't concerned when a boy, perhaps eleven or twelve, popped out from between two parked stalls and grabbed Noor's arm. She spoke to him as if she knew him, but her tone wasn't the same as the one she'd used with the women. She wasn't happy to see him. Had Shami not been asleep in her arms I felt certain she would have shoved the boy away.

"Is everything all right?" I asked.

The boy smirked at me. "My name Adit," he said in a heavy accent. "What is your name?"

I ignored him. "Is he bothering you, Noor?"

Noor looked pointedly at the boy's hand, still gripping the arm that was cradling Shami. He let go.

"Adit is a friend from when he was a child." It wasn't clear if she was telling me or reminding him.

"I am not child," said Adit.

"You think because you are a bully you are a man?" asked Noor in English, perhaps to put him at a disadvantage.

"I am telling Pran-ji where is Lali go."

"You tell Pran and you will be sorry, Adit." Noor spoke calmly and added a few words in Hindi; threats, I suspected.

Adit puffed out his chest but his eye twitched. I wasn't sure if it was nerves or a permanent condition. He spoke back to her in Hindi, throwing in a few English swearwords having to do with the female anatomy. She waited until he ran out of steam, replied curtly in Hindi and turned to me.

"My house is a little more down the street. We cannot go inside at this time but I will show you." She continued walking and I followed.

"Who's Lali?" I asked.

"Lali ran away from our house."

"Does Adit want to harm her?"

"He says he knows where she is. Probably he is lying."

Aamaal was still holding my hand, which by now was sweaty and not just with heat. I glanced down at her. She stared back with round eyes.

"What if he's telling the truth?"

"We must hope he is not," said Noor.

Noor stopped and pointed across the road. It wasn't clear which building she was pointing at. They were all narrow and tightly packed, sharing walls, like ramshackle row houses from a bygone era. Most were fronted by shops or workshops, though they were all so drab and cluttered it was difficult to figure out what many of them were selling.

"Which one's yours?"

"The entrance beside the car-fixing shop."

I looked skeptically across the road. There was a guy on the street with some kind of loud power tool that he was using on metal. None of the various pieces of metal strewn in haphazard piles nearby looked as though they'd come out of a car, but it was the only thing in sight that might have fit her description. It did have a darkened, open doorway to the left of it. It also had bars extending out from the second-floor windows like cages. There was a woman sitting in one of them looking out over the street.

"It's like she's in a cage." I hadn't meant to say it out loud and immediately wished I could take it back. What if Noor mistook my meaning?

"Yes."

"Why doesn't she come out?"

"Some women are not allowed outside."

"They aren't allowed outside . . . ever?"

"Lali was not allowed out."

"How old was Lali?"

"Older than me, younger than you."

I gasped.

"Do you have a phone, Noor?"

"I have Parvati's phone but I am not using it. I am keeping it safe for her."

"But you could use it, if you had an emergency, if you needed me?"

Noor looked at me strangely. "Needed you?"

I didn't know how to explain my fear. Perhaps it was the young boy's aggressiveness, or the horror of a world where young girls were locked away, only to be taken out to be played with like toys from a cupboard. Noor had explained that her mother had chosen not to force her into prostitution, but for how long? She'd also said that her mother believed there was nothing wrong with sex work, that it was even expected for the women in their community.

"Do you know Parvati's number? If you give it to me, I'll put it in my phone and then ring you. Then you can save my number."

"It is very kind of you but I am not needing help, Grace."

"Then do it for me, so I don't worry."

She reluctantly gave me Parvati's number. I rang it immediately.

"When you turn on her phone, you'll see my number as a missed call." I hoped I wasn't insulting her by explaining that.

She leaned over and hugged me with her one free arm. I was so startled by the gesture I welled up. It was ridiculous to be so emotional. I really didn't know what had come over me lately. Since my public shaming, I seemed to choke up at the slightest provocation. It was no wonder Noor doubted I could help her. I was barely coping with my own life, and my problems were nothing compared to hers. But in that moment I vowed to myself that if she ever was in trouble, I wouldn't fail her.

24

Grace

Over the next couple of days I almost put Madison's comments out of my head. While Noor and I hadn't talked about Madison, other than my brief rundown of Madison taking the fall for Kelsey, seeing Noor's life had put my own in perspective. I thought less about my own troubles and more about Noor. I found my mind wandering to daring if unrealistic scenarios in which I rescued her entire family from poverty. I still checked out my Hater Wall every morning but there had been no new comments since Madison had been suspended, and I no longer felt the need to reread the old ones.

I felt only a little nervous arriving at school on Friday morning. Madison would be back from suspension. I hoped, like me, she was ready to move on, but I feared she might still be looking for payback. The frustrating thing was that I did feel guilty. While I wasn't responsible for getting her in trouble, I'd let her take the fall for something I knew she hadn't done.

Thirty minutes into the day I received a note to report to the principal's office. I wasn't at all surprised to see Madison when I was ushered into the conference room. Mr. Smiley and the counselor were the only other people there. I was directed to the seat across from Madison's.

"Thank you for coming, Grace. We wanted to give you and Madison a chance to clear the air before she resumes classes."

Madison and I avoided eye contact.

"Who'd like to go first?" asked Mr. Smiley.

"Perhaps now that Madison's had a few days to reflect on her actions, she has something she'd like to say to Grace," prompted the counselor.

Madison's silence filled the room.

"Grace," said the counselor, undaunted, "perhaps you'd like to tell Madison how her actions affected you."

My own silence joined Madison's.

"We have to talk this out, girls," said Mr. Smiley. "We're not leaving here until we do."

"Is someone going to send out for pizza?" I asked.

It was a failed attempt to lighten the mood. Madison's lips didn't even twitch.

"Well, at least we're talking," said Mr. Smiley optimistically. "So, why don't you go first, Grace. How did Madison's actions make you feel?"

My hands were resting in my lap. I pressed gently on my thigh, where my feelings were inscribed for my eyes only. It ached a little.

"I'm over it. I'd just like to put it behind me."

Mr. Smiley looked disappointed. "Madison, do you have anything to add?"

Madison met my eyes for the first time. My mouth went dry. Her gaze shifted to Mr. Smiley. "I've learned my lesson, sir."

"And what lesson was that?"

"That I shouldn't betray my friends."

There was a long pause. Mr. Smiley was obviously trying to decide whether I was the betrayed friend that Madison was talking about.

"That's good to hear," he finally said. "Isn't it, Grace?"

"Terrific."

"Well, girls, you can go back to class."

Madison and I filed out. I was glad we were heading to different classes. My heart was still pounding from the malevolent look she'd given me back there. I planned to peel off the second we passed out of the office doors, but she grabbed my arm.

"Do you know that in addition to destroying my college chances you got me grounded for six weeks? You show off your skanky body to the entire school and I get punished. You know what you are? You're a dis*grace*."

She stressed the last syllable in case I couldn't work out that she was doing a play on my name.

"I don't know what to say. I already apologized for flirting with fake-Todd. I offered to go to Smiley with you to tell him Kelsey was the one texting me. It's not my fault you chose to take the blame." But I'd let her. Was it my fault?

"Unlike you, I don't betray my friends."

"What do you want from me, Madison?"

"I want everyone to know the truth about you."

"What truth? That I sent a topless photo to some random person? That I'm the least popular girl in school? Unless they've been in a coma for the past three weeks, I can assure you they do know."

"You're right about that. Your *dis-grace* is legend."

I wrenched my arm out of her grasp and walked away. I thought she'd hurl some parting shot but she didn't. She saved that for later.

The rest of the school day passed without incident. That was the way I thought of it, as if incident were the norm and lack of it was noteworthy.

I got home to find Mom at the door, as she always was these days. If hawkeyed concern was supposed to make me feel loved, it wasn't working. All I felt was suffocated.

"Did you see Madison today?" she asked. That was her greeting. No hello.

"Yeah, Mr. Smiley called us both in."

"Really? He should have told me he was going to do that. I would have come."

"It went well, Mom. Everything's okay between us now."

"What did she say?"

"She apologized."

"As if that's enough for what she did!"

"It is enough, Mom. It's over."

"What about the other kids?"

"What other kids?"

"What are kids saying about what you did? Are they treating you differently?" She'd asked me this question every day for two weeks. By now she had to know what I was going to say. Just like I knew what she was going say.

"No one's said anything. They've forgotten about it."

"Forgotten?! I assure you they haven't forgotten." And there it was. Whether other kids were still being mean or were really moving on, the one person who would never forget was my mom. To give her credit, she was sounding less accusatory and more resigned, so perhaps we were making progress.

"I'm going to take Bosco for a walk," I said. The reason for the change in subject was not lost on her.

"I'll come with you."

"I need some time alone, Mom."

"We can talk about your birthday. What would you like this year?"

"Can you buy me a new life?"

"Grace!" Mom looked devastated. I shouldn't have said it.

"Sorry, I'm just joking." I gave her a hug. "I'll be back in fifteen minutes. Please stop worrying." If she ever found out about the bullying, much less the cutting, she'd never let me out of the house.

She hovered in the doorway while I fetched Bosco and followed us out to the elevator lobby. I could tell she was debating whether to insist on coming. It wouldn't have been the first time. The relief when the elevator doors closed, leaving her behind, was almost as intense as the feelings I got from cutting.

By the time I got back, Dad was home and we sat down to dinner. Mom happily relayed my lie that things had gone well with Madison. Dad, with his own brand of vigilance, asked for details, which unfortunately required further lies. He was skeptical when I said that Madison wasn't angry, so I told him that Madison and Kelsey had invited me to eat lunch with them again.

Finally they moved on to what I wanted for my birthday. Truthfully, there was nothing I wanted, but Dad loved spoiling us with presents so I came up with a few suggestions. Then

Mom started badgering me about having a party. It was her version of spoiling. I regretted lying about Madison and Kelsey when Mom practically insisted we invite them over to help me celebrate.

"It's important to show you have no hard feelings," said Mom.

"But I've already made plans with Noor and VJ," I improvised.

"Well, they can come too. You can have as many people as you want."

"Let me talk to them and get back to you."

I escaped to my room shortly after. My excuse—homework—was legitimate for once. I had a ton. It was close to eleven by the time I broke the back of it and could turn to my nightly ritual of checking Facebook for new hate messages. I hadn't had any for a week, so I wasn't even nervous when I saw an invitation to join a Facebook group, until I saw the name. I shouldn't have clicked on it.

I'm not sure what I expected. I do know that when the page opened with my topless image, in full living color, my world turned black. I slid off my chair and sank to the floor, putting my head between my bent knees. I took deep raggedy breaths but couldn't stop my heart from pounding or my head from spinning. It was everything Mom had predicted. My half-naked image was now on the Internet. Available for everyone to see. Forever.

Finally I pulled myself up and sat down again at my computer. The possibility that my parents might see this page made me feel physically ill. I grabbed the trash can from beside my desk and held it on my lap, in case I threw up, while I scrolled through the forum. I had to know how bad it was.

It was bad.

Every comment was more heinous and humiliating than the one before, as if they were competing to see who could be the crudest. It was hardly surprising, given the name of the group.

DissGrace.

Madison may not have engineered my original downfall but she was definitely behind this. With a three-day suspension she'd had time on her hands, and judging from the comments, the page had been up since the very first day. I will say one thing for Madison: she knew how to rally support. She wasn't the only one who thought I was an ugly hag.

It was a long while before I turned off my computer, and a long while after that before I walked over to my bag and fished out the knife. It was lucky I'd kept it. It had been over a week since I'd inscribed Todd's appraisal. I'd been thinking about returning it to the kitchen. Even without Noor's support, I'd been feeling stronger. I'd thought I was done. I'd hoped I was.

This was my longest inscription yet, seven letters, two words. I was careful to line up the *U* with the *S* and the *L* so I had to wrap the rest of it around the back of my thigh. It was awkward. I thought about the femoral artery. It was so accessible, and I had the right equipment.

I knew now that people at school were never going to forget I'd stripped off for a total stranger. My image on the Internet would be an eternal reminder. The bullying wasn't going to stop. The only way to end it was if I ended it. I could make it look like an accident, though my parents wouldn't be consoled by the idea that I'd accidentally bled out while etching *UGLY HAG* into my thigh.

I had to take a break after a couple of letters to go fetch tissue so I didn't bleed on my bedspread. Wasn't I lucky to be so wealthy and well cared for that I had my own en suite bathroom? It was yet another privilege I had over Noor. I'd been insane to think I could ever tell her about this. The absurdity of voluntarily carving up my own flesh was staggering, and yet I couldn't stop. I played with my life, while she struggled for hers. She must never know.

Bosco watched from the foot of my bed, my only witness.

"What do you think, buddy? Am I crazy? Wouldn't I be doing everyone a favor by ending this tonight?"

His soft brown eyes held silent reproach.

"You'd still have Mom. And Kyle will be home at Christmas. You know, when he returns you're going to want to be with him anyway. This was never more than a temporary arrangement."

My phone pinged from inside my bag. It was probably my brother again. His timing was uncanny. I had to force myself to walk over and take out my phone. I didn't put down the knife, certain this was going to be something else I'd rather not read.

I was wrong.

The text was brief and to the point.

go to zoo sunday? noor

I sat down at my desk chair and stared at the letters I'd just finished chiseling into my flesh. They shone crimson in the light of the overhead lamp. I swiped my tissue over the *A*. I'd cut a little too deep; it was still dripping. I looked back at the message and read it again.

what time? I asked.

10 am at the flamingos

"Flamingos, Bosco, what do you think of that? I can't check

out before I've seen the flamingos." I put the knife back in my bag and returned to the bed, plopping down, phone still in hand.

ok

Bosco heaved his lazy self to his feet, padded closer and dropped his head into my lap. I lay down and curled around him, my face buried in his soft woolly fur. The steady rise and fall of his chest lulled me to sleep.

25

Noor

Without a matriarch . . .

It was my idea to visit the zoo. Grace seemed lonely and in
need of a friend, but it was Parvati I was most concerned about.
More and more she was succumbing to Suresh's domination.
She rarely bothered to fight him anymore, as if she too believed
he owned her. I'd seen so many spirits crushed among the girls
and women in my community. I couldn't bear to see it happen
to Parvati.

Parvati had always loved the zoo. We'd discovered it together
years ago, a refuge from our lives. I wasn't sure how she'd feel
about sharing it with Grace but she didn't hesitate.

"Are you sure she'll like it?" asked Parvati.

"No," I said honestly. "I think she will like doing something
with us though. She was sorry you didn't come last week."

A shadow crossed Parvati's face and I cursed myself for
reminding her.

"Was the café very grand?" asked Parvati.

"It was a waste of money. The zoo is much nicer," I reassured her.

Unlike the café, the zoo was cheap, even if we paid to get in. Of course, Parvati and I never did pay. Years ago we'd found a back entrance where we could sneak in for free. In the cooler months, I would take Shami and Aamaal whenever I had the bus fare. Recently, though, Shami's illnesses had sapped my cash reserve. The large grounds were like walking through an ancient forest. The trees were twisted giants, covered in vines and moss. I imagined that many of them, like the zoo, were over one hundred years old. It was one of the few places we could go where people weren't fighting over every inch of pavement.

Most of the cages were empty, and more animals were gone each time we visited. Only the signs were left to suggest what might once have been there: lions and rhinoceros, leopards and tigers. It must have been something to see all those animals in real life, but on the bright side, the zoo had fewer visitors now, and the animals that were left had become old friends.

"I want to see the bear," said Aamaal, staring, bored, at the flamingos. "And the deer and the spotted dog."

"He's not a dog, Aamaal." I was hoping she'd forgotten about the hyena. It was the one animal I did not like to visit.

"Do you think she'll bring Vijender Patel?" Parvati asked anxiously. I wasn't sure if she wanted to see him or was scared he would come—Parvati never flirted with boys anymore. She didn't even speak to them, if she could avoid them. I used to wish she was more cautious. Now that she was, all I felt was longing for the girl she used to be.

"I don't know. She didn't bring him to the café."

"And the monkeys, and the rhino—"

"The rhino's gone, Aamaal. I explained that."

"Did she say why he wasn't there?"

"Did you remember the lettuce for the hippo, Noor-didi?"

"Yes, Aamaal, but I've told you we really shouldn't feed him. If we got caught—"

"Do you think he's ever been to the zoo before? With his money, I bet he can see hippos and tigers in the jungle."

"There they are!" I said loudly. Vijender had come. I shot a look at Parvati. Her once-open face was unreadable.

Aamaal wrenched her hand from mine and ran toward Grace and VJ. I was on the point of calling her back when Shami wriggled from my arms and followed her. VJ had already dropped to his knees by the time they reached him. It was typical of his arrogance that he assumed they were running to him.

VJ swept both my siblings into a big hug. My stomach clenched to see Aamaal in his arms. I had to remind myself that not every male was a threat. I hadn't shared my suspicions about VJ's preferences with Parvati. Perhaps I should have. It might have put her at ease.

As we came up to them I was shocked to hear Shami burbling about a cricket match he'd watched on TV. I felt a stab of jealousy that he'd chosen to tell VJ about his new interest rather than me, but I couldn't help smiling when VJ dissected every play Shami described, and Shami glowed with excitement. Perhaps the film star could do some things for Shami that I could not. I just hoped VJ understood that if he ever did anything to hurt my brother I'd make him sorry he ever met me.

"So, what are we going to look at first?" asked Grace.

"The spotted dog," shouted Aamaal in Hindi. Though I'd

coached her to speak English when we were with the foreigners, I was happy in this instance that she'd forgotten.

"Let's start with the hippo," I said, also in Hindi. "He's much closer and we have food for him." I didn't add that I'd deliberately chosen our meeting place to be as far from the hyena as possible.

"Shami want to see spotty dog," agreed Shami. Fortunately he spoke Kannada. Shami still got his languages mixed up. He was fluent in three and had begun to learn English as well.

"What's that, little man?" asked VJ. I knew he'd cause trouble.

"Shami want to see spotty dog," Shami repeated, this time mostly in Hindi.

"The spotty dog it is, then," said VJ, as if he were in charge.

"Why do they have a dog in a zoo?" asked Grace.

"It is not being dog," said Parvati.

"It's a hyena," I said. "But really we should leave it till later. It's on the other side of the zoo."

"I want spotty dog," insisted Aamaal. She tugged on VJ's arm.

VJ scooped up Shami and placed him on his shoulders. I was on the point of objecting in the same moment that Shami squealed in delight. VJ put a hand on one of Shami's dangling legs and took Aamaal's hand with the other.

"Are we ready to go?" he asked cheerfully.

I crossed my arms. What an irritating boy he was.

"Which way do you want to go, Noor?" asked Grace.

VJ, Aamaal and Shami pinned me with identical imploring looks.

"All right," I said grouchily, "we will see the hyena first."

"Yes!" VJ crowed, swinging Aamaal's arm up in a victory punch.

VJ set off with my siblings at a slow trot, deliberately bouncing Shami up and down. Shami giggled and shrieked with far more enthusiasm than I'd ever seen in him before. It made me sad and happy at the same time.

Grace, Parvati and I followed. Parvati looked glum. I wasn't sure if she was wishing she'd brought Eka. We'd agreed, since we were spending the bus fare to come this far, that she would look for a place to sleep in this part of town tonight, far from Suresh.

"Shami seems to have taken to VJ," said Grace, calling my attention to where VJ had stopped to let us catch up and was passing the time swinging each of my siblings around like propellers on a helicopter.

"He is too rough with them."

"They seem to like it."

"Yes, they liking," agreed Parvati.

"I could give you a go," VJ teased.

Parvati flinched.

I started walking again, giving my brother's flying feet a wide berth.

Fifteen minutes later we reached the hyena. I swallowed my disappointment to find him still there. Many animals at our zoo died from poor care and malnutrition; I imagined it was a welcome release. Every time we came I hoped the suffering of this miserable creature had ended. He paced his tiny iron cage with a glassy-eyed despair that I'd seen too often in my own community. His tongue lolled out of his open mouth, skin stretched taut over jutting bones. I looked at my sister, who had come to stand beside me. Her anguished face was only part of what I hated about visiting the hyena.

Her hand found its way into my own. "Tell him the story, Noor."

The story was the other part.

Shami, who had been in VJ's arms, asked to be put down and

ran to take my other hand. It was our tradition to tell the story together. I was embarrassed to tell it in front of the foreigners but I couldn't disappoint Shami and Aamaal.

"You come from a proud line of hyenas," I began in Hindi, looking directly at the hyena. "Your mother and your aunties all loved you. Your sisters hunted while you stayed at home and played and slept and learned what it was to be a little boy hyena, beloved, in the paws of your community."

"Because girl hyenas are stronger and fiercer," said Aamaal, who knew the story well.

"Yes," I agreed.

"But hyena families stick together forever," said Aamaal. "That's why he's so sad. He misses his family."

"When will his mummy come, Noor?" asked Shami.

"Not yet, Shami," scolded Aamaal authoritatively. "We haven't told him the bad part yet."

"What are they saying?" asked Grace quietly. VJ played translator.

"One day some bad men came and stole you from your mother," I continued.

"Because mummy and sisters were out hunting," added Aamaal.

"But your mummy and sisters never stopped looking for you."

"Your sisters would never forget about you," said Aamaal pointedly to Shami.

"And one day they'll find you," I said to the hyena.

"Because family sticks together, right, Noor-di?" asked Shami.

"And a family isn't a family without a mummy," added Aamaal.

"That's right, one day we'll come and this hyena will be gone, but we won't feel sad because we'll know his mummy and sisters have come for him."

"Don't worry, darling, your mummy and sisters are on their way," said Aamaal to the hyena. "I wish I could give him a hug," she said to me.

"Well, who's for ice cream?" asked VJ. "My treat!"

"You don't have to treat us," I said.

"I am wanting ice cream," said Parvati, summoning a smile. For once I felt a rush of warmth for the film star.

"I'm treating everyone, even Gracie here. She could use a little meat on her bones."

Grace flushed and quickly turned away. Even VJ noticed.

"Everything all right, Grace?" VJ gave her a curious look. "You're not upset that I called you bony, are you?"

"You need to learn when to keep quiet," I scolded. "There is a small restaurant down this path." I took Grace's arm.

Grace and I dropped back, letting VJ go ahead with my siblings. "You are feeling embarrassed," I said.

"No, it was no big deal. Where did the story come from?"

"The first time we came here Aamaal was so sad because of the hyena that I made up a story about his family rescuing him. Later I asked my teacher about hyenas. Their families really do stay together and look after each other, just like people. I think that is why he has become crazy. He is lonely."

"You're a good sister."

"I am certain you are as well."

"Maybe I used to be."

We enjoyed another hour at the zoo before I had to take Shami and Aamaal home. I let VJ give us a ride. It was much quicker, and I worried Shami's flushed face might indicate more than excitement. The car dropped us at the end of our street.

"Can you meet next week?" asked Grace. "On Friday night, maybe?"

"I think so."

"I was thinking maybe we could have a meal somewhere."

I hesitated, but I could see it was important to her, so we agreed on a falafel place. It was on the edge of my neighborhood and not too expensive. If I set aside a little money all week, I might be able to afford something.

Deepa-Auntie met us the minute we walked through the door of our house. "Thank goodness you're back, Noor. Your ma isn't well. I think she should see a doctor."

"I'll talk to her," I said.

"Shami want to see Ma," said Shami.

"Not right now, Shami-baby," said Deepa-Auntie. "Let Noor go first."

I hurried to the ladder, scrambled up and peeked over the top. Ma was flat on her back with her eyes closed. The heat, even with the fan going, was stifling. I climbed the rest of the way and went over to the bed, perching uneasily at its foot. She didn't stir. I reached for her wrist. She had a pulse but her flesh was burning up. I noticed she had a sore on her lip again, heavy with pus.

I crawled under the bed and pulled out the fixings for tea and a tiny folded paper of pills that she didn't know about. I would dissolve some into her drink. To please her I also took the small jar of home remedy that she swore by. Shami called it her magic powder. If only it was magic, I thought traitorously. I wondered how many more illnesses like this her body could endure before death took her. Each time, she returned from them a little weaker.

I left her sleeping and made my way down the ladder, heading to the kitchen. Adit was standing in the hallway.

"She's sick again," he said.

"It's nothing. A cup of tea will revive her."

"Nishikar-Sir was asking about you."

The owner of the brothel. My heart stopped but I held myself tightly, determined not to show my fear.

"Why would he be asking about me?"

"Did you really think he wouldn't notice you forever? Your ma earns so little now. You must have seen this coming."

"You seem to take pleasure in this, Adit."

"It's just the way things are. Your mother was stupid to send you to school. You're just a girl."

"You're a boy, yet your mother didn't bother to send you to school."

"It wouldn't matter. An education is more useful for a boy, but both our fates were written before we were born. If I'm lucky, Pran will let me stay on here as his assistant."

"You call that luck, to live off the women who are trapped here?"

"What do you expect me to do, Noor? I also must provide for my family."

"I don't know who you are anymore, Adit. The boy I knew was a fighter. He would not have given in to a fate he didn't choose. There is a whole world of possibilities beyond our fifteen lanes. Don't you want more for yourself?"

I didn't give him a chance to respond. I could see my words had hit home as his cheeks colored. I pushed past him and went down the hall to make my mother's tea.

26

Noor

The big boss . . .

Ma must have known that Nishikar-Sir had asked about me, though she gave no sign of concern. She was a respected woman in our home and in the community. As powerful as he was, I was not such a valuable item that Nishikar-Sir would risk the anger of the entire Devadasi community, not to mention the non-Devadasi sex workers, by selling me without Ma's permission.

Still, I couldn't ignore his interest entirely. I'd seen it often enough. If Nishikar-Sir had decided he wanted me, the pressure on Ma would begin. But Ma had worked hard to give me a good education, and her pride wouldn't allow her to accept that her daughter needed to take over the work because she could no longer bring in enough customers to provide for her children. So over the next few days, I kept my worries to myself, making light of it whenever Deepa-Auntie tried to broach the subject. I don't think she would have let it go so easily if we hadn't both been distracted by the return of Lali-didi.

She was brought back in the night. There were as many accounts of how it happened as there were people to tell the tale. What was certain was Adit's part in it. He really had known where she was, and for the promise of a job he gave her up.

Lali-didi went back to the lockup. We were all forbidden to speak to her, but there wasn't a woman or girl in the house who obeyed. No matter how many times Pran or Binti-Ma'am chased us away, we kept a round-the-clock vigil outside the box that was her prison. We spoke to her constantly, told her what was happening in the outside world and made plans for her release. Some of us promised her wild things that we could never bestow.

Lali-didi herself spoke little. She didn't cry either, even when Pran went inside the box with her. Her silence echoed off the walls of our home in a way that her tears never had. It spooked Pran. Over the week of her confinement he went to her with decreasing frequency and none of his usual malicious glee. He tortured her with the dogged determination of a man completing a distasteful task. We all suspected Nishikar-Sir had ordered it.

On the day she was released, Pran came into the outer room, walked straight past Shami and me sitting on the floor, went to the door of the box and unlocked it. He didn't speak to us. I'm not even sure he saw us. He turned and walked straight back out. Shami and I jumped up. Other than Pran, we were the first to see Lali-didi since her return to our house.

"You're free, Lali-didi," I called out. "Pran isn't here. You can come out now."

After a few minutes of silence, I climbed up on the stool and poked my head through the doorway. Lali-didi was a shadow in the farthest corner. "Come out," I said gently. She didn't budge.

I hated the box. My fear of it had only grown over the years. But I had no choice. I climbed in. Shami's face appeared in the open doorway.

"Shami want Lal-di," he said.

I reached over and hauled him in as well.

"It's over, Lali-didi. You have to come out now. You're safe." Of all the many lies I'd told in my life, that was perhaps the biggest.

"It is over, isn't it, Noor?" she said.

"I swear I'll get you out of here, Lali-didi." Silently, I added her to my list of people who would someday share my small room in a distant slum.

"We're almost the same age but I'm not like you," she said. "I can't even write my own name. I've never been to school. My brother sold me to the brothel in Calcutta. My family was glad to be rid of me. You have a future. This is all I'm good for."

"You're wrong. It's not too late for you to go to school. When I get out, I'll make a life for all of us." The tears streamed down my face. I had to make her believe me.

Shami patted my leg. "Don't cry, Noor-di. Come out, Lal-di. You're making Noor-di sad."

The shadow moved. I reached out my hand and Lali-didi took it. We maneuvered awkwardly past Shami and out of the box. He crawled to the door and I lifted him down.

Lali-didi was thinner than I remembered her. Her crocodile arm had completely healed, but I wondered if the wounds inside her ever could. She looked around bleakly, squinting at the light. I left Shami to guard her while I went to the bottom of our ladder to shout for Deepa-Auntie.

She came running, as I knew she would, and followed me back down the hall to the lock-up. I was surprised to see Ma and several other aunties right behind her.

"It's a crying shame," Prita-Auntie muttered, waiting her turn to embrace Lali-didi. "The girl's not strong enough for the life. Any fool can see that."

For the rest of the evening, the aunties clucked around her as if she were a precious object, easily broken. Lali-didi drank the tea they served and sat quietly while they washed and brushed her hair, but her despair was written on her body. Nothing anyone did could dislodge it. Pran made a futile effort to send her customers that night. But he couldn't stand up to the entire house when the entire house united against him. Lali-didi got a single night of peace.

The day after Lali-didi emerged from the box, Nishikar-Sir returned to our home. It was Friday night, the evening my siblings and I were supposed to meet Grace for dinner. We were late leaving the house. I'd spent more time than usual sitting with Lali-didi after school. Like never before, I was aware of the narrow gap in our ages and the vast gulf in our life experiences. I was fearful of what she might do to herself.

I stayed with her until her first customer arrived, even though it meant my siblings and I would have to run to make it to the restaurant in time to meet Grace. She'd texted me twice since the zoo to confirm the meeting. I didn't know why it was quite so important to her.

When I got downstairs, Shami reported that Aamaal had a

sick stomach and was in the washroom. Together we went to stand outside the locked door. I could smell the problem from the hallway.

"Are you okay in there, Aamaal?"

"No."

"Try to hurry, we're running late."

I held myself back from scolding her, though I was genuinely getting worried about the time. Shami sank down to the floor to wait but I paced in frustration.

I was just on the point of texting Grace to let her know we'd be late when I heard loud voices coming around the corner. It didn't even occur to me to think of Nishikar-Sir. I'd been so absorbed by Lali-didi's tragedy, I'd forgotten my own danger. But when I heard a harsh male voice call my name, I felt a stab of fear. There was one way out of the building and that was in the direction of the man calling my name. The only hiding places I could get to quickly were the toilet, which Aamaal was currently occupying, and the washing room beside it. The washing room was a tiny closet, not more than four feet square, completely devoid of anything but a tap and a drain. Anyone looking for me would find me the second they opened the door, which left only the room Aamaal was currently befouling.

"Shami, you need to tell the men that I've gone out to fetch you dinner."

"Shami having dinner with Grace."

"I know, baby, but Noor needs to hide from the bad men. Can you help Noor hide?"

Shami's brow creased. "Noor-di hide," he said solemnly.

As quietly as possible I tapped on the latrine door.

"Let me in, Aamaal. It's an emergency."

"I'm not finished" came her surly reply.

"Please, Aamaal. I need to come in, quickly!"

She unlocked the door just as I heard the voices rounding the corner. I slipped in and locked it behind me. I wasn't sure if I'd been spotted. The smell in the room made me gag but it also filled me with hope. If I could find someplace to hide I was certain the men wouldn't give the room any more than a very brief once-over.

"Pran and Nishikar-Sir are coming, Aamaal," I whispered, looking down to where she was crouching above the hole. "They can't know I'm here."

She nodded in understanding. It broke my heart at how easily she accepted a dangerous situation.

"If they open the door, I will stand behind it," I whispered. "You must make sure they don't open it too far. Can you do that?"

She nodded again.

"Hello, Shami." Voices were just on the other side of the door. I recognized Pran's. "Where's Noor, Shami?"

"Noor-di buy kebabs," said Shami.

I had to smile. I almost never bought kebabs. We couldn't afford them, but they were Shami's favorite. If I got through this, he was definitely getting kebabs tonight.

"Would she leave them alone?" asked another male voice. It had to be Nishikar-Sir.

"She wouldn't leave them on the street but she'd leave them in here if she was just going out to get food," said Pran.

"I told you I wanted to see her. Why would you let her go out?"

"I'm very sorry, Nishikar-Sir, I didn't know you were coming tonight, you didn't—"

Pran's obsequious pleading was cut short by a loud thwack.

"Do you think I have time for your excuses, you useless mule? Go find the girl and bring her to me."

"She might be in there, Nishikar-Sir."

"Why didn't you say that in the first place? Are you trying to hide her from me?"

There were two more loud cracks, accompanied by Pran's whimpers. I had to admit I felt a grim satisfaction in hearing him get beaten.

I jumped at a sharp rap on the door and I pressed against the wall.

"I'm in here!" shouted Aamaal.

"Is that you, Aamaal?" It was Pran again, though his voice sounded different than I'd ever heard it, weak and frightened. "Where is your sister?"

"She went to buy food," said Aamaal.

"Why did she leave you two here?"

"I have bad diarrhea. Do you want to see?"

If I hadn't been so terrified, I would have laughed.

"These children are more effort than they're worth," snarled Nishikar-Sir. "I hope you charge Ashmita double to let them stay here."

I bristled with indignation. We were already charged for every bucket of water, the rental of Ma's bed, a share of the electricity and we bought all our own food. What more could we be charged for?

"Of course, Nishikar-Sir, we'll certainly do that."

"I've been offered a good price for the girl, Pran. I'll be back for her before morning. When she returns, lock her up."

My blood pulsed in my ears. It was true, then. That was his plan. I was trembling so much I had to sit down on the filthy, urine-stained floor.

"I understand, sir. It's just that I think Ashmita was hoping to delay a little longer. The girl's a top student, medal-winning."

"Education is wasted on girls. It only gives them expectations they have no right to. Ashmita's delayed long enough. How old is the girl, thirteen, fourteen? Does Ashmita plan to wait until the blossom has wilted? She's worth less every day."

"But the Devadasis, sir, they support each other. If you anger one—"

"Let them experience my anger! The Devadasis are born to be whores. They should know their place. If Ashmita cooperates, the girl can continue to work here. If she doesn't . . . well, I have brothels all over the country. I'll send her away and Ashmita will never see her again. See how she likes that!"

"Ashmita's been a good earner for—"

Again Pran was cut off. The door reverberated as something slammed into it. There was a muffled grunt.

"Ashmita will be dead within two years. Her earnings are already a fraction of what the young girls bring in. The lounge is full tonight because you got the young one back. We need more like her. We're doing the lot of them a favor by training the girl. Everyone expects something for nothing. Who does she think will feed those brats once she's gone?"

Loud footsteps receded down the hallway. I rose heavily to

my feet and put a cold hand on the door. I was on the point of opening it when Shami spoke.

"Why are you sitting there, Pran-ji. Do you feel sick?"

Clever boy. I didn't know Pran was still outside.

"Shut up!"

There was scuffling, at first quiet and then louder.

"Let go, Pran-ji."

"You're coming with me. It's long past time I introduced you to a little place where your sister spent many nights at your age."

No! I threw open the door and took in the scene in an instant: Shami was twisting and cowering away, trying desperately to escape as Pran dragged him down the hall. I saw the familiar light of excitement in Pran's eyes as the tears rolled down Shami's face. My little brother, who'd endured countless injections, a life of wracking coughs and constant illness, who never complained, never cried. I ran after them and leaped on Pran's back, pummeling him.

"Let go of him!" I screamed.

Pran dropped Shami as he turned his attention to me, raising his hands to ward off my blows while trying to grab my swinging arms at the same time. I felt rather than saw Aamaal join the fray. Pran howled in pain. I knew Aamaal had bitten him. I'd suffered her bites myself on many occasions. He lashed out, and I heard the sickening crack of his fist hitting flesh. It wasn't my own, so it had to be one of my siblings'. I turned to look and saw Aamaal flying through the air. She cracked against the wall and dropped to the floor. She lay still, whimpering. I left Pran to rush to her but he grabbed me from behind and threw me to the ground. As he bent over me Shami leaped on his back, a whirlwind of teeth and nails.

"Go get Ma, Shami," I gurgled as Pran easily shook him off and dragged me to my feet, one hand clutching my hair, the other encircling my throat.

Shami was off, scampering down the hall. Pran didn't even notice.

"You've been trouble since you were a child." Pran pulled me after him in the opposite direction. "I hope Nishikar-Sir does send you away. I'll be glad to be rid of you."

There was only one place we could be going in that direction. The box.

"No, Pran-ji," I pleaded. "You don't have to lock me in there. I won't try to escape. Just let me look after my sister." I craned my head over his shoulder, trying to see Aamaal. She hadn't moved from where she'd fallen. Her arm was twisted underneath her body in a way that looked physically impossible. "Please, Pran-ji, I beg you."

He laughed. "You're going to be doing a lot of begging over the next weeks, little Noor."

"STOP!" My mother had come. She rushed forward with an energy I hadn't seen in weeks and gave Pran a hard shove that made him release me, though he took a chunk of my hair with him. I winced, then ran to Aamaal, still flat on the floor.

"What do you think you're . . . ?" Ma broke off midsentence when she caught sight of Aamaal. In seconds she was at my side. "What has he done to her?" she demanded.

"She attacked me," said Pran, coming to stand over us. "You're lucky I didn't do worse."

Ma wasn't listening. She gently raised Aamaal so she could

free her trapped arm but it dangled uselessly from her shoulder. Aamaal moaned.

"It hurts, Ma," she said.

Ma laid her down again, positioning the floppy arm at her side. "Stay still, child," she said. "Noor, go get a dupatta. We need to bind it."

I jumped up, grateful to have my old ma back and taking charge. Even Pran stepped aside to let me pass as I ran to the ladder. I clambered up, only slowing when my head was above the level of our floor. Deepa-Auntie and Lali-didi were entertaining customers. I was as quiet as possible as I rushed past their closed curtains. Ma's own bed looked recently vacated. I knelt down and pulled out our box of clothes, taking Ma's cleanest and least worn dupatta. For a moment I wondered if she'd object, but this was Aamaal. I was sure she would have made the same choice.

I raced back to my sister. Shami and Ma were on the floor comforting her. Pran stood nearby. I helped Ma use the dupatta to bind Aamaal's arm tightly against her chest.

"We must take her to the hospital. Noor, go out to the main road and bring back a taxi."

"Noor's not going anywhere." Pran suddenly came to life, crossing his arms and spreading his legs in a stance clearly intended to prevent our passage.

"What are you talking about, flea-on-a-rat's-backside? Noor needs to help me take her sister to hospital. Can't you see you've broken Aamaal's arm?"

"You can go but Noor stays here."

"Why should I leave her? What's it to you?"

"Nishikar-Sir wants to meet her."

"For what purpose?" Ma knew the answer. There could be only one.

"He wants to sell me," I said, before Pran could come up with a lie.

"Not without my permission," said Ma coldly.

"There'll be trouble if she's not here when he returns, Ashmita. I won't let him take her tonight but we must let him see her, so he doesn't think you're openly defying him. Then tomorrow we can all discuss what is to be done." Pran's voice was uncharacteristically reasonable. I felt a prickle of fear.

Ma gave him a hard stare. She too was suspicious. Aamaal moaned again. Ma got unsteadily to her feet, Aamaal in her arms. For the first time I realized what this fight had cost her. Though the drugs I'd been slipping her had helped, she was still weak.

"Please let me go with them, Pran-ji," I pleaded. "I promise I'll come back."

"I'm sorry, Noor," he said, sounding genuinely regretful. "I can't do that. You must meet with Nishikar-Sir tonight. But I promise I won't let him touch you until your ma returns."

Ma looked from Pran to me, her face creased with indecision.

"I'll be back soon, Noor. If I go quickly I might return before Nishikar-Sir gets here. Look after your brother."

I held my breath, rigidly holding myself, so the tears would not fall.

"I'll be back soon," she repeated. "She had better be here when I return, Pran, or you will experience the true meaning of trouble."

Ma swept past him and disappeared around the corner and

out of sight. The harsh glare of the fluorescent light gave Pran's pointed features a maniacal glow as he advanced toward me. Shami hid behind my leg. I put a reassuring hand on his shoulder.

"If you go quietly, Noor, I won't beat you."

"You don't need to lock me in, Pran. I'll wait for Nishikar-Sir and my mother."

He laughed. It was the most chilling sound I'd heard all night.

"You'll be gone long before your mother returns, Noor. I'll make sure of that."

"You wouldn't dare. Ma will be furious."

"Perhaps, but she'll get over it. We both know which daughter she loves, Noor. She's always treated you as little more than a servant. I'm surprised you aren't looking forward to getting away from her. You'll have your own life, your own money."

"Before or after I've paid back my purchase price?" I scoffed.

"Don't worry, you'll work in another of Nishikar-Sir's brothels, possibly in Calcutta or Bangalore. Wouldn't you like to see a bit more of this great country of ours? There will be no purchase price because he already owns you. A share of your earnings will go into your own pocket from the first day. Who knows, perhaps someday you'll earn enough that you can send for the little brat." He nodded at Shami.

I hoisted Shami onto my hip and tried to walk past him. "I've heard enough, Pran. I'll wait outside for my mother."

"You will do what I tell you, Noor, or I'll wring your brother's neck, like you should have done the day he was born, sickly runt that he is."

I hesitated. Pran made a grab for Shami and we scuffled, Shami kicking out with his little legs, but even united we were no match for Pran. He had Shami out of my arms in seconds. We squared off, him holding my squirming, clawing brother, and me, my arms empty. I thought my heart would stop; the pain of seeing Shami in Pran's clutches was that great. My pride, watching Shami's determined struggle not to give in, was matched only by my agony. It was a struggle I'd witnessed every day of his life.

"All right," I said. "Let him go. I'll go with you."

Grace

I wanted to recreate my fifteenth birthday. That's my excuse. It was the best birthday I'd ever had. Up till then most of my birthdays had been little-kid birthdays: specifically, unpopular little-kid birthdays, by which I mean I celebrated with my family.

By my fifteenth birthday I still didn't have enough friends to have a party but I did have one exceptionally wonderful friend who was determined to make my birthday special. Tina said it was time we had a sophisticated grown-up evening, no parents allowed. She chose a real five-star restaurant, with napkins and fine china. She even had to make a reservation. We both got dressed up and put on makeup. We had a good giggle when we got to the place and the hostess realized it was just us.

Tina ordered truffles crostini and roast duck; I ordered scallops almandine and grilled salmon. We were both dismayed to discover truffles were just expensive mushrooms. They tasted hideous so we shared my scallops. The only rule was that everything we ordered had to be something we'd never tried before—new experiences to celebrate the new me. Tina said turning fifteen was like teetering on the precipice of adulthood. Sixteen was an adult. Fifteen was a practice run. The excitement of dating and college and careers seemed just around the corner. We couldn't wait.

I didn't tell Noor that Friday was my sixteenth birthday. I didn't want to pressure her or make it into a big deal. But it was a big deal, bigger than she could possibly have imagined. The past few weeks had been a nightmare. I couldn't believe that all my hopes and expectations of who I'd be on my sixteenth birthday could have imploded so dramatically in such a short space of time. I thought maybe with Noor I could recreate some of the magic of my friendship with Tina.

As usual it took many lies to convince my parents to let me spend the evening with Noor. It wasn't just that she was a sex worker's daughter, though that did worry them. More than that, they no longer trusted me to make good decisions without adult supervision. I told them Parvati and VJ would be there as well. I thought they might be more encouraging if it seemed that I was developing a group of friends. It didn't help. They didn't know any of my new friends, so their overprotective paranoia was in overdrive.

Mom insisted on talking me through my plans multiple times. If I hadn't known better, I'd have suspected it was the lawyer in her trying to trip me up in a lie.

"And you're going with VJ's driver?"

"Yes, that's why I'm walking to his house."

"Why can't our driver take you?"

"It's like last year, Mom. *VJ*'s taking *me* out, like Tina did."
I knew that would get to her. Mom was almost as devastated
by my loss of a best friend as I was.

"Maybe I should call VJ's mother," said Mom.

"Please don't embarrass me, Mom. I need to go out with
friends like a normal teenager."

Mom sighed. The Achilles' heel for both my parents was
always the same. They wanted my life to be perfect. To
control them, the only real challenge was to figure out how
to convince them that giving me what I wanted would
ensure that.

I spent considerable time deciding what to wear. I didn't
want to dress super-fancy like last year but I did put on one of
my prettiest Indian print dresses and a bit of makeup. I wasn't
trying to show off. I just wanted to look my best. I hoped Noor
would notice and tell me I looked nice. If it felt right, I'd admit
it was my birthday. Maybe after the falafel place we could get
cake somewhere.

When I was ready I did a quick turn in front of the mirror.

"What do you think, Bosco?" Bosco, asleep on my bed as
usual, raised his head and looked at me. "I'm sixteen. Can you
believe it? I want you to know things are going to be okay from
now on. I really like Noor and I've got VJ. So you can stop worrying about me."

I wasn't at all sure if this was the truth, but I wanted it to be.
I went over and gave his ears a reassuring rub, kissed him and
headed to the kitchen to say good-bye to my parents.

Dad was sitting at the table. "Your mom tells me you're
going out with VJ and some girls from the NGO tonight," said
Dad, trying to sound as though he wasn't crushed.

I walked over, hugged him and kissed the top of his head. He gave me a one-armed squeeze and I stayed a while with his arm around me.

"We can go out tomorrow night, Dad. It'll give you more time to plan something really super-special."

"Your mom and I could take you all out tonight for something super-special."

"We've already made plans, Dad. I'll do something with you guys tomorrow."

"It won't be your birthday tomorrow."

Mom made big eyes at him across the table.

"I'm sixteen now, Dad. Sometimes I want to be with my friends."

"You'll always be my baby girl."

"John!" said Mom in a reproving voice, though she was no better.

"You're such a dork, Dad."

I gave him a final hug before I pulled away and headed for the door. Both my parents jumped up to follow.

"If you run into any trouble, or if anyone says or does something that makes you feel uncomfortable, just call us," said Mom, hugging me at the door. I'd already told her VJ was gay. It was probably the only reason she was letting me go.

"We're just going to get pizza, Mom. Nothing is going to go wrong."

Dad opened the door and gave me another hug. "Happy birthday, my girl."

"Thanks, Dad. Love you."

I walked to the elevator. I didn't need to look back to know they were still at the door watching me.

I walked down the block before hailing a taxi. I'd already lied to my parents that VJ lived just around the corner. It would be just like them to watch out the front window.

The drive to Kamathipura took an hour, which was longer than usual. Friday night traffic in Mumbai was always terrible. I had trouble spotting the falafel place Noor had described. It was smaller than I'd expected but also a bit nicer. Most of the food outlets in Kamathipura were little more than counters with no place to sit. This one looked like a proper restaurant though it was open to the air, with just a few large overhead fans for cooling.

I was a few minutes late and disappointed that Noor wasn't already there. There wasn't a single woman in the place. I sat down at a table as close as I could get to the door, though there were only eight tightly packed tables and most were occupied. I'd been sitting about fifteen minutes when I noticed the server behind the counter staring at me. It was one of those places where you have to go up to the counter to order. He must have been wondering what I was waiting for. I got out my phone.

already at restaurant. U far? I texted.

I waited for an answer. A group of men came in and took the last empty table. I could feel the counter guy's eyes on me, though I was careful not to look his way. Men from other tables were gawping at me as well. I suddenly felt exposed in my flimsy Indian frock. I should have just worn jeans. My face burned with embarrassment. I looked at my phone again. Noor was almost thirty minutes late. I'd never felt so pathetic.

restaurant crowded. u here soon? I typed.

I waited.

And waited.

And waited.

Another fifteen minutes passed.

Nothing.

So far this was the worst birthday ever. Maybe I should have gone to her house but I didn't have the courage to walk through Kamathipura alone at night. Surely if she'd had to cancel she'd have let me know. I couldn't continue to sit there if I didn't get food. The counter clerk was clearly talking about me with one of his servers, gesturing angrily. I flushed with embarrassment. They were going to throw me out any minute. I got up and went to the counter to order a falafel and water, though I really only wanted the water. The heat, combined with my anxiety, was making me queasy.

I couldn't bear the thought of going home and giving up on this night, though it was obvious Noor wasn't coming. I'd had such stupidly high hopes, not only for my birthday but for our friendship. I took my food back to the table and proceeded to consume it as slowly as possible. It was close to eight, two hours after we were meant to meet, when I sent one final text.

can only wait a few more minutes. hope u ok

The last statement was both true and not. I was genuinely worried about Noor. She lived a precarious life. Maybe something bad had happened to her. At the same time, it seemed too coincidental that she'd have a serious problem the very same night we'd agreed to meet. A far more likely explanation was that she'd decided she didn't want to have dinner with me. On reflection, she hadn't seemed that keen. I was the loser trying to force my friendship on her. Why should she want to be my friend? No one else did.

So, on my sixteenth birthday, I sat alone in a run-down restaurant, surrounded by men openly ogling me, wishing I could disappear.

Noor didn't like me.

I felt foolish that I'd expected anything more and betrayed because I really did like her and Shami and Aamaal. What was so wrong with me? My eyes stung with unshed tears. I only wanted to be her friend. Was that too much to ask? I felt like screaming or hurling my half-eaten falafel across the room.

I didn't.

I had a better way to release tension.

The washroom sign was to the right. I picked up my bag and headed over. I was grateful to find the door unlocked, but disappointed, when I stepped inside, to discover it filthy and foul-smelling. I took the knife from my bag. Fortunately, I was wearing a dress—easier access. I hiked it up, gingerly leaned against the wall and bent my leg, bringing my canvas within reach. The first letter was an obvious choice.

T

It couldn't be anything else. My poem was almost complete.

I thought long and hard about the next letter. I wanted to write *traitor*, an indictment of Noor. But this was my epitaph, not hers. It needed to describe me, and when I realized that, I came to another realization. The word was obvious, as obvious as what I needed to do next. I'd known all along it would come to this. Even the location felt somehow right. My parents wouldn't find me. Strangers would clear me away like so much debris.

I etched an *E*.

My father's face, his disappointment as I'd left the house this evening swam into view.

The *R* took more time. My hand was shaking.

I looked around the small room. Maybe I should leave a note.

I started on the *M* but my hands were shaking so badly now I had to stop. I felt light-headed.

My phone buzzed. I looked at my bag. Who could be calling at a time like this?

"You're too late," I said grimly.

I finished the *M*.

My phone rang again. What if it was my mother checking up on me?

I glared at the bag. The ringing was interminable. Every time it ran through the limit of rings, it would start afresh moments later. In my frustration I'd made the downstroke on the *M* too deep. Blood dripped down my leg.

Whoever it was, they weren't giving up on me. It had to be my parents. It would be typical of my mom to somehow intuit something was wrong. Or maybe it was my dad making a last-ditch effort to convince me to spend my birthday with them. It could even be Kyle or Tina, wishing me a happy birthday. I put the knife under the tap and rinsed it off. The phone continued to ring as I dried the knife, reached for my bag and dropped it in. My phone, nestled inside, glowed and bleated like a living thing. I took it out and checked the caller ID.

It was Noor.

I put the phone to my ear and answered.

"Hello."

28

Noor

A small triumph . . .

The only light switch for the box was on the outside. It would have cost Pran nothing to turn it on. He didn't. In the silent darkness, with no room to move, the smell of sweat mingled with sex and blood was magnified. I thought I might suffocate. It would be some kind of victory if he found me dead. Too bad I wouldn't be around to enjoy it.

There was no need to explore the limits of my prison; I'd seen it often enough. I could do nothing but wait. My own thoughts were an unwelcome companion. I worried about Aamaal. Would they be able to fix her arm? Could Ma afford it? I worried about Shami. Before Pran took me away I'd told him to go to Deepa-Auntie. I could only hope that he had.

I worried about myself. My life was over. I would rather be dead than submit to the men who used Ma. I didn't give in to tears. I was beyond them.

"Noor-di?" It was Shami.

"What are you doing here, baby? I told you to go to Deepa-Auntie."

"Should I bring her here, Noor-di?"

"No, Shami, that would only get her in trouble. Just tell her where I am. Tell her Pran has broken his promise to Ma."

"Okay," said Shami. I heard the faintest footsteps as he left.

Only a few minutes had passed when I heard noises again.

"Noor, what has he done to you? What are you doing in there?" Joy coursed through me at the sound of Deepa-Auntie's voice.

"He's going to sell me. Nishikar-Sir has ordered it."

"No! That can't be. Your ma would never allow it." It was Lali-didi this time. It was good to hear her voice, but they had to leave before Pran caught them. How had they got rid of their customers so quickly? Surely that would arouse suspicion.

"Pran hurt Aamaal. Ma took her to hospital. He plans to hand me over to Nishikar-Sir before she returns."

"I won't allow it!" said Deepa-Auntie.

"No, you mustn't confront him! He'll hurt you."

There was silence, followed by whispering between Deepa-Auntie and Lali-didi.

"Noor, do you still have Parvati's phone?" asked Deepa-Auntie.

"It's in my pocket."

"You must call the foreigner. We have a plan."

Over the next ten minutes, we talked through their idea. It was outrageous, and I wasn't sure Grace or Vijender Patel would agree. There was only a small chance it would even work, but it was my only chance.

It was already almost eight o'clock. We had agreed to meet

for dinner at six. Grace would be back home by now. Would she even be allowed to come out again?

She didn't pick up the first time I called. I tried again. It rang and rang then went to voice mail. She had to answer. I couldn't give up. Maybe she didn't keep her phone with her all the time like I did. She lived in a proper house where her valuables weren't in constant threat of being stolen.

The seventh time I called, Grace answered.

"Hello." Her voice was wary.

"Grace, you have to help me." The words spilled out. "I'm locked in a box. You need to come here and bring Vijender Patel."

"Noor, what did you say?" The phone crackled. I could hardly hear her.

"A box. He'll need to pretend he wants a prostitute and then come and break the door. He should ask for a young girl, that's important. Do you remember I told you about Lali-didi? He must get to her."

"Noor, I don't understand—"

"He's going to sell me tonight, Grace." I was in tears now.

"Who's going to sell you?" The line crackled, beeped and went dead.

I hit redial several times and repeatedly got the recorded message telling me the caller was out of range. I cried as quietly as I could.

"Are they coming?" asked Deepa-Auntie. I could hear the doubt in her voice.

"I don't think so. I couldn't make her understand."

"I'll find your ma, Noor. I'll check every hospital."

"No, you can't. Pran will punish you if you take the night off."

"When your ma finds out, Pran will have bigger problems than me. I'll go down the street talking to men. He won't realize what I'm up to until I'm long gone."

"It's too dangerous, Deepa-Auntie. Please, don't."

Her bark of laughter was harsh and unlike her. "I've lived with danger since the day the men came to my village, Noor. The only thing that kept me going was you and your brother and sister. You give us all something to hope for. If you can escape, maybe someday we all can."

"It's true, Noor," agreed Lali-didi. "Some day you'll be an important person, more powerful than Pran or Binti-Ma'am, or even Nishikar-Sir. On that day we will laugh in their faces and walk out the front door."

The weight of their expectations could have felt like a burden, but it had the opposite effect. Their dreams only strengthened my own.

"Be careful, Deepa-Auntie."

"Don't worry, Noor-baby, I'll be back before you know it."

I leaned my head against the wooden wall and prepared to wait. The time passed slowly. Shami kept vigil outside. For a while we played a guessing game. As the hour grew late, his responses became more infrequent and his words jumbled. Finally, I ordered him to go to sleep. His silence, after wishing me good night, was almost immediate. At first it was comfort enough that I could picture his small body curled up beside the stool under my prison door.

I checked the time on the phone many times and chided myself for wasting the battery. I wished I could have slept as well. Some ninety minutes after Deepa-Auntie's departure the phone rang. My fingers trembled as I answered it.

"Noor?" It was Grace. "I'm outside your building." Her voice was as clear as if she were just outside the box. "VJ has headed inside."

"He's inside?" All at once I realized the rashness of my plan. VJ might be a rich film star, but he was a boy, sheltered and inexperienced. He didn't even like girls. If I could figure that out, surely a man with Pran's experience would realize.

"Shami!" I called through the wall.

"Yes?" I was surprised by how quickly he woke up.

"You must go tell Lali-didi that the plan is happening. VJ Patel will be asking for her."

"I'll tell her, Noor-di," he said eagerly. The patter of his feet retreated.

I looked at my phone. It was nearly ten o'clock.

I checked it a dozen times over the next thirty minutes. Finally, I heard the approach of footsteps and whispers.

"Are you in there, Noor?"

It was Vijender. I broke into a cold sweat. I was relieved and terrified at the same time.

"Hurry," I said. "Pran could show up at any moment."

"I bought us some time. Pran recognized me but I used it to our advantage. I promised him five times Lali's price to clear your room and I said if anyone disturbed me before I was finished, then the deal was off." There was a loud scraping along the doorframe.

"Are you okay in there, Noor?" It was Lali-didi. My heart pounded as I considered the danger I'd placed her in.

"You must come with us, Lali-didi," I told her, though the racket from VJ hammering a wedge between the door and frame may have drowned out my words.

"I need to go back to the lounge, Noor. You know how suspicious Pran is. He'll be worried about his money. Sooner or later he'll come looking to make sure VJ hasn't snuck away without paying. VJ has given me money for him. Perhaps it will be enough to distract him awhile longer. Should I take Shami with me?" she asked.

"No!" I couldn't bear to not see Shami before I left. "I want to take him with me."

"We can't take him tonight, Noor. It's too dangerous," said VJ.

"I promise I'll keep him safe," said Lali-didi.

"Shami want to go with Noor-di." I didn't know if he was pleading with me or them. My heart ached. What had I been thinking? I couldn't leave Shami.

"Good luck, Noor. We're going now . . ."

"No!"

"Bye-bye, Noor-di." I knew him so well. He was holding in his tears, as he had so many times before. I reached out to him in the darkness.

"Make us proud," said Lali-didi. They were her final words to me.

I shoved my fist in my mouth to stifle the sound of the sobs that wracked my body.

Minutes later, with a shattering of wood, the door fell open and VJ's head appeared in the opening. He registered surprise when he saw the state of me but quickly recovered. There was no time to delay.

VJ extended his hand to help me down. "Hurry. We haven't much time."

"Shami?" Grief overshadowed my fear.

"We'll come back for him, but we must go now."

He didn't need to tell me that, but where could we go? There was only one exit, and it meant getting past the lounge without being seen. We'd never make it.

"Follow me," said VJ. He ran in the only possible direction. I followed but was still shocked when he got to the ladder that led to our room. Suddenly we heard distant shouts coming from the direction of the lounge.

"Quick, Noor!" said VJ, taking the rungs of the ladder two at a time.

We were going to get caught. There was no way out from the second floor. Still I followed him, scaling the ladder faster than I'd ever done. I stopped in my tracks when I got to the top. Adit was waiting there.

"Come on, Noor." Adit gave me an impatient look. "I did what you asked," he said, turning to VJ, who was running across the room to the window.

"Good man." VJ dug in his pocket and pulled out a wad of cash, tossing it onto the nearest bed. Adit trotted over, snatched it up and pocketed it.

VJ was leaning out the window, where the metal cage prevented escape. I could hear the sound of running feet from the floor below. I raced over to join VJ. It took me a moment to realize there was something different about the window. The screws had been removed from one side and the metal bars pushed out from the wall, creating an opening just large enough to squeeze through.

I shot a look at Adit, who smiled proudly.

"Pran will beat you for this if he doesn't kill you," I said.

"Maybe I won't give him the chance. You were right when you said there's a whole world beyond these fifteen lanes. Why should you be the only one to escape?"

"Enough talking," snapped VJ. "You need to go first, Noor."

"We're going to jump?" I said, aghast.

"Not exactly." VJ picked up a bundle from the floor. Only then did I realize it was a rope made out of knotted dupattas. Some were so tattered it would be a miracle if they didn't tear and break.

"You go first," he said. "I'm heavier. This might not hold my weight."

I took it from him, steeling myself not to look down as I swung my legs out the window and squeezed through the bars. It took every ounce of my courage to push off and drop. For just a second I panicked and hung helplessly, my feet dangling in midair. I didn't know what to do, but suddenly I heard Pran's voice. He was in our room. It spurred me to action. Planting my feet against the wall, I leaned out and scuttled down.

I looked up to see VJ and Pran grappling at the window. For a moment Pran's face disappeared, and in that same instant VJ was over the side and coming down twice as fast as I had.

There was no time to worry about what had happened to Adit as VJ grabbed my arm and pulled me across the road. Grace was there, waiting by the open door of a taxi. We jumped in, amid the bellowing of many voices. I was shaking with terror.

The car moved off immediately but it was Kamathipura, and speed was impossible. We locked our doors, but Pran emerged from our house and chased after us. Within minutes he'd reached the car and was banging on the window. I was grateful to be sitting in between VJ and Grace, and I was more grateful still that Pran was alone. No one was coming to his aid, though I had no doubt Binti-Ma'am had to be out on the street by now, though too fat and lazy to give chase. She was probably planning the beating she'd give me when I was dragged back to her.

Pran's screaming and banging accompanied us to the end of our lane. At any moment, I was certain he'd smash through the glass. I think the taxi driver had the same concern. He kept leaning on his horn and shouting at Pran to stop. Had VJ not ordered him to keep moving, the driver would have got out of the car to fight Pran off. Finally, when we turned onto the main road, Pran had to give up after he was almost swiped by a speeding car.

I didn't turn to look at him as we roared off. I felt no satisfaction. My small triumph over Pran seemed like nothing compared to my fear for those I'd left behind.

Grace

"Are you okay, Noor?" I asked. My heart was still racing.

She nodded but seemed strangely subdued.

"You're still frightened."

"I left them all. I left Shami."

"You'll see them again soon." I tried to sound confident.

The roads got wider as we left the heart of Kamathipura, and I began to think through what to do next. I'd have to take her home, unless she went with VJ. He could smuggle her into his house more easily but I doubted she'd be very happy about it. I glanced at her. She was staring silently out the window. We were passing a collection of tarp-covered lean-tos under a bridge. Noor's tension was palpable.

"Stop," she said.

"Stop what?" I asked.

"Stop! Stop the car!" Clearly agitated, she barked something in Hindi directly to the driver.

He pulled off the road and she fumbled with the door handle.

"What's wrong?" asked VJ.

"We must get Parvati."

"Where's Parvati?" I asked.

"There." She pointed back to the settlement we just passed.

"It's late, almost eleven o'clock. Is this a good time to be dropping in on her?" I didn't add the fact that I was already unsure what the future held for Noor. The last thing we needed was Parvati as well. Miss Chanda had told us there were rescue homes for girls in danger of being trafficked but I wasn't sure that applied to Parvati.

"You are right, it is too early," said Noor.

"For what?" asked VJ.

"To help Parvati escape from Suresh. He will be awake. We must wait."

"Who is Suresh?" I asked. "And why would Parvati need to sneak away from him?"

"He takes money from men to let them do things to Parvati. He is very dangerous. He has a knife."

I jumped when someone tapped on the window but it was just an old man. I rolled down the window and gave him a ten-rupee note. It was dark under the bridge and it gave me the creeps. If there were potential murderers around, I wasn't sure it was safe to hang out there. I was also starting to worry about what I'd say to my parents. It would be midnight soon. I needed to get home.

"Well, I guess we wait," said VJ.

"Are you sure Parvati will leave with us?" I asked.

"She must."

"Okay," I said, wondering what fresh lie I could tell my parents to explain missing curfew by several hours.

I dialed Mom's cell. She picked up on the third ring.

"Grace, Dad and I were just talking about you."

Why didn't that surprise me?

"Are you having a good time?"

"Fabulous!" I forced as much enthusiasm into my voice as I could muster. "In fact, VJ's asked me to spend the night. We're watching some of his dad's old movies. They've got a full-size screening room. It's so cool, Mom. You have to see it sometime. Can I stay, Mom, please?"

Noor raised an eyebrow.

There was a long pause and some whispering with my father. She could have saved herself the effort. I knew what they were saying. They wanted me home safely tucked into bed but were thrilled that I sounded so happy.

"Can you put VJ's mom on the phone, sweetie?"

"Sure, Mom, no problem."

"She wants to talk to your mom, VJ," I said loudly, while giving Noor a pleading look.

She nodded and took the phone.

"Hello, it is very nice to speak with you," said Noor in a mature voice that was not her own. I gaped at her.

I didn't hear my mom's response, though I probably could have guessed it.

"Of course," responded Noor. "She is a good girl. I am so happy to have such a friend for VJ." Then she listened for a while. I could practically feel my mother's enthusiasm coming through the phone line.

"No, no," Noor continued. "We are happy to have her to

stay with us. It is a great honor. Yes. Thank you. Good-bye."

She handed the phone back to me without a word and looked out the window.

"I'm really sorry I made you lie for me."

She turned to me with a small smile. "I understand. Sometimes I also do not tell my mother everything."

I sighed in relief.

We waited three hours while the streets cleared and the neighborhood fell silent. The taxi driver reclined his seat and slept. VJ had promised him far more money than he'd make in several nights of driving, so he was good-natured about the change in plans. VJ did his best to distract us with stories of life in the film industry, often tinged with an underlying sadness, a lot of broken dreams and betrayals. Up till then I'd thought he dabbled in the industry to please his father, but his ability to go to the heart of a story made me rethink that. Perhaps he just needed to be behind the camera instead of in front of it.

Finally Noor deemed it late enough to go looking for Parvati.

"Everyone will be sleeping now," said Noor. "Many boys are using heroin and they are drinking. Once they sleep, they do not easily wake."

We got out of the car and approached the squatter settlement. Lights from the bridge overhead provided enough illumination to see that many people didn't even have the luxury of a lean-to covered with plastic tarp. Whole families slept right on the pavement, their few worldly goods bundled around them.

We picked our way carefully between bodies and the tent-like structures. Even this late, the heat was oppressive. The windowless polyethylene homes must have been stifling. Noor stopped and put a finger to her lips. A few steps on she raised her hand. VJ and I stopped while she went a little farther on her own, rounding a lean-to, so we could see only the top of her. She crouched and disappeared.

She was gone for what felt like a long time, though it was probably not more than ten minutes. Finally she reappeared and came round the front of the lean-to. I felt weak with relief to see Parvati behind her. I could see why Noor was concerned for her. Her hair was a straggly mess and her clothes dirty and disheveled. It was the look in her eyes that was most disturbing though. She looked hunted, like an animal that's been chased to the point where it has lost all hope of survival.

She nodded to us but didn't speak. I think she had no words for the torture she'd endured. She fell in step behind us as we walked to the edge of the camp. We were almost on the point of leaving when she stopped, though I didn't notice at first. Noor touched me on the shoulder and I turned to find Parvati standing stock-still, as if she didn't dare take the last step to freedom. Noor walked back to her and took her hand, murmuring in a soothing tone. Parvati shook her head. She leaned close and whispered something to Noor, turned around and wove her way back the way she'd come.

Noor came to stand beside us. "She is coming. She forgot something. I told her to leave it but she said it is important."

VJ and I exchanged looks. Every second we delayed increased the chances someone would wake up and confront us. In fact, I was certain I'd seen movement in the shadowy interior of a nearby lean-to. Any minute now I expected someone to raise the alarm.

We waited almost twenty minutes. Twice I suggested going

back to look for Parvati but Noor was resolute that we must wait. I was just on the point of going after her myself when we saw movement from the direction of Suresh's lean-to. Sure enough, Parvati came into view. She was running as quickly as possible in the crowded space, leaping over debris and dodging shelters. It was more than her energy level that was different.

"Is that blood?" I whispered to VJ.

"I don't think it's tomato sauce."

As she came closer the smell of it wafted off her. She paused again at the edge of the encampment, where she'd stopped before. Her final look around was one of triumph and satisfaction. Blood was spattered on her kurta and smeared on her face. There were specks of it on her trousers and sandals. In one hand a knife glinted in the lamplight. Blood dripped from its tip.

"I want we are leaving now," she said.

"Well, all right, then," said VJ, approaching her carefully. He held out his hand. "Shall I just hold on to that for you?"

She looked at it as if seeing it for the first time. "I think I must be throwing."

"That sounds like a wonderful plan." VJ still held out his hand. She placed the knife in it, careful to hand him the hilt.

Noor took Parvati's arm and gently led her to the car. VJ and I followed at a distance.

"What are we going to do?" I asked in a low voice.

"You heard the lady. We throw it away."

"It's evidence."

"Of what? I didn't see anyone commit a crime. Did you?"

"You know what she must have done."

"The only thing I know is that she was gang-raped and tortured and the guy we've left behind was responsible for that."

We reached the car. Noor and Parvati were already inside.

"It's not right, VJ. Vigilante justice is not the solution."

"Maybe not, but I'm not going to turn her in. Are you?"

We made the trip home in a fraction of the time it had taken us to reach Kamathipura. The streets were virtually empty. We decided we'd all go to VJ's house. He lived in a mansion on the seafront, and the guard was in the employ of his family and wouldn't jeopardize his job by telling stories of a bloodstained girl arriving in the early hours of the morning.

VJ brought clean clothes for Parvati to change into. I suspected he got them from a maid. They looked too modest to be his mother's. Noor and I both went into the bathroom to help Parvati clean up.

We were all exhausted from the evening's events. VJ had offered us separate bedrooms but the three of us flopped down together on a king-size bed. As tired as I was, I lay awake for a long time wondering what the morning would bring.

30

Noor

Unexpected poetry . . .

I wasn't sure what woke me. When I sat up, Parvati was coming out of the bathroom. Her hair was brushed and neatly braided. She wore the clothes Vijender had given her the previous night. She nodded toward the hallway. I got up and followed her.

"You're leaving?" I asked.

"You know I must."

"What will you do?"

"I'll find a job, work as a maid or clean the streets. I'll do anything." She considered her words. "Anything but *that*."

"Vijender's family is rich. They could help you."

"What have I told you, Noor? Foreigners and films stars—you can't trust them."

"But they rescued us."

"And I'm grateful, but I've looked after myself for as long as I can remember. I'm not going to put my life in the hands of strangers now, when I have everything to lose."

"Suresh is dead, then? You're sure of it?"

"There's no doubt." She gave a cheerless smile.

"You'll need money. I don't have much but I—"

"I don't need money." She pulled a wad of bloodstained cash out of her pocket. "This will get me to the other side of the country. I've heard Calcutta is a good place to disappear."

"Was that his?"

"It was mine. I earned it."

"You must take your phone." I tried to hand it to her, but she wouldn't take that either.

"You keep it, Noor. Someday, when they've stopped looking for me, I want to be able to contact you."

I pulled her into a fierce hug. "If you ever need anything . . ." My voice broke as I stifled a sob.

She pulled out of my arms and we faced each other. A lifetime of memories passed between us. She was dry-eyed, but her face twisted with the misery of our parting.

I wanted to see her out. She wouldn't let me. We walked together to the end of the landing. I watched her disappear down a grand spiral staircase that looked built for a cinema heroine.

When I returned to our room Grace was sitting up in bed.

"Where's Parvati?"

"She left."

"Why?"

"You know what she did to Suresh."

"VJ's family is powerful. They could help her."

"The risk is too great. She did a crime. Money cannot change that. And she is a low-caste girl. Money cannot change that either. There will be many who think that what Suresh did to her was not so bad. They will want to punish Parvati. I know it is hard for you to understand, but for us things are not always easy."

Grace looked down at her lap. I hoped I had not hurt her feelings.

"I have something to show you," she said, a strange hesitancy in her voice.

She crossed her leg and hiked her dress up over her thigh. At first I saw only a mess of cuts and wondered what kind of accident could have left such wounds. I sat down next to her for a closer look. Only then did I realize the cuts formed words. It seemed impossible. I waited for an explanation.

"It's an acrostic," she said.

"What?"

"A kind of poem. We did them in middle school. You see, in one direction it forms the word *slut* and in the other, the first letter . . ."

Her words trailed off. She must have seen the look on my face. She had carved words into her own flesh. I thought of the many scars I'd seen on the girls and women in my community— I'd never seen anything like this.

"I am not understanding," I said. "What is *hag*?"

"It's like a witch."

"And *term*?"

"I was going to write *terminal*, like *dead*. I changed my mind."

"Why did you do this, Grace?"

"I was ashamed. I felt so alone."

"But this . . ."

"It was stupid. It only made things worse. Now I have this to be ashamed of as well."

"Do your parents know?"

"How can I disappoint them again?"

I wasn't sure how to put my thoughts into words. I felt as if I were watching her standing on a bridge, looking over the side. She was safe for the moment but that could change in an instant; the desire to jump could become too strong.

"You must tell your parents," I said.

"I know." She sighed heavily.

We heard quick footsteps in the hallway and VJ rushed in through the open doorway.

"Where's Parvati?" he demanded urgently. "The police are here!"

31

Grace

I told VJ about Parvati's disappearance on our way down-stairs. He led the way into a large living room with seating for at least thirty people. I wondered if the cops felt as intimidated as I did. There were three of them seated on one side of the room. Across an expanse of Persian silk carpet sat VJ's dad and a stunning woman who must have been his mom. VJ's parents stood up when we entered and greeted us warmly. VJ sat next to them and Noor and I took seats nearby.

"As I was saying," VJ's mother said firmly, "you cannot question these children until their parents arrive."

My heart jumped out of my chest. Had she called my parents already? I wasn't sure I was ready to talk to them.

"At this time we only need to speak to the girl Parvati," said the oldest policeman. "Are you Parvati?" he asked Noor.

"No, she's not," said VJ. "We don't know where Parvati is."

"When did you last see her?"

VJ hesitated.

"She left many hours ago," said Noor.

"Do you know Suresh Asari?" The officer's tone became considerably less polite when he addressed Noor.

"Yes, he is the boy who raped my fourteen-year-old friend and made her do sex work."

The officer was momentarily thrown off balance by Noor's directness. "Do you have proof of this?" he demanded flatly.

"Why? Will you charge him?" Her face gave nothing away.

"You were seen at the encampment under the Grant Road Bridge tonight."

Noor eyed him calmly.

"Suresh Asari was found murdered shortly after you left."

"This has gone far enough," said VJ's dad. "If you have further questions, you may speak to my lawyer."

"That's fine, Mr. Patel, but you have no rights over this girl. We're taking her with us."

"This child is a victim," snapped VJ's dad. "You aren't taking her anywhere without me."

"The only victim here is a murdered boy under a bridge."

"She's just told you that the child you're looking for was raped and trafficked!" VJ's mom exploded.

"We have only her word, and what does she know of these things?"

"I grew up in a house where minor girls do sex work," snapped Noor.

"And where would that be?" The officer leaned toward Noor, while one of his younger colleagues flipped open a notebook and prepared to write.

Noor was slow to answer. She looked from the officers to me and back again.

"What will you do if I tell you?"

"We will raid the establishment." He seemed to think this answer would please her. It didn't. Her face was wreathed in anxiety.

"What will you do with the women who are working there?"

"If they're not minors and haven't been involved in trafficking, they'll be released."

"They will not be charged for doing sex work?" she asked suspiciously.

"No."

"I want to get Shami and Aamaal out," she said to me. "Pran will be very angry at my escape. He may hurt them. And I need to save Lali-didi. What do you think I should do?"

Though I didn't entirely understand Noor's distrust of police, I understood her struggle. Her mother and her community might disown her for instigating a police raid.

"This may be your best chance to get justice."

Noor stood up and addressed the officers. "I will tell you where I live. But I must go too."

VJ and his parents stood as well. "I'll go with you," said VJ.

"No, you won't," said his parents in unison.

"I'll go," said VJ's father. "Noor, you will ride with me."

The senior officer started to object but VJ's father raised his hand. "It's not negotiable."

"I'd like to come," I said.

"Your parents will be here any minute," said VJ's mom. "You must be here when they arrive." My heart plummeted.

I walked Noor to the front door and gave her a hug. "Good luck," I said.

"You too." She gave me a meaningful look.

I went back and sat down. VJ's mom left the room, saying she was going to organize breakfast.

"When my parents come, would you mind leaving us alone?" I asked VJ.

"Of course," he said. I was grateful he didn't ask for an explanation.

Minutes later we heard voices coming down the hall. A servant showed my parents in. They rushed to me, enveloping me in a family hug.

"I'll go see how my mom's doing with that breakfast," said VJ.

We sat together on the couch, Mom and Dad on either side of me.

"Gracie, why did you lie to us?" demanded my mom before I had a chance to speak. "You should have told us what was going on last night. You could have been killed."

This was so far from what I was worrying about that I was momentarily thrown.

"Mom," I said, taking a deep breath, "there are a lot of things that I should have told you."

I crossed my ankle over my thigh and hitched up my dress.

Mom gasped. Dad was perfectly silent. I couldn't bear to look at either of them, so I looked at what I'd done.

I wondered if the scars would be there for the rest of my life, like my topless image on the Internet. Was it yet another thing I'd have to explain to my own teenage daughter someday?

Finally I peeped at my mother. Her face was rigid with shock. She was barely holding it together. I put my arms around her and was relieved that she hugged me back.

"I'm so sorry, Gracie. How did I let all this slip past me?"

"Give me a little credit, Mom. I'm a teenager. Slipping things past you is what I live for."

"Grace, that's not funny!" Her voice sounded more like her, though, so it couldn't have been unfunny.

I marshaled the courage to pull out of my mom's arms and looked at my dad sitting silently on the other side of me.

I wish I hadn't.

Tears were streaming down his face.

"My baby girl," he said miserably.

"Aw, Dad, you're such a dork." We hugged, and stayed like that for a long time.

32

ⴖoor

Freedom . . .

The minute we entered the outskirts of Kamathipura I began
to question whether I was doing the right thing. All my life
experience told me police were the bad guys. I'd seen them take
bribes from the overlords who controlled us, while arresting
and abusing the people I cared about. How would this time be
any different?

As Sanjay Patel's silver Porsche cruised down our narrow
lane, I felt every person on the street watching me. Our small
lane was already clogged with police cars. It seemed the entire
force was converging on my home, though the ones who'd
arrived before us had only the lane number. They milled about
impatiently peering in every open doorway.

I jumped out the second our car stopped, not even thanking
Vijender's father. My only thought was to disappear into the
crowd in the vain hope that no one would know I was the traitor. Despite what the cops said, I knew the aunties, and even

my own mother, would be arrested along with Pran and Binti-Ma'am, even if it was only temporary. Brothels were illegal. The cops weren't going to take the time to figure out who were the victims and who were the criminals.

Unfortunately, my role in the raid was not yet over. A cop caught me before I got very far and hauled me back to the officer in charge.

"Is this your house?" he demanded.

I was so terrified I could only nod.

He put a loudspeaker to his mouth. "Let's go!" he shouted to the legions of cops flanking him.

It seemed impossible that so many people could fit inside our house but they stormed the door with purpose, rushing in like a rising tide. I tried to follow but was held back, so I watched in horror as, one after another, everyone I loved was dragged out in handcuffs. The women who shared my room were among the last. The awkward access, up and down our narrow ladder, must have slowed the cops, but it didn't deter them.

Prita-Auntie was first. She frothed at the mouth she was so enraged. It took three men to get her in a van. She kicked one of them in his private parts. I cringed to imagine how he might retaliate when they got her to the station.

Ma was next. She was too weak to fight.

"It's my ma," I screamed, struggling with the cop who was holding me. He seemed to understand and let me go. I rushed to her, putting my arms around her waist. It wasn't my intention to impede her captors but only beg her forgiveness, but they pulled me off her and threw me to the ground.

"Ma," I cried, prostrate on the pavement, as she was hustled past. "I'm sorry, Ma!"

"Find Aamaal and Shami!" she shouted. She struggled. One of the cops lost his grip. She looked back at me. "Keep them safe."

I scrambled to my feet and raced after her. "I'm sorry," I cried. I needed her to understand. "I'm sorry."

Both cops had hold of her again. They half-pushed, half-lifted her into the back of the van to join Prita-Auntie. Prita-Auntie was crying now. She looked scared. Ma stumbled and fell to her knees, off balance with her hands cuffed behind her. For a moment she just sat on the floor, defeated, as if she hadn't the energy to lift herself onto the bench. I tried to climb in to help her but one of the cops shoved me aside.

"It's my ma!" I screamed, but he held me fast.

"Leave me," Ma shouted. "I'm all right. Go!"

"Noor!" It was Deepa-Auntie, suddenly beside me, also in cuffs. I hugged her, though she couldn't hug me back.

"It's my fault," I said.

"You did well, Noor. Your ma's right, go find your Shami and Aamaal now."

The cops hustled her away.

Ma still hadn't uttered a single word of forgiveness, but I left. My siblings were more important. They were why I'd brought the police. I ran back to the entrance to our house. No more adults were coming out. I hadn't seen Binti-Ma'am or Pran.

Some children were already in vans, separated from their mothers and aunties. I raced back and forth on shaky legs from one vehicle to another. I couldn't see Shami or Aamaal anywhere. I returned to our house, where two cops guarded the entrance.

"I need to go inside," I said. "My brother and sister haven't come out yet."

"The house is clear," said one of the cops. "There are only policemen in there now. Check the vans."

"I've checked them all. Please, let me past."

"No one's allowed back in."

I looked wildly around for someone to help me. Finally, I spotted the cop who'd interviewed me at VJ's house. I ran to him and explained the situation. I was hysterical. I'm not sure I made much sense, but he followed me back to the entrance and ordered the guards to let me through.

The house felt strangely unfamiliar, though I'd left less than twenty-four hours before. The noises and smells that had filled my childhood were gone. It seemed impossible that my history could be expunged so quickly and completely. I crept down the hallway and peeked around the corner to make sure the coast was clear before rushing for the ladder. I was up it as fast as I'd ever climbed and found my siblings exactly where I knew they'd be, huddled under the bed, their arms wrapped around each other though poor Aamaal had one arm in a cast.

"Come out now." I knelt on the floor, leaned down and reached for the entwined mass of them. Aamaal shuffled them both out of reach.

"Ma said to stay here," she said.

"She didn't mean forever, Aamaal. Just until I came for you."

"That's not what she said."

"I peed," said Shami in a tiny voice.

"It's okay, Shami-baby, we'll get you cleaned up. But you must come out now."

"Not till Ma comes," said Aamaal.

"She's not coming back, Aamaal," I said, with a mixture of guilt and exasperation.

"Where's Ma?" asked Shami, his voice trembling. He'd been holding back tears a long time.

I did the only thing I could. I slid under the bed and lay next to them, pulling them into my arms. Shami was sandwiched between us. I rubbed Aamaal's back. Her body shook as she finally let herself cry. Shami put his thumb in his mouth and burrowed into me. I felt his chest rise and fall against my own. I wished we could have stayed like that forever, but I could hear the officers banging around downstairs, their shouts filling the air. This wasn't our home anymore. We had to leave.

"Come on," I said. Wiggling backwards, I dragged them with me, stood up and helped them both to their feet. "It's time to go."

We walked cautiously to the ladder, listening for sounds before we wordlessly descended. I took a final look around, knowing I would never see this place again. I waited for the relief to wash over me but all I felt was sad. Whatever else it was, it was my childhood home. I could hear voices from the direction of the lounge—stern, joyless voices. I took each of my siblings by the hand and we walked in the opposite direction, past the washroom, the kitchen, to the small room at the end of the hall.

I had to see it one last time, commit it to memory as one might revisit the scene of a murder. It was the site of so much sadness. Shami and Aamaal didn't question where we were going. Their steps didn't falter as we entered the outer room. My brave little siblings stood with me in front of the box.

The noise was nearly imperceptible, yet unmistakable. All

three of us held our breath as we strained to listen. It came again. The wooden crate, little more than a coffin, was not empty.

It didn't make sense. The door was closed but it wasn't locked. Why would anyone choose to be inside? The light was off. Even with the morning sun filtering into the outer room, it would be pitch-black in there. Could a rat have got in? It wasn't impossible. They got in everywhere else.

I let go of my siblings' hands, hopped up on the stool and opened the door. I jumped back quickly. If it was a rat, it would scurry away. I didn't want to be in its path.

We waited.

Nothing.

The noise had stopped. Yet I knew there was something in there. The hair rose on the back of my neck. The presence inside the box waited just as we did. My siblings' hands found their way back into my own.

"Hello," I said.

Silence.

"Is someone there?"

Suddenly I remembered that I hadn't seen Pran or Binti-Ma'am outside. Was it possible they were hiding in the box? It made sense. The police wouldn't think to look there. It was the perfect hiding place. Only someone very familiar with our home would think of it. I was ablaze with outrage that Pran or Binti-Ma'am would be saved from arrest by the very thing they'd used to destroy the souls of others. I let go of my siblings, got back up on the stool, switched on the light and climbed inside.

I wasn't prepared for the sight that greeted me.

Lali-didi sat on the filthy mattress, leaning back against the blood-spattered wall.

"What are you doing in here?" I asked. There was something beyond the fact of finding her in such a strange place that made me uneasy.

"Just resting."

"In here?" I couldn't keep the astonishment out of my voice. She smiled weakly.

"I've brought the police, Lali-didi. Everyone has been arrested, but you don't need to worry. You're a minor. You'll get sent to a rescue home."

"Good for you. I knew you would save us."

"So you'll come out now," I said.

"Not yet."

"But you're free, Lali-didi. You don't ever have to be in a place like this again. You're free."

"Not yet."

I didn't know what to say. Lali-didi had often been a mystery to me but I was more perplexed than usual. My disquiet grew.

"You're going to have a wonderful life. Everything's going to be okay now."

"Do you know how many times I've been raped, Noor?"

I didn't answer. I couldn't.

"Ha! Neither do I. I can't count beyond one hundred. It was many hundreds though, I can tell you that."

"It's over, Lali-didi."

"I can still feel their touch on my skin. I can still smell them, even after I bathe, like their stink seeps out of my own pores."

"You can go to school. You can be happy." Tears were sliding down my face. Lali-didi's eyes were dry.

"I am happy, Noor. I've waited for this day a long time. You marched in just as I knew you would and closed the doors on this house of torture. I planned for this from the moment you escaped last night. You came more quickly than I expected. Thank you for that." Blood dripped out of her nose. She wiped it away but it only seemed to make it bleed faster. "You should go now."

"Lali-didi, what's going on? What have you done?"

She held up a can of rat poison that had slipped down on the far side of her.

"No," I gasped. "Not now, Lali-didi. You're going to get your freedom."

"Yes I am, Noor. Yes I am."

I crawled over and pulled at her arm. "We have to get you out of here. We'll go to the hospital. There's still time."

She wouldn't budge.

"Good-bye, Noor." She crumpled before my eyes. For the first time I noticed blood leaking from her ear.

"Lali-didi," I sobbed. "Please don't do this." I pulled at her arms, even as I felt her limbs go limp.

I don't know when my siblings joined me in the box or how long we sat there. We didn't hear the heavy footsteps enter the outer room or the voices urging us to come out. I don't remember leaving Lali-didi, or climbing in a van. I don't remember the police station or the day and night we spent in detention while our futures were being decided.

Everyone I loved was in prison, everyone but Lali-didi. Only she was free.

33

Noor

What I will remember . . .

I'm woken by the mattress creaking above me. I slide out of bed, careful not to disturb Aamaal, and stand up. I have to climb up the first rung of the ladder to get my head high enough to see Shami on the top bunk. His eyes are wide open.

"Are you okay, baby?"

"My stomach hurts."

"Do you need to go to the bathroom?"

"I'm not sure."

"Well, let's give it a try."

I pull down his cover and step off the ladder to give my seven-year-old brother space to climb down. I put my hands out to catch him in case he stumbles. He's wobbly but manages to get down without mishap. His body is still adjusting to a new higher-dose medication. We've been through it all before, the diarrhea, nausea and fatigue.

I follow him into the bathroom and sit cross-legged on the

floor while he sits on the toilet. There's no shyness between us. I've ministered to his ills since he was a baby. I'll continue for as long as he'll let me.

"Do you think Ma is watching us?" asks Shami.

"Well, hopefully not right now." I smile.

"Maybe she's already been born again. She could be a baby bunny."

I chuckle. Shami can think of no better incarnation. He dotes on Aamaal's rabbits.

"Noor-di?"

"Yes?"

"I haven't done much good in my life. If I died right now, I wouldn't come back as a bunny, would I?"

"You're not going anywhere for a long time," I say firmly.

"I'd probably come back as a pigeon. No one likes pigeons. There's too many and they all look the same. I bet a lot of naughty boys come back as pigeons. Noor, if I was a pigeon would you still recognize me?"

"Of course."

There's a quiet knock on the door. I stand up and open it.

"Everything all right in here?" Karuna-Auntie pops her head round the door.

"His stomach is giving him trouble again."

She walks in, leaving the door open, and strokes Shami's hair. I only hope Varun-Uncle and Nanni are not behind her. It's the hazard of living with a houseful of doctors; poor Shami has no privacy. If I'd had any idea what we were getting into I might have thought twice about moving in with them. I wouldn't have refused—they're our salvation—but I might have thought twice.

Aamaal and I spent six weeks in protective custody after Ma's arrest. For all that time, we weren't allowed to see Shami, or anyone else. Shami was put in a home for HIV-infected kids. Luckily, since it was private and not state-run, it had liberal visiting privileges. Grace and VJ visited every day.

We all missed Ma's funeral, though it was nothing to speak of. She was given a pauper's cremation when her body was found in an alley barely a month after she got out of jail. She'd spent two nights locked up. The only people who did less time were Pran and Binti-Ma'am, who had mysteriously disappeared not an hour before the raid. Prita-Auntie was sentenced to three years for helping train underage girls. Deepa-Auntie spent several days in jail while it was decided whether she was in the country illegally. When she was finally released, Nishikar-Sir was waiting to install her in another brothel. It might have seemed like good fortune that Ma didn't meet that fate, but she had nowhere to go. With our home closed and her own health failing she lived on the street.

Some days I think Ma died of a broken heart. With her livelihood and children gone she had no way to survive and nothing left to fight for. Other days I remember the woman who endured endless nights of pain and humiliation to look after me and send me to a fee-paying school. Ma rarely praised me and never once said she loved me. She always insisted my destiny was both bleak and inevitable. Yet she kept my medals hidden in the hem of her skirt and fought anyone who tried to limit my dreams. Perhaps she died because her heart had filled to capacity. She knew the battle was over and she had won.

Karuna-Auntie came back into our lives by accident. She was doing volunteer checkups at the HIV home and discovered

Shami. She recognized him, though he didn't remember her. I'd dragged him to so many doctors, and it had been over a year since he'd seen her. Only when she reminded him of their shared passion for *manga an' napple* did he figure it out. It didn't take long for her to get the details on all of us.

She appeared at our rescue home one afternoon, standing in the doorway of the musty room that doubled as a bedroom and lounge for thirty girls. I knew her immediately, though I didn't acknowledge her. I waited to see why she had come. The disappointment would have been too much if it had been a random coincidence.

The ache of missing Shami had become unbearable. I was close to the desperation of those girls I'd read about years earlier who'd broken their legs trying to escape their rescue home. Had it not been for Aamaal, I would have tried it. I remembered Karuna-Auntie's compassion and prayed she was there to help us.

Her eyes lit up the second they fell on me and she walked straight over.

"Hello, Noor." She plopped down onto my mattress on the floor. "Do you remember me?"

Aamaal, who was never more than a few feet from me the entire time we lived in protective custody, looked up from the schoolwork I'd assigned her.

"Yes," I said.

My eagerness must have registered on my face. She looked pleased. In addition to being separated from my beloved brother, we hadn't been allowed out of the home to go to school. Prison could not have been more punitive.

"You never came back to see me. I always hoped you would."

"You would have taken my brother away." I didn't state the obvious—that I'd since brought that misfortune upon myself.

"I saw Shami yesterday."

I sat up straighter.

"How is he?" demanded Aamaal, closing her book. "How did you get to see him? Can you take us?"

I didn't speak. Aamaal had asked every question in my own heart.

"I thought perhaps we could discuss a more permanent solution."

My breath caught in my throat.

"I live with my brother's family and my mother. My mother and brother are both doctors. My brother has a wife and two children. Thankfully she's not a doctor. That would be a bit tiresome, wouldn't it?"

She paused, but when we didn't respond she continued. "We're a crowded household but we're happy. I think you would like my nieces, Noor. The eldest is studying her standard twelve. The younger is in standard eight. You're in standard ten now, aren't you?"

I blushed when I remembered the lie I'd told her.

"Standard nine," I mumbled.

"So what do you say?" Her penetrating eyes were full of kindness, just as before.

I was confused. What was she asking?

"Would you and Aamaal like to come live with us?"

Her offer was beyond my wildest hopes. "What about Shami?"

"Oh, he's already agreed," she said breezily.

Aamaal jumped up. "Yes, YES, YES!"

"Wait a minute, Aamaal," I cautioned. "How long would we live with you?"

"I've never married, Noor. The idea of deferring to a man never sat well with me. Having my own children, on the other hand, is something I've always wanted. I like you, Noor. I have a feeling you and I are not so different. And, of course, I've been smitten with Shami from the moment I met him. Now that I've met Aamaal, I can see you're an irresistible lot, you Benkatti children. I'd like to become your guardian. What do you say?"

It was a week beyond that before the legal work was completed and we came home to this apartment. I laughed when Usha-Auntie, Karuna-Auntie's sister-in-law, showed us to the bedroom we now share and apologized that all three of us would have to share a room, and Aamaal and I would both sleep in the lower bunk. It took her weeks to accept that, to us, everything about the way they lived was luxurious.

Finished on the toilet, Shami goes to the sink to wash his hands. I stand up to supervise. He isn't thorough if I don't keep an eye on him. Karuna-Auntie follows us back to the bedroom and climbs up the ladder to tuck Shami in and kiss him good-night. I switch on my night-light and pick up my Biology textbook. In two weeks I'll write the medical school entrance exam. With three doctors constantly testing me, I'm confident I'm ready, but I enjoy studying, which is lucky as it'll be another seven years before I'm fully qualified.

Karuna-Auntie leans down and plants a kiss on my forehead. "Sleep is just as important as study, Noor," she whispers. "Don't stay up too late."

"I won't."

She walks out, leaving our door slightly ajar. I stare at the page in front of me but my mind wanders.

Grace will return to Mumbai soon for her summer holidays. I'm looking forward to being together again. She graduated last year and went home for university. VJ and I have planned a welcome dinner for her.

VJ graduated two years ago and has been a rising star in Indian cinema. Last year he was in a British coproduced movie that was an international hit. When he was nominated for an Oscar everyone said his fame would eclipse his father's. He went to America for the ceremony. The paparazzi found it quaint that he brought a high-school friend as his date.

All of India watched with pride as Bollywood's heartthrob won the prize. Since VJ had remained a fixture in our own lives, our whole family was gathered around the television when he took the stage to accept.

He began his speech by thanking his father and mother. Then he thanked us, his adopted siblings. He said his brother Shami had taught him everything he knew about courage; I was surprised to discover we had that in common. I smiled when he said his sister Aamaal had taught him to live life to the fullest. It may have been true, but I'd never known the film star to have any problem living big.

I was nervous when he mentioned me. He said I'd taught him that if the future was not written as you wanted it to be, then you must write your own story. I thought about that for a long time. My life hadn't been the straight canal to the sea that Ma had predicted, but neither had it been Deepa-Auntie's mountain river full of unpredictable twists and turns. Many hands had guided my journey, not the least of them Ma's. I'd had some luck, but more than that, time and again, I'd had help. I couldn't have written my story without that.

Last of all, VJ thanked his high-school sweetheart, the love of his life, Luca D'Silva. The camera panned to the beautiful boy in the audience who blew him a kiss.

It caused a media storm that went on for months. Some said VJ's public disclosure would end his career. VJ said it launched it. He's moved behind the camera now, to tell the stories that matter to him. His father is financing his first film, a documentary on sex trafficking. He and Luca live together. They talk of getting married if it ever becomes legal.

Grace has grown stronger with each passing year. Counseling and finally confronting Kelsey and Todd, the masterminds of her downfall, helped her to move forward, but that was only a small part of her recovery. Grace and I spent her last two years in Mumbai volunteering at the NGO in Kamathipura, Sisters Helping Sisters. With Chandra-Teacher's help we've started literacy classes for sex workers. Deepa-Auntie was our first student. When Chandra-Teacher offered Deepa-Auntie a job as an outreach worker and helped her break free from Nishikar-Sir, Grace and I learned as much about the importance of confronting bullies as Deepa-Auntie did. Grace plans to become a human rights lawyer. I pity anyone who persecutes the powerless on her watch.

This summer she's bringing a boy with her who wants to intern at our NGO. Grace doesn't call him her boyfriend but I think he's important to her. Grace didn't date throughout high school. While the wounds on her leg have healed, not all damage is visible. I teased her that this boy must be serious if she was bringing him to meet us, but she just laughed and said, "He's a bit of a dork."

"Noor-di." Shami interrupts my thoughts. I get out of bed and step up on the ladder.

"Are you all right, baby? Is the light bothering you?"

"My stomach still hurts."

I climb up the ladder and settle myself next to him, leaning on the headboard. "Roll on your side. I'll stroke your back."

It's the rare night that I can't put him to sleep with a back rub.

"Noor-di?"

"Go to sleep now."

"Just one question."

"Okay, but only one."

"If I die and get born into another family in Kamathipura, will you still recognize me?"

"You're not going to die."

"But will you recognize me?"

I don't tell him the truth—that when we lived in Kamathipura, and in the years since, I've seen all of us reborn a thousand times. I see myself in the hopeful school-going girls with their scuffed shoes and faded uniforms, and Aamaal in the wide-eyed stares of young girls who know too much about abuse and too little about love. I see Shami in the wizened faces of children haunted by disease. I used to dream that one day I would have a home where I could shelter all the people that I loved, but every day, the list of people I want to save grows longer. There are already too many to be contained by four walls and a roof, so I've changed my dream. I've opened a room in my heart that I reserve for the women and children of Kamathipura. Its size and scope have no limits.

"Of course I will recognize you," I say. "Now go to sleep."

"Just one more question, Noor-di, and then I promise I'll sleep. If I'm born into another family, will you still love me?"

I pull him into my lap. He's so tiny and light he still fits easily. "If you come back as a bunny, or a pigeon or a child of Kamathipura, born to another family, I will find you, Shami. And I will always love you."

Author's Note

I first started volunteering with sex workers' daughters in Kamathipura, the largest red-light district in Asia, in March of 2013. Though I've had training in working with victims of sexual violence, I wasn't so naive as to think I was going to transform the lives of the girls I worked with. Still, I wasn't entirely prepared for the level of violence and degradation they're routinely exposed to. More disheartening still is the extent to which a large portion of society has turned its back on them. Time and again I've heard stories of girls being shunned, even asked to leave school, when it was found out their mothers were sex workers—no matter that the vast majority of their mothers had been trafficked into the life and were victims themselves.

Early in my work with the girls, I had the opportunity to edit a countrywide report on sex trafficking produced by Dasra, a leading Indian strategic philanthropy organization based in Mumbai. Suddenly my personal experiences and observations had a broader context. Though government figures are lower, according to Dasra's research, there are an estimated 15 million people in India who have been trafficked into sex work. More than a third are children, some as young as nine years old, sold into sexual slavery to satisfy an increasing demand for younger girls. Daughters of sex workers are at particular risk.

In a decade where India has seen unprecedented growth and a decrease in the percentage of the population living below the poverty line, sex workers have experienced falling wages, an increase in the number of child prostitutes and a significant decline in life expectancy. NGO workers in Kamathipura estimate that 60 percent of sex workers are HIV-positive. Many children are born infected. Tuberculosis and other diseases related to poverty and overcrowding are also rampant.

Some day I will leave India, as I have left so many other countries, but I'll take with me the memory of girls, full of hope and determination, who against all odds dream of a future beyond the fifteen lanes of their red-light community. I'll remember their mothers, who chided me for my abysmal Hindi, and the chai-wallah who, despite the congestion of goats, cows, people and all manner of vehicles, always managed to save me a parking space outside the night shelter where I worked. But for now I look forward to the hugs and shrieks of "Susandidi!" that will greet me tomorrow night when I return to my girls in Kamathipura. I still have no illusions that I've transformed their lives, but I have no doubt they've changed mine.

SJ Laidlaw
Mumbai, February 2015

Acknowledgments

It took close to two years to write this book, because it was challenging to find the light in a story too dark to tell.

I'm very grateful to the Canada Council for the Arts, not only for financial support but for the tacit endorsement that this story was worth the struggle.

I feel extremely fortunate to have worked on yet another book with my wonderful editor at Tundra Books, Sue Tate. As always, Sue provided the perfect combination of intelligence and empathy, cheerleading and honesty.

Also at Tundra, I appreciated the wisdom of my former publisher, Alison Morgan, and I'd like to mention a young intern, Sarah Essak, who was an early champion of Noor's story, even in its darkest incarnation.

This was my first time benefitting from the keen eyes of Catherine Marjoribanks, who copyedited this book, and Tundra's managing editor Elizabeth Kribs. I'd like to thank them both.

While this book is a work of fiction, it's based on lives that are all too real. Those stories were collected from many sources, but two women in particular illuminated my work with their insights. I'm grateful to Manju Vyas, who has dedicated her life to the women and girls of Kamathipura, and Namita Khatu, whose energy and smile never faltered despite the daunting task of helping the most downtrodden in a city where more than a quarter-million people live on less than thirty cents a day.

I'd also like to thank Sudarshan Loyalka, who sixteen years ago started the small NGO in Kamathipura that became my second home in Mumbai, Apne Aap Women's Collective (www.aawc.in). His vision and commitment continue to inspire all those around him.

Unwittingly, two good friends, Neera Nundy and Deval Sanghavi, cofounders of Dasra, provided assistance when they invited me to attend a countrywide conference of anti-trafficking NGOs and asked me to edit their report on sex trafficking in India. Also at Dasra, I'd like to thank Pakzan Dastoor, who oversaw the report and lent me books. I swear I'm still planning to return them.

Finally, as always, I thank my husband, Richard Bale, who reads every draft of my work from the most abysmal beginnings. He is perhaps the only person whose relief when a book is finally finished equals my own.